Cyn
Denny

D1002319

THE BONE HARVEST

STACY M. JONES

The Bone Harvest Copyright © 2019 Stacy M. Jones

All rights reserved. No part of this publication may be reproduced, distributed, or transmitted in any form or by any means, including photocopying, recording, or other electronic or mechanical methods, without the prior written permission of the publisher, except in the case of brief quotations embodied in critical reviews and certain other noncommercial uses permitted by copyright law.

ISBN: 978-0-578-55112-8
Imprint: Stacy M. Jones
First printing edition: 2019

Any references to historical events, real people, or real places are used fictitiously. Names, characters, and places are products of the author's imagination.

Book design by Sharon Aponte, Chick & a Mouse Graphic Design.

For more information and to contact the author:
www.stacymjones.com

DEDICATION

For Sonja – you make a great Liv

ACKNOWLEDGMENTS

Special thanks to my family and friends who are always a source of support and encouragement. I'm sure you must be tired of listening to me talk about the characters in my head. Thank you to my early readers whose feedback was invaluable. Sharon Aponte, a wonderfully-skilled graphic designer, a huge thank you. Thank you to Dj Hendrickson for your insightful editing. I am always grateful for the city of Little Rock and my hometown of Troy, New York for allowing me to borrow your landscapes, businesses, and city streets and adding my own twist – sometimes moving streets and locations to fit my scene but always still reflective of the area. To the residents of both – I hope you enjoy this one.

THE BONE
HARVEST

CHAPTER 1

It has been nearly a year since I was drugged, taken to a cabin near Lake Catherine, shot, and nearly strangled to death. My investigator partner, Cooper Deagnan, and I had taken what we thought would be a fairly routine missing person's case that turned out to be significantly more. In reality, it was a case I shouldn't have ever touched. My ex-boyfriend's wife was missing – a woman who had caused me serious drama in the past. I should have stayed away completely. The case quickly took a dark and sinister turn. Several women ended up dead in the Arkansas River, and I put my life on the line. Something I plan on never doing again.

The only positive was it brought me back to Little Rock from New York, and right back to Lucas "Luke" Morgan, the lead homicide detective who had been working the case. We had a tricky relationship in the past, caused by my own fear. I got over it, mostly. Luke was there for me on that case and had been there for me every day since.

Today was the one-hundredth day free of the nightmares and terror that filled my every waking night after my almost death. Months back, Luke finally convinced me to seek some therapy to deal with what I was feeling. He was sure I had post-traumatic stress, and I did. I can't say I enjoyed the therapy, but I was pleased the process brought me to the other side and feeling like myself again. If

I was going to be honest, I still have mild anxiety, but that's from worrying that when I close my eyes at night the nightmares will return. So far, they haven't. I'm going to celebrate the small victory.

It's fall, but the weather still hasn't turned. A week left in October, and I'm ready for the heat to break and the leaves to start changing color. I'm more than ready for Luke to stop looking at me like I'm going to break at any second.

"What?" I grouched, looking up from my newspaper and coffee.

"You look tired. Did you sleep last night?" Luke leaned back against the kitchen counter with a coffee cup in hand and peered down at me with a concerned expression on his face.

"You sleep next to me every night. You know I slept." I knew Luke meant well. He just worried too much. I stood and crossed the distance between us. I wrapped my arms around his waist and hugged him. At six foot, Luke was taller than I was by five inches. I could lay my head on his chest, which was comforting.

Luke set his cup down, traced a finger along my cheek and kissed me. When we parted, he pulled back. "I had fun at the lake last weekend. You should put more aloe on your shoulders. They're still pink from your sunburn."

I sighed sweetly, smiling up at him. The previous weekend we had borrowed Cooper's cabin on Lake Forrest up near Eureka Springs. We didn't swim, but rather hiked, took the canoe out on the lake and just relaxed. Apparently, my fair Irish skin still sunburns even in the fall.

Luke was overprotective. I never knew I needed to be tended to so much. I had been a journalist for many years before opening my own private investigation firm in my hometown of Troy, New York. Last year, when I moved back to Little Rock, I partnered with Cooper in his firm. I hunted cheaters, insurance fraudsters, missing people, and those who couldn't properly watch their kids on child custody visits. I wasn't used to being babied.

"What's your plan with your remaining few days of vacation?" Now that I was in his life full-time, Luke actually used his vacation days. He had taken a full two weeks off but had purposefully waited until October so other detectives could take the summer with their kids. It was Tuesday of his final week.

"I'm not going to do a thing except lie around and be lazy." Luke laughed, showing off his perfect white teeth. He was handsome.

Tall, dark coffee-colored skin, always freshly shaven and bald by choice. I was on the receiving end of many jealous glances when we were out. Luke never noticed the advances of other women, or at least, he was very good at pretending he didn't.

"Really, though," Luke added, running a hand across his bald head, "the unit secretary dropped off my mail. She said it had been building up. I think I'll start going through it so it's taken care of before I'm back at the station."

"Sounds like a plan, but don't work too hard today." I returned to the sink and sunk my hands into soapy water. I didn't make much progress as Luke pulled me back into his arms and turned me around.

He dropped a kiss against my lips and whispered, "How about we go back upstairs first?"

"I have a meeting with Cooper. But the minute I get home, you're on."

Luke swatted playfully at my backside. "Fine, but you're missing out," he groused.

Luke picked up the pile of mail on the counter. He flashed me a grin before heading up the stairs to his office. Luke officially moved into my house on N. Tyler Street soon after I decided to stay in Little Rock. He took one of the spare bedrooms for his office while I took the other. The other bedrooms served as the master and spare for the rare guest we had.

I grabbed my cellphone from the table and texted Cooper that I'd be at his downtown loft in about thirty minutes. As I put my hands back into the soapy water, Luke yelled for me, his voice filled with terror. With my hands still soapy wet, I moved quickly to the stairs.

Luke bounded down the steps, taking two at a time. The sheer look of panic on his face set my nerves on edge.

"What? What is it?"

He thrust a piece of paper in front of me. I wiped my wet hands on my pants and took it from him. Turning it so I could read, it took a few seconds to digest. It was a plain piece of white paper with block letters in big red bold ink. It simply read:

"Lily wasn't the first. She won't be the last. Like the fall leaves that turn orange and red, 23 pretty little girls harvested dead."

Luke's sister Lily was murdered at the University of Arkansas in Fayetteville when she was a freshman and Luke was a senior. Her body, just bones scattered among leaves, was found in the woods near the campus nine months after she went missing. To this day there were no suspects and hardly any evidence or clues as to what happened. Luke had never forgiven himself.

Now it looked like the killer was back or some cruel person was taunting him. Luke stared at me, his mouth open and eyes wide. I wasn't sure what to say. We looked at each other in confusion and panic.

CHAPTER 2

Luke paced the third floor of the Little Rock Police Department. His head down and his thoughts spinning as he waited for a lab tech to go over every inch of the letter. His partner, Det. Bill Tyler, watched Luke intently. Tyler hadn't said a word after Luke showed him the letter, just stared in disbelief. It was the same response everyone gave. Luke had no idea what to make of it, but he knew that it was real. The gnawing feeling that wouldn't let go, deep down in that place detectives just know, ate at him.

After reading the letter, all Luke cared about was getting to the police station to have it processed. He forced Riley out of the house, making her keep her meeting with Cooper. There was nothing she could do other than worry with him. Luke couldn't worry about Riley right now. While Luke was trying desperately not to overreact, the letter brought it all back to him.

After handing the letter over and pacing for nearly thirty minutes, Luke finally gave up the wait. It wasn't making the tech work any faster, and he needed to be productive. Luke went to his desk. He took a small silver key hidden under the mat on his desk and unlocked the very bottom drawer. Inside was a small framed photo of his sister and him on her first day of university. They both looked so young. Looking at Lily's face brought it all right back to him. Luke recalled it all - the sights, sounds and even smell - like it was yesterday.

Back in 2002, Luke had gone from being a fun-loving, university senior, whose only concern was how much alcohol he consumed and which co-ed was going to be his date on Saturday night, to life never being the same again. The photo had been taken a couple of weeks before Lily turned eighteen on September second. Other than the height difference, they looked like siblings. Her smile, especially, matched his.

Luke and Lily hadn't seen much of each other during the first few weeks of the fall semester. Lily had made friends and focused hard on her studies. Luke tried not to hover. She had seemed to be adjusting well. They had checked in with each other, from time to time, that first couple of months. They had grabbed pizza occasionally on a Saturday afternoon, but mostly they had stuck with their own friends. Life had been fairly smooth sailing.

It had been just two weeks past Luke's twenty-second birthday, which he celebrated on October eleventh, and the only thing that had been on his mind was the upcoming winter break. Luke, with Cooper and some other friends, had been headed to Key West for a week. Knowing he was joining the police academy right after graduation, all Luke had wanted was to blow off some steam before he started his final semester of university. But that wasn't what fate had in store for him.

Instead, Luke had woken up on that fateful Sunday morning on October twenty-seventh to a phone call from his mother, Lucia, asking if he'd seen or spoken to his sister. Luke had recalled seeing Lily briefly heading to a party on that Friday night, but hadn't really thought much about her since. As his mother talked, Luke had thought about covering for his sister, who he assumed had done what most freshmen did – drank too much and maybe made some bad choices.

His mother had been in a panic because it wasn't like Lily to worry her. Luke had been calm. This was Fayetteville, after all. Sure, there were some 20,000 plus students at the school, but the campus was tucked into a small town near the Ozark Mountains. It wasn't the kind of place, or at least Luke naively thought then, where bad things happened.

Luke had assured his mother he'd track Lily down and have her call home. He hadn't even rushed. Luke had grabbed a shower and woken up Cooper. Once the two were ready, they had headed to campus from their off-campus apartment in search of Lily.

Lily hadn't been in her dorm. She hadn't been at the sorority house where she had some friends. Every friend they had spoken to had told them the same. Lily had gone to a fraternity party on Friday night. No one could quite pin down how much Lily had to drink, if at all, or if she had walked home with anyone. They hadn't heard from her for the rest of the weekend.

The only bit of new information Luke had learned was that Lily had just started dating a junior. Most of her friends assumed she had gone off with him. Luke had found Chris, but he hadn't seen Lily since an early dinner on Friday. Chris had informed Luke he had gone home to Jonesboro for the weekend for his father's birthday and was just getting back. Chris' roommate had confirmed it.

Chris had offered to help. Luke had waited while Chris called everyone who might have known Lily's whereabouts. The people who had answered his call had no idea. Chris had promised he'd call Luke the moment he heard anything and had asked if there was more he could do. At the time, Luke wasn't sure. Luke hadn't known what to do.

It had been when light turned to dark, and Lily still hadn't been found, that panic started to set in for both Luke and Cooper. Luke had called his parents, who had already been en route to the school from Little Rock. Late that evening, Luke had gone with his parents to make a missing person's report at the Fayetteville Police Department, but they hadn't taken it seriously. The cops had speculated Lily had run away or was with friends. They had said they saw it all the time with university freshmen – the pressure got too much. Luke had known in his heart that wasn't true. He had vowed right then and there that he'd find his sister on his own.

By the next morning, Luke had set up a tip line and started a volunteer search of the community. The university had helped tremendously. They had put up reward money, provided volunteers, and offered the full support of campus security. Sadly, nothing had been found that day or in the months that followed. Luke hadn't gone away for winter break as he had planned. He hadn't even gone back home to Little Rock. He had stayed on campus and searched.

He had followed up on tips and tried to keep the story alive, but help had faded fast. The volunteers dwindled. The trail had gone cold.

What should have been an exciting final semester for Luke, had dragged on. He had trouble concentrating. Sitting in class had felt pointless. Not even a month after graduation, Luke had joined the Little Rock police academy with vigor. He had a promise to keep.

In late July, as Luke had studied in the police academy, Lily's remains had been found in the woods near campus by groundskeepers preparing the campus for the upcoming school year. Lily's skeletal remains had been among leaves that had fallen from the trees. No cause of death had ever been determined, and the manner had been ruled undetermined. Finally, though, the cops had started an investigation.

The crime went unsolved with few clues for the next seventeen years. Over the years, Luke had tried and failed several times to solve the case. There just wasn't much to go on until now.

The letter was the first real clue Luke had ever come across.

CHAPTER 3

Cooper's cellphone buzzed on the nightstand, waking him from his slumber. He cracked open his eyes, blinked a few times and remembered he wasn't alone. He reached over and felt the soft shape of a woman next to him. In response, she curled against him seductively and purred like a cat.

Cooper cursed and ran a hand through his messy hair. He didn't usually let women spend the night, but he had been more than a little drunk the night before and must have fallen asleep before rousting her from his bed.

Remembering what woke him, Cooper slapped at the nightstand until he palmed his phone. Cooper read the text from Riley that she was on her way. He sat with a start. His only mission was to get this woman out of his bed and out the door before Riley arrived or he'd never hear the end of it. Luke and Riley teased him incessantly about his bachelor lifestyle. If Cooper didn't see firsthand how in love and happy they were, he'd think they were jealous.

Cooper hated to even admit it to himself, but he was wracking his brain trying to think of the name of the woman who was now clawing her fingernails down his bare back. Cooper thought back to the night before. He had walked down into the River Market district, just blocks from his condo. He had run into a few friends, had a few drinks and met a woman at the bar. *What was her name?* Cooper made several more mental leaps before he landed on Holly.

Just as recognition took hold, Cooper caught her hand as she trailed her fingers around to his stomach and started to trail south.

"You have to go," Cooper said a little more loudly and abruptly than he meant. "My investigative partner is on her way here."

Holly took her hand back and yawned loudly. "I thought we'd get breakfast. I don't have to be at work until later."

Cooper moved, sliding his feet onto the floor. "Can't. Some other time. I need to get up."

As Cooper moved off the bed, Holly sat upright and wrapped the sheet around her. Her blonde hair was tousled and there was a streak of mascara under her right eye. Cooper hated these awkward moments, which is why he kicked himself every time he picked up a woman. He was a man with needs and no desire for anything complicated or long-term. Cooper tried hard not to be "that guy" but found himself there more times than he'd like to admit.

Cooper looked at her sympathetically. "Let's go out Friday night if I don't have a case." He wasn't entirely sure that's what he wanted, but he wasn't sure what else to say.

Holly looked at him sideways, a confused expression on her face. "A case? Are you a cop?"

Cooper shook his head. "Private investigator."

Holly turned her back to him and started pulling her clothes together. Cooper wanted to be a respectable guy and offer her a shower, but he also wanted her out before Riley got there.

Cooper paused a beat, his guilt getting the better of him. "Hey listen, you can shower before you go if you'd like. My friend Riley should be here soon, but I'm up now so we're good."

"Is she a girlfriend?" Holly asked, clutching the dress she had worn the night before to her chest, looking uncertain.

Cooper laughed. "Not at all. She lives with my best friend Luke. We work together." He walked Holly down the hall to the bathroom. He turned on the bathroom light, gave her a spare toothbrush, showed her where the towels and toiletries were and stepped out to give her space.

Cooper pulled himself together the best he could. He made his bed. Brushed his teeth in the kitchen sink and splashed water on his face. Cooper was just pulling a shirt over his head when the steady rain of the shower shut off. A knock on his front door followed a few minutes later.

Cooper pulled open the door to find Riley standing there, two coffees from Starbucks in hand and a worried look on her face.

"All okay?" Cooper asked as he stepped aside to let Riley in.

"Not in the least. Luke just received..." Riley stopped midsentence, her attention drawn to the hall.

Holly sauntered into the living room barefoot with her heels in her hand. She looked Riley up and down. Then she pulled Cooper close and laid one hell of a kiss on him, hotter than what got them going the night before. She trailed her hand against his crotch, patted him, and then turned on her heels towards the door. Holly shot Riley a parting look as she slipped out the door.

Riley rolled her eyes, shook her head in disgust and walked farther into his living room. She slumped down into his brown leather sofa and burst into tears.

CHAPTER 4

Cooper froze, unsure of what was happening. He couldn't remember the last time he'd seen Riley cry. Cooper moved to the couch to sit next to her. Riley handed him his coffee. After a few minutes, Riley pulled herself together.

"What's going on?" Cooper sipped his caramel macchiato.

"Luke received a letter today from Lily's killer or someone pretending to be Lily's killer. We don't know much." Riley wiped her face with her hand and took a sip of her coffee.

Cooper stopped drinking, startled by what he heard. He started to speak and stopped, unsure of what to say or where to start.

Before Cooper could form a question, Riley continued. "It was a letter addressed to Luke at work. It wasn't signed. Just block letters that stated that they had killed before Lily and will kill again. There was a crude rhyming line indicating twenty-three victims and then the strange phrase 'harvested dead.'"

Lily as a freshman flashed in Cooper's mind. She had been pretty, vibrant and ready to take on the world. Because of his close friendship with Luke, Cooper had seen Lily often while she had been in high school. Cooper had teased Lily like he would have his own sister, if he had one. Lily had given it right back to Cooper, which amused him. She had been smart and quick-witted. Cooper had felt his own pain at her loss. He could never imagine what Luke had gone through.

It pained Cooper that her murder had never been solved. He had helped Luke, on a few occasions over the years, attempt to dig up new leads. There was never much to go on. Cooper had seen, with his own eyes, what it did to Luke. He was singularly focused for years. Cooper was afraid of what this letter might do to him.

"Any clues as to where the letter came from?"

"I don't think so. Luke's at the station having them run some tests. I didn't even ask about the envelope. Luke rushed out so fast, I didn't get to ask. He didn't want me to come. He asked me to come over here and tell you. The way the letter's written you're not going to get good handwriting analysis, if it got to that. It was crude, childish block letters."

"What does 'harvested dead' mean?" Riley was right that it was a strange phrase, but it didn't have a lot of meaning for him.

"No idea." Riley readjusted herself on the couch. She sighed. "When did Lily go missing exactly?"

"Friday, October twenty-fifth, right before Halloween. Most fraternities were having Halloween parties that weekend. Lily's friends said she went to one and then no one seems to know more. They assumed she left and had walked home alone or went to another party."

"If she was heading home, how far did she have to walk?" Riley checked her phone.

"Probably less than a mile, at most, if she was headed home. Lily was at a fraternity party on Stadium Drive and either headed back to her dorm or to the sorority she had been planning to pledge. Lily had friends there, and she stayed there sometimes. That was located on West Maple Street."

"Lily went missing during the height of fall. Maybe harvest means the time of year," Riley speculated. She got up from the couch and walked into Cooper's kitchen. She rinsed out her cup before throwing it in the trash. When Riley noticed him staring, she shrugged. "Apparently I even clean a disposable cup when I'm stressed."

Riley leaned back on the counter, hugging herself. She seemed near tears, again.

Cooper moved into his kitchen and wrapped her in a hug. "It's going to be okay." Cooper wasn't sure he believed that, but they had to hold it together for Luke.

Moments later, they walked back into the living room and both sat down on the couch. Cooper ran a hand through his hair. He needed to shower and go meet Luke at the police station. He asked, "Do you believe the twenty-three part? Could whoever have killed Lily really have twenty-three victims and no one notices?"

"I don't know," Riley said, exhaustion apparent in her voice. "I'm not sure what to believe."

Before Cooper could ask anything else, Riley changed the subject. "Hey before we forget, I've got that update on the child custody case. I caught the dad with a known meth dealer during his visitation. He had the kids in the car with him. Got photos, but didn't see him buy anything. No money exchange or anything."

Cooper had nearly forgotten why Riley had come over. They had been working a child custody case. The mother was worried that the dad was back into drugs and was concerned for the safety of the two kids, a boy seven years old and the girl nine. Cooper wasn't sure if associating with a known drug dealer would help his client's case, but the evidence certainly might support it.

"I'll let the client know. I can take the case from here while you focus on Luke."

Riley nodded as her cellphone rang. She held it up to show that it was Luke. Cooper indicated he was going to shower while she took the call.

Nearly twenty minutes later, Cooper, showered and freshly dressed, walked into the living room. Riley looked at the phone intently. She looked up when Cooper came into the room. "Luke said we could come down and meet him at the station. They should have lab results back from the envelope. They put a rush on it."

CHAPTER 5

Luke, Captain Meadows, and Det. Tyler stood in the middle of the detective bureau bullpen listening to Sharon, a forensic analyst with the Little Rock Police Department.

Sharon handed the bagged letter to Luke. "We swabbed this really well, but there's nothing we can find. We also swabbed the envelope seal and postage stamp for DNA, but that will take a while. The likelihood of getting anything back is slim. Both are self-adhesive."

They nodded in understanding. When they didn't have questions, Sharon excused herself and left the room.

Luke looked to his partner Tyler and Captain Kurt Meadows. "What do you think?"

Captain Meadows was well past retirement age but wasn't ready to head out to pasture just yet. He explained, "I called Fayetteville. It's postmarked from there, and it's their jurisdiction, so we're going to have to hand it over."

"I'm not handing over a thing," Luke said determined. "They've had seventeen years to solve this, and they haven't done anything. If they had taken this seriously at the start, we might have found my sister sooner."

Captain Meadows put a hand on Luke's shoulder. "You know it has to go to Fayetteville, but I didn't say you couldn't work on it."

"What do you mean?" Luke asked skeptically. He calmed down, but felt the growing knots in his neck and back where he carried his stress.

"I made a call to the detective who handles the cold cases. His name is Gabe Barry. He's young, eager and willing to let you consult. Everyone that originally handled Lily's case has long since retired or moved on to other jurisdictions. Gabe comes highly recommended. I told him you'd give him a call today."

Luke was relieved. At least he would still have a shot at working the case within the confines of his job. But he was going to work it either way. It was just good to know he wouldn't have to risk his job to do it. Luke was just about to thank his Captain when Riley and Cooper got off the elevator. They looked around. Luke called, "We're down here."

Captain Meadows and Tyler turned to see Riley and Cooper make their way down the hall into the detectives' bullpen. Captain Meadows turned back to Luke. "Why don't we take this into the conference room. Bring the letter."

Luke waved Riley and Cooper into the conference room. The five of them sat around the table. They made their hellos, but introductions weren't necessary. The last time they had all sat around the table was just last year when Maime LaRue Brewer went missing.

All seated, Riley slid her hand into Luke's, which was resting on his thigh. He smiled over at her. He was glad she was there with him. Luke was angry and frustrated by his failed previous attempts to find his sister's killer, but this time felt different. The killer had made contact. They had at least a potential lead.

"Did you find out anything?" Cooper asked Luke.

"Nothing," Luke said disappointed. "I didn't think we would, but I was hoping. It was postmarked from Fayetteville, so we know it's local, but that's about it."

"We don't know it's local, Luke," Riley interrupted. "We know it was mailed from there, but it doesn't mean the killer lives there."

Luke paused to consider. He hadn't ever really thought about the killer being from out of state. Most people in Arkansas are from Arkansas. He assumed Lily's killer was another university student or someone local to the community. Even the majority of the students are from within the state or at least the surrounding states.

Captain Meadows spoke up before Luke could. "Why do you think that?"

"Do you have twenty-two other unsolved homicides in Arkansas that are similar?" Riley asked.

Luke appraised Captain Meadows and his partner, Tyler, for any pushback. They gave none.

"That's assuming he's telling the truth. Do you believe him?" Luke asked, moving his seat to face Riley more directly.

Riley nodded. "Why would he send the letter and lie? He got away with an abduction and murder. Given there hasn't even been a clue all these years, I would imagine it wasn't his first. I think if we act on the premise the letter is real, then we should assume the content of it is real, too."

Cooper said what Luke was thinking, "He could just be screwing with us?"

Tyler responded, "He could. But why now? Why after so many years and so close to the anniversary?"

No one had an answer. Luke had known the anniversary was coming, but until Tyler said it out loud, it hadn't really hit home.

Cooper continued, "Back then and through the years, we always thought of this as a sexual assault that got out of hand. We assumed that Lily was killed accidentally or so she couldn't identify her attacker. We never thought or had evidence it was connected to anything else. There were no other murders in Fayetteville, at the time, or even sexual assaults on campus that were similar."

"In Fayetteville or in the whole of Arkansas," Luke added. "We looked into that to see if other areas had similar cases."

"But you didn't go national?" Riley asked, her eyebrows raised.

"No, we didn't have a reason to at the time," Luke noted. "We ruled out her boyfriend. We had no witnesses and no suspects. It was right around Halloween so people were dressed up in costumes for parties so we didn't even have a good eyewitness who saw her on the road walking home. You had a few streets of mostly drunk university kids in costume focused on having a good time. No one was paying attention."

Cooper turned to Riley and added to what Luke said, "We didn't have a solid time Lily left the party, what she was wearing or anything else. Lily wasn't one to dress up for Halloween. She had even told

Luke a few days before that she might throw on her masquerade mask, but other than that, she said she wasn't dressing up."

"Her mask was light pink lace with a flower on one side. It was something my mother had bought her years prior when Lily loved playing dress-up." Remembering his sister so vividly, Luke struggled to get the words out, but he added, "It was one of her favorite possessions. It was missing too and never found. We assume she had it on. One of her friends confirmed."

Captain Meadows suggested, "Have you put all the details you know into ViCAP to see if it connects to other cases nationally?"

"No, but that's a good idea. We should be able to see if any other homicides have similar details."

Just as Luke was speaking, the unit secretary, Charlene, popped her head into the doorway, and with fear in her voice, she stammered, "Luke, there's another letter."

CHAPTER 6

Luke wasn't sure he had heard correctly. He looked around the table. Riley, Cooper, Tyler and Captain Meadows were all frozen in place, looking at him as if waiting for him to react. Luke got up slowly and walked towards the door. He took the letter from Charlene's hands. It was just a white envelope, standard letter size. It was postmarked from Fayetteville. The same block lettering as the last spelled out his name and the police station's address.

Luke turned back toward the group, but his feet were frozen to the spot. He palmed the envelope in his hand, unsure of how to hold it or even if he should. Luke knew it was possible that the same envelope he was holding could have touched the hands that murdered his sister. He swallowed the bile that rose up in his throat. Luke had never felt this close before. He stared down at the letter, unmoving, not speaking. Luke could feel the connection to the killer. Every synapse in his body was on fire. Prickly heat rose up his back. Rage burned in his gut.

Tyler cautioned, "Hold on. Let me get you gloves and a letter opener."

Luke brought his thoughts back to the present. He moved back to the table and set the envelope down. They waited for Tyler to come back. He handed Luke the items, and Luke put on the gloves.

He used the silver letter opener to slice the envelope open, careful not to disturb the contents.

Slipping his gloved fingers between the opening, Luke gently pulled out the letter. As he unfolded it, Luke was shocked by what he saw. This time it wasn't the same block lettering from the envelope and the previous letter. The plain piece of white paper was adorned with scrawling cursive. It was neat and precise. No lines dipped or angled. The black writing was clear and legible.

Luke eyed each person in the room and read the letter aloud, his voice breaking.

> *"Det. Lucas Morgan,*
> *I found myself embarrassed by the display of the first letter. I had a moment's hesitation about being caught and resorted to silly antics to conceal my real handwriting. If the goal is to give you any sporting chance to catch me, I must present a more confident front. This is my handwriting. No subterfuge this time. I want to ensure that you understand how real this is. I killed your sister and several other young girls. I like them young, ripe for the plucking. Please don't mistake that. I did not engage in sexual congress with them. There is a peak freshness of a young girl, just eighteen and on her own for the first time. A wonderment in her eyes. Her flesh soft, supple, unsullied by the world. Oh! How glorious that they go off into the world at harvest time. There is symmetry in the world reflecting back my own desires. I'm careful in my selection. You don't want any bad apples in the bunch. They must be perfect in every way. I can say with confidence, your sister was the sweetest and ripest of them all. I go unobserved. It's not your fault you haven't stopped me. I haven't wanted you to. It's no longer a challenge. A real man needs an adversary to keep the game engaging. You, Det. Morgan, are my adversary and a skilled one at that. I will help you with your investigation. I mentioned twenty-three last time. Check the University of Alabama 1996 & Chamblee University 1993. The harvest at Chamblee was my first.*
> *Until next time. See you on the harvest fields."*

Luke laid the letter on the table. His eyes widened and a wave of nausea took hold. Luke thought he might be sick. No one in the room uttered a word. Lily's face was all he saw. So young and innocent. Taken. Harvested.

After time passed, a hand on Luke's leg grounded him back to reality. Luke locked eyes with Riley and conveyed a thank you with only a look. The silent message of gratitude passed between them. Luke coughed and cleared his throat. He swallowed, but his mouth was dry.

"First thoughts?" he stammered, embarrassed by how shaky his voice sounded.

"Total psycho," Tyler offered quickly. His disgust was apparent. Luke couldn't disagree, but he needed more than that.

"Intelligent by the words he used," Riley offered. "Probably well-educated or at least well-read. Handwriting has a level of precise perfection that is hard to accomplish. If he's had twenty-three kills since 1993, he missed a few seasons. Two at least if we are assuming it was one kill per harvest season. The universities he's mentioned are in the south so he's somewhat familiar with the area."

Nodding in agreement with Riley's assessment, Cooper added, "He acts like he wants to get caught, but I don't believe that. He wants to play a game. If he wanted to get caught, he'd just turn himself in, but there's no fun in that for him."

"I agree," Captain Meadows said. "Before we get ahead of ourselves, let's confirm any facts in this letter. If it's all true, we need to call in the FBI. Tyler, get on the phone to Atlanta Police and Chamblee University to see what we can confirm. Luke, start with Alabama. We're going to need more resources on this."

"How can I help?" Riley offered.

Luke turned to her. "Why don't you go search for news reports and see if you can find anything related to these old cases. Cooper, why don't you do a general search for missing university girls. Start in the south and then go more national. Let's all meet around one o'clock and compare notes."

Each of them slowly got up from the table and gave Luke a reassuring look before they left the room. Cooper squeezed his shoulder. Riley wrapped her arms around him and whispered that he'd be okay. Luke wasn't sure he would. His thoughts right now were spinning.

CHAPTER 7

I went back home to do the research. I didn't have my laptop with me at the police station and I didn't want to take another detective's desk, not that anyone was offering. Cooper said he was heading back to his loft. Luke stayed at the station.

As I pulled into my driveway, my best friend Emma was on her porch. We developed a fast and easy friendship when I had lived in Little Rock, years earlier. Time and distance had only strengthened the bond when I had moved away for a few years. Now that I was back, friendship had easily turned to family.

"Joe saw Luke leave earlier. He said Luke looked upset. Everything okay?" Emma called out. She stepped down from her porch and crossed the distance into my yard. Her naturally dark hair had grown out from her normal chin-length bob. It was now past her shoulders, straight and pretty. A drastic contrast to my auburn tresses that were long, but never tamed. While we were about the same height, Emma was small framed and thin. We'd never share clothes, as I was positive that I'd never get her pants past my ample hips and generous backside.

I still felt numb from hearing Luke read the letter, but when Emma wrapped her arms around me, it was like breaking ice. My façade was shattered and it was hard to hold back the tears. I quickly unlocked and opened my front door. I made my way to the kitchen with Emma in tow. After pouring glasses of tea from the fridge, we sat at a small round table.

I detailed the events of the morning, including everything I could remember from the letters. Emma was my secret-keeper, so I was sure that the conversation wouldn't go beyond us.

"He sounds insane," Emma said, as I finished.

"Definitely, but with the upper hand at the moment."

"This brings back some memories I hadn't thought about in several years." Emma traced her finger around her glass. She paused as if thinking. "There was a girl missing from the University of Charleston when I was a sophomore. She was a junior. The police thought her boyfriend was involved. They never did find her." Emma looked off into the distance, not really seeming to focus on anything.

I wasn't sure if she was lost in thought or feeling as sad as I felt. I put my hand on her arm. "Unfortunately, I'm sure there are a lot of university girls that go missing. It's a strange time in life. Some, I'm sure, run away and others are vulnerable."

"I know. It's just so sad. There's so much violence." Emma sighed, stifling back a few tears. She pulled a tissue out of her pocket and blew her nose.

I took a sip of tea and eyed her suspiciously. "I know this is upsetting for all of us, but you're not usually this emotional. What's up?"

Emma smoothed a hand down her hair, tucking it behind her ears. She gave me a lopsided grin. "Sophie is off to pre-school. I was planning to take a few copywriting jobs here or there again, but I confirmed at the doctor this morning, that Sophie is going to be a big sister."

Sophie was Emma's four-year-old daughter. She was a miniature version of Emma, but with bouncy dark curls. She was smart and adorable. The thought of Emma having another child made me smile despite everything. I raised my eyebrows in an unspoken question.

"We're thrilled," Emma reassured. "We had been trying for more than a year. I thought it wasn't going to happen so I had given up hope. I had just settled into thinking that Sophie would be our only. I was excited about going back to work. It's just a shift in thinking."

Emma laughed. "And I'm hormonal."

"You can still work. It's not the 1950s."

"I know, but you know Joe. I told him, and the first thing he said was that now I didn't have to go back to work. Not that I had to. His construction business is booming so we don't need the money. It just gave me a little more to do."

"Go back to work or not, up to you, but you can always take a job here or there as you feel like it. How are you feeling?"

"Great otherwise." Emma looked at the clock above my stove. She put her glass in the sink. "I need to let you get back. Sophie gets out of pre-school early today so I need to run and get her." Emma kissed me on the cheek as she left.

I poured another glass of tea, grabbed an apple, and went up to my office. I settled into my desk and turned on my laptop to start my search. It only took a few minutes of putting in different search terms to find what I was looking for. I found a missing person's podcast that had an entire episode on Jordan Baker who went missing from Chamblee University in 1993. The podcast was from a few years ago, but hopefully, it would provide some detail.

I took a sip of tea, bit into the apple and clicked the button to listen. I found it to be more detailed than I thought it would be and spent a good deal of time taking notes. An hour later when it was over, I was convinced it was connected to Lily's case. I stood briefly to stretch my legs, checked my phone, and then got back down to work.

The missing person's case in Alabama was harder to find. Finally, after a few searches, I came up with a brief news article that indicated that a young freshman had run away in their fall semester. It offered little in the way of details and it didn't seem like there had been a police investigation. I typed in a few more search terms and found a website dedicated to the case. I suspected her parents or other family had set it up. I jotted down a few notes. Some of the details were consistent with the other missing persons' cases we were exploring.

CHAPTER 8

Luke wasn't having much luck with the Alabama case. He'd been on the phone for more than two hours. He had tried to gain some information from the University of Alabama first, before calling the local police department, but was passed from one person to the next. Finally, Luke was connected to their campus security department. He waited on hold for more than twenty minutes only to be told by a guy – that sounded too young to even be attending school there – that no one was reported missing in 1996.

Luke wasn't satisfied with the answer so he called another administrative office. Finally, after being bounced around by several people again, he spoke with a woman who wouldn't give Luke her name, but said she did recall a freshman who had "taken off and left the campus leaving her parents in a panic."

When Luke pressed if she remembered the young lady's name, the woman offered the name Francine Thomas. The woman said Francine never returned to school. The woman stressed that the only reason she even remembered was that the parents had caused such an uproar that it was impossible to forget.

At least Luke had a name. Although he had no idea if this was even the case his mystery letter writer was indicating. Next, Luke made a call to the Tuscaloosa Police Department. He was quickly connected to a detective in charge but didn't get much further with the police than he did with the university. There was no missing person's report that the detective could find on a Francine Thomas, or anyone, missing from the school in 1996.

Luke knew Riley was scouring the internet for the case, but with a name, he assumed he'd get further. As soon as he typed, "Francine Thomas University of Alabama" into the search engine, Luke found information right there on the first page. Francine's parents Isaac and Margo Thomas or someone close to the family had launched a website to provide details about Francine, her disappearance, searches, and recent events, of which it didn't look like there was much.

From what Luke read, it seems Frannie, as she was known to family and friends, had been a freshman at the University of Alabama and had disappeared one Friday night walking back from the library. Luke searched around for the date of her disappearance. A chill ran down his spine when he saw it. Friday, October twenty-fifth. That fit.

The last date in the news section of the website was more than five years ago. While someone was still keeping the website available, it didn't look like much was happening with the case. Most of the information looked like it had been added in the months and early years after Frannie disappeared. Luke didn't see a phone number on the website, but the site indicated that Frannie was from Huntsville.

After a quick search, Luke found a phone number for an Isaac Thomas. He paused, not sure what exactly he'd say to the family. He didn't want to give false hope, but he certainly needed information. Luke punched in the number. It rang three times and the call was answered by an older man with a deep voice.

After asking some initial questions to make sure he was speaking with the right Isaac Thomas, Luke gently explained why he was calling. At the mention of his daughter's disappearance, Isaac sounded hesitant to speak. Luke offered to let Isaac call him back at the police station. Luke also quickly added that his sister went missing her freshman year, too.

"I'm sorry for your loss," Isaac said directly. "We've had a lot of crazies calling us since Frannie went missing. Psychics and even well-meaning people. It's just too much for us, you understand?"

"I understand completely," Luke said, hoping to put the man at ease. "I don't want to take up much of your time, or open the wounds, but there are a few things I need to understand. Why is there no police report or information from the university about Frannie's disappearance?"

"It's simple. Both denied she was taken," Isaac said matter-of-factly. Luke could hear the frustration in his voice. "They told us Frannie must have had a boyfriend and took off with him. Frannie didn't have a boyfriend. She was a straight-A student, focused on going to law school. She didn't party. No drugs. No drinking. Best we can tell, she was snatched on her way home from the library. She didn't run away."

"The police or school officials didn't believe that?" Luke jotted down notes.

"They didn't believe a word we said. Barely even gave us the time of day. We had to do it on our own. The searches, the tip line, website, all of it ourselves. We even hired a couple of private investigators. One took our money and ran. The other gave us our money back when he couldn't even find one lead to go on."

Isaac paused. "I'm sorry," Isaac finally said softy. "You'd think I'd be past this given how many years have gone by. She was our youngest, and not knowing what happened to her has been the hardest part. Even if all we had was her body, we could have set ourselves to grieving. Just not knowing, well, it takes its toll."

Luke understood better than the man knew. While he'd give anything to have his sister back, they at least were able to bury her. Lily was at least found. It was something he and his parents had reflected back on when times were hard. Luke hadn't planned on getting too far into the details of why he was calling and making the inquiry, but there was something about the man's voice he trusted. Luke wanted to give him something.

"We can't say for sure, but we've come across some potential evidence that your daughter's disappearance might be connected to my sister's. We just wanted more information for comparison, but some of the details are similar."

"Can you tell me more?" Isaac asked.

"Not yet, but as soon as I know more, I'll call you back."

"Anything at this late stage would be nothing short of a miracle. If you call back, please just ask for me. I don't want my wife to get her hopes up. This changed us as a family. I just can't see her hurt anymore."

"I understand. Hopefully, soon I'll have some answers for you."
Luke ended the call. When he looked up from his notes, Tyler stood
in front of his desk with notes in hand.

Luke raised his eyebrows.

"Seems like Chamblee could be connected."

"Alabama, too," Luke informed him.

CHAPTER 9

It was a little before one in the afternoon before I made it back to the police station. I picked up lunch for Luke who I was sure hadn't eaten. When I arrived at the station, I climbed the wide-open staircase up to the detectives' bullpen. Luke was seated with his head down focused on a stack of papers in front of him. I made my way over and placed the bag of food down in his line of sight.

He looked up and caught my eye. "Have I told you, today, how much I love you?"

"I think three times so far. I love you, too."

Luke stood and looked around the room. Then he planted a kiss on my lips. He wasn't one for public displays of affection, especially at work. After we pulled apart, Luke sat down and dug into the food.

"Make any headway?" I glanced at his notes. Luke has his own shorthand that didn't always make sense to me.

"Some," he said in between bites, "but let's wait until the others are here so we can go over it together."

I took the chair across from his desk. "I didn't really get a chance to say it before, but I'm sorry you're going through all this. If you want me to come with you when you tell your parents, I will. If you want to handle it alone, I understand that, too."

Luke smiled up at me. "You're getting better at this relationship thing."

He was right, but it still didn't come as naturally to me as it did for Luke. Cooper's voice echoed behind me. He was talking to Det. Tyler and Captain Meadows as they came down the hall. Luke yelled to them that we'd join them in the conference room. He gathered up what was left of his lunch and his notes, and we headed into the conference room. We all took seats around the table with our notes in front of us.

Once we got settled, Luke asked Tyler, "What did you find on Chamblee?"

"Seems like it fits. Jordan Baker went missing on October 29, 1993. Basically, Halloween weekend. Except she wasn't at a party like your sister. She was in the library."

"She went missing from the library, or on the way home?" Luke asked, with a confused look on his face. He got up and went to the dry erase board at the far end of the room. He jotted down case details, forming a timeline.

"Well that's just it," Tyler continued. "No one knows. Jordan was in the library one minute and seemed like the next, she was gone. They found her notebooks and some textbooks on the table along with a few other personal items, but she was nowhere to be found. When they closed the library, they assumed she met up with a friend and left her stuff there."

"It's a really bizarre case, Luke," I added. "There is a missing person's podcast that did an entire show on this case a few years ago."

"What did they say?" Luke asked with interest.

I flipped through my notes. "Jordan didn't have a roommate because her roommate had dropped out of the university. They hadn't given her another. Jordan hadn't made that many friends because she was studying so much, at least according to her sister who spoke on the podcast. It was one of her professors, Jill Turner, who finally got suspicious because Jordan never missed class. After she missed three, Turner went to Jordan's dorm, but she wasn't there. The girl next door said she hadn't seen Jordan in a while. The professor went to the administration, got the girl's parents' number and called them. Once Jordan's parents got involved, they finally did a search of the campus and found all the school and personal items that Jordan had left in the library. The library staff had set it aside but didn't notify anyone. Although, the podcast did speculate there was a library staff person who might know more but had been unwilling to talk all these years."

Tyler looked back down at his notes and added, "Atlanta police department didn't even take a report. I called, and they had nothing. They were only familiar with the case because the podcast had renewed interest in the community. I talked to a detective in their cold cases who said maybe one day they'd take a look, but it was never an open case for them. The university line is she ran away because the pressure got too much for her. She was from Hattiesburg, Mississippi. Her parents are hardworking folks but didn't have the money to fight the system. Jordan was going to university on a full scholarship. Her family used what resources they had, but there has never been a full-scale investigation. Jordan, it seems, just vanished."

"They a black family?" Luke asked.

"Yes," Riley answered. "The victim in the Alabama case is black as well. It's too early to tell, but I wonder if that's his victim type. What did you find out there?"

Luke spent a few minutes filling us in on the case related to the University of Alabama. Similar circumstances to Chamblee University, but people saw Frannie leave the library. She had told friends she was heading back to her dorm. With Jordan, they didn't even know that much. I didn't have much to add that Luke hadn't already found out.

"What do you think?" Luke asked when he was finished going over everything. He looked around the room at us, but I wasn't sure what to tell him. I didn't feel like I had enough to say for certain that the guy was real. He could have easily pulled the details from the Chamblee case from the podcast. While not much was out there about the case in Alabama, there was still a website he could have stumbled across. Before I could explain that to Luke, Captain Meadows said what I was thinking.

He leaned his arms on the table and looked directly at Luke. "It sounds like all he told us could be found online. I'm not saying he's not the real deal, but I also haven't ruled out he's some twisted sicko screwing with you."

Cooper stood and pulled a thick file folder from his knapsack. "I'd agree with you," he said as he slapped the folder down on the table, "but I found some interesting cases in a broad search and a scary trend."

CHAPTER 10

Cooper had our full attention. He bent over the file folder and pulled out pages that were clipped together. He explained, "I had no idea the minefield I was walking into when you asked me to do a broad search, Luke. I thought I'd maybe come across a few cases. There are seventy-nine cases going back to 1990. These are the cases of missing university girls where either there was no body found, or a body was found and the case remains unsolved."

Cooper handed stacks to each of us. Captain Meadows took a handful and asked, "You said you found a scary trend?"

Cooper nodded as he handed a stack to me. "Yeah, all the freshmen went missing in October. I didn't notice it at first. Then I hit three cases in a row that were all freshmen and all went missing in October. I went back through them all again and noted that all the missing girls who were freshmen at the time of their disappearance went missing in October."

I flipped through the pages, taking in their contents. Most were pages from websites created by families or friends of the missing. Some pages were pulled off other sites including social media.

"The cases from Chamblee and Alabama are in there. Your sister too, Luke," Cooper noted.

Luke rubbed his hand down his face. "Are there any other similarities?"

"Not that I saw, but I didn't dive in too deep. I didn't screen out age, or location, or anything like that."

Cooper picked up a page and held it up. "Like this one, I wouldn't think this is connected. This girl is from UCLA and had a boyfriend who went missing at the same time. She was a senior. It just doesn't seem to fit the same circumstances as the others."

We all nodded in agreement.

"What do you want us to look for?" Tyler asked, holding his own stack in front of him.

Luke looked at all of us but seemed at a loss for words. After a few seconds, he informed us, "I guess just look through and see if anything feels like it fits. I don't even know what to narrow down. Cooper said the freshmen girls went missing in October. My sister went missing from a party and the other two have library connections. That's all we are really working with. Better to cast a wider net right now. Let's make three piles – freshmen who seem to fit, others that seem to fit, and then those cases that don't fit."

We all put our heads down to read the pages in front of us. The stack in front of me had pages with photos. Girls stared back at me. They were so young with so much potential in life snatched away. It was depressing to think about too deeply.

Every few minutes one of us would add to the piles. The freshman pile seemed to be growing more rapidly than the others. No one said much, but there was the occasional deep sigh.

When Luke added the last case, he picked up the freshmen pile and flipped through it, counting the number of cases. Then he started making two piles out of them.

"What are you seeing?" I asked.

"I'm just separating by location." Luke moved one pile to the right and indicated that they were all the cases, twenty-five in all, that were east coast and south. The smaller pile had cases out west in Oregon, Colorado and South Dakota.

"Are you thinking those don't fit?" Tyler inquired as he picked up the pile of three cases and started thumbing through them.

"They were just the odd ones out so I wasn't sure. Not that they wouldn't fit. We just seem to have a bigger cluster on the east coast and in the south especially.

"We'll need to go through these and see what more we can find out," Luke indicated. He directed his attention to Det. Tyler. "I need you to run my sister's case through ViCAP and see what else comes back. Then we can cross-reference to this list."

Luke turned to Cooper and me, "It would be great if you two could start making some calls like we did for Chamblee and Alabama. Just tell them you're a researcher for the Little Rock Police and that you might have some connected cases. If they give you a hard time, tell them to call me."

"Do you want to call the FBI in?" Captain Meadows asked Luke.

"Not yet. If we are going to bring them in, I want to at least have a better idea of what we're working with."

"What's your plan then?" Captain Meadows asked, clearly concerned.

"First I'm going to talk to my parents. Then I'm going to connect with Detective Barry in Fayetteville and go over all the evidence we have with Lily's case one more time. I need to get a better handle on that, while everyone else is running down other leads. Then we can regroup and see what we have. If we don't have a strong case that meets their jurisdiction, the FBI won't even listen."

CHAPTER 11

Luke left the police station about an hour after they wrapped the meeting. He had kissed Riley goodbye and explained that he'd better talk to his parents alone. She understood and headed home. As Luke navigated his way to his parents' Hillcrest neighborhood, the same one he grew up in, he talked aloud, hoping his sister could hear him. Luke wasn't exactly sure he believed in life after death, but he figured he'd hedge his bets anyway.

Luke asked Lily for the strength to be able to tell his parents what was happening and find her killer. He apologized again for not being there to protect her and vowed once again to bring her killer to justice. Luke thought of her smile and the bossy way she was with him. At least that brought a smile to his face. He was sure if there was a heaven, she would have center stage.

Lily might have been three years younger than Luke, but she was the bossy sibling for sure. Luke sometimes even took her advice, although he never let on, for fear it would have encouraged her to continue her bossy ways.

While he felt silly for talking to his sister, Luke really did need to summon some strength to talk to his parents. He had no idea how they were going to react. His father, Spencer, and mother, Lucia, were married for forty-one years. His mother was sixty-six and his father sixty-seven. They had Luke in their late twenties and his sister in their early thirties. Both were retired now, but when Luke was growing up his dad was an eye doctor and his mother a high school English teacher.

Luke pulled his car into the driveway of his parents' Hillcrest home, situated across from Allsopp Park on S. Lookout Road near the corner of Fairview Road. The house was grand with a brick walkway flanked on either side by fall flowers. The landscape was gorgeous. During her retirement, his mother had taken to learning all she could about cultivating beautiful flowers. This was the house Luke grew up in. He knew every nook and detail of the place.

Luke parked in the driveway and made his way into the house via the side door, which led right into the mudroom. He kicked off his shoes and made his way into the kitchen. Luke grabbed an oatmeal raisin cookie from the plate on the table and took a bite. They were soft, still slightly warm, and fresh. His mother must have just baked them.

Luke found his parents sitting in the family room. Spencer was relaxing on the sectional while Lucia read a book in her favorite chair, which was so wide and deep it seemed to consume her. It was her favorite spot, and outside of the kitchen, Luke would have been surprised to find her anywhere else. She always read there, catching the light from the window.

"Luke, honey, we didn't hear you come in." Lucia looked up from her book as he entered the room. Luke gave his mother a quick peck on the cheek.

Luke walked over to his father and sat next to him on the couch. He wrung his hands in front of him. Looking down at the floor, he blurted, "I wanted to talk to you both. I'm not really sure how to tell you, but I have some news about Lily's case."

His mother set her book down and moved closer to the edge of her seat. Luke's father looked at him with his eyes wide. Luke looked up at each of them, making eye contact for the first time. "I got a letter at the police station from a man who claims he's Lily's killer. He said that he had killed before and would kill again."

Lucia gasped loudly as Luke spoke. She got up from the chair, crossed the room and sat down next to Spencer. He put his arm around her. She urged Luke to go on.

"He said he had killed twenty-three girls. He sent another letter, which I received this afternoon. He said he had killed at Chamblee

University in 1993 and the University of Alabama in 1996. Cooper and Riley are helping. This afternoon we found those cases and several others that could possibly be connected. I'm going to head up to Fayetteville tomorrow."

His parents were both silent. They shared a look with each other and then Spencer asked, "You think it's credible?"

"I do, Dad," Luke offered sincerely. "We were able to confirm those cases he mentioned. The victims were freshmen, too. All of the disappearances happened in October like Lily. There are other things too I can't go into, but I feel it in my gut. It's the real deal."

Lucia cried softly. Spencer didn't say anything for a few moments, then turned to Luke and asked, "Do you really think it's best if you go? Maybe one of the other detectives should handle it."

Luke shook his head and sighed loudly. "You don't think I can solve the case, do you?"

Both of his parents started to speak, but Luke cut them off. "I know you've been disappointed in me, but I finally have something to go on and you want me to give it to someone else? That's how little you think of me?"

Luke got up from the couch and stood in front of them. Lucia grabbed for Luke's hand, but he pulled it back. Luke glared down at them, fighting back tears. He wasn't even sure what he wanted to say.

Spencer looked up at Luke, his eyes serious and his mouth set in a firm line. Finally, he stood and put his hand on Luke's shoulder. "Son, we think nothing of the sort. Don't be so defensive. We are just worried about you. We know how hard you've tried to solve this case. This is, well, I don't even have words for what this is. Like you, we always assumed it was another student. You're telling us it's a killer who has killed twenty-three times. We all want justice, but my biggest concern is you."

Luke calmed down almost immediately. His shoulders relaxed, and he was embarrassed for losing his cool. Luke had always felt like his parents were disappointed he hadn't found the killer. There was always a part of him that felt like a failure as a detective, as a brother, and as a man. Riley told him all the time no one else felt that way about him, especially his parents.

Luke shook it off. "I'm fine," he said.

Spencer stood watching him.

"Dad, I'm serious. I'm fine. I have Riley and Cooper to help me. Riley is going to stay here and do some research and calls for me while I head up to Fayetteville. There's a new detective there I'm going to meet."

"I pray this can finally stop, not just for us, but for all the families." Lucia reached for her husband's hand. "You'll be careful, Luke, won't you?"

Lucia looked at Luke with such worry in her eyes that he reached down and hugged her. He said in her ear, "Of course. I'll send Riley over for dinner while I'm gone. She can probably use the company."

Breaking the tension, Spencer asked, "When are you going to make an honest woman of her?"

Luke smiled for the first time since he had arrived. "Soon, Dad, soon."

CHAPTER 12

"Since when do you pout?" Luke asked Riley, who was sitting in the middle of their bed, watching him pack. Her eyes were on Luke's back as he took shirts and pants out of the closet and dresser and arranged them neatly in his suitcase. He didn't really know how long he'd be gone.

"Since you are leaving for Fayetteville while a deranged killer is on the loose."

"Are you scared to be here on your own? I know you haven't really spent a night alone since everything happened last year. You can stay with my parents, or Cooper can stay here with you."

Riley shook her head and said calmly, "You misunderstood me. I'm worried about you. You're heading up there alone. We all know how difficult this case is for you. I don't like you being there in Fayetteville without me, or at least Cooper."

Luke thought her concern was sweet but displaced. He went back to packing. "Riley, I'm fine, really I am. My parents are worried too, but I got this. You and Cooper just work on the other cases and see if there are any leads, especially the early cases. He might have slipped up somewhere. They usually do early on before they perfect their crimes."

Riley shrugged, probably knowing she wasn't going to get very far with him on this. "In all seriousness, do you really think this guy is legit? I know we found those two cases he mentioned, but he could have found them online."

"I know it's him without a question," Luke countered. He didn't really want to go over this again. He was tired of answering the question. Luke felt it in his gut. That's all he could say, and the only answer he had. Plus, Luke knew as sure as he was standing there that the guy would be in contact again. Luke was hoping he'd let more slip. Luke hated that he needed the killer to direct him, but the guy, at least with his sister, left no discernible clues. It frustrated Luke to his core.

Riley put her arms about Luke, resting her head on his back. "I know you believe him. Even though I'm trying to stay reasonable and logical, I think I know, too."

Luke turned around and hugged Riley, resting his chin on the top of her head. "I don't really want to go away and leave you here, but it's probably best we separate to get things done."

Riley squeezed him back and then moved out of his arms, sitting back down on the bed. Luke looked down at her, his face pained. "Before I leave, I wanted to ask if you have any ideas on a profile of the killer. I'm feeling a little out of my depth on this."

"Unfortunately, not a clue. I mean, so far, the three cases we have are connected to universities. If that's where he hunts, I would imagine he has to be somewhat inconspicuous in the environment. Given the span of years, he is probably well into his forties or fifties, and he's clearly intelligent. He'd have to blend in pretty well, otherwise, someone would have noticed a creepy suspicious guy. Either he's luring them away from campus somehow, or they went willingly because they knew him."

"My sister would never just walk off with a stranger," Luke said, with confidence.

"You never know," Riley countered. "It might have been someone in her classes or someone from campus. Someone could have asked her for help, or directions. Serial killers have a million tricks up their sleeves. Just don't make any judgments on her. We all go a little outside our comfort zone sometimes, especially at college. Just don't make any assumptions."

Luke knew what Riley meant. He still thought of his sister as a little girl.

"Promise me?" Riley insisted. "You might overlook something right in front of you."

"I promise," Luke said solemnly. He finished packing and set the suitcase aside for the morning. He pulled out shorts and a tee-shirt to get comfortable for the evening.

Luke walked to the bathroom to brush his teeth. Catching his reflection in the mirror, he didn't like what he saw. His tired eyes were swollen and drooping. The wrinkle across his forehead was more apparent. The case was just getting started. Luke finished up and walked back into the bedroom. As he entered the room, Riley informed him, "We had so much commotion, today, that I didn't even tell you Emma is pregnant again."

Luke was surprised. Joe hadn't mentioned that the last time they got together. "I bet they are happy. How far along is she?"

"She just confirmed at the doctor. Two months, or so, I think."

"What do you think? Should we start trying?" Luke teased her with a half-smile. He wanted to be a dad, and more importantly, he was ready to be a dad. Luke knew whether Riley believed it, or not, she would be a great mom.

"Not even close to ready for that." Riley laughed. She reached for him. Luke let himself be pulled on top of her. She kissed him sweetly. His hands roamed over her. She whispered, "We can have all the fun we want pretending to try."

Luke groaned. He was going to miss her.

CHAPTER 13

After we ate breakfast, Luke hit the road for Fayetteville. I cleaned up the kitchen and threw ingredients in the slow cooker for dinner. Then I grabbed the stack of cases Cooper had given me and another cup of coffee and headed back upstairs to my home office.

Luke had done a great job of helping me paint and pull the room together after he moved in. I had used it previously as a reading room. There had been a bookcase and chair, but not much else. We had picked out an ocean blue color for the walls, white for the trim and found the perfect white and blue pattern throw rug to cover the cold hardwoods. I accentuated it with some prints on the walls and a comfortable couch and my desk. The bookcase stacked with my favorite reads and investigative books remained.

I quickly got down to work going through the case files, one by one. I developed a system fairly quickly. I read the pages in each file thoroughly, looked up additional information online, and made calls to universities and police departments to try to find police reports or talk to detectives if any had been assigned.

I was so comfortable in my office and so engrossed in the work, that when I finally caught sight of the time on my phone, I was surprised that four hours had passed.

The cases where girls were still missing were much harder to dig up information because many investigations had stalled out completely with no new leads. Some of the detectives had retired or had moved on to other assignments within the departments. Some cases were sitting on cold case shelves. If a body had been found, there was more to go on.

I had four cases among the ones Cooper had given me where a body was found. One from North Carolina and the other from Washington D.C. were like what had happened with Lily. Only the victims' skeletal remains were found.

The cases in Virginia and New York were more interesting because the girls' bodies were found relatively early and autopsies were completed as well as thorough assessments of the crime scenes. Although from what I could tell so far, the cases were never solved, but at least law enforcement had launched full-scale investigations.

The most surprising was that the New York case had happened in my hometown of Troy. As I read the internet pages Cooper had pulled, my eyes grew wide in disbelief. I read it a few more times just to make sure. But there it was in black and white. It had to have been in someone else's pile when we initially went through them because it hadn't been in mine.

Back on October 27, 2000, a freshman from Russell Sage College, an all-girls college located in downtown Troy, had gone missing from a house party on Pawling Avenue located in Troy's Eastside neighborhood. The neighborhood was a mix of stately homes and older well-established residents mixed with Rensselaer Polytechnic Institute, known often as RPI, fraternities and university students living in flats, in the many two- and three-family houses that dotted the neighborhood.

I grew up in the neighborhood. In fact, my mom still owned her house on Locust Avenue. It was the kind of place that, even in high school, I'd felt safe at two in the morning – not that I was ever allowed out at that hour. I was having trouble imagining a serial killer roaming those streets in search of a victim.

The neighborhood was the last place where freshman Amanda Taylor was seen alive. Her body was found several miles away in Forest Park Cemetery, locally known as Pinewoods Cemetery, because it was located on Pinewoods Avenue. Locals also sometimes just referred to it as the "haunted cemetery" because, by all accounts, it was.

The more I read about the case, the more it started to come back to me. I had completely forgotten about it. I wasn't living in Troy when Amanda went missing. I was away at college. It was a few days later when her body had been found by someone walking their dog.

The cemetery was supposed to be off-limits. It was abandoned and overgrown. But that didn't stop people from taking a stroll through, or kids getting drunk and seeing how much they could scare each other, lurking among the broken headstones and tall weeds.

The entrance to the cemetery was hardly an entrance at all. It was more like a warning. It was heavily tree-covered and marked by gravel at the front and then grass. It had no paved road leading in or out. Four white pillars and closed black wrought iron gates marked its entrance. There were no signs or markers to indicate the cemetery name and barely any graves were visible from the road. Pinewoods Avenue itself was just a narrow two-lane road marked by homes and farmland. If a driver blinked, they'd miss passing the cemetery altogether.

Just beyond the gates stood the only original structure that had been built before the Forest Park Cemetery Corporation went bankrupt in 1914, and the original plans for the cemetery went unfinished. The structure was a receiving tomb made of granite and once featured a copper roof with a large skylight. It had contained 128 marble catacombs and was used for storing corpses during the winter. From the time I was young, all I could ever remember was its creepy dilapidated state. Really it was just a shell with the roof and even the walls gone. Bodies had been buried in the cemetery back to 1856, but by 1975, it was pretty much abandoned. There were close to 1,400 burials there, at least according to records.

Urban legend and spooky lore were pretty much all I knew about the place. I'd gone in with friends in high school, and we scared ourselves more than anything. Some of the old burial monuments were ornate, but sadly many have been destroyed and vandalized over time.

Amanda's body was found propped up against a large gravestone that had a wide granite base. Sitting atop the base was a solid cross with a large sculpted angel in front. The angel had broad intricately designed wings and a flowing dress. Whether it was made that way, or worn over time, the angel was missing its head and right arm, below the elbow. The statue itself was captivating in its realism, but a bit unnerving all the same. Seeing the headless angel would be enough. I couldn't even imagine the dead body of a young woman propped up against it.

CHAPTER 14

Pulling up in front of the Fayetteville Police Department on W. Rock Street, Luke realized he had missed two calls from Riley. Cell service wasn't the best on the stretch of 1-49 from Fort Smith to Fayetteville. Luke assumed that's when Riley had called, but calling her back would have to wait.

Luke couldn't check into his hotel until at least four in the afternoon. That was fine because he wanted to meet with Det. Gabe Barry before he did anything. Luke got out of his SUV and shifted his bag on his shoulder. He walked confidently into the police station and gave his name at the front desk. The cop directed Luke through the double doors and up the stairs to the detective bureau. He assured Luke that Det. Barry was ready and waiting for him.

Luke navigated the simple directions with ease. When he got to the top of the wide stairway that led directly into Fayetteville's detective bullpen, he was surprised by how much it looked like his own office. Several desks sat in the middle of a large room with other more private conference rooms and offices bordering it. A young African-American detective, shorter than Luke by a few inches and far more muscular, walked towards Luke.

"Det. Barry, I'm Luke Morgan." Luke extended his hand.

The detective clasped Luke's hand in a firm handshake. "Please just call me Gabe. I'm happy to meet you. I've looked at your sister's case a few times before you reached out. It's definitely been an interest of mine."

"Mine too for years," Luke admitted, "but there isn't much to go on."

Gabe directed Luke back to his office, which was in the far corner of the room. As Luke entered, he was taken aback by the rows of stacked boxes piled up on all sides. They were evidence boxes labeled with the familiar codes and markers. Gabe pulled three boxes from the pile and put them on a round table he had at the side of his office. He indicated to Luke to take one of the chairs.

"Do you want to start with the letters?" Gabe asked as he sat down.

Luke pulled the bagged letters from his brown leather messenger bag and handed them over to Gabe. As Gabe inspected them, Luke explained, "We called Chamblee University and the University of Alabama as well as the local police departments. But not much from either. Chamblee University denies that anything happened. The University of Alabama didn't have much because that victim wasn't missing from the university grounds, but rather walking home on city streets. They assume she just ran away. I talked to her father and he said there is no way she ran away. Neither has been heard from again. No bodies ever recovered."

Gabe nodded in understanding. Holding up the letter, he asked skeptically, "Any firm confirmation this is real?"

Luke shook his head. "Other than finding missing girls at both places he said we would, no. My team hasn't fully confirmed that this is the perp responsible. We felt it was worth exploring though." Luke wanted to scream that he knew for sure, but had decided on the drive up that a more conservative approach might get him further. But then Gabe surprised him.

"Don't tell me what you can prove. What do you really think in your gut?"

"He's good for it," Luke said confidently and relieved. "I have my girlfriend and my best friend, both licensed private investigators, looking into some other similar cases we came across. We are running my sister's case through ViCAP. My partner will give us a shout if he's got anything."

Gabe read the letters again through the sealed bag. After he finished, he handed them back to Luke.

"What do you think?"

Gabe sat back and didn't say anything for a few seconds. He seemed to mull his thoughts over. Then he said finally, "I feel like it's credible, but we don't have a team big enough to investigate them all."

Before Luke could say another word, they were interrupted by a knock at the door. A tall, thin man with skin the color of paste, like he'd never seen the sun, stood in the office doorway holding a file.

Gabe walked over and shook the man's hand. "Luke, meet Chris Starling. He's the Washington County Coroner. I asked him to go over the reports on your sister and see if he found anything of interest."

Luke got up and shook the man's hand. He had been hoping to get the medical examiner's report and bring it back to Ed Purvis, the Pulaski County medical examiner. Luke trusted Purvis far more than anyone in the field.

"Got anything of interest, Chris?" Gabe asked, as they each took a seat around the table.

"It seems from the report, all we had was your sister's skeletal remains. Is that correct?"

"That's right," Luke replied. "I've never seen the report, but were there any markings on the bones, anything to indicate— well anything?"

"Are you aware we didn't have all her bones? A full skeleton wasn't found," Chris explained.

Luke was caught off guard. No, it wasn't something he knew or had ever given much thought to. At the time that Lily's skeleton was found, most of it was intact. Even later when Luke investigated, he had never received any of the records from Washington County so he didn't know. It was a cold case, and they weren't willing to give up the reports, even to fellow law enforcement, no matter how hard Luke tried.

Luke explained, "No, I don't know that we were ever told that. I'd have to ask my parents though. I was at the police academy when Lily was found. Maybe it was something I missed in conversation, but I feel like I'd remember. What was missing?"

Holding up his own left hand and pointing with his right index finger, Chris indicated, "Her left hand was missing the bones of her middle, ring and pinkie fingers. What's most interesting is that there are saw marks on the metacarpal bones that connect the fingers to the hand."

"What does that mean?" Gabe asked what Luke was thinking.

"It looks like someone sawed off her fingers," Chris said, matter-of-factly.

Luke tried desperately not to show the emotion that he felt inside. It was a mix of rage and sorrow. This was new information for Luke. It was not something his family was told. He'd have definitely remembered that. Luke hated to think of his sister like this, but if he was going to investigate, he needed professional distance. "Any chance her fingers could have been torn apart by animals or something like that?"

"No, not at all. There were distinctive serrated cut marks on the bones indicating a saw-like motion. It wasn't stabbing but rather cutting." Chris indicated the back and forth motion with his hand.

"Anything else?" Luke swallowed.

"No, but the coroner, at the time, took photos as they should have so we have them with the report here. After you review it, if you have more questions, let me know, and I'd be happy to help."

Luke extended his hand. "I really appreciate it. I've spent a lot of time trying to get this report over the years. This has helped more than you know."

Chris shook Luke's hand, wished him well, and left.

Gabe turned to Luke. "Not that it means anything, but at least that's a bit more than we had."

CHAPTER 15

Luke stepped out of the police station after he and Gabe went over the medical examiner's report on Lily. There had been no more surprises other than what Chris Starling had already told them. Because only Lily's skeletal remains were found, the Washington County medical examiner was never able to determine a cause of death so the case had been and remained labeled undetermined, but the fact that his sister's fingers were missing was new.

Luke threw his messenger bag in his SUV and stood by the open door. He placed a quick call to his father just to confirm that his parents didn't already know about Lily's fingers. His father answered.

"What's happening? Is everything okay? I was in the yard with your mother."

"Listen, Dad, I'm at the police station in Fayetteville and just met with the medical examiner. I finally have a full report from their office. It's more comprehensive than the overview they gave us. I have a question though. When Lily was found, did the medical examiner tell you anything about missing bones on Lily's hand?"

Spencer didn't respond right away. With confusion in his voice, he said, "No, not that I recall. They just said that Lily had been found, and all that remained were bones. They matched up dental records for positive identification. Your sister was also found near her purse, which had her wallet and driver's license. I don't remember anything about missing bones. I handled all the conversations. Your mother was too upset at the time to speak to anyone."

"That's what I thought because I didn't remember it either," Luke said frustrated. "Chris Starling, the new medical examiner, gave me the report that shows photos of the marks on the metacarpals where her fingers were cut off."

Spencer asked with hesitation in his voice, "Were the cuts postmortem?"

"Dad, I don't know. To get through it, I have to believe they were. The reality is, I don't think we will ever know, but let's just assume they were to keep us sane. I'll call you back as soon as I know more. Hug Mom for me."

Luke hung up from his father and immediately called Riley.

"Hey, sorry I missed you earlier," Luke said as Riley answered. He walked back and forth on the sidewalk in front of the police station.

"It's okay," Riley said sweetly. "I figured you were busy. I was looking through those case files Cooper gave us and came across something interesting. I found a case connected to my hometown."

Luke stopped pacing. Surprised, he asked, "You mean there was a missing girl from Troy? What university?"

"Russell Sage, but she didn't go missing from there. She went missing from a party on the Eastside, actually not that far from my mom's house. They found this girl's body…" Riley trailed off. There was the sound of shuffling papers. "They found her days after she went missing in a creepy cemetery about two miles away from where she was last seen."

Riley usually had a spot-on memory so Luke was curious that she hadn't made a connection. He asked curiously, "You didn't remember this when we started looking at the cases?"

"No, I was a freshman in 2000 when it happened. I was in Geneseo. I wasn't even in Troy. I remember my mom talking about it, but I don't really remember the details. They never solved it. I guess I just stopped hearing about it and forgot."

Luke switched the phone from one ear to the other. "You know any of the cops or medical examiner involved?"

"Nothing I have here says who they are. I'll make some calls. I was going to do a newspaper search first to see what I can pull up and call my mom and see what she remembers."

"Good plan," Luke said. He looked around to see if anyone was in earshot. He said quietly, "The medical examiner here gave me some new info. My sister was missing three fingers off her left hand when they found her body. Based on knife markings on the bones, they were cut off."

"That's awful," Riley exclaimed. "Do they have an idea about a cause of death?"

"No, and unless we solve it, they never will."

"Do you have the report?"

"Yeah, I finally got it. I'm going to send it to Purvis for him to review. He might see something everyone else is missing," Luke said hopefully.

"You doing okay?" Riley asked softly.

"I'm as good as can be expected. I just can't think about what Lily went through too much or I get in my head so much I can't concentrate."

"I understand. I'm just a phone call away, whatever you need. I'll update you when I know more. Cooper will be here soon to go over the calls he made this morning and compare notes. Call me tonight after you're settled in the hotel."

CHAPTER 16

"What do you think, Cooper, you want back in?" Captain Meadows asked between bites of his steak. He was sitting across from Cooper at Doe's Eat Place in downtown Little Rock.

Cooper had hesitantly taken the meeting not sure what he was walking into. He swallowed the bite of his own perfectly cooked steak and said, "I'm really sure, Cap. I appreciate the offer to come back and be a detective again, but I have a fully-operational business that gives me the flexibility I want. I didn't fit as a detective. We both know that."

"Yeah, but the mayor is breathing down my neck to bring you back," Captain Meadows added sternly. "After saving Riley like you did last year, and the help you gave us, we need a good man like you. What will it take? More money? A promotion? More time off?"

Cooper laughed. A few years ago, Captain Meadows practically threw him out of the police station. Cooper wasn't a good detective. He was great at the nuts and bolts of detective work, but not the politics with the higher-ups, the paperwork, and the high level of crap that came with the job. He couldn't imagine going back to the police department.

"Cap, really," Cooper said, trying to convince him. "I appreciate the offer, but nothing is going to get me back. You can tell the mayor

I'm happy to consult here and there, but that's about all he's getting out of me."

Cooper watched as Captain Meadows put his fork down, surveyed his face carefully, and made intense eye contact for a few seconds too long. "I didn't think we'd get you back, but it was worth a shot. So then tell me, what do you really think about these letters?"

Cooper knew there had to have been an ulterior motive to this lunch. He took another bite of steak and chewed deliberately, all in an effort to buy some time. After a sip of his drink to wash it down, Cooper said, "I don't know any more than you do. I do trust what Luke believes. If he believes it's connected so do I, even if somewhat cautiously. If we had looked and there were no similar cases, I'd have assumed it was a fake, but we found some. It's worth exploring."

"Don't get me wrong, Cooper," Captain Meadows said seriously, "I think it's real, too. Nobody wants Luke to solve this and get justice for his sister more than I do. I just don't want to lose him in the process. I don't want him to climb so far down a rabbit hole, there's no bringing him back."

Cooper nodded in agreement. "How do we protect him from himself?"

"I figured you'd have an answer for that."

"I don't," Cooper said regretfully. "Luke is hard-headed and strong-willed. I can keep my eye on him. Riley and I are both helping him out. Riley better than anyone will keep him in check. Even when Luke hasn't listened to reason from anyone else, he will listen to her."

"That's good. Real good. If you need more support, just let me know. I'll put a detective or two on it." Captain Meadows summoned the server and slapped his credit card on the table. He waved away Cooper's attempt at payment.

"Thanks for lunch," Cooper said. Captain Meadows waved a dismissive hand at him. They both stood from the table and grabbed their keys and cellphones.

As they moved through the restaurant, Cooper assured him, "I'm headed to Riley's right now. I'll have a chat about keeping an eye on Luke. We'll let you know if we need additional support."

As they got to the door, Captain Meadows pulled it open, and Cooper came face to face with Holly, who was walking in with a group of women. Cooper nodded hello to her and tried to sidestep around her. She didn't let him pass. Holly leaned into him and planted a kiss on his lips. Cooper was taken aback. He felt like all eyes in the place were on him.

Holly pulled back and grabbed for his hand. Looking up at Cooper with a seductive smile on her face, she said in a sultry voice, "It's so good to see you after the other night. Call me later, okay?" She dropped his hand and walked farther into the restaurant, leaving Cooper feeling awkward in her wake.

Captain Meadows raised his eyebrows and slapped Cooper on the back as they made their way out of the restaurant and onto the sidewalk. Cooper turned from one direction to the other, trying to remember where he had parked his truck.

CHAPTER 17

After Luke called, I made myself a turkey sandwich, grabbed some chips from the cabinet, and called my mother, Karen. Our relationship has improved dramatically since I moved back to Little Rock. She had been dead set against the move, but once she saw my house and spent some time getting to know Luke, she was on board. She did remind me from time to time, in only the way that she can, not to mess it up.

My mother answered quickly, and after beating around the bush, I finally asked her about the murder in Forest Park Cemetery.

"You didn't take any interest in it then. Why now?" my mother asked, skeptically.

I had been hoping to not get into everything. I didn't want to worry her, but my mother saw through it as I should have known she would. I spent the next fifteen minutes going through what had been happening with Lily's case and the letters.

If I didn't just give her everything at the front end, she would have just dragged it out of me with endless questions. Like usual, my mother chastised me for being an investigator and always being in harm's way. She finally gave up the information I was seeking.

"Nobody searched the cemetery when Amanda Taylor went missing," she started. "No one could have thought she'd be in that direction. If I'm remembering correctly, Amanda had come up from downtown with friends. She was last seen on the front lawn of the fraternity house talking to some people. Her friends assumed she went off with some guy, or that she went back to her dorm. Nobody gave it a thought until late Sunday night when she had been gone for two days. When her roommate realized she still hadn't come home, she alerted college officials. They immediately called the police. Troy PD was out in full force. School officials were out. The whole town was out. But everyone was looking between the party and downtown. They looked along the river. They checked the bus route, the route she could have walked home. There was no one looking farther out toward Pinewoods, and there was no reason to search there."

"Amanda was found by someone walking their dog, right?"

"The poor man nearly had a heart attack," my mother said in an exaggerated tone.

"What was the cause of death?"

"Now that's the strange thing," my mother detailed. "They never said."

"They just never said the cause of death?" I asked incredulously. It was a small town. I knew there had to have been talk. "If not officially, then what was the gossip?"

My mother hesitated, but then whispered, "That she was pierced through the heart with what they surmised was a sharp thin sword or knife."

My mother's words sent a shiver down my spine.

She added cautiously, "That's just gossip. I don't know for sure."

"Any suspects at the time?" I asked, hoping there was one. My mother had a memory like an elephant. The woman forgot nothing down to the smallest detail. Not that I was glad a case was connected to my hometown, but at least we had my mother's memory.

"Sure, there were a few. I think they questioned every RPI boy there, every homeless person within a few blocks of Russell Sage and even a weird maintenance guy at the college some of the girls said was creepy. Nothing. I think the best and most likely suspect the cops figured was one of the RPI boys at the party. Shawn Westin, I believe his name was. He had a car, she was seen talking to him a lot that night, and he had a prior assault charge that was dropped under mysterious circumstances."

"What do you mean 'mysterious circumstances'?"

"I had heard he raped a girl in high school, and the cops didn't want to arrest a nice boy from a good family. He was headed to university after all and boys will be boys," my mother said sarcastically.

I could tell she was angry. She had never liked the "boys will be boys" excuse. I remember once when we were little a boy had hit my sister Liv. I stepped in and broke his nose. My mother gave me an extra slice of pie after dinner. When the nun at my Catholic school called her in, and she had heard how the boy was just being rough like typical boys, my mother threatened to punch her in the nose. I smiled at the memory.

"Where was Shawn Westin from?"

"Virginia, if I'm not mistaken."

"Did they have evidence to tie him to Amanda?" I asked, as I got up and walked down the stairs to the kitchen to put my dish in the sink.

"I don't know that they ever said much in the news. The neighborhood had gossip as it always does, but I don't think there was ever much. Jack Malone was the lead detective. You should give him a call and ask. I'll see him at church this weekend if you want me to tell him you need some information."

I dropped my plate in the sink and opened the fridge. I poured myself some more sweet tea. I could tell my mother was moving around as well. The sound of pots and pans clanging in the background was apparent.

Jack Malone was a retired homicide detective with the Troy police. He was also a long-time friend of my mother's. They went to grade school and high school together. He was sixty-three, the same age as my mother, and a widower. His family was as Irish Catholic as my own.

"I'll probably try to call him before you see him, but thanks. If you remember anything else, call me."

I was headed back up the stairs to my office when there was a knock on the front door. I opened it to find Cooper standing there. He thrust a page in front of me. "I found a pattern."

CHAPTER 18

I took the paper from Cooper and looked it over, not quite catching his meaning. It was just a list of cases and dates. "What am I looking at?" I asked as we walked into the kitchen and sat at the table.

Cooper took the page back from me. He pulled up his phone and showed me a calendar from 1993 and then scrolled forward year by year. "All the missing dates are Friday nights. It's a pattern. Now we have four – October, universities, freshmen, and Friday nights."

I mulled over what Cooper said. "Do we have exactly twenty-three cases or are there more?"

"There are twenty-five, but he could be mistaken and lost count, or a few of these don't fit."

"I don't think he lost count," I countered. "He seemed too precise. Let's go up to my office and go over some cases. I heard from Luke so I can update you on what's happening there, too."

I poured Cooper a glass of tea before we headed upstairs. I double-checked that my front door was locked, and we made our way to my office. Cooper took a seat on the couch and put his file folder of cases next to him. I sat at my desk.

I updated Cooper about Luke as well as Lily's missing fingers. Cooper didn't say much. He had known Lily so I imagined this was hard for him, too. I had some distance from it, never having met her. I also detailed the Amanda Taylor case in Troy.

When I was done, Cooper asked, "Is Troy a big city?"

"No, it's small. Just about 50,000 people, but it does have three universities. Small downtown, suburbs, and then some rural parts that connect to other towns farther into Rensselaer county, which bumps up to Massachusetts and Vermont."

I handed him back the case file so he could look over the case, which now included my notes along with what he had initially pulled from the internet.

Cooper spent a few minutes going through the file. When he was done, Cooper locked eyes with me. "Since you have connections, you think it might be worth going up there to investigate?"

"I hadn't thought of that," I replied honestly. "I think I'd probably want to make some calls first and see if anyone is willing to talk to me. I'd consider going if we have something to run with. My private investigator's license is still good."

As much as I like fall in upstate New York, I didn't want to leave Luke alone in Arkansas, even if he was up in Fayetteville. A three-hour drive was far better than being a flight away.

"I want to go to Atlanta and check out Chamblee University," Cooper indicated, surprising me.

I eyed him not understanding. "Why?"

Cooper leaned forward on the couch and explained, "All the cases we have, girls either go missing from parties near campus or walking home off-campus. Chamblee University is the only case where a girl goes missing from on campus. According to the killer, Chamblee University was his first. Maybe he messed up taking her right from the library, which is why his method changed."

I thought for a moment and then countered, "That's a fair point. It's so long ago though and the university is still saying nothing happened. Where would you even start?"

"I made a call earlier today. Jordan Baker's sister, Adele, is friends with a woman who works at the university. She went to school with Jordan. Adele thinks she knows more than she's been saying. She might be the key."

I shrugged. "I don't know that it's worth the trip."

"I do," Cooper said confidently. "If it was his first, he was bound to have made mistakes."

"Fair enough. When will you leave?"

"I want to check in with Luke first and see what he needs." Cooper leaned back on the couch and ran a hand down his face. He looked back at me and said frustrated, "There are just so many cases. We need something concrete to connect them. Maybe I can find that in Atlanta."

I hitched my jaw in the direction of Cooper's file of cases. He handed them over to me. I picked through the stack of pages. "In how many of the cases you looked through were bodies found?"

"Two, but like in Lily's case, all the remains found were bones. What about you?"

I told Cooper about the four cases — two with just skeletal remains and two where the victims were found relatively soon after they went missing. "It would be interesting to see if we can get any method and manner of death on the case in Troy and the one in Virginia. Maybe at least then we could find similarities in the method of killing."

"Want me to make some calls to Virginia? Is it the girl from the College of William & Mary in Williamsburg?"

"Yes. If you call them, I'll call my contact in Troy."

Cooper agreed, and I gave him my office so we weren't talking over each other. I headed down the stairs to my kitchen. I hit the bottom stair just as there was a knock on my front door. I opened it to find Luke's partner Det. Tyler standing on my front porch, looking pale and shaken.

He thrust a bagged envelope at me and choked out the words, "He says he's going to kill again this weekend in Fayetteville."

I called out to Cooper, who quickly came down the stairs and stood next to me. Tyler shifted his weight from one foot to the other as he tried patiently to wait for us to absorb the message. Cooper read the letter over my shoulder. I felt rapid puffs of air on the back of my neck. The letter was simple enough. It was addressed to Luke, like the others, and indicated that the killer was going to strike again this weekend. His crisp scrolling cursive stated:

"It's harvest time again. I'm going back to one of my old haunts. You're quite familiar with it, Lucas. It's your alma mater, and where I met your sweet sister Lily. This weekend. Make plans. I'll see you on the harvest fields."

I handed the letter back to Tyler and moved farther into my living room. I sat on one of my overstuffed chairs while they took a seat on the couch. Cooper and Tyler looked battle-worn, and we'd only just begun.

Cooper asked, "When did this come in?"

"Earlier today. We had it tested by the lab and again nothing. No prints. No markings."

I reached out for Tyler to hand me back the letter. I turned it over and checked to see the envelope. I was looking directly at the back, but couldn't see the postmark. "Where was it postmarked from?"

"Just north of Fayetteville in Springdale. We need to take this seriously."

"Of course, there's no way we can't. We will all probably need to head up there."

"Have you told Luke?" Cooper asked.

Tyler shook his head. "Captain Meadows wanted you two to see this first. He assumed one of you would want to call Luke. He also wanted me to check in to see what you've found."

Cooper spent the next half hour detailing everything. He went through each of the cases and noted where bodies had been found. He then narrowed in on the cases in Atlanta and Troy. Tyler asked questions that Cooper answered as best he could. Before I could offer any of my own insight, Cooper told Tyler that he thought he should visit Atlanta while I head back to Troy. That is after we all go to Fayetteville.

When they were done, Cooper turned to me and asked, "You calling Luke?"

"It's better coming from me."

CHAPTER 19

Riley called just as Luke stood at the spot where the groundskeeper had found his sister's remains. She told him about the letter and that the killer was going to strike again this weekend. Friday, most likely, given Cooper's assessment.

Luke hung up with her, knowing they'd be there soon. He formed a plan in his mind. He'd need to go inform the university, the police department and call in the FBI.

After Luke had called his father and Riley, while standing outside of the police department, he had come directly to this spot. He wasn't sure why. He had been there before. It's not like there would be evidence this many years later. Luke felt connected to his sister in the place where she had been found. Maybe it was because it was so close to the anniversary of when Lily went missing. No one knew Lily's date of death. They had no idea when she had been killed. Luke speculated it was probably immediately after she was taken, but with so few details, he couldn't know for sure.

Lily had been found in woods near the freshman dorms. There was a path that cut through the woods, made by students over time who walked from the dorms to the main campus buildings. It was a shortcut. Luke had walked the worn path himself countless times when he was a freshman.

Lily was found about thirty feet off the main path. Because of the dense tree coverage, it was impossible to see the spot from the path itself. Luke had checked that countless times. It was secluded enough that if Lily had been killed there, no one would have seen. They might have heard her scream, if she had, but not have been able to see her from the path.

Luke took a moment and said a silent prayer. When he was done, Luke walked back to the main part of campus and placed a call to Gabe. When he answered, Luke quickly explained the new letter and told Gabe to call the university to set up a meeting with the administration. Gabe promised he was on it.

Luke then placed a call to the local FBI field office in Fayetteville. He was eventually routed to an FBI agent. Luke explained who he was, detailed the letters, facts about his sister's murder, and the current threat. He was about to tell the man about asking for a meeting at the university but was abruptly cut off.

With a sarcastic tone of voice, the agent barked, "You don't even know if this is credible, Detective Morgan. This could be an incredible waste of FBI resources."

"If it's not," Luke countered, "are you willing to risk a young woman's life on that?"

"Let's not be dramatic," the agent said condescendingly, "I think you're a bit compromised and lacking perspective given your close connection to the case."

Luke sighed. He hated the feds sometimes. "I don't have any time to go around and around with you on this…"

The FBI agent attempted to interrupt, but Luke cut him off. "No, now you listen to me. Bottom line it. Do you want to take a look at what we have? Do you want to meet with us to properly assess this potential threat?"

"No, we are going to decline at this time. If you find something credible that connects these cases across state lines, call us back. We are sure you and the local authorities can handle it."

Luke hung up without even saying goodbye. He couldn't be bothered with them. Luke had assumed back in Little Rock that's what the FBI would be like so he didn't rush to call them in. They had way too many political hoops to jump through to get involved in cases. To be fair, Luke couldn't give them the hands-down credible proof they were after. For Luke, there was more than enough to go on.

While Luke was on the call with the FBI, he'd received a text from Gabe letting him know that the university president would meet with them as soon as Luke could make it to the building. Gabe had assured them they were both on their way.

Luke made his way to the administration building, dodging students as he moved. Luke couldn't remember a time he'd been in the building as a student. He couldn't even recall if there had been any meetings there after his sister went missing, or her body was found. There had to have been.

As Luke climbed the steps and opened the front door, he noticed a parking lot off to the left. It was filled with news vans. He hoped whatever was happening wouldn't interrupt his meeting with the president.

Luke entered the building and was immediately overwhelmed by the news media stationed in the lobby. He wasn't sure which way to turn. Luke caught sight of an opening and made his way to the stairs. He flashed his badge to the campus security blocking off the stairs and was admitted only after giving his name.

Luke climbed the stairs quickly, not looking back. Once upstairs, university personnel was in a panic, moving back and forth in the hallways in and out of offices. Luke moved down the hall and found the president's office. He pulled open the wide double doors and was immediately met with a secretary and the head of campus security, Mitchell Lake. They made quick introductions all around and then ushered Luke into the president's office.

Upon entering, University President Louis Kane came around his desk and gripped Luke's hand. "We were glad Det. Barry called for a meeting. Our next call was to law enforcement, and you saved us time."

"I'm not quite sure what you mean," Luke said, confused. "I was calling for a meeting…"

Kane interrupted, thrusting a bagged letter in Luke's direction. "We received that today. It says one of our female freshmen will be taken Friday night. To stop him, we'd need to contact you. My secretary was trying to find you when Det. Barry called. The media received a similar letter, which is why they are camped out in our lobby."

Luke staggered back, trying to adjust his eyes to the words in the letter, but he never got the chance to read it.

Kane demanded, "Who is he and how do we stop him?"

Luke held up his hand. "Give me a minute. This wasn't why we called you."

He carefully looked over the letter and was at a loss for words.

"On Friday, I will harvest my next bride from your selection of beautiful freshmen. You can't stop me. Call Detective Lucas Morgan from Little Rock. It's time the chase commenced."

As Luke finished reading the last word, Gabe entered the room, identifying himself quickly. Luke handed Gabe the letter and watched his face as he read. When Gabe was done, he raised his eyes. He and Luke shared a knowing glance.

"Well," Kane demanded again. "How do we stop him?"

CHAPTER 20

"I don't know," Luke responded honestly, feeling foolish and completely powerless not having a better answer. He was the lead detective in the detective's bureau in the state's capital city – he needed a better answer than he was giving, but Luke simply didn't have one.

Looking around the room at Kane, Gabe, and Mitchell, Luke said, "I think you should sit. I can tell y'all what I know, so far."

For the second time that day, Luke detailed the entire story from his sister's disappearance to the letters that arrived yesterday and the one they received today. He went into some detail about Riley and Cooper's assistance looking at similar cases, but Luke didn't go in-depth. As far as Luke was concerned, he didn't trust the people in front of him. While President Kane and the head of campus security seemed like they were playing for the same team, years of investigative work taught Luke to take nothing for granted.

When Luke was done catching everyone up to the most recent letter the university received, Mitchell asked, "You're really taking this guy seriously?"

"I am," Luke said straight-faced. "Even if we're wrong, what's the worst that will happen?"

"We overreact and make complete fools of ourselves, panic parents and students, and potentially ruin our reputation," Mitchell speculated. He sat slouched in the chair with his arms folded over his chest.

Luke guessed Mitchell was probably in his mid-fifties. He had told Luke that he'd been in charge of campus security at the university for the last eight years. Before that, Mitchell had said he was in charge of security at a local medical center. Luke didn't question the man's ability to provide security, what he questioned was the man's investigative background.

Luke leveled a look at him. "I can appreciate that, but what happens if you don't take it seriously and a freshman girl is kidnapped and murdered? How do parents and the media react then?"

Kane waved the conversation off. He pointed towards the door. "The story is already public. This isn't something we can hide. We have to make a statement and make it now. To do that, I need to know what law enforcement and campus security will be doing to protect us."

Turning to Mitchell, Kane said, "I strongly suggest you let these men take the lead. They are obviously knowledgeable about this case and have far more resources than your office."

Duly chastised, Mitchell muttered, "Fine. What's the plan?"

Luke explained, "I called the FBI. They weren't interested. Maybe a call from the university might help, but I doubt it. Det. Barry, what resources can we count on from your office?"

Det. Gabe Barry assured, "The police department is fully committed to anything this operation needs. We are calling in all the manpower we have over the next few days. The first thing I think we need to do is put out a warning from the university to students and parents."

To President Kane, Gabe asked directly, "Are you able to close the school this weekend and encourage students to go home?"

"I don't see how that would be possible. Not to mention we have even more students headed this way. The Razorbacks have a game against LSU on Saturday at two. We will have even more students and parents here than normal this weekend. Canceling the game is not an option for us."

Luke closed his eyes, rubbed them with his fingers. He had forgotten they were in the middle of football season. This brought a whole host of other complications he hadn't even been considering.

They'd have far more people in the city, easier for a killer to blend in, and more students to worry about.

"I think we still need to give a stern warning that we have received this letter, that we consider it credible, and then people can decide on their own the course of action," Luke said. An idea struck him all at once. He added, "Let's also pull in student leadership to help. Let's go to the sororities and fraternities and student body leadership councils and explain. The more eyes and ears we have out there on our side, keeping watch, paying attention, will make all the difference."

President Kane nodded. "That's a good idea. Let me pull in my public affairs department to craft the message to the media and let me round up other staff to pull these student groups together. Let's say we will meet tomorrow at one o'clock in the auditorium."

He picked up his office phone and began making calls.

Mitchell rolled his eyes and shifted in his chair.

Luke cleared his throat. "Is there something you'd like to say?"

"I'm not even saying I think this is credible," Mitchell started, "but if it is, why do you want to alert the whole world of your plan? Won't this drive him underground and then you won't catch him?"

Luke had thought about that. But more important to Luke was keeping the students safe. "Safety is my only priority. If I have to alert the whole school to do that, I will."

Gabe added, "These kids need to be more alert anyway. All we are asking from them is to watch out for each other. Our plan, where we will have law enforcement stationed, and what we will be doing won't be made public. I agree with Luke, the more we can have people stay alert, the safer everyone will be."

There was no more debate. Luke worked with President Kane and his public affairs staff to craft the perfect message to the public – one that expressed concern but wasn't so alarming they'd look foolish for panicking the city. They kept a nice even tone and left it up to students and parents if they remained on campus. Classes were not canceled, but if students felt safer leaving, the university would give them a pass for their absence on Friday. The statement assured the public that law enforcement was doing everything to run down leads in advance of Friday and would be out in full force from now through the weekend.

Luke hoped they were able to live up to the promise.

CHAPTER 21

Later that evening, after Cooper left Riley's house, he stopped for a drink at a bar in the River Market. He grabbed dinner and relaxed before heading to Fayetteville. Tyler was already on his way up to see Luke. Cooper was supposed to pick up Riley in the morning, but that's what was hanging him up. Cooper didn't think Riley should go.

While Cooper played it cool, he worried about sending Riley into a full-blown anxiety attack, if things got tense. Riley had assured him the symptoms had passed, but Cooper had watched what she had gone through. The last thing they needed in Fayetteville was a repeat. With everything Luke had to worry about in Fayetteville, Cooper didn't think any of them needed one more complication. Not that Riley was a complication. Luke had so much to focus on, and Fayetteville would be a highly tense situation. Cooper was concerned about Luke's focus, and his own, would be on making sure Riley was okay, rather than the task at hand.

The problem was, Cooper didn't know how to explain that without sounding insensitive. Cooper tossed the words around in his head, but nothing sounded right. He got a reprieve when the bartender slid his burger in front of him. Cooper took a satisfying bite, still distracted by his thoughts when a finger ran down his back making him sit up straighter.

He nearly choked on his food. Cooper turned to see Holly standing there with a broad smile on her face.

She took the seat next to him. "Where are you taking me this Friday?"

Cooper chewed and washed his food down with some beer. "I was going to text you," Cooper fibbed – he had completely forgotten. "I can't take you out Friday night. I have to travel for a case this weekend. I'm leaving tomorrow."

Holly withdrew her hand but looked at him defiantly. "Cancel it. I'm worth it."

"I can't cancel. That's not how my job works. I don't get a lot of say in my schedule. That's just how it goes." Cooper went back to eating, hoping she'd go away.

"I want you to cancel," Holly demanded, clearly not giving up. "I always get what I want."

Cooper nearly got his burger lodged in his throat. He took another drink and turned to her. "I can appreciate that, but that doesn't work with me. I have a complicated job so maybe I'm just not the guy for you." He turned back to his food.

Holly started to argue, but Cooper was saved by his ringing cellphone. It was Riley. He picked up his phone and stepped away from the bar. "Everything okay?" Cooper asked.

"Yeah, I'm fine," Riley said hesitantly. "I wanted to ask you a question though. I know you and Luke need me, but I don't know if going to Fayetteville with you is the best idea."

Feeling relieved but wanting to make sure he understood, Cooper clarified, "Do you mean you wouldn't go at all?"

"I have so many things to follow up on with these other cases, it might be best if I was here doing that. I just don't want to bail on Luke or let him down. Do you think he'll be angry with me?"

"No, not at all," Cooper replied, feeling let off the hook. "I was going to suggest that to you, but didn't want to hurt your feelings, or say the wrong thing. Actually, following up on all the rest would be a huge help. That way, we aren't letting anything fall through the cracks. I'm sure Luke will understand, and there will be enough people helping him up there. Do you want me to tell him?"

"I can tell him. You never got to those calls in Virginia, did you?

"No, Tyler interrupted that," Cooper noted. As Riley went over some case information, Holly got up from the bar. She walked off, shooting Cooper a dirty look over her shoulder. Cooper really hoped that the situation wasn't going to come back to bite him.

"Cooper, are you there?" Riley asked impatiently.

"Yeah, sorry," Cooper responded.

"Do you know the medical examiner, or have any law enforcement connections in Virginia?"

Cooper thought over the people he knew, but he was coming up blank on Virginia connections. "I'd just call whoever was in charge of the investigation and tell them what Luke said – that we are working on some research for the Little Rock police."

"That's what I'll do, just wanted to rule out if you had someone specific you were calling. I'm hoping since they had a body, we will have some leads."

"We definitely could use them. Are you sure you're going to be okay there alone? I can always send my stalker over?" Cooper teased.

Riley laughed. "You have a stalker?"

"That girl you met yesterday morning. She's now shown up when I was having lunch and she just showed up here at the bar while I was having dinner. You think that's a coincidence, right?"

"Stop being a player and you won't have so much trouble in your life," Riley barked and then hung up on him.

Riley was right. He made his way back to the bar. The bartender grabbed his empty glass and refilled his beer. Sitting it down in front of Cooper, he said, "You need to watch your back with that one. She's persistent."

"That bad?" Cooper asked, mentally cringing.

"She keyed a friend's car when he didn't ask her on a second date. It might be nothing, but just watch your back."

CHAPTER 22

Luke finished his third cup of coffee as he stood in the conference room at the Fayetteville Police Department. He held the cup, looked over the freshly made coffee, and debated if one more was needed. Luke hadn't slept much the night before. He and Gabe worked long into the night, coming up with a strategy for campus security. Mitchell had proven useless so they had to work around him. Luke was happy with their plan. He couldn't guarantee everyone's safety by any stretch, but they'd have a uniformed police presence and plainclothes officers working undercover.

They'd also have some younger female cops working as decoys. Luke had no idea if the killer stalked his victims ahead of time, so he couldn't be sure how useful that idea would bear out, but it was worth a shot.

He wished Riley was there, but he understood why she had stayed back. She had called him the night before, just as he was getting ready for bed, and asked if he minded if she stayed in Little Rock and worked on the other cases. Luke didn't mind, it was actually a good idea. There wasn't much she could do with him right now, anyway. Cooper was on his way. Tyler was running down some leads, and Gabe was calling other local, smaller, police departments to see how much manpower they could secure.

Right now, they had deputies coming from the sheriff's office, some state police and even cops from other local city police departments. Luke wasn't sure what else he could be doing at the moment, but he felt like it should be something. The meeting with student leaders was about an hour away.

Luke poured himself another cup of coffee, and then sat at the table to go over his notes for the meeting. He read and reread them. The information was solid. President Kane's public message, the previous evening, had been powerful and effective. He had managed an even tone, letting students, parents, and the community know the seriousness of the threat while cautioning they had no idea how credible it was, but that every precaution was being taken. It aired on the local news and was on social media. Every parent and student had received a text with the video. All bases were covered.

Popping his head into the conference room, Gabe asked, "You ready to head over to campus?"

"Ready as I'll ever be. Do you know how many we are expecting?"

"I heard fifty, and then I heard about two hundred, so really it's anyone's guess. I did hear students were receptive to helping keep campus safe."

"That's good, what I was hoping for," Luke commented. He got up, threw his cup away, and headed out with Gabe.

After a short ride from the police station, they entered the auditorium. Luke took in the scene. The room was full of students and what Luke assumed were university staff, professors and other administrators. The meeting had been closed to the public and to parents.

Luke shook President Kane's hand. "This is a great turnout. I didn't expect people to be here so early. You doing okay?"

Kane nodded. "They are eager to help. When my staff started calling student groups, there was no hesitation on their part. Their only question was what you wanted from them and when. Let's give it another few minutes and get started."

Luke went over his notes again. Gabe had wanted Luke to speak. He felt Luke was closer to the situation and could give a more impassioned plea. After a few minutes, Kane went to the podium and quieted the crowd. He thanked the students for being there and introduced Luke.

Luke stepped up, gave a weak smile to the crowd, and told the students why he was there. He talked about attending the university and told them about his sister. His voice cracked when he spoke about Lily. He rushed through that part as best he could. The last thing Luke wanted to do was break down in front of all these students and faculty.

Luke spoke about the recent threats. The students were engaged and listening. All eyes were on him. Luke had their full attention. "Most important," Luke concluded, "while I can't tell you not to have parties this weekend or enjoy time with your friends, what I can say is you are leaders on this campus. You are our first line of defense. If you are alert and aware, watching out for your peers and reporting suspicious activity, not just this weekend, but all the time – inevitably the campus as a whole and the entire student body is safer."

"Should we arm ourselves?" a voice shouted from the audience.

"I don't see a need," Luke responded. "Some of you already have concealed carry permits, which Arkansas does allow on campus now, but I don't think anyone not already carrying should worry themselves with that."

Luke looked to President Kane to see if he wanted to add anything. He had nothing to add.

Luke continued, "The most important thing is to walk in groups. Don't let anyone walk alone. Don't drink too much and wander off, or drink so much you are not aware of your surroundings. Just practice some common sense safety and you'll be okay."

"We want to do more than that," another voice shouted from the crowd. A tall, young man, with Greek letters on his shirt, stood. "We've been talking about doing walking patrols around campus and using social media to put our phone numbers out, so if anyone needs someone to walk or drive them home, we will be there."

Luke nodded in agreement. "That's an excellent idea, and on target to what we are hoping. Anything you can do to work together and to help support other students and keep an eye out, the better. Feel free to stop up here after this and we can talk with you further about some ideas."

The students began to talk to each other. Luke asked if there were other questions, and when there were none, he dismissed them.

Luke walked to the back of the stage and was talking with Gabe when he felt a tap on his back.

An attractive black woman about Luke's age offered him her hand. "I don't think you'll remember me, but I'm Brie Hall. I was friends with your sister Lily. I recently remembered something about the night Lily disappeared that I think you should know."

CHAPTER 23

I spent the better part of the morning into the afternoon trying to track down a good source of information on the Virginia case. Sara Curtis was the victim's name. Because the case was still an open homicide, it was nearly impossible to get information directly from the police department. Even telling them it was a Little Rock detective who wanted the information, they stonewalled. It was suggested to me, that if the Little Rock police wanted the information so badly, they could call themselves.

Calling Sara's parents proved more fruitful. They gave me the name of a detective, Frank Flynn, who had been working on the case for years but had recently retired. Sara's parents said he'd be more than willing to speak to me. It was a case, they said, that haunted him.

I thanked them and promised I'd update if anything was found about their daughter. I then reread the Virginia case file and made the call.

"Frank Flynn," the man answered. His voice was deep and serious, but strangely calming.

I introduced myself and explained the reason for my call. I told him about Lily's case and the letters. Finally, I noted, "We have reason to suspect that the case is connected to Sara Curtis' death."

Frank excused himself to someone on his end. It was silent for several more seconds. Finally, he said, "Sorry, I wanted to be in my office. Can you say that again? You think your case, in Arkansas, is connected to the one here in Virginia?"

"Not just Arkansas, but potentially a serial killer," I said seriously. "We are at the early stages of this, but my boyfriend, Luke Morgan, is a detective with the Little Rock police department. His sister was murdered similarly to Sara. At least we are seeing some commonality – missing on a Friday in October near Halloween and a freshman at a local university."

"That's a big leap though," Frank countered.

"True, but the letters we received said there are twenty-three victims. We flagged Sara's as a potential. Is exploring the case at least a possibility?" I asked, keeping my fingers crossed.

Frank sighed loudly. "We never did find who killed Sara. Our community is small. We get tourists in Colonial Williamsburg, which is where Sara's body was found, but still, the case should have been solved."

I saw a glimmer of hope, so I pushed. "The only information we have is what we pulled from online sources. We read that Sara's body was found, but it didn't give any more detail than that. Are you willing to share that information?"

"I assume the Williamsburg detectives won't release any information to you?"

"No, but I can just as easily have a Little Rock detective call you. I'm sure the professional courtesy will be extended."

"You'd think." Frank laughed sarcastically. "They won't share even then. I want this case solved. They pushed me into retirement, and I'm bored. How can I help you?"

"Anything you can tell me about the case I can't find online. We can start with Sara's disappearance and murder."

Frank took an audible breath. He told his story. "Sara went missing in 2008 on Halloween. It was a Friday. She was a freshman at the College of William & Mary. Sara had attended a party earlier in the evening but got separated from her friends, or at least that's how the story goes. Her body was found, on Saturday night, at the Bruton parish cemetery. It was less than a mile apart. The medical examiner put her death at about twenty-four hours prior to her being found. Where she was from Friday night to Saturday night is a mystery."

I took notes as he spoke. "How was she killed?"

"She was stabbed in the chest with a thinly pointed instrument. It wasn't anything as big as a knife blade," Frank said and then added, "but we are fairly certain she wasn't killed where she was found. The area offered no blood evidence."

I thought back to what my mother said about Amanda's murder in Troy. It, again, was eerily similar. I told him about that case, including the details of being found in a cemetery and the cause of death.

"When was that case?"

"It was in 2000," I explained. Then I thought of something else my mother said. "Does the name Shawn Westin ring a bell?"

"No, should it?" Frank asked.

"No, that was the initial suspect in the Troy case, but he was from Virginia and had been accused of a sexual assault while in high school."

"Virginia's a big state," Frank countered. "Do you know where he's from specifically?"

I checked my notes. "No, that's something I need to follow up on."

"Well, Riley, you have me intrigued enough. What's the next step?"

"I'm making some more calls on cases, and then plan to call my contact in New York. Of all the cases we have, Virginia and New York are the only two where victims were found soon after. The rest were never found, or only skeletal remains were recovered. This seems like my best shot at getting enough info for some solid leads. I think I'll be heading up to New York to explore further."

"You want some help up there?" Frank offered eagerly.

I debated for only a second. Who better to help me than the detectives originally assigned to the cases? "If you're willing, I'm sure that will be a huge help. Let me speak with the retired detective from the New York case and get back to you on the plan."

"That's good," Frank said. "I really want this case solved. Sara's parents are good people and they deserve answers, as do all the families. I'll be ready whenever you need me."

CHAPTER 24

After I hung up with Frank, I stood and stretched. I needed to call Jack Malone. While I had a few current connections at the Troy Police Department, I'd go right to the source.

After a good stretch, I looked at my phone, debating whether or not to text Luke to see how he was doing, but I figured he was too busy. It would probably be better to wait until after I talked to Jack and figured out a plan. I picked up the Troy case file again and thumbed through it. Feeling satisfied I knew all I could, I called Jack.

The phone rang and rang. I was sure I was headed to voicemail when a sleepy voice said, "Yeah, this is Jack."

I fumbled over my words and checked my clock. It was three in the afternoon in New York. Maybe he was napping. I said tentatively, "Jack, this is Riley Sullivan. I was hoping to talk to you about a case."

It sounded like the phone was set down and then rubbed against clothing. Jack grunted and apologized for having been asleep. "Retirement is getting the better of me. That and the golf course," he said laughing. "How can I help you?"

I started to explain, but he cut me off.

"The Amanda Taylor case. That was a tough one. Aren't you in Little Rock now? Why are you looking into that?"

"I am in Little Rock," I confirmed, "but I've got a situation here that seems like it might be connected to that case."

"Really," Jack said, now wide awake. He whistled. "How would that be connected down there?"

I went over every detail of Lily's case, the murder in Virginia, and the letters. With each detail I dropped, Jack responded with shock. When I was done, it was his turn to shock me.

"Did Luke's sister or the girl in Virginia have missing fingers?"

"Lily did. Three fingers on her left hand to be exact – pinkie, ring finger, and middle. I don't know about the case in Virginia. Frank, the detective there, didn't mention it. I didn't think to ask. Why?"

Jack didn't answer, but instead asked, "How did you say the girl in Virginia was killed?"

I knew but doubl checked my notes just to make sure. "Frank said she was stabbed in the chest with a thin, but pointed blade of some kind."

"It was probably an ice pick," Jack said, solemnly. "Riley, I think our cases are connected."

"Was Amanda killed the same way?"

"Yes, and the killer was so violent that he left a round impression on her skin. We believe it was where the blade met the handle. That's what our medical examiner figured anyway. We did some comparisons, and that's what they found. That's not public though, so don't let that slip."

I let that sink in and felt my stomach rumble. There wasn't going to be a way to shield Luke from that, as much as I wanted to. "You still didn't answer me about the fingers."

"This is definitely not for the public," Jack warned, "but yes, Amanda was missing the same fingers as Lily. As I said, you've got me convinced these cases are connected. When are you coming up here? I think it's best, if we are really going to jump into investigating, that you're here."

Surprised, I asked, "You're willing to help me look into this? Won't this step on toes? It's got to still be an open case, right?"

"It's very much an open case, but Troy doesn't have the money to spend on cold cases," Jack explained. "They won't let you anywhere near it, but if I want to dig around on my own time, I can. I already have the clearance. I just hadn't had the motivation. All my leads ran dry."

"Frank offered to help us, too. Should I tell him to head to New York?" I wrote a text to Cooper to let him know that it looked like I'd be heading to New York sooner rather than later.

"Definitely. Tell him to bring whatever he has on his case, and we can get down to work. I've got a few things to handle in the next few days. Can you be up here by next week? What do you say we meet on Tuesday morning?"

"That should give me enough time. I'll let Frank know. I can't thank you enough for your help. This will really mean a lot to Luke," I said gratefully.

I was ready to get off the phone, but I wanted Jack's advice. Maybe I shouldn't have, but I explained what was happening with the most recent threat in Fayetteville. "I'm worried he's just toying with Luke, but don't want to tell him that."

"Could be, but better safe than sorry," Jack countered. "I wouldn't be surprised, though, if the guy is sitting there watching the law enforcement and the university's response, but not planning anything. Some killers reach a point where the game becomes more satisfying than the kill."

I let those words sink in, thinking that Jack was probably on to something. Just as I was about to hang up, Jack loudly cleared his throat. He started to say something and then stopped. Dead air hung between us for a few seconds.

When Jack finally spoke, it came out rushed. "Your mom seeing anyone?"

"Are you asking if my mom is dating anyone?" I asked, and laughed a little. I didn't mean to, it just slipped out. "No, my mom hasn't dated anyone since my father more than thirty years ago."

"Huh," Jack blurted. "Do you think she'd say yes if I asked her out?"

I was trying really hard not to laugh. He sounded so sincere. I knew Jack had lost his wife, of nearly thirty years, to cancer two years prior. I guess he was ready to be back out there.

"Jack, there's only one way to find out."

CHAPTER 25

Luke caught sight of Cooper standing in the back of the auditorium just as Brie Hall had introduced herself. Luke excused himself, for a moment, from Brie and yelled out to Cooper to get his attention. He waved Cooper to the stage.

Luke guided Brie down the steps at the side of the stage and around to where Cooper was standing in front of it. If Brie had something to say, Luke was glad Cooper was there to hear it. Luke made introductions and suggested a quieter place to talk. When Brie suggested her office in the fine arts building, they took it.

Luke yelled over to Gabe, to let him know they were heading out, and asked if he'd like to come with them. Gabe waved them off, telling them he'd stay back and continue planning with the university.

Once seated in Brie's office, Luke noticed how nervous the woman seemed. Back at the auditorium, she had appeared strong and confident. Now Brie had a worried look on her face and was wringing her hands.

"You said you went to school here with Lily," Luke said, hoping to get her talking. He wanted to make her as calm as possible. He was worried she'd shut down. Luke was also trying to place her because he didn't remember speaking to anyone by her name back then.

Brie nodded. "Your sister was the best. We became really fast friends. I lived next door to her in the dorm. I've always wanted to tell you. I'm so sorry for your loss. I can't imagine what your family has been through."

"Thank you, it hasn't been easy, which is why these letters have renewed my hope of catching her killer," Luke explained, hopefully. "You said you know something about that night?"

"I do," Brie said. She nervously tapped her finger on her desk.

Luke caught her eye. Brie stopped and sat back in her chair. Calmly, she began, "I tried to tell the cops at the time, but no one listened to me. I was at the party with your sister that night. Lily hadn't been drinking, neither was I. Neither one of us was feeling that great earlier in the evening. We thought about not even going out. But Lily was going to meet some girls in a sorority she was planning to pledge, and I was hoping to see a guy I liked."

Brie paused. Tears formed in her eyes. Luke offered her a sympathetic smile.

"You have to know when Lily wanted to leave, I offered to walk her home, but she knew the guy I liked had just walked in. She told me to stay. I guess she didn't want me to miss my chance at talking to him."

Luke smiled. It sounded like Lily. She was always looking out for other people like that. Puzzled though, Luke said, "There's something I don't understand. I spoke to a lot of the girls Lily was with that night, but I don't remember talking to you. No one mentioned your name."

"I don't know who you spoke with, but I assume you talked to the girls Lily had headed to the party to meet. Lily had a few different groups of friends. I wasn't friends with the girls in the sorority. I wouldn't assume they'd even know about me. As I said, Lily and I lived next door to each other in the dorm. We also had an English class together. I didn't go out to parties very often, but as I said, a guy I liked was there that night."

That made sense to Luke. It bothered him now that back then he didn't explore further. His focus was only on the girls, he had heard, Lily was with at the party. He never explored other friendships she might have had. He wanted to chalk it up to his inexperience, but it felt like the weight of another failure.

Luke leaned forward with his arms on the table. "I've always been curious. The girls I thought Lily was with at the party weren't even able to give me a time that she left, or tell me how much she'd been drinking. Do you know what time Lily left?"

"I do," Brie said quietly. "I think we need to back up though. There's a reason none of those girls could answer those questions."

Luke raised his eyebrows, his curiosity immediately piqued.

Brie went on. "Some of the girls Lily planned to meet at the party were there. But when we came in, they wouldn't talk to her. They brushed Lily off, giving her the cold shoulder. Lily was upset, but you know how she was, she ignored it. Lily said that one of the girls was a little jealous that she had been dating her new boyfriend, Chris. I guess this other girl liked him. They banded together and left Lily out. I think it's one of the reasons she left early."

"What time did she leave?" Cooper asked. He jotted down some notes as Brie talked.

"It was right around ten. Lily made the joke that she was probably the lamest freshman there. That she'd be home asleep by ten-thirty on a Friday night. It took about fifteen minutes to walk back to the dorm."

"Did you see her after that?" Luke asked hopefully.

"Yeah, that's the strange thing. I watched Lily walk out the door. Then I went in search of the guy I was there to see. I talked to him for a short period of time. He grabbed another beer and suggested we head outside to the front porch. Once I was out there, I was surprised to see Lily just down the road, talking to a history professor – Aaron Roberts. I recognized him because, back then, it was a joke around school how cute he was, and how he didn't look like a professor. Everyone wanted to take his class."

"Did my sister know him?" Luke wondered. He wasn't sure where this was going. He shifted in his seat and looked over at Cooper who looked back at him and shrugged. This was all new information for them.

"Not that I was aware of," Brie responded, "but they seemed really engaged in conversation like they had known each other so maybe they did. He was parked at the curb, leaning against his car. Lily was standing in front of him. I wanted to yell to her, but she was too far down the road to hear me."

Cooper inquired, "Did Lily look like she was enjoying the conversation?"

"She did," Brie affirmed. "Apparently felt safe enough with him that she got in his car and left."

Cooper and Luke shared a look of surprise. No one had told them anything like this back then or even through the years as Luke looked into his sister's disappearance.

Luke looked back to Brie. She was crying. Luke started to speak, hoping to say something comforting, but she waved him off.

Brie said regretfully, "I tried telling the cops this at the time. They said they'd look into it. When I followed up, the detective said that I had to have been mistaken because Aaron Roberts said he was out of town that weekend. They said he had an alibi. They said I must have been drinking and got mixed up."

Luke leaned forward. "Is there any chance you were mistaken?"

Brie shook her head. "I'm confident in what I saw. As I had said, neither of us were drinking that night. Neither of us felt great. We had both taken some cold medicine before we left. We were young, but neither one of us was stupid enough to mix that with alcohol."

Luke didn't say anything. He was processing the information.

Brie took his silence for doubt. She locked eyes with him and said forcefully, "I wasn't drunk. I wasn't confused. I know exactly what I saw, but I couldn't get them to believe me. I don't know what kind of alibi he had or even if the cops really talked to him, but he was there that night. Lily got in his car, and that was the last time I ever saw her."

CHAPTER 26

Luke reached across the table and grabbed her hand. He looked Brie in the eyes and said, "I believe you. I'm not doubting what you're saying. This is just all new information for me, and it's taking me some time to process."

"You have to understand," Brie sniffled, "I've been carrying this for a long time. I had tried to get the cops to believe me then. I had told some of the other girls we lived with at the dorm. I had told my parents, but everyone kept trying to convince me I must have been mistaken. I knew I wasn't, but nobody listened to me. Over the years, I assumed it must not have been important."

Luke understood exactly how she felt. "Do you have any idea where Aaron Roberts is now?"

"No, if I'm remembering correctly, he left after the spring semester."

Luke started to speak but Cooper interjected, "We were seniors when you were a freshman and I don't remember him at all. But then again, I didn't know many people in the history department. Do you know how long he had been at the school prior to that point?"

"He was new our freshman year," Brie indicated. "That's why I thought it was strange that he knew Lily. She wasn't taking any history classes. She hadn't even declared a major. I don't even know how she would have met him."

The three of them went back and forth on a few more questions, trying to pin down details. When Luke was sure he had everything he needed, he thanked Brie and promised they'd be in touch. Luke also told Brie that if she remembered anything else not to hesitate to call.

Once out of the fine arts building and standing on the sidewalk, Luke turned to Cooper. "What do you think?"

"I believe her," Cooper said confidently. "It's a shame we didn't know about her then. I can see how she was missed. Lily was supposed to be at the party with that other group of girls. Not one person had hinted at anything different. Sounds like now we might at least have a lead to run down."

Luke and Cooper made their way back to the police station to meet with Det. Gabe Barry. Det. Tyler was there, too. Luke made introductions and caught everyone up to speed on the meeting with Brie Hall. The four of them took up space in the Fayetteville Police Department's conference room – more of a strategy war room, as Gabe described it.

Gabe asked, "That was a long time ago. You think her memory is solid?"

Luke ran a hand down his face. He tried to think objectively. "I do. It really seemed like Brie's been carrying this around with her for a long time. She didn't embellish. She didn't create a big story of it. She just stated what she remembered. It was traumatic for her. She carries a lot of guilt, it seems, for not stopping my sister from going with him and for not getting anyone to listen to her back then."

Cooper waited for Luke to finish and then added, "Brie also didn't say the professor was guilty of anything. She just said she saw Lily talking to him and get in his car. He could have just driven her home. We don't know what happened. The part Brie was most frustrated by was that the cops told her she didn't see what she did. That's what was suspicious to her."

Det. Tyler turned to Gabe, who was sitting directly across the table from him. "You got the detective's notes from back then?"

"I do," Gabe answered. "But there's no mention of this guy. There's no mention of any guy. The detective, at the time, simply states that Lily left the party with the intention of walking home, and she was never seen again."

"Well that's what we got, too," Luke said sarcastically, "but that doesn't seem now like it's anywhere close to the truth."

"Luke, I'm not questioning you," Gabe countered. "I'm just telling you what the report said. Mistakes were clearly made."

Det. Tyler interrupted, "Why don't we just go to President Kane and ask to see this guy's record. See what the university knows about this guy. If he worked here, there must be some record of him."

Luke nodded. "I don't know what they will give us—"

Luke didn't get out his full thought because Cooper interrupted. He turned his phone so it faced Luke, "You think this is the guy? I found him on LinkedIn. Says he's still local to the area."

Luke took Cooper's phone and read the profile details. History professor. Worked at the University of Arkansas when Lily disappeared as Brie said. There were gaps in his employment history, and he seemed to bounce around a lot. He was originally from the Washington D.C. area.

Luke handed the phone back. "I'd say that's him. We have an address?"

Cooper typed a few things into his phone. He looked back up at them. "Says here he lives about ten miles from here, heading closer to Springdale."

Gabe offered, "We can go have a talk with him, Luke. See what he remembers."

All eyes were on him, but Luke wasn't sure what he was feeling. He didn't expect it to be this easy to track the guy down. Luke thought he'd have a little more time to mentally prepare. "I think maybe you guys should go. I'll sit this one out. I've got a bit to do here."

Cooper eyed him. "You sure?"

"Yeah," Luke confirmed. "I think if you and Tyler go, you'll have better luck and be more objective. If this is the guy sending letters and I show up at his door, what's going to happen? I just think you'll get further questioning him if I'm not there."

CHAPTER 27

I thought with Luke gone, the days would have crawled by for me. They didn't. It was like a mad dash to get things done before I left for New York. I had spoken to Luke on Wednesday evening, and he had told me about Aaron Roberts. Cooper and Det. Tyler had gone to the man's home, but he wasn't there. They tried a few more times and assumed maybe he was out of town.

Luke sounded stressed, as anyone would be, but there was something else in his voice. A weariness I'd never heard before. I avoided telling him the cause of death in the Virginia and New York murders, and thankfully, he hadn't asked. I just didn't have the heart to tell him that the girls had been stabbed in the chest. There would come a time for that, but it wasn't now when he was in the middle of an active threat. I had told Luke about the girls' missing fingers, which was what sealed the deal for us that the cases were connected.

Missing on Fridays, in October, was compelling, but it hadn't been enough for me. The fact that they had been freshmen, killed the same way, and that the victims' fingers were missing, was what finally convinced me the Virginia and New York cases were connected. If the rest were connected, I couldn't understand how the killer could so easily commit these crimes undetected. It also puzzled me why these were the only cases where bodies were found fully intact so quickly after the murder.

If it was all the same killer, why leave bodies just in Virginia and New York? These murders weren't his first. They were right in the middle – 2000 and 2008. It was this fact that kept tripping me up. I spent Thursday following up on cities where skeletal remains had been found. Few wanted to give me information over the phone, but I managed to get a handful of confirmations that victims had been missing fingers on their left hands. The pattern remained.

Late Thursday afternoon I also had an appointment with my therapist. I just wanted a check-in before I left town. I was concerned that the stress of the case and worrying about Luke might trigger an anxiety attack. She cautioned me to keep my stress levels in check, and then offered some breathing exercises, knowing that less stress wasn't always possible with my line of work.

Now early Friday evening, I sat in my kitchen, moving my dinner around on my plate. I'd barely touched the lasagna I'd made. I had already texted Luke and Cooper to wish them luck. They had a solid plan in place, and really there was nothing more they could do. It didn't mean that a million things couldn't go wrong.

I was flipping through a news app on my phone when there was a knock at my front door. I answered to find Emma standing there. "Let's go get ice cream," she said with a mischievous grin.

"Ice cream?" I asked, looking back at my kitchen and my uneaten dinner.

"Yeah, come on," Emma encouraged. "You're just sitting in there stressing about what Luke's doing. You need a break. We can walk over to the new place on Kavanaugh."

The new ice cream shop had replaced the Starbucks on Kavanaugh Boulevard, one of the main streets that ran through my Heights neighborhood and connected to Hillcrest, where Luke's parents lived. I was completely bummed when Starbucks left the spot, but there were several other Starbucks in the city. I just liked being able to walk there, and they had a decent patio.

Emma was just trying to take my mind off things. I grabbed my phone, some cash and locked the door behind me. It was a quick walk, and once I was there, I was glad for the company.

We both ordered. I grabbed a mint chocolate chip milkshake and Emma had a hot fudge sundae that looked delicious. As soon as we were at the table, she dug in. She looked up at me and laughed. "Pregnancy. Don't judge."

I held my hands up. "No judging. Glad you're enjoying it. I have no appetite, otherwise, I'd have had the same. I'm nervous about Luke."

"How's he doing?" Emma asked between bites.

"He says he's got it covered. Cooper told me that Luke did back off and let him and Tyler question a professor who was seen with Lily on the night she disappeared. That was good. Maybe Luke understands his limits this time."

"I hope so," Emma offered. "We both know how bad it can go when you mix personal with a criminal case. Speaking of mixing personal with work, how are you feeling about going back to stay with your mom and sister?"

"I'm okay. It will be nice to crash at my mom's while I work on the case," I said, taking another sip and then regretting it. I drank too fast and my head was stinging. I held the spot on my head.

Emma frowned. "You're as bad as Sophie sometimes. I'm glad you think it will be okay. You haven't really been back since your sister Liv started dating your ex-husband. I didn't know if it would be awkward."

"It shouldn't be," I said and really hoped that was true. My sister Olivia had been dating my ex-husband for close to a year now. "I'd like for them both to be happy, I just don't get what they see in each other. Maybe it's true and opposites attract."

"How long do you think you'll be up there?" Emma asked, taking the last spoonful. She wiped her mouth with her napkin and pushed the bowl away.

"I don't know, but I'm hoping not long. I'm excited that I won't be going it alone," I explained, finishing off my milkshake. I picked up my garbage and Emma's and dropped it in the can by the door. Returning, I added, "A detective from Virginia is coming up to help me along with Jack, the detective in Troy. They both handled the cases directly back when they occurred. Both seemed pretty motivated to find the killer."

"That's great you'll have help," Emma said. Giving me a motherly look, she added, "Just try to stay out of harm's way this time."

CHAPTER 28

A lot of private investigators and even cops hated surveillance, but not Cooper. It was one of his skills. Even if he had to sit for hours and had five minutes of action, it was worth it to him. He knew it was a long game. Some investigators wanted to knock down doors, interview perps, and shakedown people for information. Cooper was content to wait in the shadows and let the action come to him.

It was late on Friday evening just before eleven o'clock. The night had been quiet. Luke's team and two others had been out since five that evening. The decoys went to parties. Cooper had walked the streets himself several times, watching for any suspicious activity. Nothing all night. It had been quiet.

Cooper sat in his truck with Det. Tyler near a row of sorority houses. Luke was with Gabe positioned at another location. Most of the university kids they saw were walking in groups. The most action they'd seen was about an hour before when a girl, obviously drunk, took a tumble on the sidewalk, but her friends helped her back up, and they went on their way.

Det. Tyler asked, "You really think this guy was going to tell us his plan?"

"I don't know, but better safe than sorry."

"I know Luke really feels like this guy is the one. I hope he doesn't have him out here just chasing his tail."

Cooper agreed with that. He'd watched Luke through the years invest time, his own money, and more energy than one person should have into the case to get nowhere. He wasn't sure that Luke would recover if all this was just a game, someone screwing with him for the fun of it.

The ping of Cooper's cellphone cut through the stillness. It was just Luke reporting in that all was quiet where they were stationed. Another thirty minutes passed by. Cooper was ready to call it a night. The throngs of kids walking back and forth had slowed to a trickle. Most, Cooper assumed, had heeded their warning to make it a quiet night.

Cooper was just about to ask Det. Tyler if they should change up their location when Cooper spotted movement at the side of a sorority house. The house was big, three floors and wide. People were home or at least Cooper assumed so with the number of lights that were on. The yard was heavily tree-lined. Cooper caught sight of a guy walking down the street. He stopped in front of the house, looked around and then walked up on the grass. He stopped again and looked around. He took off in a jog around the side of the house and out of Cooper's sight.

The guy had been dressed in dark clothes, looked older than a student, and had something in his hand Cooper couldn't quite make out. Nudging Tyler, Cooper asked, "Did you see that guy?"

"Yeah," Tyler responded, his eyes also fixed on the house. "Let's go check it out."

The pair made their way out of the truck and took the same path as the guy down the street. As they stepped on the grass in the front yard, a woman screamed. Cooper looked at Tyler and the two men took off in a sprint around the side of the house. There they found a man in front of a side door of the home, trying to open it. He was saying something Cooper couldn't hear, but each time he pushed against the door, it would give an inch and be pushed back at him. Cooper assumed someone on the other side was trying to keep him out.

Tyler drew his gun. Cooper tackled the man to the ground. The man gave no resistance. Cooper rolled him over to look at his face. He was older than Cooper, but he wasn't sure by how much. The man yelled to let him up and something about his daughter living at the house. Cooper rolled off the man and got to his knees. The man struggled to a sitting position.

"What are you doing?" the man said, wiping dirt off his face.

Det. Tyler aimed his gun at the man. "Keep your hands where I can see them."

Two girls stepped out of the side exit. They were both panicked. "He was trying to break in!" they shouted in unison.

The man turned to them and shouted right back. "I'm here for my daughter. She goes to school here."

Cooper grabbed the guy by the shirt and yanked him to his feet. "Explain, now. Who is your daughter?"

The man stumbled over his words. "Her name is Amy. She lives here."

The two girls looked to each other and then back to Cooper. The dark-haired girl said, "There's no Amy here. No one uses this door. He didn't knock. He slammed against it and tried to get in."

Cooper asked the man for his name. He got no response. Tyler got out his cuffs and slapped them on the man. As Tyler escorted the man to the front of the house, Cooper assured the girls they were safe and to go back inside.

As Cooper came around to the front of the house, he texted Luke and told him what was happening. By the time the police car pulled up, which was going to take Tyler and the man to the station, the response from Luke was even more confusing.

Luke texted: *Same. Just apprehended a man trying to break into the freshman dorms. Claims he's a father. No one knows his daughter. Headed back to the station now.*

CHAPTER 29

Luke looked at the man sitting across from him dressed in a dark polo shirt, jeans, and a pair of beat-up running shoes. He told Luke his name was Craig. Luke didn't believe the man was a father. No one seemed to know his daughter. There was something about the man's story Luke just wasn't buying.

"I'm going to ask you again to tell me why you were trying to break into a freshman dorm." Luke leaned back in his chair like he had all the time in the world.

"I told you," Craig said, putting his head in his hands. "I was there to see my daughter. I heard on the news about the threats at the school. I came to see if she was okay."

"Why not call her?" Luke countered.

Craig stammered, "I tried, but she didn't answer so I was even more worried."

"I see," Luke said, not believing a word of it. "Give me her number. I'll call her right now, and we can assess her safety."

Craig didn't budge. He just watched Luke. Finally, he said, "I don't want her involved in all this. I'm not giving you my daughter's phone number."

"Well you can't be too worried about your daughter then," Luke said smugly, drumming his fingers on the tabletop. "She doesn't live in that dorm. I have the school checking for her records right now. What about her mom? How can we reach her?"

Craig shook his head. "We're divorced."

"You don't seem too worried about your daughter right now." Luke leaned forward, pointed at Craig and said angrily, "Why don't you just tell me what's really going on here. I'm going to know one way or the other if your daughter even exists soon so you might as well be out with it now. Otherwise, you're wasting my time."

Craig said nothing. Luke watched his face for any recognition. He knew the man was lying, but he wasn't sure of his angle. Luke stood and kicked the chair back behind him. "I'm going out there to give you a few minutes to get your head right. When I come back in, I want some answers."

Again, Craig said nothing. He just sat calmly at the table with his hands folded in his lap.

As Luke left the small interrogation room, he ran right into Det. Tyler. "Cooper said you brought someone in. What do you have?"

"Don't know. It doesn't make a bit of sense to me. The guy claims his daughter lives at the sorority. He was trying to go in a side door. The girls we talked to said no one of that name lives there."

"I got the same situation in there," Luke said, pointing at the door. "He looks like a dad. He says he's divorced. Couldn't reach his daughter and was going to check on her. The dorm monitors don't know of anyone by the daughter's name. Gabe is running down leads at the school to see if his kid exists. I should hear back any minute."

"I passed my info off to Gabe, too." He added with frustration in his voice, "The guy isn't giving up anything. I have nothing to go on. I don't even know for sure if a crime was committed. I don't think pushing on a door to get in would qualify as a break-in, especially when he's got no weapons and no burglary tools. He wasn't yelling at the girls or nothing."

"Same with this guy. I find it strange there are two that happened near the same time – tonight of all nights." His phone pinged. Gabe sent a text, letting Luke know that there was no one at the school with Craig's daughter's name.

"This guy's a fraud," Luke said definitively. "Cooper still out there on surveillance?"

"Yeah, everyone is still in place other than us. I'm going to take another crack at this guy." Tyler walked back down the hall. He stopped briefly to look at papers on a nearby desk and reentered the room.

Luke went back to the interrogation room. Pushing open the door, he looked at Craig calmly sitting there. Luke demanded, "Well your daughter doesn't exist. You've got one last chance to tell me or I'm throwing you in a cell."

"You don't have anything on me," Craig countered angrily.

Luke held up his hand and counted down his fingers one by one. "Lying to me, pretending to have a kid on campus to get access to a dorm, and scaring students when you tried to break into the dorm will at a minimum give you a trespassing charge." Then he added with emphasis, "Trust me, I can get creative from there. Those kids at the dorm you scared will certainly back me up."

Craig's eyes shifted. It was the first break in the man's body language.

Luke took his seat and stared at the man across from him, thoughts spinning through his head. Luke got an idea so he tried a different approach.

"Look, Craig," he said, sitting on the edge of his chair leaning in, "I don't actually think you're a bad guy. I think someone set you up to distract us. Why go down for someone else's crime?"

Craig's eyes snapped up and met Luke's. "If that were to happen, and I'm not saying it is, what kind of trouble would I be in?"

Luke shrugged. "Maybe none if you can help us out. It's really up to you at this point." Luke leaned back and didn't say another word. He got the crack in the armor he was looking for. Now all he had to do was wait.

After a few minutes, Craig admitted, "You're right. Someone gave me directions on what to do, where to go, what to say. He paid me five grand to do it."

Not exactly what Luke was expecting so it took some constraint to hide his surprise. "Who was it?"

"I really don't know. I swear," Craig conceded. "I've been out of work for a while so the money was great. The job was listed on the dark web in a chat forum. The guy was looking for someone to come to the school and try to get access to the dorm. He gave the specific date and time, too."

"What was the plan after that – once you got access?"

"Nothing, honestly," Craig replied. "I was just supposed to try to get access. If I did, I had to tell the guy how. If I didn't, I had to tell him that, too."

"Who was this guy? What did he call himself?"

"The Professor. I'd never seen him in the chat before, and haven't seen him since. He seemed to get on there and then was gone."

"How'd you get paid?"

"I had asked that and the guy never answered. One morning, the money was in an envelope on my doorstep. It creeped me out. I never told the guy my address. But the money was there."

"Anything else you need to tell me?"

Craig looked down at the table.

Luke prodded again. "If there's something else, this is the time to tell me."

Craig said cautiously, "I don't know what this means, but he told me I'd meet you. I'm supposed to tell you that he won this round. That he'll see you on the harvest fields next time."

CHAPTER 30

Luke struggled to breathe. He couldn't believe what he just heard. Luke's mind raced, running through the possibilities. Were they set up or was a girl taken right under their noses? Luke wasn't sure. Luke feared a student was missing, and they didn't know. How long would they have to wait until some poor family came in and filed a missing person's report? It brought him right back to his sister Lily and the day his own parents had gone to the police station. A mix of fear and anger rose up in Luke's chest.

If no student was missing, could this guy really have played Luke? Made him and the university run all over the place like puppets and terrorize a community for nothing? That was a far cry better than a missing girl, but Luke didn't like being at someone else's mercy. Before Luke could ask Craig anything else, there was a knock on the door that made them both jump.

Luke took another hard look at Craig, who sat with a blank look on his face. Det. Tyler stood in the doorway. His face was flushed and there was a line of sweat at his brow. Det. Tyler waved Luke out.

Once the door was securely closed, Tyler, in rushed speech, told Luke the same story he just heard right down to the final taunting threat. Tyler added defeated, "What do you think?"

"I don't know." Luke pinched the bridge of his nose. "No one has reported anything from the field. There have been no disturbances, but I'm not sure what this means. Heads are going to roll if it means we were screwing around with these two while he took another girl."

"We did everything we could," Tyler said softly, more to himself than Luke.

"We did," Luke agreed. He looked down at the floor, thinking it through. He looked back up at Tyler. "Let's call Gabe and tell him. Maybe they can get some extra patrol units out and start canvassing. Better to actively think we've got a missing girl than sit here and do nothing. After that, keep grilling your guy to see if he'll give up anything else. I'll do the same. Let's meet in an hour."

Tyler agreed and pulled out his phone. Luke went back into the room. He closed the door securely and it clicked into place. It was the only sound in the room. Luke watched Craig who hadn't even turned to make eye contact with him. He yanked the chair out from the table and slammed himself down. Luke slapped his hand on the table. "We've got a big problem here."

Craig finally made eye contact. "I've told you everything I know. I swear."

"You need to go over every detail again."

Craig sighed but did as Luke requested. When he was done, Craig added, "I don't understand why what I did was so bad. It's not like I hurt anyone or broke in really. I was just trying to see if I could. I wasn't going to hurt anyone."

"How do you know no one was hurt while we had to focus on your little stunt?"

"What do you mean?" Craig stammered. He shifted in his chair. The legs scraped against the floor as he moved in his seat.

"You already said you know about the threats at the school. We've had cops out all night trying to keep this campus safe. Your little stunt diverted resources. What if you were the diversion he needed to snatch a girl while we were focused on you?"

"I don't understand what you're saying. You think the guy who contacted me is the one making the threats on the school?" Craig swallowed visibly. He looked suddenly shaken and sick.

"Not think, know," Luke stressed. "He's playing a game with us, and either you're in on it or you're just a pawn. I'm not sure which yet. You better hope a girl wasn't taken tonight."

"Listen, man, listen. I didn't have anything to do with this. I swear. He just paid me to see if I could get into that dorm. That's it."

Luke leveled a look at him. "But he told you what to do and when to do it, right?"

"Yeah, but I don't think that means anything."

"Are you stupid?" Luke asked sarcastically. "Someone you don't know asks if you can break into a freshman girls' dorm and report back to him if you could and how you did it. You think there's any good reason for that?"

Craig looked around the room, his eyes not landing on any one spot.

Luke saw fear take hold as some recognition finally hit that man. "You're thinking about what I'm saying, aren't you?"

"I really didn't think there was any harm," Craig said, squeaking out each word. "You have to believe me."

"What else do you know about him?"

"Nothing, I swear," Craig said, pleading. "Go check my computer. I know you can do that. See where he found me. You can see all of our communication."

Luke stood, fairly certain he wasn't going to get any more from him. "We are going to be doing that and more. Meanwhile, we've got more than enough to keep you here for a while so get comfortable."

Luke left the room. He stood in the hall, trying to catch his bearings. He checked his phone and noticed there was a call from Gabe. Luke punched in the other detective's number.

"What's happening there?" Gabe asked.

Luke went over the details that he knew to date. Gabe assured him that there was no missing person's report yet, but cautioned that it was early. Luke asked for officers to take Craig to a cell. Luke was determined to go back out and start canvassing himself.

CHAPTER 31

On Saturday, at close to noon, Cooper and Det. Tyler stood on the front steps of Aaron Roberts' house. Luke had urged them to go while he finally caught a few hours of sleep. He had stayed out until five that morning, driving around and canvassing. Thankfully, no one was reported missing, but there was the nagging question of who had paid the two men to break into a dorm and sorority and divert police attention. It wasn't adding up for Cooper.

Aaron Roberts' home was a two-story with a wide front porch. It had a heavy wood door and no doorbell that Cooper could see. He knocked and waited. He knocked again, loudly this time.

The floor creaked behind the door and Cooper knew someone was home. The door was pulled open, leaving Cooper standing face to face with a man who was a little taller than him, had a solid to stocky build and close-cropped brown hair and glasses. "Can I help you?" the man said.

Cooper introduced himself and Det. Tyler. He confirmed that the man was, in fact, Aaron Roberts, who had worked at the University of Arkansas, some time ago. Cooper asked if they could speak with him.

Aaron showed no signs of discomfort or fear. He opened the door wider and let them in. As they entered the small, sparse living room, Aaron busied himself with picking up newspapers, magazines, and a few empty cups. He took the items and headed into the hall, calling over his shoulder, "Feel free to sit. Can I get you anything to drink?"

Cooper and Det. Tyler sat on the couch and declined the drink. When Aaron returned, he asked, "You said it's something related to my time at the university?"

Det. Tyler spoke first. "Do you remember a student by the name of Lily Morgan?"

Aaron sat back in his chair. "I've had a lot of students over the years. The name sounds familiar…"

"She went missing and was later found murdered," Cooper deadpanned.

Aaron's eyes grew wide. He sat up straighter in his chair and leaned forward. "Now that you mention that, I do recall it. I remembered a girl went missing during my time there, but I couldn't recall her name. It's been many years."

Cooper made direct eye contact and asked calmly, "Do you remember meeting Lily?"

"I don't believe she was a student of mine."

"That's not what I asked," Cooper said directly. "I asked if you remember meeting her."

Aaron stayed silent for a moment too long. Cooper could tell the man was contemplating the truth so he didn't give him the chance to lie. Cooper pointed at him and said, "Let me rephrase. We have a witness who saw you, at least once, with Lily, so we know that you knew her."

"It was complicated," Aaron admitted. He got up and walked across the room and looked out the window.

"Complicated how?" Det. Tyler asked.

Cooper noticed the edge in Tyler's voice. He was squinting and rubbing his eyes. The stress and lack of sleep from the night before were getting to all of them.

Aaron turned back to them. "Lily and I went out a couple of times."

"What the hell does that mean? She was barely eighteen years old," Cooper said agitatedly. He stood and walked towards the man. Tyler was on his feet in seconds, holding Cooper back. Cooper knew losing his temper, right now, wouldn't do anyone any good, but he wasn't ready to hear what the man had to say, especially, if he was headed in the direction Cooper thought he might.

Aaron let out a sigh. "It means, we met for coffee a few times. We had met at a lecture, and we struck up a conversation. That's all that happened. I was interested. Lily was smart, charming and beautiful, but as you said, she was just eighteen. She wasn't interested in me."

"What did you do about that?" Cooper asked, narrowing his eyes.

Aaron threw his arms wide open. "Nothing. I didn't do anything. I certainly didn't kill her, if that's what you're asking. I was with her the night she died. I always felt like I could have done more to protect her."

"Could you have?" Cooper asked.

"No," Aaron said with defeat in his voice.

"Tell me about the last time you saw her," Det. Tyler urged.

Aaron looked back out the window. Cooper wasn't sure what he was looking for, and it was a bit unnerving. Aaron was forthcoming, or so it seemed, with information, but there was something Cooper didn't like about him.

With his back still turned to them, Aaron finally explained. "I saw Lily that night walking home from a party. I pulled over and we had some conversation. I asked if she needed a ride home. She said no at first, but I cautioned her about walking alone so late at night, particularly on Halloween. I gave her a ride back to the dorm and that's it." Aaron cleared his throat.

"That's not it," Cooper said sarcastically. "What aren't you telling us?"

Aaron turned around. He started to speak and stopped. He chewed at his bottom lip. "I didn't bring her all the way to her dorm. We stopped a few blocks before. She said she wanted to see a friend so I let her out. I've felt guilty all these years for not making sure she made it into her dorm."

"What friend?" Tyler asked. He sat back down and nudged Cooper's side to do the same. They both took a seat on the couch. Cooper was sure Tyler was hoping it would put Aaron more at ease, but he didn't care. He wanted Aaron to feel as uncomfortable as he did.

Aaron shrugged. "I really don't know. She asked me to pull over. She thanked me and got out. That's the last time I saw her. I didn't actually see her meet anyone. She just walked off heading in the same direction as the school, but for whatever reason, she didn't want me to drive her there."

"You did nothing to make her uncomfortable?" Cooper eyed him.

"No, of course not."

Det. Tyler instructed Aaron to run through the situation again, and then a third time. Cooper noticed the man's answers remained the same. Most would think that was good. For Cooper, and he knew Tyler, it was a sign the man had rehearsed what he'd say if the cops ever came calling. There was no additional detail. He didn't leave anything out. Aaron told the same story exactly the same way three times. Cooper and Tyler shared a look.

They didn't have anything to arrest him, and Tyler didn't have the jurisdiction even if they had.

Before they left, Cooper asked one last question. "Why didn't you ever come forward at the time? People were frantic searching for her. You were the last person to have seen Lily."

"I did though," Aaron indicated. "I told someone in the family."

Cooper stared the man down. Cooper knew for a fact no one had heard about this man then. Aaron looked away, wouldn't hold eye contact with him. Cooper felt a tug on his arm, and let Tyler lead him out of the house.

Back in Cooper's truck, Tyler asked, "What do you think was more suspicious – him lying about telling Luke's family or that he never asked why we were asking those questions about Lily?"

CHAPTER 32

Late in the afternoon, after I had spoken to Luke, who had just woken up from a nap, all I had wanted was a little time to relax. I was glad that no one had been taken from the university. I hoped it would give us all a chance to regroup. Luke told me he was going to stay a few more days in Fayetteville because he had more leads to run down, and then he would be home.

I didn't think I was going to get the chance to see him before I left for New York, but we'd Skype or something I was sure. Thankfully, we had the kind of relationship that could handle the distance. While we missed each other, neither of us fell apart without the other – especially when the separation was work-related.

I spent time puttering around the house, not really sure what to do. Emma was busy with Joe and Sophie. Cooper was with Luke. I liked my alone time, but it had been a while since I had any when I wasn't working. I went to my bookcase and grabbed a spy novel I hadn't had time to read. I decided to go find a patio, a beer, and dive into a good story.

Nearly thirty minutes later, I sat comfortably on the patio at Dugan's Irish Pub in downtown Little Rock. The patio faced two relatively quiet streets. The chair was comfortable, the patio nearly empty, and the beer in front was the right temperature for a Guinness. I was waiting for the very delicious sandwich I had ordered. It was the only place in the city where I knew I could get a good RLT, which was Irish bacon, known as a rasher, lettuce, and tomato, with a fried egg on it, too.

I opened my novel and got six pages in when Rhoda dropped my plate in front of me. We made some quick small talk. I had gotten to know her with how frequently Luke and I ate there. She didn't even need to ask my order anymore. That's how good she was. She left me alone to eat, and I dug in, savoring each bite.

I lost myself in my novel and my food for quite a long time. Movement from the corner of my eye disrupted my reading. People had joined me on the patio. There were murmurs of conversation but not enough to make out actual words. I continued to read.

Rhoda brought me another beer and removed my empty plate. A few words from the gathering crowd caught my attention. I put the book on the table and turned my head around to assess. There were several people standing on the patio staring at the television. I couldn't see it from my vantage point, could only hear it. I got up and moved over to the crowd.

"What's going on?" I asked a guy who looked to be in his twenties.

With shock in his voice, he said, "A girl is missing from the University of Arkansas at Little Rock. She never went back to her dorm last night."

My stomach dropped at his words. On the screen, a local news reporter stood in front of the missing girl's dorm, discussing the details of the case. The reporter indicated that the young woman had just turned eighteen. She was a freshman and went missing after a night out with friends. It seemed from her friends, that she wasn't feeling well and went home alone from a bar. That was the last anyone saw of her, at least that they knew right now.

My phone rang from the table where I had left it. It was Captain Meadows. I answered before the call was picked up by voicemail.

"Did you hear?" he asked.

"Do you know any more than what's been reported in the news?"

"Not really. I've got another detective down there now, but I want Luke. Do you want to call him and break the news?"

I didn't, but of course, I would. "I'll handle it."

I hung up and called Luke. He didn't answer so I left him a message to call me back as soon as he could. I tried to not sound panicked, but I don't think I succeeded. I searched for Rhoda and thrust more than enough cash at her to cover the bill and a tip, and then I went to find my SUV.

Once inside, ignition started and seat belt securely on, I called Cooper. Thankfully he answered. He hadn't seen Luke all day.

"Cooper, there's a missing girl here. She's a freshman at the University of Arkansas at Little Rock. It's been on our news here already. We need to tell Luke."

Cooper let out a string of expletives. "I'll tell Tyler and we will go meet Luke together. What's your plan?"

"I don't have a plan," I said, as I navigated out of the parking lot. "There's nothing for me to do. It's not like I can jump in the middle of this. Captain Meadows said he wants Luke back as soon as possible."

"Trust me," Cooper said, "he will come racing back after he kicks himself for not being a mind reader. While we were running around Fayetteville trying to stop him, he struck in Little Rock. How could we have been so stupid?"

"There's no way we could have known," I countered but wasn't sure I believed it myself. We had been duped. We had believed the words of a serial killer. One of us should have had better sense. Luke had enough to worry about so it should have been Cooper or me.

"I need to go find Tyler." He hung up.

Several minutes later, as I was turning onto my street, my phone rang again. It was Luke's mother. I figured she was calling to ask if I'd heard about the case. What she said nearly made me crash.

Lucia sobbed, "Spencer found a girl's body across the street from our house on the Allsopp park trail."

CHAPTER 33

I immediately turned my SUV around and headed back towards Hillcrest. Lucia told me I was her second call. The first was to the police. She explained through tears that Spencer was sitting in his favorite spot on the living room couch, waiting for the cops to arrive. Lucia said he was clutching his chest, and she was concerned for his heart. I could hear her lovingly tell him to take slow, deep breaths. She told me she had to go and hung up.

I couldn't even imagine the shock they must be feeling. To have their own daughter murdered and then find the body of a young girl, in the woods, across from their house. I assumed it was the girl missing from the previous night. I hadn't heard about anyone else. I knew if it was her that it was a sick, twisted message for Luke. It also meant that the killer knew where his parents lived.

I looked down at my phone wondering if I should call Luke. I picked it up and put it back down, talking myself out of it. I was stalling the inevitable. Luke would be informed, but I was hoping maybe there was a way we could get him back to Little Rock before having to tell him. He had a long drive in front of him. I was concerned about his safety on the road.

Once in Hillcrest, I turned from Kavanaugh onto Beechwood. I didn't make it very far down the road. People were congregating on their lawns and standing in the roadway. The road was also blocked by cop cars so there was no way I could drive any farther. Luckily, I found a place to park without blocking a driveway. I grabbed my bag and walked towards Luke's parents' house.

Two cops were standing guard at the barrier that blocked off the road where Beechwood turned into S. Lookout. There was yellow crime scene tape roping off the point where the trail started. Off to the right was a grassy area and then the walking path down into the woods.

I approached the two cops, fingers crossed they'd let me through. It's not like I had a badge or anything official to flash at them. They stood talking to each other, both looking pale and nervous. They were young.

"Excuse me," I started. "I'm a friend of the Morgan family. Lucia called and explained what happened. Can I get through to see them?"

"No one is allowed back," one officer said sternly.

"The Morgans are Det. Luke Morgan's parents. He is out of town right now working a case in Fayetteville. I'm his girlfriend. I really need to be there for his parents. Please call Captain Meadows."

The one cop who hadn't spoken looked me over. He stepped away and picked up his walkie. I was too far to hear what he was saying. He looked back at me and then back into the woods. I turned to see what he was looking at. I didn't see anything, but then a moment later, Captain Meadows appeared at the top of the trail. He hitched his head at me to follow him. I thanked the officers as I passed by.

"Lucia called me," I explained. "I thought since Luke wasn't here, it might be good for me to check on them."

"It's good you're here," Captain Meadows said, patting me on the back.

We didn't walk back down the trail the way he came. Instead, we walked towards the Morgans' house. As we moved farther away from the crowds and cops standing guard, Captain Meadows stopped. "I don't know what kind of game this sicko is playing, but this is as bad as I've seen."

It was completely unlike Captain Meadows to share information with me or any civilian, not on the police force. I hoped this meant I had gained some of his trust over the last year. Private investigators and cops can either have a cordial or completely adversarial relationship depending on the personalities involved. I went to great lengths to prove to Captain Meadows I was friend, not foe. I hoped this was the turning point in our relationship.

"Were you able to confirm it's the missing girl from last night?" I asked, looking beyond him at the trees. Some of the leaves had turned color but not enough had fallen to give me a line of sight.

"We were. It's definitely her."

"How long has she been dead?"

Captain Meadows ran a hand down his face. "We can't be sure yet. Purvis, the medical examiner, is down there removing her body now. He said she was probably killed some time in the middle of the night."

I thought back to what the other detectives, back home in Troy and in Virginia, had said. I was hesitant to ask, mostly I was scared of the answer, but I pushed forward. "By any chance was she killed from a stab wound to the heart? Did she have missing fingers off her left hand?"

Captain Meadow's eyes grew wide. He gave a curt nod but didn't say anything. After several moments, he said, "I assume since there's no other way you could have known those details that you've seen other cases like this."

It was more of a statement than a question, but I knew he wanted details. "I have. In that stack of cases Cooper pulled, there were cases with similar details. I went through them and stumbled on a couple of cases where they found the body soon enough to do a proper autopsy and collect evidence. They have some commonalities like being stabbed in the heart with a thin blade and fingers cut off from the left hand. One of them, strangely enough, is from my hometown in New York."

Captain Meadows stepped back. "There's a case connected to where you're from?"

"Yes, the girl went missing right around the corner from my mother's house."

"You think the killer knew about your connection to Luke?"

"No, definitely not. The case was from long before I ever moved to Little Rock or met Luke. I was in college and away from Troy when it happened."

"That's one heck of a coincidence," Captain Meadows said.

I agreed, but I had no other explanation. "I know the detective that was on the case. I had planned to go to New York, this week, to see what more I can find. The detective on the Virginia case is meeting us."

"You should still go. Don't let this stop you."

"What if Luke needs me? This is going to crush him."

Captain Meadows put a hand on my shoulder. "I've got Det. Tyler informing Luke about this. The best thing you can do is go to New York and work that case while Luke works this one."

I hated to admit it, but he was right. "I'm surprised you're going to let Luke handle this."

Captain Meadows cracked the first smile I'd seen on his face since we received the first letter. "You think I could stop him? I'd rather make it easier on both of us and just give him the case."

He was right, again, and got no argument from me. I knew Luke would fight to take the case regardless. I followed Captain Meadows to the Morgans' house.

CHAPTER 34

Luke gripped the steering wheel. His eyes were focused on the road. He was on a mission to hunt down and bring to justice the man who killed his sister, countless other university girls, and made him look like a fool. Luke didn't care if justice was a guilty verdict in court or a bullet through the brain. Either way, Luke was putting an end to this.

Earlier in the day, Cooper had come to the hotel to tell him that a student from the university in Little Rock was missing. To say that Luke completely lost it would be an understatement. He had been so angry he was sure that some of the words he had used were completely made up, combinations of curses that would shock most. Cooper had sat in the chair and watched Luke until he wound himself down. Cooper was good like that. He gave Luke the space he needed to lose it, knowing that eventually, Luke would regain his calm, cool and collected demeanor.

They had been sitting there talking things through when Det. Tyler had rapped on Luke's hotel room door. He stepped into the room, looking worried and upset. He had stumbled over his words but broke the news to Luke that the girl's body had been found. Tyler had paused to let Luke absorb the news before adding where the body had been placed. Instead of an outward display of rage, Luke had simply seethed.

Luke had immediately packed his things and checked out of the hotel. Before Luke left, he had called Gabe to see if he could question Aaron Roberts. Luke had not liked the details that Cooper had provided about that interview. The man seemed a creep at best. Roberts was also unaccounted for and not in Fayetteville during the Little Rock murder, so checking his alibi would need to be done. Luke had not met the man, but he trusted Cooper's opinion that something was very off with Aaron Roberts.

Cooper and Det. Tyler were headed back to Little Rock, too. Tyler planned to go with Gabe to speak with the university president again and finalize any last details before they called their surveillance mission a success, in Fayetteville, at least. It was an abysmal failure as far as Luke was concerned.

Gabe also processed the two men who had broken into the dorm and sorority. Neither had given any more information. Luke knew where to find them if the time came. Cooper offered to drive Luke back and retrieve his SUV later. Luke declined. He wanted time on the road to gather his thoughts before arriving in Little Rock. Luke needed to hit the ground running.

Luke had been on the road for more than an hour, and as each mile passed, he replayed how it all went wrong. He tried to convince himself that he shouldn't have so blindly followed the note and the word of a psychopath. His captain, though, assured Luke that was exactly what he had to do. Captain Meadows postulated that the murder could have taken place anywhere, and even if Luke was in Little Rock, he couldn't have stopped the abduction and murder. Cooper and Tyler had echoed the same.

Deep down Luke knew they were speaking the truth. There was no way he couldn't have acted on the tip. Even if he was in Little Rock, there was no way he could have known the university was a target. But that didn't make Luke feel like any less a failure or give him any solace. Now, more so than ever, Luke just wanted revenge. The psychopath, who called himself The Professor, had brought Luke's parents into this.

The idea that the man had planted a body while watching Luke's parents' house terrified him. It made his skin itch. Riley was with his parents. He had spoken to both his mom and dad and briefly with

Riley. He was glad she was there. It was one less thing he needed to worry about. Luke's father was strong. They would get through this just like they had his sister's murder. The only difference was this time Luke wouldn't fail at catching her killer.

Luke plotted and planned the rest of the trip. He was used to facing setbacks in investigations and coming back stronger. This is what he needed right now.

Once Luke finally arrived back in Little Rock, he navigated from the interstate to his parents' house. Purvis, the medical examiner, already had the body. Luke wanted to check on his parents and assess the crime scene for himself. Captain Meadows had said the crime scene techs had already come and gone. Dusk was falling and Luke wasn't sure what he'd be able to see, but there was no way he wasn't going to the scene.

As Luke pulled down Beechwood, two uniformed cops stood at the barricade. He drove towards them and stopped. Luke waved them over, showed his credentials and they let him pass. Most of the department either knew Luke or knew of him, but he appreciated they still had a job to do. Turning down S. Lookout, a street Luke had been down since childhood, he was suddenly overcome with grief – raw, real emotion. It took him off guard and the tears flowed. He choked back the sobs.

Luke pulled into his parents' driveway right behind his father's car. He put his SUV in park and tried to regain his composure. The tears kept coming. Luke wasn't sure how long he sat there, but before he realized it, his father stood at his side window, a look of sympathy and concern on his face. Luke wiped his eyes with his hand and got out.

Spencer embraced him in a hug. "Sometimes you just need a good cry."

His father offering support when Luke knew Spencer needed it more broke his heart. It forced him to pull himself together and stand back from his dad. "You okay, Pop?"

"As well as can be expected."

Together they walked to the end of the driveway and looked across the street. It was roped off still, but there was just enough daylight left for Luke to go over and take a look. Before crossing the street, Spencer said, "I'll show you the spot. They have it marked off, but I'll show you exactly where she was. I take the dog for a walk over there every day and she was right there near the footbridge, but down enough, wedged against it so you had to be right there to see her."

"Where's Riley?"

Spencer looked back at the house. "She made us dinner. Riley and your mother have been asleep for about an hour. I can wake her when I go back in."

They crossed the street and entered into the woods to assess the spot where the girl's body had been found – the second time the two had to undertake such a task. It may not have been Luke's sister this time, but it wasn't any less personal.

CHAPTER 35

I stood at the edge of the trail, on Fairview, and watched Luke search the ground looking for clues. Spencer had woken me up when he had come back in the house. I immediately went to see Luke.

I had not been to the site, yet, but was hesitant to walk down the dirt path, to where Luke stood. I knew I had to, but my feet didn't want to move. Going to the spot where a young woman's body had just been found was proving more difficult than I thought it would be.

Earlier in the day when I had shown up to Luke's parents, they immediately welcomed me. Spencer and Lucia were both thankful that I was there, not that I felt I could do much for them. They were amazing people and loving parents. They made me feel as comfortable as I do with my own family. I was there to provide support, but I felt just as supported in return. Spencer had looked as exhausted as Lucia did scared. I had felt a mix of both.

While I was there, I learned the victim's name. I had missed it when I first caught the news at Dugan's but heard from Captain Meadows that it was Cristina Sawyer. She had been a freshman at the university and from a small town about fifty miles outside of Little Rock.

Now standing on the edge of the wood, watching Luke, I assessed the section of Allsopp Park, where her body had been left. The small section of woods had two entrances – off Beechwood to the west, and Fairview, where I was standing, to the east. Both streets ran perpendicular to S. Lookout. Cristina's body was found in a tiny section of the total park and trail. The U-shaped Fairview made a tiny island in the overall dense park. If you entered at Beechwood, you'd walk east, and then have to cut south along the trail where Fairview cut into the woods. Once around, you'd keep following the trail east.

It was a strange part of the park to leave a body. It was close to homes, hard to enter because of a lack of street parking, and shallow. There were other parts of the park that offered better parking nearby and were denser, meaning a body placed there might have taken days to be found.

The killer wanted to leave a message. He wanted her to be found. The calculated risk was worth it to let Luke know he could get to his parents. The spot was carefully planned.

Near the entrance at Fairview, there was a small wooden footbridge, which covered a section where the earth dipped low. The bridge allowed the trail to be flat. It was down in the dirt, next to the bridge, where Cristina's body had been found. Captain Meadows said she was propped up against one of the posts. Her head had slumped forward, but her body had remained upright. Her hands were in her lap. There was no blood on the ground.

Captain Meadows theorized that she had been killed elsewhere and placed at the spot. No one had heard screaming, and she was close enough to homes that someone might have heard. Captain Meadows didn't think the killer would take the chance to kill her at the spot. He wanted to leave a message, but he didn't want his game to end, just yet. I agreed with Captain Meadows that she had been killed someplace else. It seemed the evidence backed that up, too.

Luke crouched down surveying the ground by the footbridge. I called his name so I wouldn't startle him. Luke looked around and once he saw me, he stood. As soon as I got close enough, he pulled me into him.

"I talked to my dad a little, but really, how are my parents doing?" He ran his fingers through my hair.

"Better than to be expected, I think. Your mom was more shook up than your dad, but maybe he just hides it better." I kissed him and then stepped back. "What happened in Fayetteville?"

Luke ran though the events in detail, right up to the moment that Det. Tyler had informed him, and Cooper, that the girl's body had been found.

"Is Gabe arresting those two men?"

"He did," Luke explained. "He made the arrest on burglary charges and was going to question them again."

"That professor, Aaron Roberts. You have any feeling on him one way or the other?"

"You'd have to ask Cooper about that. I didn't interview the guy. I figured he'd talk more to Cooper, especially if he knew Lily was my sister."

That made sense. Luke bent down to look at the ground again. He checked the spot where the footbridge connected to the ground. He stood again and looked back up at the road, but it wasn't visible from where we were standing.

"What are you thinking?" I asked, walking over to the spot.

Luke turned all the way around, checking out every direction. "I was just trying to figure out how he got her in here without being seen. I know it was the middle of the night, but still, there isn't much street parking. It's dark as hell out here, full of sticks and debris. It's hard to stay on the trail in daylight let alone at night. Plus, he'd be carrying her. I'm wondering how he pulled it off."

"There's some parking down Fairview," I offered. There's no way he would have parked on Beechwood or on S. Lookout. There wasn't much room for cars to pass. It was too obvious and suspicious if someone happened by, even in the middle of the night.

"That's true." He moved past me and walked up the part of the trail I had just come down. He called over his shoulder. "This is definitely easier to walk than coming in from Beechwood."

Night was coming pretty rapidly and there wasn't much light left. I followed close behind Luke. As he approached the road, a man stood there quietly. I wasn't sure if he had been watching us or not, but he was definitely unexpected.

"Can I help you?" Luke asked. He stomped some dirt off his shoes on the roadway.

The man pointed to the house across Fairview. "I live right there." He stuck his hand out to shake Luke's. "I'm Ryan. I think I saw the killer last night."

CHAPTER 36

"Tell me everything you saw," Luke said. He looked to me, and I looked at the man, waiting for more explanation.

"My dog woke me up last night to go out. It was just before three. I had looked at the clock, annoyed with him. He doesn't usually have to go in the middle of the night. I let him out in the backyard. I stood on the back porch waiting for him. I don't know what caught my eye, but I saw a light over here, like a flashlight. I didn't think anything of it at the time. We get kids out here, sometimes, walking the trail at night."

"What makes you think it was the killer?"

"Well," Ryan said tentatively, "the light didn't move. Normally, when kids are walking along the trail, the light keeps moving. This time it stayed in the same area so I got curious about what they were doing out here. I let the dog back in, and I kept watch. We may get the occasional kids coming through here at night, but it's a safe neighborhood."

"How long did you wait?" Luke asked.

"It was probably twenty minutes. I had no idea what was happening, but the light was just sitting in one spot. I wondered if, maybe, it was a homeless person, but then I noticed the car parked along the road. Nobody parks there."

"Did you get any of the car details?"

The man bit at the inside of his cheek and eyed Luke like he didn't want to tell him. Luke raised his eyebrows at him and encouraged him to say whatever it was he had to say.

Finally, Ryan admitted, "Yeah, I got curious so I crept out, through the far back gate, and walked up the road in the opposite way, coming towards the front of the car. It had Texas tags and was a Jeep, one of those smaller SUVs. I wrote down the tag number. It's in my house, I can get it for you."

"Why didn't you want to tell me that?" Luke asked curiously. He didn't have any anger in his voice. If anything, he sounded impressed.

"It's what happened next that I didn't want to say."

"And what was that?"

"When I was close enough to read the tag number, I heard the rustling of leaves and someone moving in the woods. I assumed they were walking up the path so I ran back and hid along the tree line." Ryan pointed up, maybe, thirty feet from where we were standing. "I moved far enough back so I was standing in the trees, so when he turned his lights on, he wouldn't be able to see me."

Luke looked at me. His face registered the same shock I felt. I didn't think there was any way there'd be a witness, let alone something this promising.

"Did you see him?" Luke asked hopefully.

"Just in the shadow," Ryan explained. "The car was definitely his. When he got in, no interior light came on, but he was probably a little taller than you, heavier build, but not fat, just stocky. He was average. There wasn't anything that jumped out at me."

Ryan added, "He drove right past me but was looking straight ahead. I'm sure he didn't see me."

I was riveted by how close this guy came to the killer. He was lucky he wasn't seen.

After a few beats, Luke asked, "Did you go into the woods to see what he had been doing?"

"No, that's why I'm so upset with myself. I went back inside and figured I'd come out in the morning, but I was running late for work so I didn't get the chance. I work for the gas company. My wife called me and told me what had happened."

Ryan looked down and kicked the dirt with his shoe. He looked up at Luke and said sincerely, "Do you think she was still alive? Do you think I could have saved her? It was just too dark to see anything, and I didn't have a flashlight with me. I never would have thought…"

Luke reached out and put a hand on his shoulder to comfort him. "Listen, she was dead long before he put her here. There's nothing you could have done. I promise you that. You can help us now though."

"Anything, whatever you need," Ryan assured.

"Go back to your place and get me that tag number. Tomorrow, I want you to come down to the police station and give a formal statement. I want you to work with a sketch artist, too. I know you may not think you remember much about him, but maybe as you're sitting there and the picture comes to life you might remember more."

"I'll be there." Ryan headed back to his house.

Luke waited until he saw him go inside and the door shut behind him. "What do you think?"

"I think we might have gotten a lucky break on this one."

"I don't know if it's as lucky as you think," Luke commented. He looked back into the woods. His gaze was far off.

I wasn't sure where his mind just went. I reached out and tugged his arms. "What do you mean?"

"Look at the hoops he's made us jump through. He's been doing this for years and hasn't gotten caught. I don't think it's going to be as easy as we have this tag number, pull his registration and there's the killer. He might have taken the risk to bring her body here, but I'd be really surprised if that car leads us back to him."

I started to speak, but Ryan came back out of his house. He walked over to where we still stood and handed Luke a slip of paper with the tag number on it.

Pointing down the road, Ryan said to Luke, "My wife just reminded me that the neighbors on the other side of Fairview have cameras facing the street. As he looped around Fairview to go back to S. Lookout, it might have picked him up."

"I'll head over there now. I'll see you in the morning."

As Ryan left, I said, "Even if it's not his car, at least maybe there's a video of him. I really don't think he'd have someone else leave the body."

Luke agreed. I told him I'd meet him at home after he went to see if he could retrieve any surveillance footage. I knew he'd spend some time with his parents, too. What started as a boring day, heading out to read at the pub, turned into one of the most stressful and upsetting that I've faced in a long time. I was ready for the day to end.

CHAPTER 37

It was mid-day on Sunday. Luke had his whole team assembled in the police station's conference room. Cooper and Det. Tyler had made it back from Fayetteville. Riley had come to the station about an hour before the meeting and brought Luke the breakfast he had failed to grab before rushing out of the house that morning. Captain Meadows had even come in on a Sunday.

Luke was ready to go over the events of the last forty-eight hours. A lot had happened, and Luke was head down and focused on making sure they were all on the same page going forward.

"Gabe, can you hear us?" Luke asked, leaning towards the phone that had been set in the middle of the table. They were conferencing him in from Fayetteville.

"I'm here," Gabe's voice boomed from the speaker. Luke lowered the volume just slightly, but the reception was strong and clear.

Luke cleared this throat and started. "It seems crazy that the first letter was just a few days ago. Now we have another death. We were played in Fayetteville while he struck here. You all have told me we couldn't have done anything, and I agree, but we need to bring him to justice now."

Luke detailed for the group everything he had found the night before, including Ryan, the neighbor, who had come forward with information. Luke also explained that he had tracked down the other neighbor with the surveillance camera on their house. The homeowner had been more than happy to give Luke anything he needed. The guy, a veteran, had some high-tech surveillance monitoring his property. Like the rest of the community, he was angry that a girl had been killed a block from his house and was eager to do anything to catch the killer.

Luke had the department's tech guys going over that footage. Luke explained that Purvis should have the autopsy done on Cristina Sawyer today.

Luke walked to the big dry erase board he used with every homicide case he worked. He used it to tack up photos, write notes, and make connections. He liked having a visual of the case. The board right now was empty except for one lone photo of a Jeep Compass, which Luke just added.

He explained, "After running the tag number that Ryan provided, it confirmed what I had suspected. The car was a rental. Not only a rental but a stolen rental at that. The rental place is out near the airport. I called around until I finally found the owner of the company at home. He confirmed the Jeep was one of his. He immediately went into the office to look at the records. I met him there. It wasn't rented out. They had no record of anyone taking that vehicle. They are closed on the weekend so someone could have easily stolen it Friday night and returned it without them ever being aware."

"It's that easy to steal a car from their lot? I thought car rental places had better security than that?" Cooper asked, a bit surprised.

"You'd think they would, right?" Luke agreed. "They didn't. While they have cameras up and a fence around the perimeter, the surveillance system has been broken for years. There's a lock that was broken on the fence and the office lock was picked. No alarm system either."

"The killer must have done some advance prep to know all this," Riley suggested.

The group agreed, adding comments at once about the kind of advance work that would need to go into pulling off the robbery, abduction, and murder.

Luke quieted them down. "This had to have been carefully planned like I think all of them were. He knew in advance where my parents lived, probably even watched the neighborhood to see what kind of activity goes on at night, and the accessibility of the woods. I wouldn't be surprised if he had walked it before in the dark to know the terrain."

Captain Meadows asked, "The crime scene techs get anything from the Jeep?"

"They are still going over the evidence they collected," Luke explained. "It's a rental so there could be a million prints. Given how meticulously this looks like it was planned, I assume the killer wore gloves and wiped it clean when he returned it. I don't think he'd be so sloppy as to give us a print. But the tech did find what they thought might be drops of blood in the back and some fibers they need to test."

Up until now, Gabe had been quiet. He asked, "Have you thought beyond this case that this might be his regular pattern – stealing rentals for body transport? It's certainly risky, but given most bodies aren't found right away, nearly all the evidence would be lost and never tied back to his vehicle."

"That's exactly what I was thinking," Luke concurred. "I also wondered if maybe that is why the abductions happened on Friday nights. Not all, but some rental places are closed on the weekend so it gives him access to steal and return before anyone knows a car is missing. We got lucky this time with a witness. Many people are in and out of rentals. They are cleaned between use, no one would be the wiser. Evidence would be easily destroyed or so contaminated it would be useless."

Captain Meadows interjected, "We can't assume he does it the same way all the time. It's definitely something to consider, but let's not hang our hats on it just yet."

"Agreed," Luke said. "I'm definitely open to wherever the evidence leads us." Luke changed subjects to cover additional evidence, but a knock on the conference room door interrupted.

One of the tech guys poked his head in the room, apologizing. He entered the room and walked over to where Luke stood and handed him a tablet. "We've got a visual of him. It's pretty solid."

Everyone got up from the table and crowded around Luke to watch the video. He clicked play. On the screen, the Jeep Compass came to life. The killer was headed up Fairview back toward S. Lookout. The timestamp indicated it was three-eighteen in the morning, which fit with what Ryan had said. The position of the camera was such that it didn't pick up the tag number. Had Ryan not been out there, it would have just been one more Jeep among a sea of many.

The man driving, clearly visible, had both gloved hands on the wheel. A dark cap was pulled low on his head, but his side profile was clear. The man never looked at the camera. He seemed to have no idea it was even there.

Luke clicked the video again, and they watched it twice more. He turned to the tech guy. "This is great. When you get the chance, grab me a few good still photos from the video."

The tech guy headed out with the tablet, promising to return with photos within the hour.

Once seated back around the table, Det. Tyler said, "Well that certainly confirms the neighbor's story, even the time."

Luke detailed, "Ryan is down with the sketch artist now, and they are working up a photo. We can show him this to confirm as well. Then we can work with both and see what we have. Let's get this photo to Gabe too, and see if either of the two men can identify him. I know they said they never saw him, but maybe they did and didn't realize it."

"Can we rule out Aaron Roberts?" Gabe asked.

Cooper responded, "I don't think we can. If the photo was head-on, I think I could tell you one way or the other, but with this side shot, we'd need a comparison. They have similar looks. Aaron was wearing glasses. I just can't be certain."

Det. Tyler agreed. "I can't rule him out either. This guy and Aaron have the same build, but with the hat on and no glasses and the angle of his face in the video, it's just too hard to tell."

"Gabe, can you pull him in for questioning and see if you can get his alibi for the weekend?" Luke asked. "Cooper and Det. Tyler were focused on Lily's case, but we know he wasn't home the first time we went to question him but was back by Saturday mid-day, which certainly doesn't rule him out."

CHAPTER 38

After a quick break, the group went back to sifting through the evidence. Luke tried not to jump from topic to topic, but it all flowed together.

When there was a lull, Captain Meadows spoke up. "You all know me. I like to take the careful approach, but I don't think there is any way this isn't connected to what went down last weekend in Fayetteville."

He shifted in his seat and read some notes he had in front of him. "I want to go over more evidence, but while things are still pending, tell me more about this dark web connection. Looks like those two guys in Fayetteville connected with the killer in some chat room. Do we have any more detail on that?"

"I can answer that," Gabe said, his voice strong and confident from the middle of the table. "Both of the guys that we arrested said they met the man they called The Professor on a dark web chat app called Blather. We have a detective undercover in there as we speak. He set up a fake profile and is hoping The Professor comes back in. The main server for the site as far as we can tell is India. We aren't getting much user info that's for sure."

"Do you really think he'd go back in there?" Cooper asked.

"You never know," Det. Tyler offered with a shrug. "If he's connecting with people who are willing to do his bidding, I don't see any reason for him to stop. It might be something he's comfortable enough to continue given the anonymity. Gabe, do you know how many total users in that chat?"

"Thousands," Gabe responded, sounding frustrated. "We can barely keep up with the chatter that's going back and forth. You have the option of taking a conversation private if needed or you can chat in the open among users. It shows how many are on at any given time, but not all the screen names. You can lurk in there without giving yourself away."

"He might have enough cover to keep going back," Luke concluded. "Worth a watch either way."

Captain Meadows agreed. "Luke, let's pull in one of our own guys to coordinate with Fayetteville. They can both look at running down some leads in this chat room. We know he operated in there so let's put some resources there. I don't know that he'd go back, but it offers such anonymity, he might."

"You don't think he'd be smart enough to know we might put someone undercover in there?" Cooper asked.

No one responded so Cooper turned to Riley. "You've been quiet. What do you think?"

"He seems to be upping his thrill level," Riley suggested. "He's been killing in secret all these years and getting away with it. I think he's taking more risks to increase the excitement and thrill of the kill. He got bored. I don't think it gives him the challenge he desires. He said as much in the letters to Luke. Each kill isn't having the same effect it used to. More risk gives him greater excitement."

Luke asked, "You think he'd operate in the chat room regardless of what we might do?"

"I think that's why you know about the chat room at all," Riley said definitively. "I think yes, he's smart enough to know the cops might put someone in there undercover, but I think that's what he wants. I don't think he would have had those two stooges break into anything in Fayetteville for no reason. You were already focused on the university. He had already turned your attention from Little Rock to Fayetteville. He had no reason to distract you further. I think you have to assume any information you gathered from those two was information he wanted you to have."

"Do you think that's true of information here in Little Rock?" Captain Meadows asked.

"What do you mean?" Luke wondered.

"If he's upping his thrill could he have known the neighbor was going to see him or noticed that the camera was focused on the road? If he really did scout out the neighborhood ahead of time, could he have seen that camera and purposefully went in that direction, allowing us to see him?"

Riley said, "I think we got lucky with the neighbor being outside. The camera maybe he knew about. He never turned to look. It didn't pick up the tag on the vehicle so maybe that was another clue for us. I don't think he'd lead us directly to the car. That's too much risk."

"He had no way of knowing that neighbor would be out there that night," Cooper added. "Luke, didn't he tell you his dog never needs to go out at night?"

"He did."

Cooper added, "Then it's not like the guy lets his dog out each night at three. It just worked in our favor that happened."

"I'd agree with that," Riley added.

"Are we safe to assume then that anything we got because of Ryan he'd have no idea we know?" Det. Tyler asked.

"I think that's probably safe to assume," Luke said.

"Luke, you went to the rental place, but you don't know how he got there, right? No idea if he flew in or drove there?" Captain Meadows asked.

"No idea. I don't think he'd be stupid enough to leave his own car right there and steal another. That's something we still need to run down." Luke made a note on the board about the car rental place and a question next to it about the killer's transportation there.

Captain Meadows said to the group, "Seems we have some promising leads. Some potential evidence in the car. A photo we can match with the database. What's the plan?"

"I want to try to look at this case separate from the rest," Luke explained. He tapped his finger on the table as he thought about how to explain. "My initial goal was to look at Lily's case, but there's little evidence to go on. He thinks he outsmarted us, but really, he handed us a fresh case. I don't know that he even realizes he left an evidence trail. This case needs to be my sole focus."

"I'm glad you're saying that, Luke," Captain Meadows agreed. "I can't have you or Tyler take your eyes off this one. Let Riley and Cooper run down some of the leads from the cold cases in other jurisdictions. If the cases converge, they converge, but right now let's just look at the evidence in front of us on this case only."

CHAPTER 39

The group took a quick break. Gabe hung up, letting everyone know he'd loop back around during the week if he had any updates about Fayetteville and to provide some coordination about the undercover work on the dark web.

While on break, Luke's cellphone rang. It was Purvis. "What do you have for me?" Luke asked. Their long-standing professional relationship and friendship no longer required pleasantries.

Luke listened intently to what Purvis detailed. The details of Cristina's last moments brought up disturbing images of what Lily could have gone through at the hands of the same killer. Luke viscerally felt the terror his sister might have felt. He swallowed hard and thanked Purvis.

After ending the call, Luke walked to the restroom to compose himself. He splashed some water on his face. He stared in the mirror and gave himself a pep talk, trying desperately to refocus his attention on the current victim. Luke reminded himself again that he had no concrete proof that his sister died the same way so there was no point running through it in his head. He pushed back the images of what might have been Lily's last moments on Earth.

Walking back to the conference room along the narrow hall, the department's sketch artist walked towards him. She handed Luke a sketch. "Your witness was better than I thought he'd be. Once he started, he was able to give a decent level of detail."

"This is good," Luke said, looking down at the sketch. He thanked her and walked back into the conference room. He went to the board and hung up the photo. The man's face was slightly tilted but still facing forward. His face was full and his hat was pulled low blocking the shape of his forehead and hairline. His eyes were wide-set, nose straight, lips set in a firm line. There wasn't much distinct about him. He looked like an ordinary guy. But it was better than nothing.

Pointing to it, Luke explained, "This is the sketch that Ryan did with our artist. The killer looks similar to the video. Now that you're seeing more of his face, can we rule out Aaron Roberts?"

Cooper and Tyler looked at the photo and then to one another. They looked back at Luke and said no in unison. Cooper added, "If you put glasses on him and took off the hat, it could be him. It's that close, but I still can't say for sure."

Tyler readily agreed. "Aaron and this guy look like average guys. Nothing really distinct. They aren't someone you'd cross the street to get away from. They aren't the kind of guys I think most women would be afraid of. They look normal."

"That's why he's gotten away with it for so long," Riley added. "He's someone that blends in. Someone creepy or that stands out isn't going to be on and off a university campus, stalking neighborhoods and killing girls without anyone noticing. He's the kind of guy who you'd see and then forget in two minutes."

"We can speculate all we want about this guy later, let's get back to the hard evidence," Captain Meadows demanded, getting them back on task. "Before you left the room, Luke, you had a call from Purvis. What's the update?"

Luke sat back down at the table. "Purvis put the time of death between midnight and two, which means sometime right in the hour or hours before he placed her body in the woods. She died from being pierced through the heart with a thin sharp blade-like an ice pick. There was a small round marking where the handle was slammed into her chest. It was a single stab wound. The killer knew just where to pierce her heart. Purvis said thankfully it looks like her fingers were cut off postmortem."

"What fingers were severed?" Det. Tyler asked.

"Her pinkie, ring finger, and middle of her left hand," Luke explained.

Tentatively Riley spoke, "I know that you don't want to consider any of the previous cases, but this is the same information given to me about the case in Virginia and in New York. Those were the only other cases where a body had been found soon enough to know the method of death."

"What do you mean the same – the fingers?" Det. Tyler asked, confusion on his face.

"All of it," Riley said. She pulled a notebook from her bag and flipped through pages. "Right here, both the detective in Virginia and my hometown gave me the same information. Both medical examiners indicated the victims were pierced through the heart with the same kind of blade. Both had the same bruised marking and missing fingers."

"Are you planning to run down leads on those cases?" Det. Tyler wondered.

"I am, well the New York case specifically. I'm heading to New York this week. The detective on the case is a family friend. I should have fairly good access. The detective from Virginia is meeting us. Both are retired now and want to solve this as much as we do."

"Cooper, are you going with Riley or you staying here to help us?" Captain Meadows asked, giving Cooper a look that Luke caught.

Luke wasn't sure what it meant, but he was sure the two had a conversation about these cases Luke hadn't been privy too. It unnerved him.

Cooper shifted in his seat. "Actually, that's what I wanted to talk to everyone about. I was thinking about going to Atlanta. It was his first kill or so he claimed. I was hoping to dig around. Maybe because it was his first, he made some mistakes. The girl was taken from the library, not outside like the others. Now that we have a photo, I might be able to pass it around and see if anyone might recognize him. Think it's worth the trip?"

"It might be," Luke offered, his voice sounding more frustrated than he meant. He was happy for Cooper's help. "I don't think you'll really know that until you get there, but it might prove useful."

"Do you need me to stick around instead?" Cooper asked, sounding unsure.

"Not really," Luke said. "Actually, the more I think about it, the more it might make sense to dig in and look at what he claims is his first. As you said, there are differences. That's going back, though, so who knows if any leads will still be there."

"I spoke to the victim's sister, and she has someone who might know something. I really don't know what, if anything, I'll uncover, but I'd like to try. If nothing materializes, I can head up to New York to help Riley."

That sounded like a solid plan for everyone. Cooper would be driving to Atlanta the next day. As they broke for the day, Riley told Luke she'd see him at home and she left. Captain Meadows and Det. Tyler left as well.

As Luke walked with Cooper to the parking lot, he asked, "Does Captain Meadows not trust me to handle this case?"

"What?" Cooper asked, clearly confused. "Why would you think that?"

"The look between you when he asked if you were sticking around here to help."

Cooper laughed and put a hand on Luke's shoulder. "You've got nothing to worry about. He dragged me to lunch a few days ago to try to get me back at the police department. He said because of all the attention I've been getting for saving Riley, he'd been getting some pressure to get me back on the force."

Luke wasn't surprised to hear that. Captain Meadows had asked Luke if he thought Cooper would. Luke was adamant that there's no way Cooper would say yes, but was curious nonetheless. "What'd you say?"

"No way no how," Cooper chuckled. "There's not enough money in the world to go back to all those rules, regulations and paperwork."

"I didn't think so."

CHAPTER 40

Late on Sunday evening Luke and I lay in bed together, my head resting on his chest and his fingers drawing circles on my naked back. He kissed me on the top of my head and asked, "Do you think he's going to go into hiding until next year this time when he's ready to kill again?"

Luke's question was a mood killer for sure. We had been lying in the peaceful moments after some pretty terrific sex. My mind had been a million miles away from murder, but I understood why he was asking. Luke felt this was his one chance and was worried he blew it. He was worried the guy was going to go back underground again.

"I could be wrong, but I don't think that's what he'll do. He started this game, and it's a challenge. It's a chase. He's not just going to put it on hold for a year."

"Do you think that means he'll kill again sooner?" Luke asked, stress apparent in his voice.

"I would hope not. If he did kill again, it would be a change in pattern for him that's for sure. That is if his only murders are university-age girls once a year. We have no reason to suspect it's more, but we have no reason to rule it out either."

"I'm worried because as you said earlier, he seems to be enjoying the thrill of getting away with this. He's taking more risks. Sometimes with serial killers, the cooling-off period becomes shorter and shorter as time goes on because they need to up their excitement to be satisfied with the kill in the same way." Luke shifted and rolled to his side to face me. We were eye to eye now and his hand lightly rubbed my arm.

Luke was right. That's what some serial killers did. Not all but some shortened the time between killings as time went on. Some just got more proficient in how they went out picking a victim, some had more time on their hands at certain points in their lives, and others needed more and more excitement.

"We should figure out why he's killing in the fall. He references harvest time so I'm wondering if that has particular meaning to him. Does it just fit into his schedule then or has he selected the time because of its meaning?"

"Most of the language he uses would suggest that's his preference," Luke speculated. "It's also when I'd think freshmen are at their most vulnerable in the first few months away from home for the first time."

"That's true," I agreed. I looked over Luke's face. He had started to get little lines around his eyes. I wasn't sure if it was stress or just natural aging. I searched his face as he searched mine. We always had kind of an unspoken language between us.

"Are you going to be okay in New York? It's been a while since you handled a case alone."

I kissed him sweetly on the lips. "My mom will be there. My sister, too. It's probably time I went home for a visit. I'm going to be staying at the house. I have support there if I need it."

"Yeah, but your mom and sister aren't investigating the case with you. It's not the same," Luke protested.

"I won't be alone," I countered. "Jack Malone, the Troy detective, will be there helping me. My mom has known him forever. He will watch out for me."

"Tell me more about the case. I was so distracted up in Fayetteville, I never really got a chance to hear about this one. I think it's both strange and a very lucky break it's in your hometown."

I agreed with Luke. It had felt strange since the moment I saw the details. Too much coincidence, but it happened so long before I even visited Little Rock there was no way there was a connection or anything to do with me personally.

As we lay there cuddling, I detailed some of the case to him. Luke had only been to my hometown once when he and Cooper had gone up the year before to clean out my house and move me permanently to Little Rock. He didn't have much frame of reference. I got to the part of the story where the victim's body had been found in the cemetery and Luke shivered.

"What?" I asked.

"That's creepy. Cemeteries don't usually freak me out, but that place sounds awful."

"Well, the lore is that it's one of the gateways to hell," I countered.

Luke grimaced. "That doesn't help. I think these are the details we need to understand about this guy. How would he ever know about that cemetery, or the terrain within it, unless he'd been there before? The bodies aren't just left near rivers or random woods. They are in very specific places that the killer must have scouted out beforehand. I'm wondering if that has any meaning, too."

"Do you think he purposefully left certain bodies to be found?"

"Cristina Sawyer here definitely," Luke explained. "That was all shock value. He wanted me to know how easily he could get to my parents. The others I can't be sure. Leaving my sister in the woods near the school always felt like he was trying to taunt us, like look how close she is and yet still out of sight."

"Maybe that's a metaphor about him. Maybe he's someone that blends in so well that nobody would ever know what lurks just out of sight."

"I think to get away with it for so long, he'd have to be, which is why he's going to be so hard to catch." Luke looked at me with concern. "Just be careful. Don't trust anyone too easily."

"I'm more worried about you than I am about me. I'll be fine." Then I cautioned him, "Don't try to go this alone. Depend on your team here. Let them help you."

"I think I'm just going to miss you. What am I going to do without you butting into my case?" Luke asked with a straight face. Then the corners of his mouth turned up in a smile.

"You'll survive without me, but I'm only a call away," I reminded him. "Listen though, do you really think you're going to be able to fully separate this case from the others in the past? I know you said you wanted to, but what does that mean exactly? There's already evidence in common."

Luke sat up and rubbed his forehead. "I want to try. This would be easier if it wasn't connected to Lily. With each bit of new evidence, I keep imagining what Lily went through. While there are commonalities among the cases, I want to try to see this case through a clean lens, just the facts for this case only."

I understood, but it seemed impossible to do. I sat up and rubbed Luke's back.

He turned his head to look at me and added, "That doesn't mean that I'm going to just ignore any evidence you and Cooper might find. If things connect, they connect, and we can use it to bolster our search for him. I just can't make assumptions based on what he did in the past. I need to focus on the now."

"I get it. Hopefully, we can end this quickly and get back to normal for us. We had such a good time at the lake."

Luke gently pulled me back on the bed with him. He snuggled into me. "We really did. When you get back from New York, whether this case is still going on or not, we need to get back to spending more time together. We both get too wrapped up in work."

"Agreed." As I watched his face, I felt it in my stomach. That knowing, the feeling that this is who I want to spend the rest of my life with. I always put up too much resistance, too many walls. I kissed him. When we pulled apart, I said simply, "I love you."

CHAPTER 41

When Luke arrived at his desk the next morning, another letter waited for him. It had come in Saturday's mail. The unit secretary saw it first thing on Monday morning. It was addressed to Luke like the others. It was handwritten and postmarked from the Hillcrest post office near Luke's parents' house.

The killer had been in the neighborhood at least a day before the murder. He had to have mailed it before the murder even took place. Luke picked up the letter again. It was short but said all it needed to say.

Ready. Set. Go. You've got your clues. Now find me.

Luke bit his lip reading it over and over again. The killer was taunting him. Riley had been right. It was just a game to him. He didn't go back underground. Luke had no idea where the guy was. He had no idea if he was going to kill again. For all Luke knew, he was stalking another university campus right at that moment.

"I heard we got another letter," Det. Tyler said, sitting down on the corner of Luke's desk.

Luke looked up, thankful for the distraction from the disturbing thoughts that ran through a loop in his mind. Luke handed him the letter.

Det. Tyler read the letter over. When he was done, he asked, "How do we change the status quo and get in front of this? It's been a long time since a perp pissed me off this much."

"We know he stole the Jeep on Friday, but if he was in Hillcrest before that, then he was driving something else. Do you think he went into any of the stores or shops? I don't want to fully release his photo to the public but we have enough of a sketch and side profile we can go to some of the stores and see if he was there by any chance."

"I can't think of a better idea until we get some more concrete evidence to run with."

The two left the police station and drove out of downtown Little Rock up into the Hillcrest neighborhood. Luke parked at the curb and the two started their search. They walked in and out of shops that lined the street, talking to shop owners, employees, and even customers. The man didn't look familiar to anyone. A stop by the post office didn't yield anything either. The photo of the killer didn't look familiar to anyone, but there were a lot of people in and out, and the killer simply could have dropped the letter in the mailbox outside.

Luke felt defeated. He tried to be realistic, but he had hoped for a break. He walked back towards his car with Det. Tyler. A woman yelled Luke's name. He turned just in time to catch the paws of an excited golden retriever who jumped up on him. Luke was knocked back by the force, but he smiled and rubbed the dog's ears in the exact spot Luke knew she liked.

"Bailey, what are you doing?" Luke cooed at her.

In response, the dog licked at his hand and nuzzled her head into him. Luke saw Bailey's poor frazzled owner running towards him. Amy and Bailey had been Luke's neighbors before he had moved in with Riley. Luke would give Bailey treats through the fence, and throw a ball occasionally for her. There were a few times when Amy was out of town that Luke had even watched Bailey at his place.

Amy finally caught up with them. "Luke, I'm so sorry. We turned the corner and Bailey must have caught sight of you. She took off. Pulled the leash right out of my hands."

Luke petted Bailey, who had her paws firmly planted on his thighs. "No worries at all. I feel bad for not stopping in more to check on you both since I moved. I miss the old neighborhood."

Luke introduced Det. Tyler and Amy.

Getting Bailey back under her control, Amy looked up the street at the turn from Kavanaugh to Beechwood. She brushed the hair out of her eyes. "I heard what happened near your parents. I can't believe a guy would leave a body there. Are you investigating?"

"Yeah, we think the guy was here in the days before he killed the girl."

"That's terrible. Have you found anything?"

"Not yet, but while you're here why don't you take a look. You know the neighborhood well. Maybe you saw him."

Tyler handed Amy the photos. "This is a sketch from a witness, and this is a side profile of him from a surveillance camera."

Amy handed the leash to Luke and took each of the photos from Tyler. She studied each carefully. She said hesitantly, "I can't be one-hundred percent sure, but this might be the guy that Bailey growled at last week."

"I've never heard Bailey growl," Luke said surprised.

"You're right, she doesn't ever. She's friendly to everyone – kids, other dogs, cats. Nothing bugs her. I've been working from home a bit. Last Thursday I took a mid-afternoon walk. It was nice out. I walked down here to get coffee at Mylo's and left Bailey outside by one of the chairs on the sidewalk. You know her, you tell her to stay, she stays. I was inside when all of a sudden, I heard her growling, then barking. I immediately ran out to see what the commotion was. Actually, a few of us ran out. Everyone knows Bailey."

"What did you see?" Luke asked, completely intrigued by the story. He lived next door to Amy since Bailey was a puppy, and he never once heard the dog act afraid or vicious around anyone.

"There was a guy walking down the sidewalk, probably twenty feet past us by the time I got outside. I yelled for Bailey to stop, but she was up on all fours and barking at him even as he walked away. I called out to the guy thinking he must have done something to her. He turned around and angrily shouted that I needed to have the dog locked up. It was an ugly exchange."

Amy held out the sketch. "This looks like the guy. He had the same kind of hat pulled low and a similar face. I've also never seen him in the neighborhood before, and you know how small it is. If you don't know them personally, you at least have seen them. No one at Mylo's knew him."

"What else can you tell me about him?" Luke asked. He thought there was really a chance it could be him.

"He was taller than you, Luke. Not by much but a little. He had a heavier build, not fat, just maybe like he still worked out a bit. What I remember the most was the scowl on his face. He was a handsome guy in some regard but that face – he looked mean."

"What happened after that?"

"Nothing," Amy explained. "He kept walking down the road. I bent down to make sure Bailey was okay. She seemed fine, and eventually stopped barking when he got in his car and left."

"Did you see what he was driving?"

Amy shook her head. "I didn't get a good look. I was focused on Bailey."

"What do you think, Luke?" Det. Tyler asked. He took the photos back from Amy's outstretched hand.

Luke crouched down and petted Bailey. He looked up at Tyler and Amy. "I think I trust a dog's instinct."

CHAPTER 42

I stood on the sidewalk looking up at my mother's house. It was a large center hall Colonial that had four bedrooms, a massive eat-in kitchen, a living room, and a formal dining room that no one ever used except for homework when we were kids and the holidays. I don't know why I just stood there with my bags in hand on the sidewalk. I looked back at my rental parked in the driveway. No one was home. My mother had texted me that she had run to the market to pick up some groceries.

My sister, Liv, was living with my ex-husband, Jeff. The two had started a relationship last year.

It was a weird relationship, but if it worked for them who was I to stop them. Jeff was out of town though so I probably wouldn't see him on this trip, which was fine by me. My sister said she was going to crash at my mom's house while I was there. Liv had been my assistant when I ran my investigative firm in New York prior to moving back to Little Rock. She was supposed to answer the phone, help write reports, and handle billing. She did very little of anything, but I still paid her. Now, she didn't work. She offered once again to help me with my case. I wasn't sure what that would amount to, but if she insisted, I'd figure it out.

I picked up my bags and made my way up the front porch steps. These were the same wide steps I sat on as a kid reading a book and waiting for my friends. It was a relaxed neighborhood. The kind where neighbors not only knew each other but looked out for each other, too.

Once inside, I carried my bags to the second floor to my old bedroom. My mother had kept it fairly similar since the last time I lived at home full-time, which was college. Walking past my sister's room, it seemed my mother had kept her bedroom the same as well.

I put my suitcases on the floor and dove headfirst into the comfortable queen size bed. There was a certain comfort to being back in my mother's house. I had an easy childhood for the most part. My parents divorced when I was very young. My father came back long enough to get my mother pregnant with my sister, and he left again. He went back to Ireland, and we were raised by my mother and her extended family of siblings. My cousins were like brothers and sisters. I had close friends both in the neighborhood and school. There were a lot of happy memories.

That's why the stark contrast of a homicide right down the street was so jarring. It didn't fit. Not that I thought we were immune from crime, but something like a homicide of a university-aged girl mere blocks from the house seemed incomprehensible to me.

A flood of memories from childhood, sleepovers, fights with my sister, and spending days staring at this ceiling pining over some boy or another filled my head. I snuggled more into my pillow and was just starting to drift off to sleep when I heard my mother's car in the driveway.

Groaning, I pulled myself out of bed to help bring in the groceries. I got to the middle of the stairs and was met with my very excited and energetic yellow lab, Dusty. He had been staying with my mom since my move to Little Rock. The two of them had been quite attached. Dusty was good company for her. She took him everywhere.

He practically knocked me over in his excitement. It had been more than a year since I'd seen him – if Skype didn't count. When I Skype with my mother, I Skype with the dog, too. He likes it. He's even happier to see me in person. I rubbed his head and ears as I tried to navigate past him down the stairs. I wound my way around the banister into the hall that runs straight back to the kitchen. My mother carried two bags and kicked a third with her foot.

She looked up at me. "It's just toilet paper. I dropped it so I kicked it along."

I shook my head and headed out the back door to find her car alongside mine in the driveway. I picked up the rest of the bags, looping their handles over my arm to get them all at once. I closed the trunk and made my way back in, dropping the bags on the counter.

"I thought I'd make some lasagna for dinner," my mother said. Then looking over her shoulder at me, giving me that look, she added, "You'll be home, right?"

And with that, I'm back to being a kid living at home. "Of course, I'll be here."

I helped my mother unpack, putting veggies and fruit in the fridge and other items in the cabinet.

"I thought you'd want to eat healthy while you're here," she commented, taking a look at the width of my hips.

"Keep looking. I got these from your side of the family so you're to blame."

"But your sister..." she started.

"Don't even." I finished.

She laughed. It's a familiar routine we have had for years. My mother has a great figure. She's short, medium build, and has short stylish blonde hair. My sister Liv is built just like her. I am built like my father and his side of the family – tall, curvy, and auburn hair. My face instantly gets red if I smile, laugh and take a few steps. It's that typical Irish complexion.

We bumped around the kitchen, old routines falling back into place. I reached high to put some cake mix boxes on the shelf when she grabbed my arm. "I forgot to tell you I invited Jack to dinner. I hope that's okay."

"Jack Malone, the detective?"

"Is there another Jack we know?"

I shrug. "I could have just met with him tomorrow, but that's fine."

"Well," my mother started, hesitation apparent in her voice, "I didn't exactly invite Jack to dinner for you. I invited him for me."

I raised my eyebrows in a knowing look. "He asked you out finally?"

"What do you mean finally?" She pulled tomatoes out of the bag and washed them.

I sat in one of the kitchen chairs. "When I talked to him about the case, he indicated to me he was interested. He sounded like he'd been interested for some time."

She looked at me, the corners of her mouth turning up in a smile. It was nice to see my mother happy. I didn't think I'd ever seen her date or even be interested in anyone. "I think it's great, really. You deserve someone. Jack seems like a great guy. I just hope he's as good a detective and not distracted being smitten by you."

For that, she threw a dinner roll at me. I caught it and took a bite.

My mother frowned. "Carbs."

I rolled my eyes and headed back upstairs to unpack.

CHAPTER 43

"I'm thinking about getting a breast reduction." Liv carried plates to the table. "Jeff said he'd pay for it. My back is killing me."

Sometimes I didn't quite know how to respond to my sister. I was just glad that Jack hadn't arrived yet. After taking a shower to get ready for dinner earlier, I had called and checked on Luke. He told me about running into his neighbor and her dog. I agreed with him that it was a good lead. Dusty wasn't one to bark, but he'd let me know when danger was present. Luke told me he had checked on Cooper, too, who was on his way to Atlanta. Luke seemed to think it was a fool's errand, but maybe Cooper would find something.

"What do you think?" Liv asked, bringing me back to the present.

"About surgery?"

She stood with her hand on her barely existent hips. "Yes."

"If it makes you happy, do it. Just don't talk about it with Jack here. Try to pretend we are normal people who don't talk about boobs at the dinner table."

My mother laughed. "How long are we going to have to pretend?"

"Until you marry him," I deadpanned. The knock at the front door was perfect timing. My mother froze in place like she was a sixteen-year-old girl and it was her first date. I went to answer it. I pulled open the front door and came face to face with Jack, who I hadn't seen in years. He had a full head of salt and pepper hair, the same piercing green eyes I remembered and a shy smile. He didn't look anywhere close to his sixty-three years.

He thrust a bouquet of fall flowers at me. He shrugged. "I wasn't sure what to bring."

I smelled them and smiled. "My mom will love these."

He followed me to the kitchen, waved to my sister and gave my mom an awkward hug. After bringing a few more items to the table, the four of us sat down to dinner.

My mother didn't waste any time showing her disappointment in my career choice.

Turning to Jack, she asked, "If you had a daughter, would you want her in Riley's line of work?"

Jack was mid-bite and looked over at me. He chewed and swallowed hard. "Thankfully, I only have sons." Diplomatically he added, "If I had a daughter as smart as Riley, I think I'd be okay if she was safe."

"Safe," my mother said, pointing her fork at me. "Riley hasn't always been safe. Did you tell Jack you were shot and strangled last year?"

Jack dropped his fork and it clanged on the plate. I hadn't told him. It wasn't something I ran around telling people. I also worried that if I told him he would tell me not to get involved in this case and refuse to help me out. My mother sat with a smug look on her face. We both knew exactly what she was doing. I couldn't blame her. I nearly died, but I wasn't going to give up work that I loved.

"Are you okay?" he asked, concern written all over his face.

"I'm fine," I assured. "It was just a case we were working that got out of hand. I've had a year to heal. I'm pretty much good as new."

Turning to my mother I pleaded with my eyes and said, "Mom, can we just eat dinner, please?"

She went back to eating. My sister started chatting endlessly about friends and people in the neighborhood. Jack and my mother talked about gossip from church. I was grateful the spotlight was no longer on me.

After dinner, my sister and I cleaned up while Jack and my mother sat in the living room talking and eating dessert.

"Why do you have to worry her?" Liv asked as she dried a plate.

I washed a fork and knife before rinsing and dropping them in the drainboard. "I don't mean to worry anyone. I love what I do. I am stepping back some. I'm not even working the active case this time. Luke has that. I'm looking into this case that happened nineteen years ago."

Liv finished drying the rest of the dishes. "I remember the case, you know. It terrified me for years." She dropped the towel, cut herself a slice of chocolate cheesecake and sat down at the table.

Because I had been a freshman and away from home, the case didn't hit that close to me. I was physically removed from it. I had completely forgotten my sister would have been in high school. She was two years younger than me so she would have been a junior.

"What do you remember?" I asked, releasing the plug to let the soapy water go down the drain. I picked up the dishtowel my sister had just set down and dried my hands. I also cut a piece of cheesecake and joined my sister.

"I was at a party the night she went missing. We had been in the woods a few blocks from here. Someone had a keg. I wasn't drinking, but just hanging out. Mom was working a nightshift at the hospital. I remember thinking I had to get home before eleven when she would call to check on me. I remember walking back and passing right by the frat. They had a huge party that night. Some guy hit on me as I walked by, called out for me to come to the party, but I keep walking. Mom would have killed me if she knew I had snuck out. She still doesn't know. I never told her. She got even more protective after that night."

"Did you see anything?" I wasn't surprised my sister had snuck out. She did that a lot when I was at college. Liv was a wild child. It wasn't always easy on my mom because she had to work, sometimes in the evenings. She was a nurse and didn't have that much control over her schedule.

Liv gave a weak smile. "I always wondered if I had seen her that night, I don't think I did. There were a lot of people in front of that house. When they found her body, it was even worse."

"What do you mean?"

"Everyone in the whole neighborhood was terrified. People started wondering if there was a killer among us. Some people started accusing each other. Suspicion was cast around. It just kind of tore things apart. My friends and I were scared to go anywhere."

I picked up Liv's dessert plate with my own and put them in the sink. I'd wash them later. Sitting back down I asked, "I don't remember any of this. Even when I was back home here, my mind was still focused on college. Were there rumors going around at the time about what could have happened?"

"Yeah," Liv said seriously. "I think most people assumed it was that guy at the frat or one of her professors. There was one that was known to be a flirt or at least that was the rumor. My friend's sister went to college with the victim. There were some rumors that a professor had dated some of the girls or wanted to date them. I can't remember now."

I didn't remember any of that. I had heard from my mother about the guy at the frat but nothing about a professor, not that it was uncommon at university campuses. Maybe my sister could help with this case after all.

"Do you remember the professor's name?"

"No, but my friend might. I can ask her," Liv offered. She pinched the bridge of her nose. She looked back at me. Her voice quiet, she said, "I went there once."

"Where?"

"To the cemetery where they found her body," Liv explained. "Someone dared a group of my girlfriends. It was a creepy place anyway and that just made it worse. Nobody knew where she had been killed. We went to the angel statue where they said her body had been found. It was so sad thinking about her being there all alone."

Liv started to cry. I had no idea this case had affected her this much, but I guess I should have known with it being this close to home.

CHAPTER 44

Cooper had settled fairly quickly into his hotel in downtown Atlanta. He had a meeting tomorrow evening with Adele Baker, the victim's sister, but tonight the plan was simply to get the lay of the land. Shortly after arriving, Cooper had sat down at the desk and went over his case notes. He didn't have much, and that was part of the challenge.

Cooper had taken the toughest case. He knew that. He hoped Luke was getting a good deal of evidence in Little Rock, and Riley certainly had connections to help her in her hometown. Cooper, though, wanted to start at the beginning or at least what the killer had said was his beginning.

This case was different for a few reasons. First and foremost, the victim, Jordan, was not a party girl, not that Lily or the other victims were per se, but Jordan was not known to drink, go to parties or do anything other than focus on school. She had few friends, and outside of being in the classroom and library, she didn't go very far.

For Cooper, that meant the killer had to have been within a small circle of people that ran in the same sphere. It wasn't like Jordan was snatched on the street or from a public place. She vanished from inside the university library or at least that's how it looked from the evidence.

Cooper's hotel was only a few blocks from the university campus. He had planned to walk it tonight while it was dark. Not that the campus would look how it did in 1993, but it certainly would give Cooper more of an idea than he had just by looking on the website.

He headed down to the hotel restaurant to grab a quick bite for dinner. While he was eating, Cooper received several text messages from Holly. He responded that he was out of town for work and not sure when he'd be back. She sent several messages back detailing her annoyance with him. It was enough that Cooper silenced his phone and put it in his pocket.

He had made a mistake with Holly; one he was surely regretting. It reminded Cooper that there probably wasn't any woman who would be able to deal with the unpredictability of his work.

After paying his tab for dinner, Cooper headed out to the street. He walked the quick few blocks to the university campus and stood looking at the entrance from the sidewalk. It was one of many entrances. The campus was set in the middle of the city but sectioned off enough that one could tell the concrete sidewalks from the red brick walkways that made up the campus. It was easily accessible though. There was no security blocking the entrance and none that Cooper saw around.

Cooper stepped onto the campus grounds and walked around. He tried one building but the door was locked. Black wrought iron lampposts peppered the walkway. There were call boxes for emergencies every several hundred feet. He passed some students, but for the most part, it was quiet. At nearly ten in the evening, it was well past the close of classes for the day.

Cooper made his way across the campus until he came upon a large open grassy area and the library far off in the distance. Cooper remembered what the building looked like from photos online. The building looked more modern than the rest with its large windows and concrete design. It was one of the only buildings lit up on campus. Cooper had no idea where the dorms were in relation, but the library was his primary focus.

He followed the walkway until he reached the steps. Cooper noted the sign at the entrance that indicated the library closed at eleven. He had about forty minutes to look around. The librarian at the desk closest to the door smiled at Cooper as he walked in. He walked past her and farther into the library, but she called out to him.

"Excuse me," she said. "I need to see your university identification?"

Cooper turned to face her. "I'm sorry, I'm not a student here."

She frowned. "Then I'm sorry, you can't access the library. It's only for students, faculty, and staff of the university."

Cooper approached her desk, offering her his private investigator's license. "I'm an investigator from Arkansas. I'm looking into a missing person's case from a long time ago. The victim went missing from the library. I just want to have a look around."

She looked uncertain. "I'm not sure I can authorize that."

Cooper smiled at her. "I swear I won't be long. I just want to take a quick look around. There's hardly anyone in here."

The librarian, who did not look like a student, but not much older than Cooper looked across the room. She said sternly, "I'll give you a few minutes, but I won't stay open late for you. We close promptly at eleven."

Cooper thanked her and walked quickly among the long tables that lined the first floor. There were stacks of books on each side and an elevator in the back. Cooper did a quick walkthrough just taking in the setting. It looked like a typical university library. Upstairs held more tables and stacks, and on the third floor, he found some quiet meeting spaces and a more comfortable reading area that had couches and chairs. Two students were checking their phones, and another was packing up her books to leave.

Cooper saw nothing out of the ordinary. He wasn't sure which floor Jordan had disappeared from but he suspected it was the first from one report he had read. He couldn't remember the details right now.

Instead of taking the elevator, Cooper found the stairs. He bounded down the steps. When he got to the first floor, he paused. The steps continued so he followed. He checked his phone for the time. He still had about twenty minutes. The stairs led to a basement, which was a maze of hallways and doors. Cooper tried a few but found them all locked. There was no one down there and not much access to anything. He did see one door that went out of the back of the building, but he assumed if he opened it an alarm would sound. Cooper made his way back to the first floor.

He approached the librarian who looked anxious to leave for the night. "Could you tell me where that basement door goes?"

She looked taken aback by the question. "You weren't authorized to go into the basement," she scolded. "But if you must know, it goes out to a service area where delivery trucks come in for mail and other shipments."

Cooper thanked her and opened the door to step outside. She called him back. "I know what case you're working on. It's Jordan Baker. I'm Hope. Adele probably told you about me."

"Adele said you went to school with Jordan. She said you might be willing to talk to me."

"I did," the woman responded. She ducked her head low and got even quieter. "I wasn't sure about talking to you, but..." She looked around again like someone might be watching. She leaned over the counter. "Adele doesn't even know this, but I never believed the university's story. If you come back tomorrow night, I'll give you a tour and tell you what I know."

CHAPTER 45

I slept late the next morning, later than I generally do back in Little Rock. I missed my mother and sister leaving. I didn't hear a peep. I even missed a couple of texts from Luke, updating me on his progress, which wasn't much from yesterday. With neither my mother or sister home, I lounged around until it was nearly time to meet Jack and Frank at noon.

Frank had arrived the night before. Late in the evening, he had texted to let me know he had picked up a rental car and was staying at a nearby hotel. He had refused my mother's offer to stay at the house and even Jack's offer to stay with him. Frank had said he wanted to create his war room at the hotel and enjoyed the quiet.

I drove the few miles from my mother's house out Pinewoods Avenue, which headed away from the suburbs and into a rural part of the county. The winding two-lane road was narrow and commanded my full attention.

Jack and Frank were already pulled over onto the shoulder of the road in the small dirt patch that sat in front of the cemetery's wrought-iron gates. I crossed the lane and pulled in next to them.

Jack had told me before he left last night that he had called in a favor and received permission for us to be on the cemetery grounds so we were sure not to get into trouble. Not that the local cops would do much more than chase us off, but legal access was always preferable.

I looked in the car mirror and tried unsuccessfully to tame my hair. This was my first face to face with Frank. I was trying to impress. I needed him to take me as a serious investigator not just someone with a true-crime hobby.

Frank was a bigger guy, bigger than I had imagined. He was tall and broad-shouldered. His deep voice matched the man in front of me. Frank looked a bit like Luke, if Luke gained about fifty pounds of muscle. I was pretty sure Frank, if he wanted to, could bench press me. All the worry I had about impressing him was out the window, because as soon as I got close enough, Frank wrapped me in a huge bear hug.

"I'm glad you got me off the couch and back working. This case has been haunting me every day of retirement." Frank squeezed me an extra second and then let me go. "My wife thanks you, too. She was tired of my brooding."

I stepped back, a bit overwhelmed by his affection. Definitely not the norm for homicide detectives. With Frank's thick southern drawl, he came across as completely genuine. He had an infectious smile.

Jack explained that he met with Frank early that morning and compared notes on their cases. They were both shocked by the similarities. I would have been offended for not being invited, but I figured they needed to have a talk cop to cop.

"You ever been in here?" Jack asked. He looked at the gate and back at me.

"A couple of times in high school like every other kid around here," I admitted cautiously. Jack had been a cop when I was in high school. I'm pretty sure he already knew I had been in here. I recalled more than once Jack was among the cops who showed up to shoo us off property and break up a kegger in the woods.

"Does your mother know?" The corners of his mouth curled into a smile.

I leveled him with a look. "You can date my mother, but you can't rat me out. Got it?"

Frank laughed and slapped Jack on the back. "You're dating her mother! You old dog."

Jack laughed and admitted, "It only took me nearly fifty years to ask her on a date. I've wanted to since we were fifteen."

"Small towns," Frank said. Then he got serious. He asked with apprehension in his voice, "Now what's the deal with this cemetery? My case in Williamsburg, the victim was found in a cemetery but not one that looked like this."

Jack briefly explained the history of the "haunted" cemetery and the lore that went along with it. Frank, for all his muscle and brawn, looked a bit nervous. His eyes darted over the overgrown landscape.

"Are you afraid?" I asked.

Frank ran a hand down his face. "Not afraid. I just don't mess around with the supernatural. Give me a perp I can get my hands on any day of the week. This haunted crap is for someone else."

"It's not really haunted," I countered. "It's just a local legend."

"Well, that legend comes from someplace." Frank shuddered.

It amused me to see such a big man spooked, but in all fairness, I wasn't looking forward to it either. Not that I believed all the lore myself, but it was creepy nonetheless.

The front entrance was locked so the three of us piled in Jack's truck. We headed down the road and turned into the long driveway that led into the Troy Country Club. Once a good distance up club's main road, we pulled over to the side.

We walked into the cemetery from the wooded side. Jack and I took the lead with Frank right behind us. We stepped carefully as we walked. Almost immediately we came upon broken headstones. Some were broken and lying on the ground, others were left with jagged stone poking out above the high grass.

Farther in, we hit the point where wide sections of stone and brick dotted the ground. It was the spot of the original road. Still, there was no clear walking path. There were areas of tall grass and then other areas that had been more matted down over the years from people walking. Some areas had nothing but dirt.

The leaves had already turned their vibrant fall colors and had fallen to the ground. Sticks and dead leaves littered the ground. Most of the monument statues were missing their heads and other limbs. The cemetery had long ago been vandalized, but no one was ever really sure where the heads and missing limbs had gone or if they had ever been there in the first place. The lore of the place had more fully cemented in people's memories than the historical record so sorting fact from fiction was a challenge.

I knew we were coming close to where Amanda's body had been found. While it had been years since I had been in the cemetery, it left a lasting impression. Up ahead the tall grass cleared to a spot that was just dirt. There were several large monuments, but the tallest and most prominent, or honestly, the most terrifying, was the headless, armless angel. She sat atop her stone three-tiered base. A shiver ran down my spine when I took sight of her.

The image was terrifying, but I had to remind myself this was someone's final resting place. The grave marker was for the Hollister family. Around the large headless angel were smaller markers for members of the family. I said a quick silent prayer as I encroached on the family.

Frank caught up to us. He looked at me and back at the angel. "Why does it look like she's bleeding from the neck?"

That had been another bit of cemetery lore – that statues were bleeding. It certainly looked that way, but there was a more plausible explanation.

Jack, who didn't seem to be afraid of anything, responded, "It's not blood, I assure you. It's a red moss that when wet can look like blood. Trust me, there's nothing haunted here."

As if the dead wanted to test Jack's resolve, a large branch or something fell at that very moment. The loud crash against the eerie quiet made us all jump.

CHAPTER 46

I spun around, looking for anything that could have made the noise, but there was nothing. Just wooded silence again. The trees on all sides made it impossible to see too far into the dense woods. The noise had sounded like a tree splitting and a large limb crashing to the ground, but there was nothing within sight.

"What was that?" Frank asked.

"I don't know," Jack admitted, his voice not quite as confident as before. "Let's just take a look at the spot and get out of here. While I don't believe in ghosts, let's not test it."

"Where did you find Amanda?" I asked, hoping to just get on with this as Jack said.

Jack pointed to the base of the front of the angel. "Amanda was propped up right here. Her head was slumped forward. She had one hand in her lap and the other tossed off to the side. She wasn't dirty. It didn't look like she had struggled. This didn't look like the place she had been killed."

"What made you think that?" I looked around at the base of the monument.

Jack paused and seemed to bring himself back to the memory of seeing her body. He explained, "There was no blood here. With a chest wound like Amanda had, there would have been blood. The area also wasn't disturbed like there had been a struggle. She had simply looked placed, propped."

"That's the same in my case," Frank interjected. "The victim had been propped up against a gravestone. Nothing quite as large or terrifying as this one, but still the same. She looked staged like the killer wanted us to think she had simply passed out next to the gravestone. You really couldn't tell until you were right up next to her that she was dead. It was like he wanted to terrorize whoever found her."

"Frank, in your case, do you think the killer wanted the victim found?" I asked.

"Found without question," Frank said definitively. "He left her in a historic churchyard cemetery. Tourists are in and out of the place every day. He had to have known the victim would be found and quickly."

Jack shook his head. "I can't say the same here. Look at this place. We are lucky someone found her at all. My biggest question was always how he knew about this place if he wasn't from around here."

"It's not exactly a secret, Jack," I countered gently. "It's on the internet. Ghost hunting sites reference the spot. There are even YouTube videos of people wandering around here. The headless angel always makes an appearance. But I will say, he had to have walked back here before he left the body. I can't see someone finding this on the first try."

"Good point," Jack said.

"That's what he did in Little Rock," I added. "He left the body in a wooded area across from Luke's parents' house. The cops there don't think it was his first time in the area either. It seems he scouts the location ahead of time."

"He'd have to. There's no way this was random," Frank agreed. "Just imagine how dark this place is at night. Where would he have parked?"

"Definitely not at the front gates. The houses across the way are quick to call the cops. There are some back entrances and then there is the way we came in," Jack explained.

"Is through the country club property the easiest way in, Jack?" I struggled to remember how we had come in when I was a kid. There was a back way but I couldn't quite place where it connected or how accessible it might be.

"We decided at the time that the killer probably came in through the country club, probably not far from where we parked. Given he was carrying a body, that would be the easiest and most efficient way. There are drop-offs in the back and hills that would make it not only inaccessible for him but dangerous. I don't think he'd risk falling or getting hurt while carrying a body."

"Is the country club closed at night?" Frank asked.

"Yes," Jack said. "The killer could have easily pulled up the same road we did, navigate over to the side, park more off the shoulder than even we did, cut his lights and head into the woods. It's so dark up here that he could go unnoticed, especially if it was in the middle of the night."

I looked around the cemetery. I wondered if Amanda had been killed someplace nearby. It was certainly desolate enough and back far enough into the cemetery no one would have heard her scream if she did. Killing her at the cemetery seemed more likely than any other place. The rest of Troy is fairly residential. Given the proximity of where she was last seen to the cemetery, I couldn't imagine another place unless the killer lived in Troy, and he killed her at home.

I moved around to the other side of the monument. There was nothing out of the ordinary. "Jack," I called. "Did you ever find where Amanda had been killed?"

"No, we never did," Jack lamented. "We had a spot we thought and there was some evidence, but nothing to say with one hundred percent certainty."

"Did you give any thought that she might have been killed someplace here, just in a different location?"

"We had. In fact, we turned over the whole cemetery as best we could. We did find some blood farther into the woods that did test positive for Amanda, but there wasn't enough that would have indicated a kill spot. It had rained between when we think she was killed and when she was found. It could have washed the evidence away."

"Can you show me?"

Jack led us back farther into the cemetery. The farther back we went, the darker it became. Jack seemed to take note of certain trees as markers because he'd touch one, pause and realign direction. Finally, we reached the spot. There were several small graves and an area that was mostly dirt. The graves were so old, I couldn't read the names or information.

"We think he might have killed her here," Jack indicated. "There was blood all around this area. It wasn't just in one spot."

Frank asked, "Did you have a theory of how he got her here?"

"We think he picked her up near the party. Either he snatched her off the street or convinced her to get into his car. There were a few of us who thought the killer might be someone Amanda knew so she went willingly since we never heard reports of a struggle anywhere along her path."

Jack paused. His face looked pained.

The case had clearly taken its toll on him. My sister had strongly suggested that it had affected the entire community in a way that I hadn't remembered. I hated making Jack relive these moments.

Jack finally continued. "We think he might have convinced her to drive out here with him. Maybe he teased her about going to a 'haunted' cemetery or maybe it was just a good lovers' lane kind of spot along the country club road. Either way, we think he convinced her to take a walk into the cemetery and killed her or he killed her near the car and carried her body in, but that wouldn't account for the blood we found unless he was walking around looking for a place to put her."

I took in what Jack said, thinking over the step by step of the killer and what would have made sense. My head snapped up at the sound of a low persistent growl. I spun around, but there was nothing there.

Jack and I shared a knowing look. Hearing growling was one of the phenomena known to the cemetery. I had never heard it before and by the look on Jack's face neither had he.

Frank looked at both of us. "Let's get out of here." He didn't wait for us. He was yards ahead of us before Jack and I got our feet in motion.

CHAPTER 47

Luke was back at his desk, going over every shred of evidence when the unit secretary dropped another letter on his desk. She gave him a sympathetic smile and walked away. The secretary had been told to watch for any new letters and not to open them. Basically, any mail for Luke was to be directed to his desk immediately.

"We knew it was coming," Tyler said, standing over Luke's desk waiting for him to open it. "This guy can't seem to do anything but gloat. Where is this one postmarked from?"

With gloved hands, Luke picked up the envelope to appraise the postmark. It was from Atlanta this time. Luke told Tyler and then he carefully opened the letter. Setting the envelope aside, he read aloud. The killer dropped the formality with this one.

Lucas,

I had hoped that you would have been more of a challenge, but I think I might have cheated. It was a good test for you. You went where I told you and found the evidence that I left for you. I know you are angry that I presented your father a little gift. You both, I'm sure, have had so many questions about how your sweet sister died. I was giving you the show up close and personal. Did you like it? Did it answer any questions for you? I'm sure you are left with many more questions, but I gave you enough to

start the chase. You know about the dark web now. You know how I catch my helpers. The breadcrumbs have been dropped. Get following.
The Professor.

Luke slammed the letter back down on the desk and pounded his fist on top of it. "I'm going to kill this scumbag."

Tyler sat down. "I get it, Luke. Read the letter again though."

"Why?" Luke asked.

"Just clear your head and read it again."

Luke read it again. It pissed him off as much the second time as it did the first. He looked up at Tyler completely frustrated. "What am I missing?"

Tyler walked over and took the letter out of Luke's hand. "He told us he uses helpers. The case in Little Rock wasn't the first time. What do these helpers do? And look at what he doesn't mention. He doesn't indicate we know about his car rental or that we got a photo of him or that there was a witness."

Luke sat back in his desk chair. Tyler was right. The Professor had called himself by the name he had used on the dark web. Luke wondered if he was, in fact, a professor. The killer easily took college freshmen.

Luke mulled over how often he had helpers and what exactly they did for him. Luke immediately thought of Aaron Roberts and how he had driven off with Lily. Had he been one of the helpers, too? Or had he been the killer? Luke didn't know if Aaron was involved at all, but it was the first thought that crossed his mind.

Tyler was right. There was a lot The Professor wasn't saying regarding the evidence Luke did have. "Do you think he knows about the witness or catching him on camera?"

"I don't," Tyler responded, sitting on the edge of Luke's desk. "He alludes to the evidence we found in Fayetteville, but he doesn't say anything about evidence in Little Rock other than leaving the body in a place where he knew you'd find her. The rest he doesn't mention at all, and I think he would."

"Do you think we should put the photo out yet?" Luke asked.

"No, I think we keep it close to the vest for now. We need to make sure Riley and Cooper have a copy, but we don't go wide with the news yet. We have the upper hand or at least I think we do right now."

Luke stood and stretched. "Let's head to the campus and talk to some of the victim's friends and see what exactly went down on Friday night. Maybe they will tell us more than they initially said in their statements."

Det. Tyler went to his desk and gathered his things while Luke waited. He reached into his desk drawer and pulled out a file. Tyler held it up and indicated, "I have their statements here. We had some initial reports that they were downtown, but they weren't, they were at a bar in the Riverdale area."

"Where did they go?"

Tyler flipped open the file. "They went to The Fold for dinner. Then they went to another bar around the corner – literally named Around the Corner – and spent the rest of the night drinking and meeting up with people. Most people in the area just call it the bar, since it's the only one."

"Was the victim drinking? She was only eighteen," Luke asked. They walked down the stairs and out into the parking lot. They got in Luke's car.

Tyler laughed. "Do you remember college? Did you drink when you were eighteen?"

"Yeah, I guess I did," Luke lamented. "I feel like an old man." He navigated out of the police station and headed towards the university.

Tyler and Luke drove the rest of the way in silence. Luke kept replaying the letter and thinking about what they could be missing. He still didn't have enough pieces of the puzzle to start to make anything fit.

After arriving at the university campus, Tyler and Luke walked to the freshman dorm. They showed their badges to the kid at the front desk and asked for specific students by name. The kid called several numbers and only reached one person. The young woman, Katie, said she'd meet Luke in the lounge on the second floor. Luke and Tyler headed upstairs.

Luke navigated down the bland hallway. There were doors on each side and the walls were painted a neutral tan. Overall the environment seemed sterile. Luke followed the directions the kid on the first floor had given him and soon found the lounge. It was a large open space with a television, pool table and couches. It was empty.

Tyler and Luke took a seat on the couch and waited. Luke pulled out his phone and started to send Riley a text when a voice at the doorway interrupted him.

The young woman, who looked significantly older than eighteen, said, "Are you here to arrest me?"

CHAPTER 48

After leaving the cemetery, we made our way back to Jack's truck. Navigating back out through the woods, I had the distinct feeling we were being watched, but I couldn't figure out from where. There was no one else out there that I could see anyway. I thought once I left the cemetery and crossed the threshold back onto country club property, I'd feel better. I didn't. There was a heavy presence with us that I was having trouble shaking. It seemed I wasn't the only one.

"Either of you feel weird?" Frank asked. His eyes were trained on the trees. "I felt like something was behind us the whole time we were walking out."

Jack raised his eyebrows. "Me, too. It's just the place. I hate going in there, but today felt particularly heavy."

Jack watched the trees along with Frank who still hadn't looked away. I turned to watch, too, but there was nothing.

"What do you think about the murder? Learn anything you didn't know before?" Jack asked, leaning up against his truck.

"I think I can say with near certainty the cases are related at least to the one that just happened in Little Rock. All the details are nearly the same even how he left the body. Did you have any witnesses to anything?"

Jack reached into his truck and pulled out a crate that contained files. "I have copies of everything. I'm not supposed to, but this case got hold of me and didn't let go."

Frank, who still looked shaken, asked, "Can we do this someplace other than here? I can't concentrate like this."

Jack and I both agreed. We got in Jack's truck and headed back out to the front gates. We decided to meet back at my mother's house. We gave Frank the address. Jack said he was going to pick up lunch for us. I texted my mother to see if anyone was there.

She let me know we'd have the place to ourselves for a while at least.

When I arrived home and got settled in the kitchen, I texted Luke to ask how everything was going. I didn't hear back so I called Cooper. After quickly catching him up to speed about my day so far, he told me about his trip to the library.

"He could have easily gotten her out that back entrance," Cooper detailed.

"Any cameras in there?" I pulled out some plates and silverware to set the table. I wasn't sure what Jack was bringing back for lunch, but I wanted to be prepared.

"I can ask, but I doubt it. Today there are, but that was 1993. I don't remember cameras being as prevalent as they are today."

"That's true. Do you think he lured her down to the basement and out the backdoor?"

"I don't know," Cooper said seriously. "I was curious how he could have gotten her out of the library without anyone seeing, and that's one way at least for now. I'm hoping to learn more this afternoon when I speak with Adele. I'm heading back to the library to talk to Jordan's friend Hope tonight. She was clear she doesn't believe the university's story that Jordon simply ran away."

"Has Hope told her story before?" I asked, trying to remember if I heard her on the podcast.

"No," Cooper confirmed. "Adele told me that Hope has never spoken about it publicly. She hasn't even been able to get Hope's story out of her. She said the woman seemed afraid. Because Hope works at the university, she's been trying to keep a low profile. But from what Adele said, she's never agreed with how the university or the cops handled this case."

"She's willing to talk to you?"

"That's what Adele tells me. Adele explained to Hope that Jordan's disappearance might be connected to more murders. Adele said that she convinced Hope to speak with me. I didn't know who she was when I first went into the library, but when I was leaving, she told me who she was and that she'd speak with me later this evening. I took that as a good sign."

Cooper and I ended our call just as someone knocked on the front door. It was Frank.

As he came in, he inquired, "Jack said that the fraternity house the victim was last seen at is right around here. Can you show me?"

I led Frank to the corner of Locust and made a right onto Pawling. The sidewalks were wide enough for us to walk side by side. He took in the large homes and manicured lawns. "It's hard to imagine a girl going missing from this neighborhood."

"My sister said she was coming home that night and walked right by the fraternity party. She was in high school and snuck out. Our mother still doesn't know, but it's terrifying that it could have been her. But that's how safe we considered this neighborhood. She was walking alone at night."

"Your mom doesn't know she went out?" Frank asked. We crossed the next side street and were about a block away from the fraternity.

"My mom is a nurse and back then she had to work an evening shift. She'd get home by midnight, but sometimes my sister would go out and be back by then."

Frank nodded. "She didn't happen to see anything did she?"

"Not that she can remember. She said some guys yelled for her to come to the party but that was it. I thought about asking her again though to see if anything can jog her memory."

"That's a good idea," Frank looked at the fraternity house. "This it?"

"Yeah, this is where Amanda was last seen according to the reports that I was able to gather."

I turned back toward where we had just walked from. "If you turn around and head back towards my mom's house, but instead of turning on her street you kept going, you'd be walking in the direction Amanda supposedly went that night. Russell Sage College is a little more than two miles into downtown Troy. The victim could have easily walked back."

Frank looked down the road and back at me. "But is that really the direction she went that night?"

CHAPTER 49

Back at my mom's house, we found Jack in the kitchen. He had arranged the plates and silverware that I had left on the table. Jack had already dug into the pizza he brought. He held up a large slice and said between bites, "I figured you might miss the real thing."

I smiled. "I certainly do."

Frank and I both helped ourselves to the pizza and wings. Jack had outdone himself for a mid-day lunch, but I wasn't complaining. I couldn't remember the last time I had allowed myself to eat either.

Frank asked Jack the question he had posed to me outside. "Did the victim really head in the direction of school? I ask because you found her body in the opposite direction."

Jack wiped his mouth with a napkin. "That's one of those lingering unanswered questions. All the witness statements we have said Amanda walked back toward her dorm. She had gotten into an argument with her boyfriend and wanted to go back. She didn't want to wait for her friends so she started walking at a little before eleven."

"No one went with her?" Frank asked.

"Not that we know of or anyone would admit," Jack said.

"What about Shawn Westin? He was an initial suspect, right?" I asked.

"He was. We interviewed every guy at that frat house. We initially thought maybe we were looking at a date rape case that got out of hand or some junior psychopath. Westin had a prior rape case thrown out. He had been charged as an adult so it wasn't sealed. But the case was dropped. Everyone else had a clean record and nothing suspicious popped up on any of them. Westin also had a car. He was arguing with the victim before she left. He was a primary suspect for a while, but there was barely any case on him."

"Did anyone see him after Amanda left?" I asked what I felt was an obvious question, but it hadn't been answered.

"Yeah, of course. That's why we had to clear him," Jack indicated, but then his voice got low. "I will say though, there was a window of about an hour, maybe less after Amanda left that nobody can account for him, but Westin swears he was there."

"I want to see if I have this correct. I feel like I have a million pieces and want to make sure I'm connecting the dots right," Frank said. "Amanda goes to a fraternity party with friends. She's there for a few hours, but some time a little before eleven she had an argument with her boyfriend, Shawn Westin, and left. By all accounts, she walks off alone. There's no confirmation she ever made it back to her dorm. A few days later, a dog walker finds her body propped up against that monument in the cemetery. She had been stabbed with what looks like an ice pick and has three fingers missing."

"That's it exactly," Jack confirmed.

Frank slapped the table. "That's my case. Nearly all of it from start to finish, minus a fight with a boyfriend."

Turning to me, he asked, "All right, Riley, you said we've got a serial killer on our hands. How are we going to catch him?"

I picked up their plates and put them in the sink. I washed them, talking over my shoulder. "That's kind of the million-dollar question. I think we know for sure he does some recon of the area and maybe even the girls before he takes them. He kills them the same way, at least in the cases where bodies have been found, and there are missing fingers. I think we need to work up some sort of profile on him. Not an exact science, but a start. We know the commonalities in the cases. We have info from his letters. Luke has a photo he's going to be sending me, too. Let's start with those witness statements, Jack. Maybe there's something in there that will jump out for me and Frank."

Jack excused himself from the table and went outside. He came back in with the large crate of files. He put it down on the table. "Let's start digging in."

Over the next two hours, we each read through every statement, looked at some crime scene photos, and dug through Jack's old case notes. Frank finished reading and then would hand it off to me. I took notes of my own. Nothing jumped out at me until I hit on one particular statement.

"I think I have something," I said seriously, silently rereading the statement again. I lifted my eyes from the statement and looked right at Jack. "You interviewed a girl who lived down the hall from Amanda and was also at the party. She indicated that Amanda had been seen several times talking off campus with one of her professors. The girl was concerned about his intentions towards Amanda. That is familiar to Lily's case. A professor was seen talking to her on the night she disappeared. He's one of the people, if not the very last, to have seen her alive. Our killer also calls himself The Professor."

Jack took the statement from my hands and reread it. "I remember this vaguely, but it didn't amount to much that I recall." Jack leaned over and dug through the crate. He didn't find what he was searching for so he took the pile next to Frank and dug through that.

Jack handed me the file he had been looking for and explained, "His name is Michael Bauer. He was a history professor. Amanda hadn't declared a major yet, but she had indicated an interest in American history. Bauer admitted that he had met with her a few times to talk coursework."

I took the statement from Jack. "Had Bauer been at the university long? Was he a tenured professor?"

"I don't think so," Jack recalled. "He had been giving some sort of lecture series. I don't think he taught regular classes, but he was around enough he got to know some of the students. I had talked to other professors who had done the same with students. There didn't seem to be anything out of the ordinary."

Frank watched us, interest growing in his eyes. "The witness said she had seen them off campus together? That doesn't sound like academics to me. Is that normal here?"

"It could be, maybe," I speculated. "It really depends on where they were seen off-campus. The university sits in downtown Troy. There are many coffee shops, bars, and restaurants around it. I think context is important. It may be nothing, but a friend of hers was concerned enough to have brought it up to the police. Was he cleared for the night of her disappearance?"

Jack ran a hand through his hair. His face turned a crimson red. "We never asked. He was never considered a suspect or even a person of interest. His story checked out. We heard nothing about anything inappropriate. Do you think we made a mistake?"

"I have no idea," I said softly, not quite sure if he did or not.

CHAPTER 50

Sitting in the lounge in the dorm at the University of Little Rock, Luke was taken aback. He looked at the young girl. "Why would we be here to arrest you?"

Katie didn't respond. She came into the room and sat across from Luke and Tyler. She was thin, had long blonde hair and was attractive. Luke took in her clothes. He didn't know one designer from the next but she looked like she came from a family with some money.

Katie folded her hands in her lap and cast her eyes downward not looking at Luke. He wasn't really sure what to think, but clearly, she had something to hide.

"Katie, it's really important that no matter what it is, you tell us," Luke started. More sympathetically he added, "We are so sorry your friend was murdered, but we need to find out who abducted and killed her. If you know anything, you have to tell us."

"I called my parents this morning. I didn't tell them anything, but my father said I should call his lawyer if I needed to." Katie lifted her gaze from her hands and looked Luke dead in the eyes. "Do I need to call a lawyer?"

Luke looked at Tyler, who shrugged. Luke tried to find a way to put the girl at ease but not compromise the investigation. He felt like he was walking a tightrope. Luke chewed on his bottom lip. Finally, he appealed, "Katie, I'm only here because I think you were a witness. You were one of the last people to see Cristina alive. If you know something, you need to tell us."

"How about immunity?" Katie challenged. She lost her demure demeanor and crossed one leg over the other. She leaned back in the chair and stared defiantly at Luke.

"I can't offer you that," Luke responded, frustrated. "That's not for me to decide. Immunity would come from the prosecutor's office in exchange for your testimony. I'm just here trying to have a conversation and find out more information about what happened that night."

Det. Tyler interrupted. "Katie, I'm not sure what's going on, but your friend is dead, and who knows who's next. Luke lost his sister potentially to this same killer. All we want is to catch the guy. We don't care what else you might have done."

Katie looked at Luke. "Is that true, about your sister?"

"Yeah," Luke said sadly. "She was your age. Just a freshman like you and your friends. One night, she went to a party and never came home. It took a long time to find her body. All I want is to catch this guy."

When she didn't respond, Luke lost his temper. "If you lie to us or hold back information that impedes the investigation you could be in even more trouble than for whatever it is you're avoiding telling us."

Katie frowned, a slight crack in her staunch posture. She looked unsure of what she should say.

"I'll tell you what I know, but I don't want to get in trouble," Katie finally said, stressed.

Luke couldn't make her any promises so he just sat back and waited. Tyler did the same.

Katie watched them closely. Her body relaxed and she relented, "That night we all just wanted to have a good time. I didn't think it would do any harm. Cristina had said she had done it before and so had the rest of the girls. I guess Cristina couldn't handle herself."

Luke had a suspicion Katie meant drugs, but he needed more. "You didn't think what specifically would do any harm?"

"I got some ecstasy from someone I know, and we all took some," Katie said flippantly. "This isn't my fault. All the girls took some. Cristina said she had done it before, but she couldn't handle herself."

Det. Tyler interjected, "You've said that twice now, that the victim couldn't handle herself. What exactly does that mean? Did she behave differently from the rest of you?"

"Not at first, but then she got paranoid," Katie said, an edge of annoyance in her voice. "We were dancing and enjoying the band, and she started killing our high. Cristina went to the bathroom at the bar, then came back out and said she was scared. She said someone was watching her. Cristina was always a baby if you know what I mean."

"I don't know what you mean at all," Luke barked. "This is someone who was supposed to be your friend. Obviously given what happened to her, she had every reason to be afraid that night."

Katie tried to defend herself, but Luke cut her off. "What happened next?"

"She left. I told her if she wasn't having a good time, she should leave." Katie looked down her nose at Luke.

"Where did she go?"

"I don't know. I didn't pay attention to her. She was being a pain. She kept asking one of us to go back to the dorm with her, but we were all having a good time. When no one would leave with her, she left."

Luke shot Tyler a look. It took everything Luke had not to throttle her. She wasn't any kind of friend he'd want to have. Frustrated, Luke asked, "Do you know how she got home?"

"No," Katie said quickly.

There was something in the girl's voice that made Luke question her honesty. "Do you have anything else you think we should know?"

"I'm done with this." Katie smirked. She stood and walked out of the room before Luke could say another word.

Luke waited for the door to shut behind Katie. He exhaled slowly. Turning to Tyler, he questioned, "What do you make of that?"

"I have no idea," Tyler said, looking as shocked as Luke felt. "I don't think I've ever had a young witness be so defiant. She's got to be hiding something."

"What?"

"She might know where Cristina went after she left the bar."

"I thought so, too," Luke commented. He got up and headed for the door. "I think we are just going to have to talk to those other witnesses."

As Luke pulled open the lounge door, Tyler asked, "Do we care about the ecstasy?"

"Not really. We have bigger fish to fry. It's going to show on the victim's toxicology report anyway. At least now we know where she got it."

Tyler agreed, and the two made their way down the hall. As they approached the stairway, a dark-haired girl wearing leggings and a tee-shirt approached. She smiled shyly at Luke. As she passed by him, she clasped Luke's hand that was at his side and kept moving. A small piece of paper pressed into the palm of his hand. He made no move to read the note now or any movement that would indicate she had given him anything. He didn't know who was watching.

Luke and Tyler walked quickly down the steps and through the first-floor hall. Once they were outside, Luke said, "That girl slipped me a note. Let's get back inside the car before we read it."

CHAPTER 51

Luke couldn't wait until he settled into the driver's seat. He got in the vehicle and immediately unfolded the note. Loopy handwriting on the blue-shaped star that had a sticky backing read, *"I know. We all do. Meet me in 20 minutes at Mylo's."*

Luke showed the note to Tyler and started the car. He put it in drive and headed to the location. He didn't speed, but he was hard-pressed to keep it at the limit. Luke turned his head briefly to look at his partner. "What do you think?"

"I think she doesn't want her friends to know she's about to rat them out," Tyler replied.

Luke felt the same. They drove in silence back to Hillcrest. Luke parked easily enough. As they walked into the coffee shop, Luke got a call. He held up the phone for Tyler. It was Riley. Tyler walked in, while Luke took the call standing on the sidewalk.

Riley explained what she had learned that day and about the professor, Michael Bauer. It wasn't a name that rang any bells for Luke, but he encouraged Riley to pursue the lead. He offered to run some background on him if she needed it. She told Luke that while it wasn't a lead, it was an unanswered question. Luke felt for the detective. He didn't know if he would have asked for the guy's alibi either.

Luke hung up, promising Riley he'd call her later that evening. He entered the shop and made his way to the counter. He took in the long list of coffee and espresso drinks and settled on a plain coffee. Riley would tease him that he was boring, but he liked what he liked. He found Tyler in the middle of the shop near the large window with a perfect view of the sidewalk entrance. He had his own coffee in front of him and scribbled in a notepad.

Luke took a sip and savored it. It was strong and perfect. He hitched his jaw at Tyler. "What are you writing?"

Tyler laughed. "It's not anything important. My wife wants me to stop at the grocery store on the way home, but if I don't write down what she wants, I'm going to forget. My brain has too much in it, can't fit in anything else."

"That's a good excuse. I'm stealing that for later," Luke joked. He leaned back and stretched. He hoped this girl showed up. He checked his watch again. They were still a few minutes early.

Luke flipped through his phone. He got an update text from Cooper. Sounded promising. Both Riley and Cooper seemed to be making some headway. He hated to admit it, but he wanted to be the one to bring this guy down. Not that he hoped Cooper or Riley wouldn't find evidence, Luke just wanted the satisfaction of solving it himself.

Tyler interrupted Luke's train of thought. "She's late. You think she's going to show?"

"I do. Let's give her a few more minutes. Maybe there was some traffic."

The two sat for a good fifteen more minutes. Just as they were about to give up, the girl walked in. She walked by Luke's table and jerked her head in the direction of a far back corner away from the window and front door. Luke and Tyler followed.

Once they sat down, the girl introduced herself. "I'm Megan," she said quickly. "Sorry I'm late. As soon as you left, Katie rounded up all of the girls that were out with Cristina that night to tell us about what you had to say. Katie told us what she told you and then cautioned us to keep the same story. Katie's really scaring some of the other girls that we could all get in trouble so we had to make sure we kept our stories straight."

"What's her deal? We know about the drugs, but there's something more than that," Luke said, catching Megan's gaze.

The girl looked around the room. She leaned in closer to Luke. "I'm pretty sure Katie knows who killed Cristina."

Luke tried not to show a reaction on his face. "Why do you say that?" he asked calmly.

"Katie gave us the ecstasy that night. Cristina wasn't reacting well. At the bar, Cristina went to the bathroom right before she left. When she was in there, Katie told us all to encourage Cristina to leave. She pushed hard for us to get Cristina to go. Nobody really cared whether Cristina was there or not, but Katie was adamant. When Cristina came out of the bathroom, Katie pretty much told her to leave, that we didn't want her there anymore if she was going to act like such a baby. She kept goading her, being really mean. The other girls followed along."

Tyler said with skepticism in his voice, "Katie said that Cristina wanted to leave. She told us that Cristina was paranoid, not reacting well, and wanted to leave."

Megan smirked. "Of course, Katie would say that. Cristina did feel uncomfortable. There was a guy at the bar who had his eye on Cristina as soon as we walked in. He was alone and did not take his eyes off of her. He tried to act sly of course, not to make it obvious, but it was obvious to me."

"Did anyone else notice?" Luke asked.

"Maybe, I'm not sure. As I said, Katie gave us all ecstasy so everyone was pretty wasted at that point. I don't do drugs. I just pretended to take it and played along. I was completely sober. I saw what was going on."

"Did this guy approach Cristina or try to talk to her?" Tyler asked.

"No, he just sat at the end of the bar and watched her."

"Did Katie talk to him or seem to interact with him in any way?"

"No, I don't think any of them noticed him, to be honest."

"I assume then that Katie and the other girls succeeded in convincing Cristina to leave, correct?" Luke pressed.

Megan nodded. She looked down at the table and wouldn't make eye contact.

"What happened after Cristina left?"

"I was planning to go with her." Tears welled up in Megan's eyes. "I feel awful. When Cristina walked out, I was right behind her.

I felt bad about how everyone was treating her. But I didn't get far. Someone spilled water all down my back."

Megan's eyes met Luke's. "It was the whole cup. I was soaked. I turned around to see what had just happened and shake the ice out of the back of my shirt. It was Katie. She stood there laughing. I started to argue with her, but then remembered Cristina."

Luke had a million questions, but he wanted to ensure Megan kept talking so he didn't press when she took a beat. He waited as she dried her tears. "What did you do next?"

Megan blew her nose. She wiped her tear-stained cheeks and started again. "By the time I turned around, Cristina was gone. I shot out of the bar but didn't see her. I called her name. I ran out into the main road and that's when I saw her getting into an SUV. I called after her again, but she never even looked in my direction. She was gone, and that was the last time I saw her. I called a rideshare right after that, thinking maybe I'd meet her back at the dorm, but she wasn't there. I was worried. I called around to some of her other friends, but no one had seen her. I called her parents the next morning when she wasn't back."

"Did you give a statement to any of the cops the other day? I know I didn't read anything like what you just told us," Luke said, perplexed.

Luke had read a few of the girls' statements, but all of them said Cristina didn't feel well and she left. Luke didn't think Megan was lying. He just didn't understand why this was the first time hearing this.

"Katie met with all of us Saturday morning and told us we had to get our stories straight. I think she might have threatened some of the other girls as she did again today. I don't know if they don't remember what happened or if they were lying, but no one mentioned Katie stopping me from following Cristina."

"Did she threaten you?" Det. Tyler asked.

"She didn't have to," Megan admitted. "I pretended like I had been so wasted I didn't remember anything. I didn't even bring up Katie spilling water on me. I made sure she heard me talking to the cop. I didn't want her to stop me from telling you what I know. I watch enough cop shows. I figured there would be detectives on the case, and I'd tell my story then."

"You're going to have to come down to the station and give a formal statement. We have some photos we need you to look at, too," Luke cautioned. "We can keep your name out of this, but you have to give us the statement. We have more questions as well."

"That's okay, but let's go now because they think I'm with my boyfriend."

CHAPTER 52

By six that evening, I was tired from a long day of investigating. Jack and Frank had left late in the afternoon. Frank headed back to the hotel to compare notes on his case to Amanda's. I pored through some more statements. I took Dusty for a long walk. We played catch in the backyard if you can call it that. I threw the ball, and every once in a while, he'd go get it. Mostly, I threw it and he looked at me wondering when I was going to run after it and bring it back. He'd give me a little side glance like I was stupid to keep throwing it.

Finally, he had gotten bored with me and stood at the backdoor to be let in. I gave him some fresh water and a snack. I had some leftover pizza. My mother was out with some friends so I was on my own for dinner. The house had been quiet, and eventually, I made my way back upstairs and turned the television on in my room. I snuggled into bed.

I must have dozed off because the next thing I knew my sister Liv was standing over me, shaking my leg. I blinked my eyes open. "What?"

Liv sat on the edge of the bed. "I think I remember something about that night the girl went missing."

I sat straight up. "You do?"

"Yeah. I got thinking about that night after we talked. Remember how I used to keep a journal all the time?"

I nodded. Liv journaled all the time. She had notebooks full of drawings and poems and notes about her day. Not that I ever snooped, but she was always buried in one.

"I got thinking about that night, and I probably journaled it. The guys who were calling me over as I was walking by were cute. It wasn't every day I had college boys flirting with me. I probably wrote about it."

It sounded reasonable to me, but it'd been years. I looked at her skeptically. "Do you have any idea where those journals are now?"

"They're here but up in the attic. I don't like going up there by myself."

"I'll go with you." Liv always had a fear of the attic even though it wasn't scary at all as far as attics go. In the hall right next to the bathroom my sister and I had shared when we were young, there was a door. It led to the attic steps. My mother generally kept the door locked, but the key had always been on her dresser under her jewelry box. Liv stood at the door as I went to my mother's bedroom to find the key.

The same six-drawer wooden box that had sat on my mother's dresser for all of my youth was still there. I picked it up and sure enough, the attic key was there as well. I entered back into the hall and waved the key at my sister. "Don't look so glum. I promise there are no monsters in the attic." I unlocked the door. Liv followed behind me, keeping a close eye out for spiders. Every few seconds, she'd jump a little.

"It's not the monsters I'm worried about," Liv protested as we climbed the attic steps, "it's the spiders."

"I'll protect you."

"You always do. Remember when you beat up Timmy Jacobs for me?" Liv asked as we hit the landing.

That was a name I hadn't heard since probably fifth grade. "What made you think of that?"

"I ran into him the other day. He asked about you. His nose is still crooked from where you bashed your big head into his face. I'm pretty sure he can't have kids because of you."

"He deserved it. He made you cry and got me in a chokehold. What else was I supposed to do other than slamming my head into his face and punching him in the balls?"

Liv laughed. Timmy never picked on my sister or any girl ever again. Timmy was apparently the second boy I had punched for my sister. I didn't remember getting pie after that altercation like the other.

The attic was fairly clear. My mother would never be accused of being a hoarder, actually, she was the opposite. She barely kept anything. I didn't have anything at her house. Years ago, when I moved out, I took nearly everything I wanted with me. My sister, on the other hand, was the saver.

Liv went to the far corner and dug through boxes that had been arranged in neat piles. At the third box, she victoriously pulled out a gray hardback journal. "Here it is!" she called out proudly.

I sat next to her cross-legged on the floor. Liv frantically flipped through pages. Pointing to one page, she beamed. "This is it. I knew I wrote something that night."

I tried to contain myself. For all I knew, it was just a description of the boy that flirted with her. I waited as Liv read to herself.

Finally, Liv plopped the journal in my lap and pointed to one of the paragraphs. "Read that."

I took in my sister's adolescent scrawl. It was easy enough to read, but each word caught me more and more by surprise. My sister not only detailed the interaction with the fraternity boys, but she had also indicated that there was a girl walking up ahead of her on the sidewalk.

Liv noticed her because the girl was wearing pants that my sister liked. Liv had also written that just as she was turning the corner onto our street, a car had pulled up next to the girl who was still on the main road. It made my sister nervous. She didn't indicate why in her writing, but she described the car as a dark blue sedan. She had even described the driver. He sounded suspiciously like the composite sketch of the killer in Little Rock. Liv saw the girl get into the guy's car.

The rest of the journal entry was about earlier in the evening at the party she had gone to and some boy she liked. It was obvious that at the time my sister saw no significance in the interaction she had witnessed.

"Well, what do you think?" Liv asked curiously.

"You never told anyone about this?"

"No, I didn't even remember until we talked about it the other night."

"What about back then? When they said a girl was missing, you didn't think seeing a girl get into a car was important?"

"I didn't," Liv regretted. "I wasn't watching the news back then. I was focused on stupid high school stuff. Mom told me a girl was missing, but I didn't know what she looked like. That girl got in the car willingly. She seemed to know the guy so I never connected it might be important. I'm not even sure now that it is. Is it?"

I looked at my sister. I wasn't sure if telling her how close she came to the killer was a good idea. She was easily spooked. I hesitated for a few seconds too long.

"That was the killer, wasn't it? I saw him." Liv's face contorted in fear.

"I think so," I explained, reaching out and rubbing her arm. "You wrote a pretty good description of him. I know it's been years, but did this jog your memory? Is there anything else you remember?"

Liv took a deep breath and closed her eyes. When she opened them, Liv looked right at me. "They knew each other. I had picked up my pace walking by the frat house because even though the guys were flirting, I was still scared because I was alone. You know how much Mom used to caution us about them. I picked up my pace and nearly caught up with the girl. She crossed our road as I turned down it. That's when the car pulled over to the curb. I remember her saying hi and walking over to the passenger side window. He never got out. I was nervous at first as his car pulled over, but then she knew him so I didn't think twice about it."

"Could you hear what they were talking about?"

"Sort of. She told him she was walking back to her dorm. He asked her if she wanted a ride. She got in. He never once got out of the car."

"Anything else?"

"The last thing I heard him say was that it was a nice night for a drive. It was."

CHAPTER 53

Luke spent the late part of the afternoon into early evening taking Megan's formal statement. She was an excellent witness. Luke wasn't exactly sure of his next move, but it was looking like he was going to have to bring Katie in for formal questioning. Luke was sure Katie was involved somehow. He just didn't know to what extent. He thought back to what the killer had said about helpers. Was Katie one of his helpers? Did she even realize it if she was?

Tyler provided Megan several photos of men from surveillance footage and from lineups. She studied each carefully and surprised Luke when she readily picked the photo of the suspected killer. His face, although a bit grainy from the surveillance photos, was still clear enough to be seen.

"It's him," Megan said without any hesitation. "I got a good look at his face. This is the same hat he was wearing in the bar."

That was all Luke needed. He was grateful for the lucky breaks this time around. He hated that another girl had to lose her life.

Luke followed Megan out of the conference room. He called to her with one last question. "How often does Katie supply drugs?"

"Never," Megan said definitively. She took a few steps back towards Luke. "That was the surprising thing about that night. The girls drink and some of them heavily. I've only known them for a couple of months, but we've never done drugs. Katie never had ecstasy or any other drugs before. The other night was a first."

After Megan left, Tyler and Luke sat at their desks talking over what they had learned and developed a plan of action.

Tyler had his legs kicked up on his desk and his chair leaned back. With his head tilted back and his eyes on the ceiling, Tyler concluded, "You know we have to bring Katie in. I hope she talks to us before she lawyers up."

"Do you think she was involved?" It was hard to believe a girl like Katie knowingly set up another girl to be murdered because that was essentially what it was. Certainly, things like that happened, but Luke struggled to make sense of it.

Tyler brought his chair into a forward position, "I think she's involved somehow. Whether she knows it or not, I think she's connected with the killer. I can't really picture that girl we met digging around in a chat room on the dark web though. Maybe he connected with her in another way."

"That's what I was thinking," Luke admitted.

"Do you think the killer used helpers? What would be the point? Does he toy with people or do you think this is how he catches his victim?"

"Serial killers don't normally work with other people," Luke said, thinking through the question. "He could easily snatch and grab girls without involving anyone else. If I had to guess, getting other people involved amps up the excitement for him. Maybe he's getting off on seeing if people can connect the dots or knowing that there are people out there who could come forward to give details to the police."

"You think he's keeping them quiet somehow?" Tyler asked.

"I think he might, but I'm more curious how he gets them involved, to begin with. The guy in Fayetteville was in financial trouble and needed the money. Money worked for him. Is the killer taking time to find the right victims and researching people to help him? That's a lot of leg work for one murder."

"It looks that way." Tyler moved some papers around on his desk and gathered his things to go. "I need to head out for the night. Let's get back at it in the morning."

Luke waved his partner off. He leaned back in his chair and closed his eyes. He didn't have much to go home to without Riley there. Luke missed her. He checked his phone to see if she had texted. There was nothing. He'd call her later.

Luke pulled out the file folder Tyler had given him with the girls' statements. He checked them against what Megan had said. They were just initial inquiries taken by the uniformed cop. Luke read each of them. He didn't see anything about the details Megan had mentioned in any of the statements. Luke read them again. Something about the way they were all worded bothered him. He shuffled through them one more time. That's when it hit him. The wording was too alike. Witnesses usually told a story a little bit differently from each other, even people standing next to each other during a crime. The details of the girls' statements read like a story they had copied from each other.

These statements were nearly identical both for the information included and what was left out. It was clear to Luke that at least part of what Megan had said was true. The girls had been coached before giving a statement. Luke wouldn't have been surprised if someone had written up a statement and had given it to each girl to read.

They all indicated that Cristina had not felt well and that she left. There was no mention of drugs, even heavy drinking. There was no mention of Cristina being goaded into leaving, and definitely no mention of water being dumped on Megan or even that she had followed Cristina out of the bar. The statements were basic, specific about time and why Cristina left. Each girl said the same thing in the same way.

Luke put the folder down on the desk. He was sure now that Katie had coached them. He texted Tyler and told him to meet at the station early so they could bring Katie in for formal questioning. Luke put his files away and locked up his desk.

CHAPTER 54

Cooper walked down to the lobby of his hotel at close to eight-thirty that evening to meet with Adele. He had spent the day canvassing around the Atlanta neighborhood near the university. He had walked through wooded areas, doing a cursory search in the brush and leaves. Not that Cooper thought after all these years, he'd just stumble on Jordan's remains, but he wanted to see what the killer was working with as far as location was concerned.

He also wanted to clock the distance and accessibility of the library. Cooper found that there were more than a few places to go. If the killer didn't want the body found – and that seemed to be the case – it was more than doable even within a few miles.

Cooper took a seat in the far back of the hotel restaurant, steering clear of the late dinner crowd. When the server arrived, Cooper ordered a soda and explained he was waiting for someone. He read the menu in front of him more than a few times. He should have been hungry, but wasn't. Reading the menu gave him something to do. He checked his phone, too. Adele wasn't late. Cooper was just anxious to speak to her.

Finally, out of the corner of his eye, Cooper noticed an attractive black woman with her hair twisted in braids on top of her head. She had bright red earrings and a matching red patterned shirt and flowing black pants. She was stylish and commanded the room as soon as she entered. He sat up in his chair a little straighter. Cooper felt underdressed in jeans and a pullover shirt.

He stood and gave an awkward wave. When Adele caught Cooper's eye, she smiled and made her way over to his table. Adele extended her hand first. "I'm Jordan's sister Adele. We spoke on the phone. It's a pleasure to meet you."

Cooper stumbled over his words. Finally, he got out, "I grabbed a table away from other people so we could speak freely."

When she was seated, Cooper slid his menu in front of her. "Hungry?" He was suddenly ravenous.

"Starving, actually," Adele admitted. "Would you mind if I ate? It was a long day in court, and I never got lunch. It's well past dinner time, too."

Cooper raised his eyebrows. "Are you a lawyer?" Cooper hadn't searched Adele's background before the meeting. She had been on the podcast but he didn't recall her profession. Cooper usually searched his witnesses before he met them, but he hadn't this time. He felt ill-prepared.

Still looking over the menu, Adele said offhandedly, "I'm a criminal defense attorney. I'm just wrapping up a fairly complex case that's been taking a lot of my time."

Cooper was impressed. "I appreciate you taking the time to meet with me. I know it can't be easy going over this case again and again."

Adele smiled and closed the menu. She looked directly at Cooper. "Finding what happened to my sister is my primary mission in life. Being an attorney is what keeps food on the table. I'd move heaven and earth to find my sister."

"Understood," Cooper said. The server came over at that moment and they both ordered.

After the server left, Cooper stated, "I know I didn't give you much background on why I was asking to meet, but I thought we could start there."

"You said Jordan's disappearance might be connected to a case in Little Rock. Is that correct?" Adele asked, unfolding the napkin on the table and placing it in her lap.

"It's more complex than that." Cooper took a sip of his drink and explained it.

Over the course of the next forty minutes, Cooper detailed more than he thought he would and everything he knew about the cases to date. They paused a few minutes to eat after the server dropped off their food, but then got right back to it after a few bites. Cooper answered questions Adele had and explained to her about what had happened in Fayetteville and subsequently the newest murder in Little Rock.

Cooper finished by explaining to Adele the reason for choosing to look at Jordan's murder. He detailed all the reasons he thought the killer could have made mistakes and laid out his case for being in Atlanta.

Adele interrupted. "You don't have to convince me. Everything you've said makes sense. People don't disappear without a trace, leaving no evidence behind – especially not someone like my sister. She wasn't in a high-risk group. Frankly, she wasn't in any risk group. She didn't have a boyfriend or hardly any friends at all here at school. She didn't drink or do drugs. She wasn't into a partying lifestyle. Jordan didn't have issues with people. She kept her head down, always focused on her studies. I've looked into every angle of this case. Telling me that it's connected to a serial killer – a stranger abduction makes sense now."

Cooper saw the relief on her face, but he wasn't sure why. He questioned gently, "How much have you investigated this case yourself?"

"All of it. Me alone for years," Adele said with frustration in her voice. "The cops didn't take a report that Jordan was even missing. The university never even admitted she went missing from the library. Their statement to this day is she left her books and went off with a boyfriend. No one was looking for my sister so I did. I pulled together volunteers. I contacted that podcast. I've contacted the media over the years. I took extra investigative courses outside of the ones normally required for my criminal law degree. I talked to her professors and her classmates. I've talked to nearly everyone who would listen."

"You seemed relieved when I said it was potentially a serial killer. Is it hard knowing your sister is probably deceased?" Cooper asked cautiously. He took another drink.

Adele chose her words carefully. "I have long since accepted that my sister is dead. We may not have had much money growing up, but we come from a loving supportive family. We were fortunate not to have the dysfunction that some families have. I have parents that have been together for fifty years and love each other as much today as they did back then. Jordan had no reason to run away. If she was alive, she would have been in contact."

Tears formed in Adele's eyes, but she quickly regained her composure. "I've felt all these years like I've failed my sister because I couldn't find her and bring her killer to justice. Knowing it might be a serial killer absolves me from some of that guilt. That's not something I was prepared for or would even know how to investigate. Knowing now, I can help however you need me."

"You said you have a potential witness?"

"I do," Adele explained. "She works at the university library now. Her name is Hope. She was working at the library the night my sister went missing. Because Jordan spent so much time in the library the two had become friends. For whatever reason, she never came forward with what she knows. She had hinted that her story would answer a lot of questions, but could put her at risk in her standing with the university."

CHAPTER 55

Cooper paid the bill at the restaurant after refusing Adele's money. The two walked together towards the university. Cooper commented, "You're very strong. Not many people could take on what you have all these years."

Adele gave a weak smile. "You do what you have to do. But it has consumed a lot of my life. I've lost relationships because men couldn't understand my desire to keep going. My parents were concerned about me for a while. They thought it had turned into an unhealthy obsession. I need to find the truth. I hate thinking of my sister, even her remains, out there without a proper burial."

"Luke, the detective who I told you about, has been the same way with his sister. Since the moment we got the call in our dorm that Lily was missing, Luke has been full steam ahead. I think he was relieved he finally got a letter from the killer. Any shred of information is more than he's ever had."

They walked in silence for a few more minutes and then Cooper added quietly, "I really worry about him. I hope this time he gets the answers he needs."

"I can understand that," Adele offered. "When you have nothing, no idea what happened to a family member, it's hard. There are a million scenarios that run through your head. But answers, even ones that are painful to hear, are better than nothing. Sometimes understanding, you can make peace with it. I hope that beyond just answers, we get justice, especially if there really are more families like mine connected to this case."

"That's all that Luke is hoping for as well." Cooper didn't know how Luke was going to be able to handle it otherwise.

Meeting the family of a missing person was never a comfortable situation for Cooper. He felt out of his element, often stymied and unsure of what to say. He hated not having answers for them so he completely understood what Adele meant. Even upsetting and painful answers were better than none.

They had time to spare before Hope would give them access to the library and share her story. Cooper wanted to see the path Jordan would have taken on her many trips to and from the library and her dorm. As they turned from the city sidewalk onto the campus in the same place Cooper had entered the night before, he asked, "While we wait for Hope, will you walk with me the path your sister would have taken from the library to her dorm? I think it will give me some perspective."

"I can," Adele said hesitantly, looking up at him. "But you know she went missing from the library, right?"

"I know that. I'm not questioning that. I just want to see the path your sister would have taken each night. I'm wondering if someone could have been watching her," Cooper detailed. He stopped walking, hoping that Adele would take him. He had no idea what dorm Jordan had lived in, and the information wasn't available anyplace.

Adele seemed to hesitate only for a moment. She walked off to the right of where they were standing. Cooper followed. They walked a winding path for close to ten minutes. They finally reached a section of buildings that Cooper assumed was the dorms.

Adele pointed to the last building on the right. "That was Jordan's. There were a couple of different ways she could have gone, but she usually took the shortest route. She had told my parents it was always well lit, and she had never expressed fear of walking alone, even at night. My parents had asked her more than once."

The two walked the rest of the distance to Jordan's dorm. Cooper checked out the front door and the large green space in front of the building. He looked around. It was all fairly open. Cooper imagined if someone had been watching Jordan, she eventually would have noticed unless they were inside one of the buildings.

"Let's go this way," Adele said. She cut across the grass until they reached a sidewalk. They walked directly by a dining hall. They kept walking and eventually Cooper found himself near a side entrance to the library. The door was marked for staff and locked.

"You have to have a special key card to enter from the side," Adele indicated. "It was like that when my sister was here, too. It's just for library staff."

"Where does it go in the building?"

"Directly into the basement. There are stairs that lead down. You can walk through a hall and then access the elevator to go the first and higher floors."

Adele and Cooper made their way to the front of the library. Cooper checked his watch. It was nearly eleven. He was struck again by how quiet the campus was in the evening. They had seen a few students walking on campus, but otherwise, it was quiet and peaceful. For a campus that sits right in the middle of a city, it surprised Cooper how few people were out at that time of night.

Together they climbed the steps to the library and entered the front door. Hope stood behind the desk in the same place as she had the night before. She came around and gave Adele a hug. She shook Cooper's hand. "All of the students are gone for the evening. I can officially lock up. Let me lock the front door and then we can talk."

Cooper and Adele walked to the center of the room and took a seat at one of the tables. Hope joined them a few minutes later. As she pulled out a chair and sat, Hope said, "I want you to know I tried to come forward earlier with my story. I had told a school official when I was still a student. They promised to look into what I saw, and then when I asked about it, they told me I had to have been mistaken. They cautioned me that if I made trouble, I could lose my scholarship. Then I got a job here and didn't want to lose it."

"I understand and no judgment," Cooper said. "I'm just glad you're willing to talk to me."

"Adele," Hope started, "I always wanted to tell you what I knew, but the school assured me I was wrong. They even threatened me that I could be sued. A couple of years ago when you did that podcast, I wanted to come forward, but fear got the better of me. I'm so sorry."

"Really," Adele said, reaching her hand across the table and grasping Hope's, "you and my sister were friends, please, anything you can do to help now is all that matters."

Hope sat back and looked at both of them. "I know who took Jordan."

CHAPTER 56

"I don't think I heard you correctly. I thought you said you know who took Jordan," Cooper asked incredulously. Could Hope really have known and not have said all these years?

Hope raised her hands in surrender. "Let me rephrase. I have a suspicion about who might have taken her. I can't know for sure."

Cooper looked at Adele who sat on the edge of her seat. Her eyes were fixed on Hope, clearly waiting for an explanation.

Hope looked directly at Cooper and started slowly, "I worked in this library when I was going to school here. Jordan would come in all the time. I think she spent more time here when she wasn't in class than she did anywhere else."

"That's true," Adele interrupted. "She always said she was here more than in her dorm."

Hope nodded. "She was and she sat at the same table." Hope pointed to a table across the aisle and two rows down from where they sat. "Jordan was here so much I think other people knew it was her spot because no one ever sat there in the evening. Sometimes Jordan would read upstairs, but more than not, she was at that table."

"You said you thought you knew who took her?" Adele prodded.

"Right, I do. Probably a month before Jordan went missing, one of the professors… well, he wasn't really a professor. He was a lecturer. Michael Hayes was his name. He must have struck up a conversation with Jordan at some point because when she was here, he would often show up and they'd talk."

"What is a lecturer?" Cooper was a bit fuzzy on the term. He had no idea how that differed from a regular university professor.

It was Adele who answered. "A lecturer is someone who may teach a class or two but isn't a professor working full-time at the university. They often have another job and expertise in a subject. Many focus on research, too."

"Would they move around from university to university?"

"They could. Some teach at different universities or even online. Some will move around depending on their research or specialty."

Cooper wondered how that might fit the killer's pattern. He fits in a university environment, knows several universities and kills unnoticed in different locations. It clicked for Cooper and he was anxious to hear more.

Leaning into the table, Cooper encouraged, "Tell me about this Michael Hayes, everything you can remember."

"Michael was young then, probably not more than thirty years old. I don't have any background on him. I don't know where he got his degrees or where he was from. I do know that after Jordan went missing, I never saw him again, the rest of that term or any other. He had taught one class, an American history class."

Hope corrected herself. "It wasn't really a class. It was more like a lecture series. They were open to everyone, both faculty, and students. I think they even had some open to the whole community. Michael was an expert on the Civil War or something like that. I'm not sure I'm remembering correctly. But anyway, he started coming to the library at the same time as Jordan, and they were friendly with each other."

"My sister was studying to be a doctor. She was taking biology, calculus, chemistry. She had no interest in history," Adele countered. "I wonder what they talked about."

"Do you think Michael had a romantic interest in Jordan?" Cooper suggested.

"I did think that at first, but I didn't think that Jordan would have been interested. She was all about her studies. Maybe she just enjoyed the attention. Michael was an attractive guy. He was pulled together, well-spoken and intelligent."

"This is all interesting," Cooper acknowledged, but he still wasn't connecting the dots. "Why do you think this guy took Jordan?"

"Well, the thing is, most times he'd come into the library right through the front door like anyone else. Other times, I'd see him in here, but had no memory of him coming in. At the time, one of the other women who worked here also commented that Michael was in the library, but she wasn't sure how he came in. Finally, we figured maybe he was slipping in the side staff entrance."

"Could professors and other university staff come in that way?"

"No, it was just library staff." Hope frowned. "I noticed that he wouldn't always come to Jordan's table though. Sometimes, he'd call her to the back. Cooper, you know those steps you walked down towards the basement, which also goes outside? That's where I mean."

Cooper turned to look at the back hallway. There was room to stand there talking, but the door to the stairway was right there. As he found the day before, all he had to do was walk down a flight of stairs and there was the door that opened to the delivery entrance.

"Do you think he was trying to hide being here or was he just walking in the easiest way without realizing he was supposed to use the main door?"

Hope folded her arms across her like she was cold, but the temperature was comfortable to Cooper. "I don't know. He kind of lurked around here so I used to think at the time maybe he didn't want anyone to know he was here. Once someone even saw Jordan and him talking in the basement."

"That's odd." Adele looked at Cooper, but he didn't have anything to offer.

Cooper wasn't sure where Hope was going with this still. "Tell me about the day Jordan went missing," he directed gently.

Hope shifted in her seat. "I wasn't working, but I was here studying. I was trying to find a book in one of the stacks upstairs. I happened to look down and there was Michael coming out of the back hall. The library was fairly empty at that time of night. He approached Jordan but didn't sit down. He said something to her and she followed him. I watched them walk through the back and then they were out of sight. I didn't think much of it at the time. Looking back that was the last time I ever saw her."

They were all quiet for several moments. Adele asked, "Did you know Jordan went missing right away?"

"No," Hope said sadly. "That was part of the problem. I didn't know for nearly a week. And even when I found out, it was probably another few weeks until I learned she had gone missing from the library. I didn't even connect it was that same night for a while, but thinking back, I realized I hadn't seen her since that night. I immediately went to my advisor and then a school administrator. They both told me that Jordan ran away. They assured me that the lecturer was probably just talking to Jordan. I remember one of them telling me she saw Jordan at one of his lectures. I didn't think anything of it at first, but it's bothered me ever since. Especially because he was gone right after Jordan."

"You didn't see him on campus or back in the library after Jordan disappeared?" Cooper asked. He had taken out a small black notebook and jotted down notes.

"No, at the time I thought it was strange. He was just gone."

"Couldn't his lecture series have just been completed?" Adele suggested. She pinched the bridge of her nose. Cooper wasn't sure if it was stress or agitation.

"That's what everyone told me, which is why I didn't think about it, but there's something else. When I went back to find all the information on that semester's lecture series, it was scrubbed. I couldn't find a thing. Other lecturers who were here that year, yes, but nothing for Michael Hayes. It was like he didn't even exist."

CHAPTER 57

I curled up in an oversized chair my mother had bought for my bedroom when I was in college. It was the most comfortable chair I had ever sat in and the oldest thing in the bedroom. My mother had bought a new bed and made some slight changes to the room sometime after I officially moved out. Even with the changes, it still felt like my bedroom.

After Liv and I discovered her journal, she spent at least an hour worrying about how she could have died that night. I tried to calm her down and reassure her, but I was just as freaked out as she was thinking about how horribly it could have gone.

I had called Jack to see if he had any old photos of Michael Bauer in the files. He told me he'd search. In the meantime, I would search for the man online. I also needed to see if Luke could send me the composite sketch to see if anyone looked familiar to Liv. Not that I thought she'd recognize him after all this time. She certainly couldn't be considered a reliable witness, but her memory of the man was similar enough to the killer Luke caught on surveillance video.

Before my mother came home, we had decided to leave her in the dark about Liv's discovery. My sister wasn't too keen on disclosing, even after all these years, that she had snuck out that night. Telling my mother Liv had potentially caught sight of the killer and was possibly the last person to have seen the victim alive was not high up on the list of things either of us wanted to share. We played it cool when my mother had arrived home and my sister left shortly after. My mother was in her room now watching television, and I was waiting for Luke to call.

He had texted me when he left the station and indicated he had a small break in the case. I was excited to hear and to share with him what my sister had told me. I tried reading a book to distract myself. I had even texted Cooper, but he hadn't responded.

Before my patience completely ran out, my phone rang. I clicked to accept the call and blurted, "I think my sister saw the killer and was possibly the last person to see the victim alive." I had held it in for so long, it all came rushing out at once.

There was silence on the other end of the phone. I'm sure Luke was processing and taking it in. After a few seconds, I heard the shock in his voice. "Tell me everything and then I'll fill you in on what's happening here."

I spent the next twenty minutes going over every detail of my day and capping it with my sister's discovery. "I feel so lucky that she was safe that night. I don't know if anything will come of it, but it's another bit of information we didn't have before. I feel like we are building slowly over time. That cemetery though is creepier than I remembered."

Luke laughed. "I didn't think you believe in ghosts."

"I don't know if I do or not, but it's not someplace I want to spend time regardless. We got talking though and I agree with Jack that the killer had scoped out the spot and knew the area. But enough of this case, tell me what you know."

Luke detailed for me what he found out from Katie and Megan. I agreed with his assessment that Katie must have had some contact with the killer beforehand whether she knew it or not. It made me wonder if the case here was similar.

Luke finished by saying, "Captain Meadows wouldn't let you interview Katie anyway, but I wish you were here. I think you could probably get more out of her than I can. She seems like a tough nut to crack."

"Does she have money?" I asked. Dusty came into my room at that moment seeking my attention. I patted his head and rubbed behind his ears the way he liked.

"She acts like she has money, but I don't really know. I think I should probably talk to some of the other girls first and see if I can get them to crack before taking another swing at Katie. Why did you ask if she had money?"

"I was thinking that if she came from money, she might feel a little more entitled and that's why she's being so defiant with you. But maybe not, it was just a thought."

"What do you think about me interviewing the other girls first?"

"I like it. Do you think Megan can tell you who the weakest girls are? She would know who might crack first. If you have a bunch of statements, it's going to be harder for Katie to lie."

"True," Luke said agreeing. "I can always use the drugs if I have to, but I'd rather not go that direction. I'm not looking to arrest her unless I find out she has a direct connection to the murder. I just want to know what she knows."

I shifted in my chair, tucking my feet underneath me. I pulled the blanket around me a little tighter. I stifled a yawn and asked, "How are you doing? I know you were pretty stressed coming back from Fayetteville. Are you in your groove yet?"

"I'm getting there. I feel like we are getting some lucky breaks. I just hope they continue. It would be better if you were here."

I smiled. I knew how Luke felt about me and how much he loved me, but it was good to hear. "I wish I was there, too. But it's not as bad being back home as I thought it would be."

Luke grunted in response. I heard movement like Luke was changing clothes or moving the phone around. "What are you doing?"

"Getting into bed. I just took a shower. I figured talking to you was the last thing I'd do tonight. I like hearing your voice before I fall asleep. Tomorrow I've got a rough day interviewing those girls."

"Just be your charming self, and I'm sure they will be falling all over themselves for you."

"You think I'm charming?" Luke asked, his voice husky and low.

"Of course, I think you're charming. Sexy, too."

"What are you wearing?"

I looked down at my gray shorts and tee-shirt. Not sexy in the least. I knew Luke well enough to know what his mood was when his voice was low like that. I wondered where this conversation was heading. Not that I was opposed to a little dirty talking but my mother was right down the hall. I got up, moving Dusty as I went, and closed the door.

"What are you thinking about?" I used the sexiest voice I could muster.

It was met with silence.

"Luke?" I asked and waited. "Luke, are you there?"

Luke snored softly. I laughed aloud and then worried I woke my mother. Here I thought we were going to have a little fun and he fell asleep on me. Even Dusty looked at me with a doglike smirk.

CHAPTER 58

The next morning Luke was ready to go. He had a game plan in place to interview the girls. From what Megan had told them, Luke knew he had enough leverage. Just like the day before, none of the girls had answered their phones or returned his earlier calls. He'd have to track them down.

Luke had picked Det. Tyler up at the station, and after grabbing some coffee, they hit the university's administration office to obtain each of the girls' class schedules. The woman behind the desk hesitated for only a second. Tyler reminded her nicely that a freshman had been murdered and they should do everything in their power to cooperate. She relented and took each of the girls' names.

Within minutes, the woman had clicked her keyboard, walked to the printer and returned, holding out several pages of class schedules. She even offered them a campus map so they could find the buildings easier. Luke and Tyler set off in different directions to interview each of the girls. There were seven in total not including Katie and Megan. They split the list in half with Luke taking four and Tyler taking three.

Luke walked clear across the campus until he found the humanities building. Once inside, he checked his watch. Five minutes left until the class period ended. He found the classroom and stood outside the door. Within minutes, the doors of all the rooms opened and a wave of university students rushed towards him. Luke had no idea what the girl looked like. He hadn't planned for these many students at once. Luke needed to find Amelia. He did the best thing he could think of and called her name loudly in the hallway.

A kid in a gray sweater pointed to a girl who had already walked by Luke. He nodded his head to the kid in thanks and followed after the girl. Luke caught her as she took the stairs down to the front door of the building.

"Excuse me, Amelia," Luke called. He reached out and put a hand on her shoulder. She jumped under his touch. "I need to speak with you."

She looked up at Luke. She didn't argue. "We can meet over there," Amelia said, pointing to a bench under a tree not far off from the building.

As they sat, Amelia asked, "Are you a lawyer?"

"No. Why would you need a lawyer?"

Amelia didn't respond. Luke pointed to the badge on his hip. "I'm with the Little Rock Police Department. I'm Det. Lucas Morgan. I'm here to talk about Cristina."

Amelia immediately got up to leave.

Luke reached his hand out to her arm. "You don't have to talk to me if you don't want to, but some of the other girls already have. I know about the drugs. I know quite a few things. All I need from you is to confirm it."

That was the approach Luke and Tyler had agreed upon that morning. If they went into the interviews acting like they already knew everything, Luke hoped they'd confirm Megan's story. Luke hoped that once they got the girls talking maybe they'd provide some other details.

Amelia asked with hesitation in her voice, "Who told you?"

"I'm not at liberty to share that with you. We've talked to enough of the girls that your stories add up. You're better off just telling me what you know."

Amelia wavered. She took a step to walk away and then turned back. She looked at Luke and the spot next to him on the bench.

"If you didn't hurt Cristina, you don't have anything to worry about. I have no reason to believe you've done anything wrong. I just need to make sure that I have a full understanding of what happened that night from all of you."

Amelia came over and sat. She folded her hands in her lap, but wouldn't look at Luke. Frustrated, she said, "I didn't even want to go out that night. I had a paper to write. Katie kept bugging me to come along. Then she got this idea that we should all do ecstasy."

Amelia looked Luke directly in the eyes. "I don't do drugs, Detective. My parents would kill me if they knew. Katie said it was fun. All the other girls were doing it. I thought okay just this once. I did have fun until Cristina started acting weird."

Luke held his hand up to stop her. "Before you feed me a lie, we know Katie encouraged all of you to tell the cops the same thing. That Cristina was sick and she left. We know that's not the real story. Why don't you tell me the real story?"

Amelia protested, but Luke held firm. When she still didn't say anything, Luke cautioned, "You can get in trouble lying to the cops. You might need that lawyer then. Is Katie worth getting in trouble? You're worried about your parents finding out about the drugs. I don't think they would take well to you lying to the police."

"Katie said she was going to call a lawyer for us if we needed. That's who I thought you were," Amelia said finally.

"Why would you need a lawyer?"

Amelia bit her fingernail. "I don't really know. Katie has been acting really strange. She told us all what to say, and then she said we'd all get in trouble if we didn't say exactly that. I don't know what we'd get in trouble for, to be honest. I thought the drugs, but then she told us she told you about that."

"Tell me about that night. Everything you can remember."

Amelia did just that. Luke had been right, once she got talking, Amelia told him everything. She had taken part in being mean to Cristina to get her to leave. Although as Amelia said, she had been a little wasted and didn't remember exactly what she had said. She admitted that Katie was the ring leader. Much to Luke's dismay, she did not remember the man that Megan saw. To be fair, Megan seemed to have been the only sober one so far.

"Do you have any idea why Katie would want Cristina to leave that night?" Luke pressed.

"Katie never really liked Cristina but the rest of us did so that's why Cristina still hung around."

"Any idea why Katie didn't like her?"

"No idea. It doesn't take much for Katie not to like people. They wear the wrong clothes, have the wrong hair, don't have enough money. Katie can come up with anything."

"Is there anything else you think I should know?" Luke asked. He could tell that Amelia was growing tired. He didn't want to push too hard in case he needed to speak to her again.

Amelia hesitated. She chewed on her lip and confided, "I think Katie has some secrets she doesn't want anyone else to know. She made a comment once that her parents had to bribe the school to let her in. There's other stuff, too. Katie said recently that someone found out some of her secrets and she was going to do everything she could to keep him quiet. I have no idea what that means, but it sounded bad and scared the rest of us."

CHAPTER 59

After wrapping up three more interviews that were similar to Amelia's, Luke met Tyler back at the car. Luke had garnered the information he was hoping and then some. The three girls Luke interviewed after Amelia had readily given up information, especially information on Katie. They cracked faster and easier than Amelia. All seemed pretty fed up with taking orders from Katie.

All of the information Luke had gathered fully supported what Megan had told them. One girl had even disclosed that Katie's secrets had more to do with her father and how he made money than it did with anything Katie was doing. It seemed her father was into some illegal business, which Katie knew all about. The girl suggested that someone was blackmailing Katie with the information.

Tyler relayed a similar experience with the girls he had interviewed. "They were more than ready to give Katie up. They backed up Megan's story and two of them indicated that Katie had stopped Megan from leaving the bar by dumping water down her back. Katie set up Cristina."

"I think I might have a motive for that." Luke filled Tyler in on what Amelia had told him about the blackmail. Luke was sure if the killer had gotten to Katie, that's what he could have used.

"That's a pretty strong motive for setting up your friend," Tyler commented. He ran a hand down his face and wondered, "Do you think Katie knew Cristina was being set up for murder?"

"I'd like to think she was being played much the way those two guys were in Fayetteville." Luke sat behind the wheel trying to focus his thoughts. "Where do we go from here? If we call Katie into the station she might lawyer up. I think we should head back to her dorm and talk to her again. Really confront her this time."

"I agree." Tyler looked at his watch. It was before noon. "Did we get her class schedule, too?"

"Right here," Luke said, holding up the page. "She should be heading to lunch at the dining hall near her dorm. I asked Amelia what Katie did for lunch, just in case we had to go back and talk to her."

Luke and Tyler exited the vehicle and walked back in the direction of Katie's dorm and the dining hall, which was right next to it. Luke hoped Katie would talk to them, but he had a feeling she would resist. The only ace Luke had was that he knew enough to pretend he knew about Katie's father, and it seemed she'd protect him at any cost.

They caught up with Katie as she was leaving her dorm, headed towards the dining hall. Luke called her name.

She turned to look at him, an angry expression plastered on her face. "Why are you still bothering me, Detective?"

Luke walked right up to her so close in fact that he had to look down to see her. He towered over her. "Your friend was murdered. We would think that you'd want to do everything you can to make sure her killer is brought to justice."

"I'm not going to pretend to care," Katie huffed. "I already talked to you and told you everything I know. This is harassment."

Neither Luke or Tyler said a word. Luke would throw her in the squad car if needed. His anger at her self-righteousness grew.

Katie shoved past Luke and walked towards the dining hall. Luke and Tyler were right on her heels. She turned back to them. "You can't follow me. I'm going to call my father."

"That might be a good idea. Sounds like your father might warrant his own police investigation," Luke taunted.

Katie's eyes grew wide. Luke could tell she was afraid. She stammered, "What do you mean? What do you know about my father?"

"I hear things," Luke said. He shoved his hands in his pockets and rocked on the balls of his feet.

"What did you hear?" Katie asked nervously, looking around.

"We heard that not all of his business dealings are legal," Luke said matter-of-factly.

"But that's not why we are here, Katie," Tyler offered. "We just need your help. It sounds like you're under a good deal of stress. Maybe you should tell us. We can help you."

"You can't help me," Katie said, sounding defeated.

"I don't think she wants our help," Luke said sarcastically. "Actually, maybe you're just like your father, Katie. You'd do anything to get ahead, even if it's illegal."

Katie didn't say anything, but she also didn't walk away.

Luke turned to his partner and pressed harder. "I think Katie set Cristina up for murder." Turning back to Katie, he asked accusingly, "How much did he pay you to sacrifice your friend? No, I'm sorry, not your friend, some girl you didn't like very much."

"I didn't get paid." Katie looked down at her feet. Her eyes snapped back up.

Luke knew, at that moment, that Katie realized she had just admitted her guilt.

Katie pleaded, "I didn't know he was going to kill her. You have to believe me. This just all got so out of hand."

Luke looked at Tyler and unspoken words passed between them. Luke stood defiant but Tyler put his hand on Katie's shoulder. "Let's go down to the station and have a talk. We believe you didn't know, but you can help us now."

Katie locked eyes with Luke, but he didn't budge. His anger grew and he struggled to get a hold of it. Luke knew before they spoke Katie had done it, but to hear her admit it was a punch in the gut. Luke hoped no one like Katie had set up his sister. He was afraid of what he'd do to them if he knew. "This is your one and only chance to redeem yourself, Katie. Don't cooperate and I'm perfectly okay throwing you in jail."

Katie looked to Tyler who had been going easy on her. Not that they had planned to play good cop, bad cop, but they had been partners for so long, they balanced each other.

"He's serious, Katie," Tyler stressed. "Luke wants to catch this killer. You know far more than you're telling us. You have a chance to cooperate or you can go to jail. It's really up to you at this point."

"Let's head to the police station," Katie said defeated.

CHAPTER 60

Cooper met Adele at a coffee shop down the road from his hotel. After Hope's revelations the night before, Adele had taken the day off and asked Cooper to meet with her. Cooper was more than happy to oblige.

Before they had wrapped with Hope, Adele had her run through the day her sister went missing again. She asked a series of really solid questions, which impressed Cooper. Hope had given them a tour, even showing them where she was standing when she said Michael Hayes approached Jordan. Hope had been correct, she had a clean line of sight, but had been standing far enough back she remained unseen. They tested it a few times.

Cooper met Adele around lunchtime. After ordering their coffee, they took a table in the back. Before they were even seated and comfortable, Adele asked, "What did you think about what Hope had to say?"

"I'm not sure what to think. It makes logical sense that someone lured your sister out of the library. That's really the only thing that makes sense if you think about it. I wish someone would have taken Hope's reports seriously at the time because her information will be nearly impossible to verify now."

"Do you think she was telling the truth?" Adele sipped her coffee.

"She seemed credible to me. I didn't get any red flags about what she was saying. You cross-examine witnesses for a living. Did you believe her?"

"I do," Adele said thoughtfully. "It also makes sense to me why she dropped it and hasn't brought it up again. The police wouldn't take a missing person's report, the university either. Who was she going to tell? If the university threatened her and said Michael Hayes had been cleared, why would she believe any different?"

"It doesn't look like she really believed that though." Cooper took a bite of his bagel. It was better than he thought it would be for a chain shop.

"I think it's probably been bothering her all these years, especially since she can't find any record of him even being at the school."

"I'll need to spend more time on Michael Hayes and see if I can find anything. Do you know what kind of information these lecturers have out there?"

"I occasionally teach a law lecture series. Whatever university I'm holding the lectures for usually has my bio, my background, sometimes even law articles available that I've written. Today, there would be information on the university's website. Back in 1993, you're dealing with a different scenario. It wasn't digital like it is today."

"You'd think though if this guy is still teaching, he'd have something online now though, right? Do you have your own website or something like that to promote you as an expert?"

"I do," Adele explained. "There is a bio page on my firm's website, but I also have social media accounts and my own website, which highlights my work."

"There should be a trace of him."

"I would think so."

Cooper frowned and shook his head. "That's the problem. When I searched, I didn't find anything. No website, no social media. There are so many people named Michael Hayes, though, that it's too broad of a search for my database. I need some narrowing fields."

Adele rubbed her brow. "We are going to have to see if someone from the history department was here back then and if they remember him. We can't go into my sister's case, but maybe we can come up with a good story and see if they have any information."

"Any ideas?"

Adele thought for several minutes. Cooper sipped his coffee and watched her. He also took in the shop, which was filling up with university students.

Finally, Adele suggested, "What about if I just say I'm doing some research for a case and his name came up and we had some info that he had been a lecturer here. That's fairly straightforward. We just need to go to the history department and not call. Calling gives them a chance to say no."

Cooper liked the way Adele thought. He pulled up his phone and typed in the university's address. Once on the site, Cooper searched the history department and looked at photos and bios of professors. There were two that had been at the university back in 1993. One of them was the head of the department. Cooper handed his phone over to Adele. She took it and scanned the page.

"Seems like Professor Marlow might be the guy," Adele agreed. Handing Cooper's phone back to him, she pointed to a few lines on the screen. "He was here back in 1993 and his bio says he has a focus on the Civil War."

The two cleaned off their table and left the coffee shop. They walked the few blocks back to the university and used the map provided on the website to locate the history building. It was two buildings down from the library.

They found Professor Marlow sitting behind his desk in a small cluttered office. It was a smaller space than Cooper would have thought for the head of a department. There was a desk and a small table off to the side, which was piled high with books, stacks of papers, and magazines.

They stood in his doorway, but the man didn't look up from his desk. Cooper wasn't sure if he realized they were standing there. He rapped once on the door. Finally, the man looked up.

Adele walked in and extended her hand. "Professor Marlow, my name is Adele Baker, a local attorney. I was looking for some information I thought you might have."

Professor Marlow smiled at them and waved them in. "Sorry, my office is a mess. I'm retiring at the end of this semester and clearing out a few things. What can I help you with?"

Adele stood at the edge of his desk while Cooper stood back a few steps. Adele asked, "I'm wondering if you remember a Michael

Hayes who gave a lecture here years ago. I'm trying to track him down for some information on some of his research, but I'm having trouble locating him."

Professor Marlow rubbed his chin seemingly lost in thought. He went to a cluttered bookcase and pulled out a binder. He flipped through page after page. Professor Marlow unsnapped the binding and pulled out a page.

He handed it to Adele. "I don't remember much about him, but this is all I have. Over the years, I've kept notes on every lecturer that I've brought to the school. My memory fails me sometimes, so I keep their information on hand. I didn't have much on Michael Hayes, but it was a good lecture series from what I can recall."

Adele read over the sheet. Cooper peered over her shoulder. There was no photo, but it listed his graduate degree from the University of Virginia and a concentration in military history and the Reconstruction era after the Civil War. There was little else to identify him.

Cooper looked up at Professor Marlow. "Do you remember him at all?"

"Not really. He was recommended by a professor here at the time. I can't remember his name. Hayes showed up, gave a few good lectures and left." Professor Marlow stared at them blankly.

Cooper couldn't read much on the man's face.

"Was he ever invited back?" Adele handed the paper back to Professor Marlow.

"No," he said curtly.

"Was there a reason?"

The professor sat down in his chair and looked up at them. "He was too flirty with some female students so we felt it better he was not invited back."

"Any student in particular?" Adele pressed.

"What did you say your last name was?"

"Baker."

Professor Marlow looked back at Cooper. He folded his arms across his chest and stared right back at the man.

Professor Marlow stood. "I need to get back to work. Have a good day."

Adele stood staring at the man, but he had gone back to rifling through papers on his desk. Cooper tugged her arm to go. As they crossed the threshold of the doorway in retreat, Professor Marlow called out to them. "I really am sorry about your sister."

CHAPTER 61

Luke wasn't in the habit of buying potential suspects lunch, but he wanted Katie to remain open to talking. He had been rough on Katie on purpose, and he knew there was a chance he was going to be rough on her again back at the station. In order to win himself some good favor with her, Luke had offered to stop for lunch. They had swung through the drive-through of a local place and each of them grabbed something to go.

Katie sat in an interrogation room eating her salad while Luke and Tyler polished off lunch at their desks and discussed strategy. Tyler would spend time digging into Katie's father's background while Luke would interview Katie formally.

Tyler popped a few fries in his mouth and washed it down with a soda. "You think you'll get what we need?"

"If not, I'm going to give you a crack at her. I don't want to be as firm as I was at the university because I really don't believe she knew she was setting Cristina up for murder, but I'll use it if I have to."

Luke finished the rest of his lunch and threw his trash in the garbage. He heard his phone chime. He pulled it from his hip and saw a text from Cooper, who indicated they had a name and some potential leads. Michael Hayes. Luke tried to remember why the name sounded familiar, but he couldn't place it.

He walked down the hall towards the interrogation room. Just before he entered, Luke remembered the conversation with Riley the night before. He pulled out his phone and sent Cooper a quick text, letting him know that Riley had something suspicious on a Michael Bauer. He suggested the two should probably compare notes.

Luke turned his phone on silent and entered the room. He found Katie sitting quietly with the remnants of her lunch wrapped up in the bag at the side of the table.

Katie looked up at Luke. "I'd really like to get this over with as quickly as we can."

"That's going to be entirely up to you." Luke took a seat across from her and put his notepad and pen down on the table. He didn't think he'd need to take notes though; the entire interview would be recorded both video and audio.

"Where do you want me to start?" Katie shifted in her seat and brushed the hair away from her face.

"When was the first time this man," Luke paused, realizing he was assuming. "Was it a man?"

"I only corresponded with him via text so I can't say for sure, but he came across like a man. The first time was near the middle of September."

"You said you only corresponded via text? I assume you have his number then." Luke leaned his forearms on the table.

Katie rolled her eyes. "I'm not dumb. I already tried calling the number. Generic voicemail. I tried looking it up. It's one of those burner phones. It doesn't go to anybody."

Luke tried not to smile. She was smart. "Tell me about the first time he contacted you."

"I got the text while in class but didn't see it until later. It just said something like I was going to help him. I deleted it. He asked three or four more times over the next couple of days. He wouldn't give me a name or tell me anything about him. I should have just blocked his number."

"Why did he want your help?" Luke sat back and grabbed the pen and jotted a note. He didn't want to have to dig through the audio and video later.

Katie rubbed her eyes and sighed deeply. "He kept texting me that he wanted my help meeting a girl he liked. I thought it was some guy from one of my classes. I tried several times to ask him who he was. I even asked a few guys in our classes if it was them, but no one knew what I was talking about. He wouldn't tell me. I tried arguing. I tried ignoring him. I also tried playing along. Nothing worked. After some texting back and forth, he mentioned Cristina by name. I have three classes with her so I started focusing on guys in our classes."

"Did you tell Cristina about the texts?"

"Not right away, but after he mentioned her by name, I did."

"Did you tell anyone else about the texts?"

"I told some other girls and the few guys I asked, but then I stopped talking about it." Katie looked towards the door and then took another sip of her drink. She watched Luke carefully.

Luke assumed she knew what questions were next. "When did you agree to help him?"

"After he brought up my father," Katie admitted softly. She toyed with the cup in front of her, avoiding eye contact with Luke.

"What did he know about your father?"

"Do I really have to get into that? I don't want to get my father into trouble. This is exactly what I was trying to avoid."

Luke leaned back and watched her. He debated on how hard to push her. At some point, someone would have to uncover what Katie's father was doing, but it wouldn't be Luke's jurisdiction, and so far, he hadn't heard more than speculation about a crime. "You don't have to get into it with me right now, but it's important I understand what this person knew, how they could have known it and how serious the threat was. Does that make sense?"

Katie nodded. "They knew about my father's business dealings. Things I heard growing up but didn't know for sure. He threatened to expose my father. I figured it could get him in serious trouble."

"Did you ask your parents if what the person in the text said was true?"

"No. I didn't want them to worry. I thought I could handle it."

"Obviously not," Luke said, frustrated. "Tell me what led up to the night Cristina went missing. I've heard from all of the girls that you convinced them to follow your lead in getting Cristina to leave by herself so was that your idea or his?"

"His. He picked the night and the bar," Katie explained, rubbing her eyes again. Katie's voice was steady, but to Luke's dismay, she had not even a hint of remorse. "He told me all I had to do was go out with my friends and bring Cristina along. He told me to make sure we were all drunk and having a good time, and to leave Cristina behind or convince her to leave. All I was supposed to do was make sure she was separated from us."

"You didn't think that was strange? You weren't concerned about your friend's safety, leaving her alone with this person who had already threatened to expose your father?"

"I didn't think he'd kill her! I just thought he wanted to meet her and ask her out."

"Katie, come on. You're a smart girl. Guys ask girls out all the time. They don't need to go through this elaborate hoax. They don't text their friends anonymously and then threaten them with exposing their parents to law enforcement. You had to have some clue this wasn't normal."

They stared at each other for several long minutes. Finally, it was Katie who broke the stalemate. She said coldly, "Sometimes things have to be sacrificed for the greater good."

CHAPTER 62

I had lazed my way through the day, but it was time for real work. After meeting my mother and sister for an early lunch at the Whistling Kettle in downtown Troy, I headed to the Russell Sage College administration office to see if I could find more about Michael Bauer. It was a quick walk from the restaurant, just a few short blocks. I was pleased to see how much the downtown area had been built back up. There were more shops and restaurants that lined the narrow streets than at any time in my recent history. The stately brownstones still looked the same, but it was clear life had sprung back in the city. And with it, the arrival of hipsters.

I wasn't such a fan of them with their tight cuffed jeans and unruly beards. They all looked like clones of one another – like they had been dropped from the sky from Brooklyn. Maybe it was the price of progress.

Lunch had been good. It was nice to catch up with my mother and sister. It was even nicer, that they were both so consumed with their own lives, that neither had pressured me much about my own. For a while, my mother had been focused on when I was going to marry Luke. She asked nearly every time I had called if we were any closer to a marriage proposal. I was closer to being ready. All I had to do was say the word and Luke would propose. He'd been ready for longer than I was even thinking marriage. His fearlessness was one of the things I admired most about him.

I checked the campus map one more time and realized that I was standing right in front of the building I needed. I pulled open the large wooden door and came face to face with several students on their way out. I stepped out of the way. They all looked so young.

I navigated through the first floor to the reception area. A woman, probably well into her fifties, sat behind the desk. She was on the phone and held up a finger asking me to wait. I smiled in response. I stood back, feeling a bit awkward. I hadn't even thought up a reason why I'd be asking about Michael Bauer. I hoped they could direct me to his office if he still worked there.

The woman finished her call. She stapled papers, slamming the stapler down. "Sorry, it doesn't always work. You really have to hit it." She put the papers in a neatly arranged pile of others on the side of her desk. "What can I help you with?"

I approached. "I need to find information on a professor. Even his office number or phone extension will do. I'm looking for Michael Bauer. He teaches history."

"There's no one here by that name."

"Are you sure?"

She leveled a look at me. "I've worked here for nearly twenty years. I know everyone. There's no Michael Bauer here."

"Was there a Michael Bauer? It would have been right around 2000. I'm fairly certain he taught here."

"That's a long time ago, Miss. What do you want with him?"

"I um," I stuttered. I exhaled and went with the truth. "I'm an investigator working on a case. I just thought he might have some information to help me."

The woman frowned. She turned to her computer and tapped her fingers aggressively against the keys. "I shouldn't give you this information. But it's so long ago now I can't see how it matters."

I felt a glimmer of hope. "I really appreciate that. I don't even know if he has the information I'm looking for, but if he does it could be a huge break for me." There was no way I was telling this woman the case he was connected to. She'd probably throw me out.

The woman put on her glasses and looked at the screen. "No," she said sternly, peering up at me over the rim of her glasses. "Michael Bauer has never been a professor here. It does look like he might have taught a few lectures for the history department. We have no information that can help you."

Dejected, I walked out of the building. As my feet hit the sidewalk, I felt a hand on my shoulder. I turned to find a young woman about my age. She had blonde shoulder-length hair and a bright smile. "I'm Paige. I teach in the history department here. I think I know who you're talking about."

She looked back behind her at the building and turned to me with a concerned look on her face. "Let's talk someplace else. Can you meet me at the Whistling Kettle in twenty minutes? I want to grab something from my office first."

"Sure, no problem."

I walked back to the Whistling Kettle. The hostess joked with me that I liked the place so much I was back again. I asked for a table a little farther removed from the rest so Paige and I could have some privacy. At that point, most of the lunch rush was over, so the hostess obliged my request.

I ordered some tea and waited. When Paige walked in, I stood and waved to her from our table.

Paige put her bag down next to her and got comfortable. She ordered some tea as well. After the server left, she dug through her bag. "I brought some information that I thought might be of help to you." Paige handed me a file folder.

I laid the file in front of me on the table and thumbed through the pages. It contained information about Michael Bauer's lecture series and some biographical information. There was no photo of him in the file. The information seemed solid. He had his Ph.D. in history with some expertise in the Civil War. He had gone to the University of Virginia. Nothing seemed unusual or out of place to me.

I looked back at Paige. "Do you happen to have a photo of him or know what he looks like?"

"No, I wasn't here then. This is all we had."

I closed the folder. "It looks like he was only here at the university in the summer of 2000 into the fall. He had two lecture series running. Is that true?"

Paige took a sip of her tea. "From what I know he gave a lecture over the summer for faculty and then another to students in late September going into October. There was an older professor here when I started. He was the head of the department. He used to talk about Michael Bauer all the time. He didn't like Michael; he said he flirted with the female students. Some of the female staff went further and said that Michael made them feel uncomfortable, but no one pinpointed why. Many have wondered if he could have been involved in that girl's disappearance and murder."

I tried to hide the shock on my face. I had thought Michael Bauer was a potential lead, but I hadn't realized anyone might have suspected him. Jack believed the man at face value. He wasn't one to make mistakes.

"Was that gossip or was there proof to anything?"

"Mostly just gossip, but I remember one of the other professors saying something like Michael had asked him to say he was with him the night the girl went missing. The other professor said that he wouldn't lie."

"Are any of these people still here at the college?"

"No, the head of the department passed away a few years ago and most people have moved on. The college forbade Michael Bauer from ever coming back to teach. They don't mess around with the safety of our students."

"Do you have any idea where I can find Michael Bauer now?"

Paige finished the last of her tea. She tucked the folder back in her bag. "Oh yeah, he lives in Troy. He's from here, I guess. Do you know that old Colonial-looking house on South Lake with the wrought iron fence and horseshoe driveway? That's his. I assume he still lives in Troy."

CHAPTER 63

I should have waited for Jack, but he was golfing with Frank. It was too cold for golf, but they must have found a place still open this late in the season. The two really hit it off. They promised me they were strategizing while playing the back nine, but I knew they were just enjoying retirement – not that I blamed them. Jack said he'd go with me later and to just wait for him. He cautioned me not to go alone, but I was anxious to talk to Michael.

I'd driven by this house a million times in my youth. The house was on a well-traveled route and sat far back from the road, high up on a hill. The property was dotted by mature trees and was neatly landscaped. It was marked in front by a horseshoe driveway that remained gravel. It had never been paved over. It was one of those grand houses that you drive by enough that you start to wonder its story and about those living in the place.

I slowly made my way up the drive, gravel crunching under my tires. There were no cars visible, but maybe there was a garage or something farther back or on the side of the house. I pulled up just shy of the front door, put the car in park and got out, taking in my surroundings. Stones crunched under my shoes, which sounded twice as loud against the eerie quiet. I knocked once and then twice. There was no answer.

I hesitated only for a moment, deciding if I should have a look around. I shouldn't but the temptation was too great. I took a quick glance toward the road and then made my way to the side of the house. There were no doors and the few windows were all covered. I walked around to the back. The trees, with their barren branches, were dense. I could hear my heart beating, my anxiety ratcheting up. By the time I reached the back of the house, I was sweating on a chilly fall day. I cursed myself for not waiting for Jack, but I didn't turn back.

There was nothing but woods in the back of the house. The yard was smaller than I would have thought, but if the owner cut down some trees, they'd have a bigger space. There was a small patio with tables and chairs and a built-in pool surrounded by wrought iron black fencing. It was closed for the season. Other than that, it was just a dense forest of trees. I looked at the back of the house. All the windows were covered by blinds or drapes. There was nothing that looked abnormal.

It was when I turned to leave that I caught sight of two windows almost flush with the ground. They were basement windows. Curiosity got the better of me. I crouched low near the windows and took a look. I had to lie on my belly to get up close enough to see through them.

The windows were dusty and obscured most of the interior from sight. It was also dark. There were no lights on in the basement. From what I could see though, it was a typical basement. The ceiling was low, there were shelves visible and the floor looked like it was dirt. There didn't seem to be much down there.

I scanned the shelves and caught sight of what I thought might be a pink mask. The color stood out in the otherwise drab space. The mask had lace and reminded me of the one Luke had said his sister had on the night of Halloween. It sat on the third shelf from the top with other items, an ornate hand mirror and what looked like women's clothing. It held my attention for a few seconds longer.

A rustling sound made me jump and drove me to my feet. I stood quickly and turned around to look out between the trees. I didn't see anything. Dread washed over me. I hightailed it out of there quickly. My phone rang loudly as I was getting into the car. I lowered the volume without even looking to see who it was. Once securely in my car, I locked the door. I took one last look at the house before turning down the driveway.

As I exited, a car turned up the other side of the driveway. I locked eyes with the driver. Was it Michael? I didn't stop to ask. I slammed my foot down on the gas as soon as the road was clear. They watched me as I departed.

I lived close. I could have walked to the house so it only took me a few minutes to make it back home. My hands were shaking as they gripped the steering wheel. Sweat beaded at my hairline.

It was only once I was in my driveway that I checked to see who had called. It was Jack. I let myself in, and Dusty rushed me as soon as I entered. I scratched him behind the ears as I called Jack. "Sorry I missed you. I'm just getting home."

"When I got back from golfing, I went through some of the witness statements again. Shawn Westin's statement is bothering me. I never could clear him completely. There was that hour window. People saw him at the party late that night, but there is another gap we never accounted for after about two in the morning. Maybe he took Amanda and killed her and then kept her body in his truck. He could go back to the party and then go out in the middle of the night and stage the body in the cemetery. It's possible."

"It certainly is, I guess. Where is he now?" The more I knew about the case, the less Shawn Westin felt like the right guy. A date rape gone wrong doesn't end with a stab through the heart and fingers cut off.

"He's here. I thought he would have moved away. He stuck around after university and got a job in some tech company in Albany. Frank did a couple of searches and found him for me. We should pay him a visit." Jack yelled something to Frank, but I couldn't make out what he was saying.

I thought they were just golfing, but it seemed they got some work done after all. "We can do that. He doesn't feel like the right guy to me anymore but maybe he knows something he didn't say before."

"What time should we pick you up?"

"Give me about an hour. I need to take care of a few things."

Jack ended the call. I went to my bedroom and changed my clothes. My back was still damp with sweat, which made me shiver against the cold fall air. I took a long hot shower and then put on a cozy sweater and jeans. I dried my hair and ran a brush through it. I sat in the chair and opened my laptop and did a search on Michael Bauer. I stumbled across a wealth of information.

CHAPTER 64

Cooper and Adele were back at his hotel comparing notes. He had offered to bring his laptop down to the hotel lobby, but Adele asked if he had a table or desk in his room. Cooper did so she suggested they meet there instead. Cooper agreed it was certainly more private.

Cooper was seated at the desk while Adele took a chair near the window. "What did you think of Professor Marlow?"

Cooper tried to weigh his words carefully, but then just opted for the truth. "I think he's covering up something. I have a feeling there were more people than just Hope who suspected the man. At the very least, Michael Hayes was known to be inappropriate with female students."

Adele rubbed her forehead. "Why didn't my sister tell anyone that he was bothering her?"

Cooper turned the desk chair to face her. He said gently, "Maybe he wasn't bothering her. I know everyone thinks of your sister as a bookworm, totally focused on her studies. I'm not saying she wasn't. Is there a chance Jordan could have simply liked the attention?"

Adele balked at the idea.

"Think about it," Cooper encouraged. "Jordan didn't have many friends. She wasn't really experiencing university like most freshmen.

Here was a man who was taking an interest in her. I'm sure a lot of university freshmen would have felt flattered. It doesn't mean your sister did something wrong."

"I know," Adele groaned. She made eye contact with Cooper. "We were raised pretty sheltered. I'm sure she was flattered by the attention. I just wish it hadn't gotten her killed."

Big fat tears spilled down Adele's face. Cooper wasn't sure what to do. He hesitated for only a few seconds and then went over to her and sat on the edge of the bed near the chair. Cooper reached out and put a hand on her shoulder. Adele put her hand on top of Cooper's. The two sat there like that for a few minutes while Adele cried.

After a few moments, Adele pulled herself together. She chided herself for the outburst and smiled at Cooper. "I really appreciate your support in this. I've not had any help with my sister's case. I've been carrying this alone for a long time. My parents are older. They don't like to talk about it. Friends and work colleagues treat me like I have the plague. Like if I talk about it, it could happen to them. I really appreciate you just being here."

Cooper felt oddly comfortable with Adele. "I do know what you mean. When my friend Luke lost his sister, I felt paralyzed. There wasn't much I could do, but it wasn't my loss. I knew Lily and cared about her, but I wasn't family. I've always felt like I had to keep it together for Luke, but I was grieving, too. I felt the loss, not like he did, but I felt it. It's been hard especially the times over the years Luke has tried to look into the case. He loses himself completely. I feel a sense of obligation to help get this solved, not just for your family but for Luke's and all the others."

Adele gave him a sad smile. "You're a good friend. Luke is lucky to have you."

Cooper stood, feeling uncomfortable by his admission. "We aren't going to solve this by sitting around feeling sorry for ourselves. Let's try to track down Michael Hayes."

Adele reached for his hand and squeezed it. "It's okay to have feelings, you know. We both can't be tough all the time. You seem like one of those guys who avoid emotions at all cost."

Cooper ran a hand through his hair. "You caught me. I'm the strong silent type." He laughed at his own joke.

Adele laughed, too. "Let's find Hayes."

Cooper sat down at the desk and Adele pulled up her chair. Together they searched several websites and social media platforms but were coming up with nothing. There was no Michael Hayes to be found that matched his description and background. If Hayes was just about thirty in 1993, Cooper figured the man would be in his mid-fifties now. They were coming up with a blank.

"It's like he doesn't exist," Adele said frustrated.

"He exists. I'll start looking at some of the universities on the list and see if they have heard of a Michael Hayes. I'm going to ask specifically for the years of each murder. If we can't track him down now, at least we can see if he had a connection to other colleges."

Adele checked her watch. "That's a great idea. I have to head to my office for a bit. Call me if you find anything. Can we meet tomorrow?"

"Sure." Cooper walked her to his door.

Standing in the hall, Adele reached up and gave Cooper a hug. "I really do appreciate all you're doing to help me." Adele kissed him on the cheek before she turned and left.

Cooper stood there for several moments. He traced his fingers along his cheek where Adele's kiss had lingered. There was a chemistry between them Cooper hadn't been expecting. Not that it meant anything or was something he was going to explore. It just surprised him.

Cooper watched Adele walk down the hall. Before stepping onto the elevator, she turned and waved. Cooper waved back and then stepped into the room, the door sliding closed behind him.

Cooper rubbed his eyes and yawned. This case was taking a toll. Years of not finding answers and running into dead ends were catching up with him. Cooper picked up his cellphone and stared at it. He wasn't sure who to call. He pulled Luke up in his contacts but didn't have much solid to report. Cooper tossed the phone back on the bed and went back to his computer.

For the next couple of hours, Cooper called each university where a victim had gone missing. He pretended to do a background check on Michael Hayes for future employment. Many of the universities had not heard of him or Cooper was routed to human resource personnel who would need to get back to him with employment dates. That's all Cooper needed to verify. He just needed to know if Michael Hayes was teaching any lectures at the universities the same years the victims went missing.

In the end, Cooper confirmed that Michael Hayes was at four of the universities the same years that victims went missing. It was not enough to convict the man, but Cooper felt a growing confidence in his gut. He finally felt like he was on the right track.

CHAPTER 65

Hours after the interview with Katie, Luke still reeled from the girl's coldness in playing a part in someone's murder. Luke had even contemplated arresting her, but Det. Tyler and Captain Meadows had talked him out of it. Both believed that while Katie was cold, they didn't think she meant any real harm to come to anyone. They agreed that no good would come from arresting her right now. They convinced Luke they were right. Even though Luke was uncomfortable with letting Katie off the hook, he made the strategic investigative decision to let it ride for now. Luke swore though that he still considered arresting her.

Before Katie was driven home by Det. Tyler, because Luke could not stand another second looking at her, he had confiscated her cellphone. He put an immediate call into her cell provider with a warrant for all call and text records. Katie provided Luke the number the killer had been texting from, but Luke hadn't done anything with it yet. He was biding his time. His plan was to hold on to the phone and see if any texts came in from the killer.

Luke clicked through files on his computer, not even sure what he hoped to find. He was so focused on what was in front of him, it took him a moment to register that Captain Meadows slid a bagged letter across his desk. "This came in while you were interviewing Katie. It's postmarked from Gettysburg, Pennsylvania."

Luke cursed. He turned the bag right side up and took in the killer's now-familiar handwriting.

Lucas,

You disappoint me. I thought you would have made some progress by now. I've been watching the news carefully and you seem to have absolutely no leads. I know you may be keeping clues close to the vest, but you seem no further along than when we started this little game. I thought you were a worthy adversary. You've disappointed me greatly. You've let your sister down once again. The mouse only lets the cat chase for so long before he grows tired and retreats back to his home. I say farewell for now. Better luck next year on the harvest fields.
The Professor

Captain Meadows studied Luke's face carefully as he read the letter. Luke felt his boss eyeing him with each word he read. When Luke was done, he had a smile on his face. "He thinks he's won. He really has no idea that we have as much information as we have."

"I thought you'd like that." Captain Meadows sat at Tyler's desk. "What's your plan now?"

Luke held up Katie's cellphone. "I'm going to figure out what I want to say and text him, pretending to be Katie. I've got a call into the provider so we can ping the location. He moves around so much, I need up to the minute info. We know he was here. We need to know where he is now. It looks like he's moving north. A letter postmarked from Georgia and now Pennsylvania. First, though, I'm going to the bar to see if anyone interreacted with this guy and see if there is surveillance coverage. The uniformed cops said no when they checked the bar, but I want to confirm for myself."

"Do me a favor and call Gabe in Fayetteville first. I want to see if we have any leads from the dark web."

"Will do."

Captain Meadows got up. He made it across the room and turned back to Luke. "Get some rest, too. I don't want this case consuming your life."

"No worries, Cap. I've got it under control this time."

"That's what I like to hear."

As soon as Captain Meadows was gone, Luke put a call into Gabe. The detective was quick to answer, but unfortunately, said everything was fairly quiet in the chat rooms. He promised Luke they'd keep at it. He also told Luke that Aaron Roberts produced a solid alibi for Friday night. He had been in Texas and was nowhere near Little Rock.

Before they hung up, Luke was struck with an idea. He asked Gabe to take another crack at Aaron Roberts related to his sister's case and see if the man was hiding any skeletons in his closet. Maybe Roberts was nothing more than one of the killer's helpers like Katie and the two men. Maybe that was why he drove Lily home that night. At least if Gabe was digging around in the man's past, Luke hoped they might stumble on something. Gabe agreed.

Luke gathered his things and left the station. He drove to the bar the girls had been at the night Cristina went missing. Along the route, he checked for security cameras but nothing jumped out.

Luke rolled up to the dive bar and was surprised to see cars in the lot. It was early still and the place didn't strike him as somewhere people went until late into the night. They had no food menu. The drinks were cheap and the clientele ran from locals to university kids. Luke always thought it was kind of an after the regular bar kind of place.

Luke pulled open the door and the six men inside, sitting on barstools, turned to look at him. It was like Luke was interrupting some sort of meeting. As Luke took a step inside, they all turned back to their drinks. Most of them looked older than Luke. He'd probably place them well into their fifties and beyond.

Luke slid up to the bar and motioned for the bartender. Luke flashed his badge and handed him the photo and composite sketch. "I'm looking into the disappearance and murder of the university student. This was the last place she was seen. We have reason to believe a man abducted her after leaving this bar. From our understanding, he was here at the same time. Does he look familiar?"

The bartender studied the photo and sketch, taking each one and lifting it to his eyes, then setting it back down. He handed both back to Luke. "I've seen him for sure. I don't know his name. He's been in a few times. He doesn't drink, which I thought was odd. Why come to a bar, especially here, and not drink?"

"What do you mean he doesn't drink? Does he just sit here?"

"He orders a beer but nurses it until it gets warm. A couple of times, he's carried it to the bathroom with him. When he came back, the bottle was empty. I didn't catch on at first, but it's a small place, and he's kind of an odd guy."

It didn't surprise Luke that the guy didn't drink. Most people who thrive on control don't do things that let their inhibitions slip. "You got any surveillance in here?"

"No, we never did. I tried to get the owner to install it, but he's too cheap. Look at the place though. It's falling down. We aren't going high-tech now."

"Understood." Luke looked around the bar, hoping something would strike him out of the ordinary but there was nothing. It was small. He imagined when it got crowded people were elbow to elbow.

The bartender poured one of the patrons a drink and then wiped down the counter. Luke called out to him. "You ever talk to the guy? Find out anything about him?"

"Not really. The guy was in here maybe three or four times. He'd sit, nurse a drink. He might have talked to other patrons but otherwise, he kept to himself."

Luke's attention diverted to a man at the end of the bar who had interrupted the conversation. Luke looked down the length of the bar at him. "I didn't catch what you said."

The man got up from his seat and walked towards Luke. He took the photos out of Luke's hand and appraised them. He handed them back. "I've talked to him. He's not from around here. He's from up north."

"How do you know that?"

"I heard him on the phone once. I caught a couple of words. When he was done, I asked him where he was from because it wasn't the south."

"What was his response?"

"He looked like I scared him. Like he was really surprised anyone noticed. My wife is from the northeast, and you know as sure as I'm standing here, that accent isn't easily hidden."

"Did he say anything?"

"He got a real sly smile on his face after a couple of seconds and then told me he was from the home of Uncle Sam."

Luke raised his eyebrows. "Uncle Sam? Like the guy with the white beard on the posters?"

"That would be the one."

"Where would that be?" Luke had no idea what that meant. The home of Uncle Sam. Luke thought he was a fictional character, some general representation of the government or something.

"Don't know. I thought he'd lost his damn mind."

CHAPTER 66

Jack and Frank picked me up in front of my house. As soon as I sat in the backseat, I detailed everything I had found on Michael Bauer including his education, background and that he often lectures at universities each summer and fall.

I explained, "Michael Bauer is fifty-five years old and has been lecturing since his twenties when he was a Ph.D. candidate. He primarily travels in the northeast and south with occasional trips to the west. He's highly intelligent, from Troy, and comes from a family of considerable wealth. He could easily be the killer."

Frank turned around to look at me from the passenger seat. "That's kind of a jump. Those are some interesting facts, but you got anything else?"

"No," I said dejectedly. "I only just started looking through. I have to cross-reference universities he's lectured at with dates of murders, but I thought it was a good start."

"It is," Jack admitted. He switched lanes on the bridge to turn onto the highway. "Let's get the interview with Shawn Westin over and we can talk more."

Frank dug around in the bag he had on his lap. He pulled out a file folder and handed it back to me. "We have everything in there. Shawn went back south for a few months after graduation. He came back though and got a job in Albany. He commuted by train to New

York City to take graduate courses at Columbia. He's unmarried, works for an investment firm, and sits on a few nonprofit boards."

I read over the file, taking in everything that Frank had just said. It put to rest all the questions about where Shawn had gone after university and what he had done. He was here in Albany. If he was the killer, there was no other university connection like there was for Michael Bauer. If Shawn Westin killed Amanda, I'd be hard-pressed to make the case that he killed the rest, at least with the information in front of me. It just didn't feel right in my gut. I told that to Jack and Frank.

Frank responded before Jack could. "It's a lead, that's all it is. We don't know what we don't know. Let's ask him some questions and see what he has to say. At the very least, he might know more about that night than he told Jack the first time."

I couldn't argue that point. We rode the rest of the way in silence. I wanted to get back and focus my efforts on Michael Bauer. Nearly twenty minutes later, the three of us rolled up to a simple two-story house in a nicer part of Albany, near St. Peter's Hospital. I checked my watch. It was close to seven. Shawn should be out of work by now, and the lights in the house indicated that at least someone was probably home.

I lagged behind Jack and Frank as they made their way to the door. Jack rapped twice loudly against it. A woman, with dark red hair tied back in a ponytail and wearing simple jeans and flats, answered the door.

"Is Shawn Westin home?" Jack asked.

The woman looked at the three of us and turned to yell for Shawn. A man smaller than I was imagining walked towards the door. He couldn't have been much taller than I am. He had closely cut blond hair and was drying his hands on a dishtowel.

The woman moved out of the way for Shawn. He looked us over and then recognition took hold. He remembered Jack. "How can I help you?"

Jack made introductions and asked if we could come in. Shawn obliged. The woman made herself scarce as the four of us sat in the neat, modernly furnished living room. I had to admit that Shawn had good taste or the woman did.

"I remember you," Shawn said, looking directly at Jack. "You're a cop. The detective that was involved when Amanda went missing. How can I help you after all these years?"

Jack looked to Frank and then back at Shawn. "What can you remember about that night?"

Shawn sat back. He looked toward the ceiling. When he looked at us again, his eyes were watery and red. "Amanda and I got into an argument and she left. That was the last I saw of her. I've always been mad at myself for not stopping her from leaving. I was a drunk college kid. I was in a world of my own, one that didn't have things like murder. I had no idea that Amanda wouldn't have made it safely home. I thought we'd patch things up the next day."

"You had a vehicle then, right?" Frank pressed.

"Yeah, a lot of us did."

"You were also missing for about an hour when no one can account for you. Is that correct?" Frank leaned forward on the couch and rested his arms on his knees. He was an imposing guy even sitting.

Shawn fumbled over his words. He regained his composure and explained, "I was angry with my girlfriend. We had a huge argument in front of our friends. I went upstairs to my room and slammed the door. I sat there and got high. I didn't want to see anyone or talk to anyone until I calmed down. I don't know how long I was up there. Next thing I knew, a few of the guys came looking for me. I don't even remember now who that was. I'm sure it was in my statement from then. By the time I went back downstairs, Amanda was gone."

"When was the very last time you saw Amanda?" I asked.

Shawn looked me dead in the eyes. "We were arguing on the front lawn. I thought she was flirting with one of her professors. I saw them a couple of times in downtown Troy. I had heard rumors, too. I thought maybe they were having an affair or something. I didn't like him. I didn't like my girlfriend flirting with another guy."

The three of us exhaled loudly at nearly the same time. It was a familiar story. I was about to ask for the name when Jack spoke first.

"I reread your statement before coming today. You didn't mention anything like that back then. Why the change?" Jack asked accusingly.

Shawn shrugged. "Age, I guess. Perspective. I was embarrassed then. I had an ego. I didn't want to admit I was even worried about my girlfriend cheating on me. The fight wounded my pride."

"And now?" Frank pressed.

"It's not about me," Shawn admitted. "It never was. I've regretted that fight every day since then. I was a stupid kid. I was arrogant. It took me several years to grow up."

"Where were you after the party ended? We can account for you later in the evening. Your fraternity brothers saw you there, but what about when everyone went to sleep?"

"I crashed, too. It had been a long night."

I believed Shawn. His body language was open. He answered questions directly. There was nothing about him that indicated he was lying or trying to withhold information. We were on a fishing expedition with the wrong man, and I hoped it ended soon. All I wanted was the name of the professor, but Frank and Jack pressed on before I could get a word in.

"When did you know that Amanda was missing?" Frank asked.

"Sometime the next day best I can remember. I tried to call her. I got one of her friends who told me Amanda never came home. I went down there to her dorm immediately. I searched the campus. I looked all over, talked to every friend."

Shawn got choked up. His voice was cracking. "When the news broke that her body had been found, it destroyed me. I stopped going to classes. I had to go to counseling. I was a mess."

Frank started to speak but my frustration hit a level that I couldn't contain myself anymore. "Who was the professor that you thought was flirting with Amanda?"

"Michael Bauer. Amanda wasn't the only girl he flirted with, but he paid particular attention to her."

"Do you think he could have taken her?"

A light went on behind his eyes. Shawn sat on the edge of the couch. "Is that who you think did this? I never put it together, but yeah, I do. He lives in Troy, you know? There was a rumor at our frat that his house had a skeleton dressed as a woman in the basement. He was a creep."

"What?" I asked incredulously.

"Years before Amanda was murdered, a couple of frat brothers broke into his house, that creepy white one, up on the hill. In the basement, they saw a skeleton in a woman's dress. They all thought it was like a Halloween decoration or something, but one of the guys was positive it was real."

CHAPTER 67

Before we left, Shawn explained the story or at least lore he had heard about Michael Bauer. It was Michael's parents who had owned that house where he lived. His father was a professor at one of the local universities. Shawn wasn't sure which one. His mother had passed away when Michael was young. His father had died when he was off at university. As the only heir, the house was his. Michael had been living in it for years.

Shawn Westin explained that the man was a bit of an enigma. There was a story once passed around that he had been engaged in college, but the woman had broken his heart. Other than flirting with university-aged girls Shawn said no one ever saw him with women. They wondered if he had any friends at all because on the few occasions they saw him in Troy, he was always alone.

I found it strange that a group of fraternity brothers would know so much about a local so I had pressed Shawn for understanding. He explained that one of the fraternity brothers, who had grown up in Troy, wanted to see the inside of the house. When Michael was out of town, they broke in. It was a dare to check out the house. What they found had left them all freaked out. Both the house and its owner had become the basis for passed down lore and speculation.

It was the first I had ever heard the story, but it wasn't surprising. Growing up, I had no idea who owned the house, but it sat back on the hill behind its wrought iron fencing screaming to be explored by nosy residents of our community.

The skeleton in the basement, however, was a bit surprising. I didn't recall the house ever being decorated for any holiday other than Christmas. I certainly never went to the house at Halloween. I would have remembered that. I'd have to ask my mother if she had ever heard a similar story.

"I thought I saw women's things on a shelf in the basement," I admitted once we were back in the car.

Jack turned abruptly. "What do you mean you saw women's things in the basement? I told you to wait for me."

"I know but you were busy so I just checked it out. He wasn't home."

"He could have been. If you really think Michael Bauer is the killer that was a really risky stupid move," Jack admonished. He turned back and focused on the road, leaving me feeling like a kid who had been scolded.

"I think that's the point, Jack. We don't know if he's the killer or not. If he is, we can't approach him like that. It will spook him and scare him off."

"What do you mean?" Frank asked.

I tried to find a way to explain so they'd understand. "The killer wants to play a game. That's why he sent the letters to Luke. He wants to show he's smarter than everyone. The killer has an above-average intellect. That was obvious in the letters, and he's gotten away with this for so long. Not to mention, he sent Luke on a wild goose chase in Fayetteville while he was killing in Little Rock. I don't think there is anything about this he hasn't planned."

I paused for a second to see if they had questions. I went on, "If Michael Bauer is the killer, we can't go to him like he is. We have to approach him and act like we need his help. We need to act like we need his intellect to sort through something. Even at that, he might see through it. No matter what, I want to see what's in that basement."

"How do you propose we do that?" Jack asked. "We can't get a search warrant."

"I don't know yet," I admitted. My phone buzzed in my pocket just as we were pulling into my driveway. It was Cooper. I'd have to call him back.

As the car came to a stop, I asked, "Can we agree that we don't think Shawn Westin had anything to with Amanda's death?"

The two looked at each other. "I don't think he did," Frank said.

Jack added, "He's either an exceptional liar and threw us Michael Bauer to redirect us or he's telling the truth. I'm inclined to believe him. He had a very short window to do anything."

"Let's not forget my sister believes she saw the victim get into another car as she walked along the road so that certainly fits with what Shawn said happened. They fought outside. He went up to his room and Amanda left. It fits."

"What's our next step?" Jack asked, turning around in the car to look at me.

"I want to know more about Michael Bauer. I want to know his background. He has a website. I want to see if any of the universities he's taught at were a match to years a victim was killed. Then I think we pay him a visit."

Frank offered, "I can easily check Virginia and see if he was at any of the local universities during the time our victim was killed."

"Did you say he was a lecturer during the summer and fall?" Jack asked.

"Yes, he's basically an expert in the Civil War. He'd go to a university and set up a lecture series. He'd be there for a short period of time. His bio said he uses the winter and spring to work on research. If he's the killer, he's got the whole summer to know the lay of the land. He can easily scope out incoming freshmen at orientation."

Jack turned to Frank. "When you call around to ask about Michael Bauer, also ask what lecturers they had for that summer and fall. We don't know if he always used his real name. This way, we can assess who was there, even if they don't have anyone by his name.

"That's a great idea." We planned to meet in the morning. We all had research assignments. Jack was also going to think through a solid plan for getting into Michael's basement.

"Tell your mother I'll call her later," Jack said as I put my feet to the pavement.

I entered the house through the front door. Dusty met me at the door wiggling around at my feet. My mother and sister were in the kitchen. Their voices were light and full of laughter. The scent of warm chocolate filled the house.

"I'm home!" I yelled as I made my way through the hallway, pulling my sweater over my head and tugging my tee-shirt back down over my tummy. My mother had cranked up the heat. "What smells so good?"

My sister held up a messy chocolate croissant. "I found a new recipe I wanted to try. It's kind of like breakfast for dinner. They don't look so good, but they taste delicious." She took another bite of the pastry.

My mother gave me a hug. "There's real food for dinner if you're hungry. How's the case going?"

I eyed her suspiciously. She normally hated my work. I said tentatively, "It's okay. I think we might have a good lead or two."

My mother sat back down at the table with my sister. I fished around in the fridge pulling together some leftovers. My mother noted, "Jack said you've been working really hard. I don't love what you do, but he says you're good at it."

I smiled at her. "He's mellowing you in your old age."

She threw a dishtowel at me. "I like having you here. If I argue with you, you'll leave."

"That's true." I finished making my plate. Liv devoured another chocolate croissant. "Mom, what do you know about the house on the left as you turn onto Route 2 from Pawling? The white one that sits back up on the hill."

"I know that family has been strange since the day they bought that house in the sixties. There have always been stories about them. What do they have to do with anything?"

CHAPTER 68

Luke never finished his research the night before because his father had called and asked him to stop by the house. Dinner had been waiting for him when he arrived after work. His mother had cooked especially for him. She wanted to ensure Luke had a homecooked meal. He appreciated it more than he could express.

After dinner, Spencer had taken a serious turn. He had pressed Luke about the progress in the case, and more importantly, how he was doing. Luke assured both his parents that the case was going better than expected and that he was fine.

Spencer had reminded Luke that therapy was still an option. Luke had sat stone-faced and listened. He wouldn't disrespect his father, but Luke didn't need the reminder. He still carried the shame of having to go to therapy the first time. He knew everyone needed a mental health checkup now and then. Luke knew how important mental health was and that there was nothing wrong with therapy. He knew all that. He'd even encouraged guys he worked with to see a therapist. He encouraged Riley last year, too. He just felt foolish that he had been so weak that he needed to go.

It galled Luke that he had become so laser-focused on bringing his sister's killer to justice that he had worried his friends and family, enough so, that they thought he needed a break and to talk to someone. Luke was forced to go. The police department hadn't given him the option. Luke would like to say that he learned more about himself or got some great coping skills. He didn't. He participated fully. He talked, listened and shared. He walked away feeling the same. Something did change though. Luke made the decision then and there that he'd hide his desire to catch the killer better than he had prior, and that's exactly what he had done for the last five years.

After Luke assured his parents, he went home. He barely made it in the door before his eyes closed. He crashed hard. Luke didn't even have a chance to call back Cooper or Riley.

After arriving at the station the next day, Luke sat at his desk staring at Katie's cellphone trying to think of a reason why she'd need to text the killer. The cellphone company had sent Luke a readout of her texts earlier that morning. If Luke was going to pull it off, he'd have to pretend to be her. The Professor wasn't stupid. Luke was sure the killer would know a fake.

All Luke needed was a few messages, and they'd be able to trace the cell tower location. Some research into the number showed it was from a common cell provider. It was a pay as you go phone so personal details would be missing. Luke contacted the company and worked with them to ping the phone's location. The data he had received so far was just as he suspected. When the killer was texting Katie, he had been in Little Rock and in the Hillcrest neighborhood where he had mailed the letter. The phone was not pinging now at all. The company suspected the user had either ditched the phone or disabled it. Luke hoped not.

Luke needed an up-to-the-minute location. Getting the killer to communicate was the best way to do that so they could ping the location in the present time. Luke jotted down some practice notes on what to write in the text.

Det. Tyler read over the text messages, too, to see if there was anything relevant, but most of the texts had been exactly as Katie had described. Actually, she had been more honest about the texts than Luke had given her credit for. Luke better understood why she complied. The guy came across like a complete psychopath.

Luke cleared his throat. "You think if I pretend to be really angry that he killed my friend that he'd respond?"

Det. Tyler looked up from the pages he was reading. "Possibly. You really think he's going to care?"

"He might care if she gets agitated enough she might tell someone. I want to hint around that without saying it. I don't want to put her in danger."

Tyler shrugged. "Try it. Let's see if you can pull off being an eighteen-year-old girl."

Luke shot him a look, but Tyler just laughed. Luke wrote a text, deleted it and wrote it again. He wanted to misspell something, but the words were simple. The text read: *You killed Cristina! I'm in trouble. What do I do?*

Luke didn't expect an immediate response, but he still watched the screen carefully for a few minutes. Finally, he set that phone down and picked up his own to call Cooper. It rang a few times before he answered.

"Hey, man, sorry I missed you yesterday. How's it going in Atlanta?"

Cooper excused himself to someone on the other end and then responded. "Good. I'm running down a few leads. I think I know how the killer got the victim out of the library."

Luke listened while Cooper laid out all of the information he had found, including the information on Michael Hayes, his connection to other schools, and the ease with which one could take someone from the library without being seen.

When Cooper was done Luke asked, "Is that the only viable suspect?"

"Yes. I have no other leads to go on. It's been too much time. Hope was one hundred percent credible in my view. I only wish someone had believed her back then."

"Have you spoken to Riley?"

"She hasn't called me back. She find anything yet?"

"Riley's got a Michael Bauer she's interested in for the case up there. Nothing credible so far. I don't even know if she's spoken with him. Michael is a common name, but worth cross-referencing with her. The Professor could be going by an alias."

"I'll call her again. If we're running down the same guy we might as well work together."

"Are you staying in Atlanta?" Luke asked absently. He checked Katie's phone again to see if the killer had responded. The phone remained silent.

"I don't know," Cooper said.

Luke caught some hesitation in his voice. "Is there a reason to stay?"

"I umm…" Cooper's voice cracked.

"Out with it."

Cooper exhaled loudly. "I seem to have some chemistry with the victim's sister. It's weird. We are nothing alike, but we've kind of bonded. Nothing has crossed a line. I just want to make sure she's good with me leaving now. I've been a support to her while I've been here."

Luke chuckled. He'd always known Cooper to avoid commitments with women. His friend prided himself on being able to detach. Where Luke admittedly wore his heart on his sleeve, Cooper's emotions remained behind a fortress. To hear Cooper even think about asking a woman if she was good with him leaving amused Luke. "I think you should do whatever makes you feel comfortable."

"Yeah, I might, but I'm going to check with Riley, too, and see if she needs anything." Cooper said goodbye.

Luke remembered something. "Coop, any chance you know what the home of Uncle Sam means?"

"Riley could tell you. The home of Uncle Sam is Troy. She knows history better than I do. Why?"

Luke's mouth fell open. Could the killer really be from Riley's hometown? Before Luke could respond, Katie's phone chimed. "I have to go, Coop. I'll call you back."

Luke hung up his cell and picked up Katie's phone from his desk. He held it in his hand for a moment before reading the text. He was immediately disappointed. It was a text from one of Katie's friends. Luke shook it off. He got a lead from Cooper. That would have to be enough for now.

He called Riley immediately, but it went straight to voicemail.

CHAPTER 69

Cooper hung up with Luke confused by the question about the home of Uncle Sam. He set his phone down and looked around his empty hotel room. Cooper knew it was probably time to leave Atlanta, but he felt a tug to stay. He needed at least to see Adele one more time. Cooper figured she'd be at work, but tried her cell.

Adele answered faster than Cooper had anticipated, and he stumbled over his words. He felt a bit strange, like a kid calling for his first date. He brushed it off. "Sorry to bother you at work. I did some research on Michael Hayes. I was able to confirm he's been at four universities when a similar murder took place."

"What were the circumstances of those cases?" Adele asked. The anticipation in her voice was apparent.

"The victims, all freshmen, disappeared after leaving Halloween parties. No one other than your sister disappeared from the school itself. None of the girls on those four cases have been found."

"Why do you think my sister is the only one missing from on campus?"

Cooper switched the phone from one ear to the other. He sat down in the comfortable chair Adele had been in the night before. "The man who calls himself The Professor claims your sister's case was the first. I was most interested in the case because of that and because your sister was missing from campus. I can't know for sure, but if I had to guess, I'd say he wasn't as organized then. He probably didn't have the planning he had in later cases. I think he realized the risk he was taking and minimized his direct exposure on later cases. Basically, he figured out how to take the girls without being seen so publicly."

Adele didn't say anything.

"You okay?" Cooper asked gently.

"It's just not knowing where she is. It's too much some days. Do you think she will ever be found?"

Cooper didn't want to lie, but the truth was harsh. Even if Jordan was found now, she'd be skeletal remains and possibly not even intact. Cooper knew Adele could take the truth, he just didn't want to be the one to deliver it. He sidestepped. "I don't know. It's been a long time. I'd say the chances are low. Have you ever held a service for her or anything like that?"

"No, but maybe once you catch the killer we will. Would you come to it?"

"Yes, I'll be there for you," Cooper said emphatically.

"I'd like that." Adele hesitated. Then all at once, she added quickly, "Do you have time to see me today?"

"Absolutely," Cooper said far too quickly and enthusiastically for his liking. His voice dropped an octave. "What time will you be available?"

"How about dinner? I'll text you the time and place."

Cooper smiled as he hung up. He kicked his feet up on the bed and tried to figure out what he was feeling. He rolled a few thoughts around in his head. The simplest answer was that Cooper wanted to get to know Adele better. He didn't care about their differences. He didn't care that they lived nine hours apart. Cooper was genuinely attracted to her and not just to how she looked. Adele was smart, thoughtful and sweet. When they were together, he felt comfortable and like himself. She put him at ease.

Cooper's daydream was cut short by a text. He picked up his phone from his lap and sweat formed at his brow as he looked at the photo. Holly was sitting outside his condo door. The text read: *I'm not leaving until you see me. Where are you?*

This had to stop, even if it meant Cooper had to get confrontational. He immediately texted back:

I'm not home. Won't be home anytime soon. We can't see each other anymore. I'm not looking for anything more than what we had.

Holly responded just as quickly. Dread washed over him as he read her words.

You'll pay for this.

Cooper did not respond. He went into his phone settings and blocked her number. Cooper hoped that in the time he was out of town, Holly would wind herself down and get over it. His truck wasn't there for her to mess with. His condo was secure. What harm could she do?

Cooper got up and stretched feeling a sense of finality with that situation. He grabbed some notes off his desk and called Riley. The phone rang and rang, but she picked up.

"Can you talk now? Luke suggested we update each other."

"Yeah, hold on. I'm moving a few things for my mom in the attic."

A major commotion echoed through the phone. Things were dropped and clunked to the floor. What sounded like a box was being dragged across a floor. "Sorry about that," Riley said. "I'm trying to get a few things done for my mom while I'm home. I've been meaning to call you back."

"I think I've got a name and a lead. Luke said you found something similar. There is a Michael Hayes who is a lecturer on the Civil War. He apparently goes to different universities and teaches a lecture series. I have five universities, including here, he's connected to when there has been a disappearance."

Riley sucked in a sharp breath. "I have a Michael Bauer. He is connected to the case here in Troy and fourteen others. You think they are the same person?"

"I don't know," Cooper said honestly. Although, he didn't believe in coincidences. "Can you find much on your guy? I can't find anything on mine. Not even a photo."

"Michael Bauer has a website," Riley explained. She rattled off the web address and some additional information about the man. "Coop, he's here in Troy. He's from here. This guy is local."

Cooper hadn't been anticipating that, but he thought back to Luke's earlier question. "You need to talk to Luke. He's trying to run down something about the home of Uncle Sam."

"That's here."

"I know. It seems all roads lead back to Troy. Should I come up?"

"Are you done there?"

"I'm meeting with Adele for dinner tonight. I can catch a flight in the morning. It's a fifteen-hour drive up there. I'd rather leave my truck here and fly. I'll rent a car when I get there. Any nearby hotels?"

"You can stay here. I'll pick you up from the airport. Just text and tell me when you're getting in," Riley said definitively.

Cooper didn't argue. It would be good to see her. Cooper really didn't want to drive all that distance but if he left his truck in Atlanta, it was a good excuse to return and see Adele. He was looking forward to their dinner that evening more than he cared to admit.

CHAPTER 70

Luke sat at his desk, frustrated he couldn't reach Riley, even more frustrated, the killer hadn't responded to his text. He typed a few words in the search engine, and sure enough, Cooper had been right. The home of Uncle Sam was Troy, New York.

The popular legend was that the name "Uncle Sam" came from Samuel Wilson, a meatpacker from Troy who had supplied rations for American soldiers during the War of 1812. Wilson had stamped his packages "E.A. – U.S." When someone asked what that stood for, a co-worker jokingly noted that it was for Elbert Anderson, a local contractor at the time, and Uncle Sam, referring to Samuel Wilson. The U.S. had actually stood for the United States, but a legend was born regardless.

Whether the legend was true or not, Samuel Wilson was real and Troy certainly took the story and ran with it. There was a monument for the man and even artistic statues that had dotted the downtown area at one time. Visitors could even check out Samuel Wilsons' burial plot in Oakwood Cemetery. There were businesses named in his honor as well.

Luke loved history and read extensively but he'd never heard this story. He guessed that beyond the northeast, most people probably hadn't heard it before either. The killer had made a reference to the place. He said that's where he was from. Luke didn't know if the man was serious or not, but he had some connection to Troy, that Luke knew without question.

Wrapping up the rest of that research, Luke mulled over his next move. He checked Katie's cellphone again and fired off another text: *If you don't respond I'm going to the police. I don't care what you say about my dad.*

It was impulsive, but Luke hoped the killer could feel the urgency. Luke drummed his finger against his desk. He thought about what Cooper had said about Michael Hayes and what Riley had told him about Michael Bauer. Neither had mentioned anything about his sister's case or the current. Luke looked on the University of Arkansas Little Rock website for anything about a speaker over the summer and fall but came up blank.

Luke placed a call to the administration. After being routed to a few different offices and then finally sent to the head of the history department, Luke found the answer he was seeking. The university did have a lecture series that summer and fall held in collaboration with a couple of other area universities. The speaker's name was Hayes Bauer. Luke sat up straighter in his chair. That couldn't be a coincidence.

"I need everything you have on the man," Luke said forcefully to the head of the history department.

"I don't know if I can just release that information to you, Detective. We do have privacy laws to consider."

"I can get a warrant," Luke pressed. "I can explain to the media how the university is refusing to cooperate in a homicide investigation into one of its students. It's bad enough you might have brought a serial killer to lecture your students. If I were you, I'd cooperate fully."

The man spoke in a hushed voice to someone in the background. Luke was placed on hold for a few minutes. When the man came back, he said, "I can email over to you all the credentials we have on the man. He would not allow us to video his lecture series or photograph him. He was a bit…eccentric."

"How long was he at the university?"

"From July first through last week of October, he stayed in university housing."

"Has that place been cleaned after he left?"

"I have no idea," the man said. "I doubt anyone has used it since though. We don't have that many people coming in from out of town this time of the semester."

"Don't allow anyone else in that space. I'm sending over a crime scene team right now."

The man agreed. He gave Luke the address which was near campus. Luke waved Det. Tyler over to his desk and yelled out for Captain Meadows who had been standing in the hall near the detective bullpen.

"We've got a possible suspect," Luke said quickly. "It's really too much to get into right now but Cooper and Riley stumbled on a lecturer who is at universities the same time as the victims disappear. He's using different variations of his name. Riley hit on a Michael Bauer while Cooper has a Michael Hayes. They are still running down leads to confirm, but I thought it best to just check out the university here and sure enough, Hayes Bauer. He was here from July up until a week ago right after the murder."

"Good work," Captain Meadows said. "You both get over there and start interviewing people to see what you can find out about this guy. I'll make a call to CSI while you're on your way. I'll send a unit to the address right now to keep people out of the space. You never know who the guy you talked to will tell. The last thing we need right now is an audience."

Luke grabbed everything he needed from his desk, including Katie's cellphone. As he walked out of the station to his car, he placed a call to Brie Hall from Fayetteville. She had given them the scoop about Aaron Roberts so maybe she'd know about other lecturers. Luke still wondered how Aaron Roberts fit into the puzzle. He'd been waiting for a call from Gabe with an update.

As the phone rang, Luke thought for sure he'd get voicemail, but on probably the tenth ring, Brie picked up. She was talking to someone else as she answered so Luke waited for a beat until she said hello.

"Brie, it's Luke Morgan. I need to see if there was a lecturer at the university when my sister was there. He would have given a lecture series on history, specifically the Civil War."

"I can talk to the history department. Is there a name of the lecturer?"

"We have a few. Just check to see if there was a lecture series, and if there was, who gave it. I can cross-reference from there."

Brie agreed. Before she hung up, she asked, "How's the case going there? We've been hoping there'd be a break soon."

"This might be the break we need. As soon as you can get me that information the better." Luke hung up. He didn't mean to be so direct or impersonal with her. He was just singularly focused on getting to the spot where the killer might have recently slept.

CHAPTER 71

I finished making up the spare room for Cooper. I had called my mother earlier and she was more than happy to have Cooper stay with us. Cooper had saved my life after all. I knew my mother felt forever in his debt.

I was arranging the last throw pillow when a knock at the front door interrupted me. I was waiting for Frank and Jack so I hoped it was them. We needed to have a short planning meeting before we speak with Michael Bauer. I was ready to go now, but Jack wanted to talk it out first.

My sister yelled up the stairs that she'd get the door. A few seconds later, Jack's and Frank's deep voices filled the downstairs hallway. I placed some bath towels on the chair and yelled that I'd be right down. Cooper probably wouldn't appreciate throw pillows and fresh towels, but my mother liked things a certain way when she had guests.

I found Frank and Jack sitting in the living room. I plopped down on the loveseat across from them. "I have a few updates but what did you want to talk about, Jack?"

Jack looked over at me. I could tell by the look on his face the news wasn't good. His tone was careful and reserved. "We," he started, looking over at Frank, "don't think you should go with us to interview Michael Bauer."

"Why?" I asked, immediately defensive.

"Riley, you were nearly killed last year," Jack said. He looked at me with sympathy. "If what you're saying is true, that this guy has been at several of the universities, we could be dealing with a serial killer. Who knows how he will react if he thinks we are hot on his trail? You don't even know if he's seen you with Luke. If you show up there and he knows you're connected to Luke, he could bolt before we have any real evidence on him."

I hadn't thought of that, but even still my goal was a reaction. I wanted to see what he'd say. I wanted to be there to gauge his reaction. Jack had let him off the hook the first time. And while I trusted Frank, I didn't know his interview style. I was more than prepared.

"I'm going," I said forcefully. "You two wouldn't even be looking at this case if it wasn't for me. If he's seen me with Luke and runs, then we will hunt him down. Besides, I know what to ask and what buttons to push. The goal isn't just to talk to him but to see in the basement, too. I know I saw women's clothing down there and potentially the pink mask Luke's sister was wearing."

"I told you she'd insist," Frank said resigned, looking at Jack. "I don't think three of us should go. I think that will look too suspicious. You and Jack go. Drop me off a block before the house and I'll take a look around the property while you're inside."

We both watched Jack, waiting for a response. He relented. "If I put you in harm's way, your mother is going to kill me."

I stood to leave. I teased, "So, you're less concerned about me and more worried about making your girlfriend angry?"

"Something like that," Jack muttered, following behind me out the door.

We rode the few blocks in silence and dropped Frank off at the light on Pawling and Route 2. It was less than a five-minute walk to Michael's house.

After Frank got out, I looked at Jack. "You ready for this? I don't even know if you believe this is the guy but Cooper said a Michael Hayes was a suspect on the case in Atlanta and a few others. The names are too similar. The background's the same. I'm fairly certain this is the guy."

"Let's just keep an open mind," Jack cautioned. "I don't want to make assumptions. We are focused only on how he can help with

Amanda's case. I agree with what you said the other night. We have to make him believe he can help us. We have to show him we aren't a threat."

Jack pulled up the driveway the same way I had gone the day before. This time there was a dark-colored sedan parked in the back of the house. It was the same car I saw yesterday. I sucked in a deep breath, suddenly not sure of myself. This was not the time to have any sort of panic attack. I reminded myself that Jack was there and Frank would be outside. I was safe.

Jack and I approached the house slowly, taking in the surroundings. As we stood on the porch, Jack was poised to knock, but the door opened before he could. There stood a man. He was close to six-foot, dark hair and solid build. He wasn't fat but he wasn't lean either. He was for lack of a better word – solid. His demeanor was totally relaxed.

"Can I help you?" he asked, holding the door open wide. He held a glass of wine in one hand and a book in the other.

Jack confirmed that the man was Michael Bauer. "I'm Det. Jack Malone. This is Riley. She's a research assistant of mine. I interviewed you on a case from a long time ago. It's a cold case for us now, and we are just taking a second look. I think we uncovered some information where we could use your assistance."

"My memory isn't great, but I'll help if I can," Michael offered and stepped back to let us through.

We stepped into a center hallway. The wide plank wood flooring gleamed. It looked original but had been well-preserved. The living room, off to my left, didn't have one piece of furniture out of place. There was no clutter. It didn't look lived in. It was a bit like stepping into the pages of *Town & Country Magazine*.

"The house is grand isn't it?" Michael remarked.

Embarrassed, I could only imagine the look of awe on my face. "Yes, it is. I grew up in the area and wanted to check out the interior for as long as I can remember."

"I'll give you the tour when we are done, but for now let's sit in the living room. Anything to drink?" Michael offered, holding up his wine glass.

We declined. Jack sat on an antique sofa while I sat nearby perched on the edge of a red chaise. Michael took a high-back chair near the fireplace. He appraised us. "How can I help?"

Jack asked, "Do you remember the murder of Amanda Taylor? She was a Russell Sage student found murdered in Forest Park Cemetery."

Michael pressed his fingers together in his lap. "I recall. I think I might have even known the girl, not well, but through school." He turned to look directly at me. "I have a Ph.D. in Civil War studies. I've always been fascinated by history. The heroes and villains and especially how it can repeat itself if we are not careful."

I don't know if it was the way his dark eyes were piercing mine or how he spoke in clear, clipped sentences but a chill ran down my spine.

"You did," Jack confirmed, bringing Michael's attention back to him. "You had met with her a few times. I had interviewed you after we found Amanda's body."

"That's right. Someone thought I might have been the last one…" Michael's voice trailed off. His phone had chimed. He excused himself and looked at it.

His phone wasn't expensive looking. It was a cheap pay-as-you-go phone.

Michael held it up after reading. "Just a friend. The games they like to play." Michael laughed a deep mirthful laugh like we were all in on the joke.

CHAPTER 72

Jack looked at me as Michael laughed. I could tell he felt as unhinged as I did at the moment. We were there to discuss murder, and he was cackling. We watched the man until he stopped laughing.

"Back to what you were saying, Detective," Michael said, finally reining himself in.

"We think you might be able to help us with Amanda. We have reason to believe someone stalked her before they killed her. Given you met with her several times, are you aware of anyone stalking her in the weeks leading up to her disappearance?"

Michael stared off into space. I wondered what was going through his head. I knew he stalked her, picked her up that night and drove an ice pick through her heart. I knew it as surely as I was sitting there. I wondered if he relived the details.

Michael looked at me. "She had a boyfriend as I recall. He was a bit jealous. We had a meeting downtown at a restaurant and he came storming in once. Is that the kind of thing you're talking about?"

"Anything you can recall is helpful. Amanda was a pretty girl. She was young. I'm sure there were many men interested in her."

"I'm sure. I don't know of anyone besides the boyfriend. Amanda was a sweet girl that I recall. She was very focused on her studies. The boyfriend seemed to be an unneeded distraction."

"When was the last time you saw her?" Jack inquired.

Michael's phone chimed again. He read it and smiled. He typed a quick reply back and tucked the phone back in his pocket. When he looked back at us, Michael fumbled for words. "Saw her? I think it was a couple of days before. I don't really remember. It wasn't important at the time."

"You didn't by chance see her the night she disappeared? Maybe you had given her a ride home?" I pressed.

Michael looked at me with a blank expression on his face. "That doesn't sound like something I would do."

"You have no idea who could have done this to her then? Nothing that might help us?"

"I don't know who, but didn't say I couldn't help." He smirked.

"Amanda's murder was graphic and brutal. Given your study of history, do you have any idea what kind of person would do something like this?"

Michael was quiet for several moments. When he spoke, he looked directly at me. "Those murder experts, you see on television, would probably tell you that it was someone full of anger. Someone who hated women, who took his rage out on an innocent. Given what I know of history, isn't murder always brutal? Love, lust, and money are your common motives. I think this was different. If I had to guess, and it's only a guess, it's someone who loves women. Someone who maybe wanted to preserve her innocence for an eternity."

Jack leaned forward on the couch. Red flamed up his neck and face. I shot him a cold stare and interrupted. "That's an interesting theory. By killing her, he is letting her stand still in time."

Michael nodded. "Take how she was killed or at least the rumor of how I heard she was killed. I don't think that's ever been released. I heard she was stabbed in the heart."

"She was," Jack said, his voice strained. His expression was firm, mouth in a solid line, his eyes boring into Michael.

I wished I could reach over and smack Jack and tell him to relax. I knew Jack saw something in Michael he had missed the first time. It was unnerving him, but I needed him to keep it together.

"The heart is a symbol of love, Detective. Maybe the killer loved Amanda in his own way. He pierced her heart in a way he couldn't do otherwise."

"And her fingers?" Jack asked his voice booming and angry.

"What about them?"

"They were missing. The three fingers on her left hand cut off." Jack held his fingers up and pressed them down one at a time. "Middle, ring, and pinkie. What kind of sick creep does that?"

Michel inched forward in his chair and turned so he was fully facing Jack. He said angrily, "I don't know that I'd call him a sick creep. Maybe the fingers meant something to him. It is after all the ring finger. Maybe he wanted to be married to her even in death."

We had ruffled him. The tension in the air was thick and prickly. I watched Jack and Michael square off without either of them saying another word.

It was Michael who relaxed his posture first. He laughed and waved his hand. "Of course this is all just conjecture. I'm just a history professor. I study murder in the context of the time. I don't think we have any romantic killers like that today. Amanda probably just rejected the wrong man."

"It wasn't just Amanda," Jack slipped. We had made the decision not to talk about any of the other victims. We were going to stay focused on Amanda only.

Michael narrowed his eyes. "What do you mean?"

"Nothing. He didn't mean anything," I assured, trying to recover quickly. "We heard some chatter from some detectives down south that this case might be connected to others, but we have no proof of that. Just some wild and crazy speculation."

Jack stood. "We appreciate you talking to us. If you remember anything else, let us know."

"Definitely. As I said, anything I can do to help." Turning to me, Michael said, "You want that tour now?"

Jack shook his head at me. I knew he wanted to get out of there. I wasn't going to let an opportunity pass. I wanted to see the basement. "Sure, a quick one."

"I'll wait here," Jack said sternly.

Michael walked me through the home. Each room was as grand as the next. I lost count, but I thought there were five bedrooms in all and at least four full baths. There was a library, a billiards room, and a large dining room. There was also a large modern kitchen that had been updated at some point. A set of stairs off the kitchen I assumed led to the basement.

Michael caught me looking at them. "I don't go down there much. There is an old kitchen and some storage, but feel free to have a look around. I'm going to ask Jack a question."

I smiled at my good fortune and made my way down the old wooden steps. Down about ten steps, I hit the basement floor. The dirt floor and low ceiling gave a cramped, cold vibe. The space was enormous. The heating system took up an entire corner. Cobwebs hung from nearly every beam. Liv would freak out completely. She'd have already turned and run back. I had a mission though.

I made my way to the back of the basement, which is what I would have been seeing from the outside. I stood in front of the shelves with my back to the windows. Stacked rows of wooden shelving that seemed as old as the house lined from floor to ceiling. The women's clothing and mask weren't there. The shelves had been wiped clean. Even the dust was gone.

My phone buzzed in my pocket. I knew I had missed a few calls while we spoke to Michael. I pulled it out to see who it was. Luke had called five times and now text. It read:

The killer is in Troy. I've been texting him for the last hour from Katie's phone. When he responded, we got a close location. Near Route 2. I'll be in Troy tonight.

I looked around unsure of what to do. I knew now for certain I was standing in the killer's basement. I stared at the text for another moment, trying to fight the wave of panic that washed over me. I moved around the shelves to go back upstairs but slammed right into Michael. His large frame knocked me back. I stumbled and landed on the cold dirt floor.

He reached out a hand to help me up. I didn't take it but got myself upright.

"Jack is ready to leave," Michael said, as I brushed past him.

He called to my back, "You like those shelves? They are original to the house. I just cleaned them. They are too close to the windows and you never know who is looking in."

I ran up the basement steps. As I ran past, I grabbed Jack, who had been waiting for me in the hallway, and pulled him out of the house.

CHAPTER 73

"Riley, calm down. You're safe," Luke said into the phone, as he moved around their bedroom, pulling clothes from the closet. It had been an eventful day, but he worried about Riley. "You're home now. Let me talk to Jack."

"Is Riley okay?" Luke asked when Jack got on the line.

"She's okay. We were in the house when you sent that last text. She was standing in the basement. Michael Bauer startled her. He's a weirdo. He said some pretty messed up things. It shook me, and I've been a homicide detective longer than you've been alive."

It was a significant lead no doubt, but Luke didn't want to jump the gun. "We don't even know for sure he's the killer. I'm waiting for confirmation from the prints and DNA we pulled from university housing."

"If he's not the killer, then he's one sick freak on his way to be. What's the plan?" Jack asked, but he was distracted. He said something to Riley, who responded that she was fine and everyone was overreacting.

"I'm not sure yet. I'm waiting for the prints to be pulled. I'm heading up there on a four o'clock flight. I'll be there at eleven. Cooper will be in earlier. Let's all meet in the morning and go over the plan. Is there anyone who can do some surveillance on Bauer?"

"You think he's going to run? He's tied to this community. That's his house. I don't think he will go far."

"I don't know. I want to be cautious," Luke said absently as he arranged clothes in his suitcase. "Thanks for paving the way with Troy PD for me. I appreciate them giving us the professional courtesy to handle this. Do you have the interview with Michael set up?"

"Yeah, I've arranged it at the Troy Pub. If you look it up, it's called Brown's Brewing but everyone knows it as the Troy Pub. We have a private room upstairs. Riley knows some people, called in a favor. It's private and out of the way. Casual."

That was exactly the kind of spot Luke needed. If this guy was The Professor, he'd be shocked to see Luke. He wanted the element of surprise. Michael Bauer wouldn't see Luke until he stepped into the room with him. They didn't have enough info to arrest him, and Luke figured calling him to the police station would be too suspicious.

Jack cleared his throat. "Listen, Luke, just remember, the Troy PD courtesy only goes so far. If he gives you access to the house, that's one thing. If he balks and you need a warrant, you'll have to bring in a detective. I ran it by them. They are on board with whatever you need. If it solves one of the city's worst long-standing cold cases, all the better. We just have to do it the right way."

"Trust me, Jack. The last thing I want is this psycho getting off on a technicality. I'm doing this by the book, but first and foremost, I need hard evidence. You think this guy will confess?"

"Today he came pretty close. He gave one of those serial killer confessions in the third person. He detailed all his reasons why someone would kill like that. But we caught him completely off guard when I mentioned other murders. His face turned white. His eyes shifted around. He was spooked. Riley played it off well enough. I think he's probably suspicious but doesn't know for sure. Either way, the faster we can move the better."

"I'm on it. Heading to the airport now. Can I talk to Riley?"

"She just headed up to take a shower. I'll have her call you when she's out."

Luke ended the call. He gathered his things and raced back down to the first floor. The day had been a whirlwind. After finding that Hayes Bauer had taught a lecture series at the university in Little

Rock, Luke and an entire crime scene unit had raced to the campus. He had received no hesitation from the administration who opened the apartment and gave Luke full access.

Luke couldn't believe his luck when he found the apartment uncleaned. The bed was unmade. Trash still in the can. There was even toothpaste still in the sink. The man had left a week earlier than planned, and the room wasn't scheduled to be cleaned for another two days. There wasn't a visiting professor using the space for another month so there had been no rush.

While Luke stood in Bauer's former temporary residence waiting for the crime scene techs to do their jobs, Katie's cellphone had chimed. Learning the lesson from the first time, Luke hadn't gotten excited. His heart had raced when he read the text.

I'll expose your father, and then I'll kill you like I did your friend. I know where you live.

Luke had immediately sent Det. Tyler to put Katie in protective custody. Luke had not expected the man to be so direct, given the tone of the previous texts. Luke expected a threat but not to that extent. He had responded back, hoping to deescalate.

I won't tell. I need your help with what to say. That cop won't leave me alone.

A few minutes later, Luke had received a text asking if the detective was Det. Lucas Morgan. Luke smiled as he typed back that it was and how much he was harassing the victim's friends for information. Luke had loved that he got a text back explaining how clueless the killer thought Luke was and that Katie had nothing to worry about. That had been the last text.

Luke had called the phone carrier and received the ping location. After pulling it up on a map, Luke's heart beat even faster. The dot blinked on a street, not even a couple of miles from Riley's mother's house. He warned her immediately having no idea where Riley was at the time.

Luke made his way through security and into the waiting area. Once seated, he called Riley's cellphone again. There was no answer so he sent her a sweet text and told her he'd see her soon.

Luke watched the passengers come and go. For a moment, he wished to be as carefree as most of them appeared. He knew that most people had their own life problems. But probably none of them were on their way to hopefully not only confront their sister's murderer but bring him to justice. Luke could only hope that was going to be the outcome.

He had very little solid evidence to go on. It was all circumstantial related to the Little Rock case only. Luke had no idea how he'd ever connect the man who called himself The Professor to the other murders. Being at a university at the same time wasn't alone a reason even to be labeled a suspect. No one even believed the cases were connected outside of a handful of them.

There was no evidence related to the letters that Luke received. There were no eye witness accounts of the murders. Seeing a person with the victim, even if they were last to see them alive wasn't a crime. Maybe someone would remember something once the killer was identified, but most cases went back so many years that it was unlikely.

There was no DNA evidence that they could find, even in the Little Rock case. If the DNA from the room matched Michael Bauer then they'd know for a fact he was the man who gave the lecture in Little Rock. They'd also connect him to other universities where he used the alias. They could make a strong circumstantial case, but those were won and lost with juries. Justice would hinge on the opinion of twelve people.

According to Riley, even the items she saw in Bauer's basement were gone. Luke was stymied on how to bring The Professor to justice. He needed more than luck on his side.

CHAPTER 74

I pulled right up to the curb at the Albany Airport. I didn't have to wait more than a minute and Cooper made his way out. I popped the button and the hatch opened in the back of the SUV. Cooper threw his bags in. "You're right on time."

"I'm never late you know that."

Cooper slid in the passenger seat and buckled his belt. "It's been a long couple of days. Confusing, too."

"Was the case in Atlanta confusing? It was so long ago. I don't know how you found anything at all."

"It wasn't the case. It was the victim's sister," Cooper deadpanned. He shot me a knowing look.

My eyebrows raised. "What about the victim's sister was confusing exactly?"

"I had dinner with her last night."

"I don't have time to do this verbal jig. Just spill it."

"I'm not really sure how it happened," Cooper explained. "The victim's sister, Adele, is beautiful. I've never seen a woman so striking, but it's more than that. She's smart and kind. She's hardworking and dedicated. We just clicked from the start. I felt comfortable with her even at the most uncomfortable times."

I stopped at a light and looked over at him, a bit perplexed. I'd never heard Cooper talk about a woman like this. Actually, Cooper never talked about women. "What's gotten into you? You never mix professional with personal. She must have been some girl."

"Woman," Cooper corrected. "She's all woman. She carries herself with such…" Cooper struggled to find the right word, starting and stopping. Finally, he settled on, "Grace, maybe. In the face of such tragedy, she's held it together on her own. She's really successful."

Hitting the foot on the gas, I asked, "How far did this go?"

Cooper shook his head. "Dinner and I kissed her when I walked her to her car last night. That's it. Before, how I used to be, that's not for me anymore. I'm going to see her again when I pick my truck up in Atlanta on the way back."

"How's she feeling? You're down there to investigate her sister's disappearance. It had to be weird."

"Funny enough, we talked at dinner about how weird it wasn't. She feels the chemistry, too. In fact, she's the one who kissed me on the cheek first. Had she not done that, I would have kept it totally professional, even though I wanted something else."

I understood. It was a case that brought Luke and me together back when I was a reporter. It was a child that had been shot in the southeast part of Little Rock. I was the first reporter on the scene, even before the body had been removed. The thin wall that normally stands between a reporter and their story was shattered that day.

"I hope it works out for you," I said and meant it sincerely. Cooper deserved a good woman.

"What's been happening here?"

I spent the rest of the drive filling Cooper in on everything that I had found related to Michael Bauer. He cross-referenced his information on Michael Hayes. By the time we pulled into the driveway and parked, we were both convinced they were the same person, and he was the killer.

"Luke will be here tonight. I don't know what he will be up for, but I thought about driving him by the house. He's interviewing Michael tomorrow." Cooper grabbed his bags while I unlocked the front door.

Dusty rushed us wagging his tail and nudging Cooper's leg with his nose. He looked up at Cooper with his tongue out and a grin on his face. He liked him, but what wasn't to like? Cooper leaned down and pet him.

My mother called from the kitchen. "I saved some dinner for you, Cooper, if you're hungry. Riley, bring his stuff upstairs."

Cooper smiled down at me. "You're like my own personal concierge."

"Your room is top of the stairs on the left." I left him standing in the hall. He could carry his own bag. I gave him a little wave for good measure. Cooper laughed and proceeded to carry his bag up the stairs. Dusty followed.

"I thought I told you to help Cooper upstairs?" my mother asked as I entered the kitchen. I snagged a few chips from the bowl she had on the table.

"Cooper's got it. He wasn't going to let me carry it anyway. The room is made up for him."

"What time will Luke be in?"

"He should be here in an hour or so. I checked the website and his flight is on time."

I moved around the kitchen fixing a plate for Cooper. He didn't say he was hungry, but I knew he would eat. My mother had made meatloaf, mashed potatoes, and green beans. Not a favorite of mine. I set his plate on the table, called for him and grabbed another handful of chips.

"Mom, you said the other day that the family living in that house on Route 2 was strange. We didn't get a chance to talk about that. What do you know specifically?"

My mother poured herself a glass of unsweetened tea and sat across from me at the table. She brushed condensation off the glass with her fingers. "They have lived in that house as far back as I can remember. The early sixties I believe. The mother died early on. It was just a father and son."

Cooper walked into the kitchen. He stood on the threshold as my mother spoke, but she caught sight of him and stopped. She stood to hug him. "I'm so glad you're here. I was just explaining to Riley about a local house and the family that lives there."

"It's Michael Bauer's house," I explained.

Cooper nodded and sat at the table. He dug into his food, praising my mother's culinary skills in between bites.

"Is that the suspect, Michael Bauer, the son?" my mother asked, her eyes on me in more than curiosity. I knew the look. She gave it when she thought I was about to stir up trouble. "It wouldn't surprise me in the least if he had killed that girl. As I started to say, the father and son were strange. Don't get me wrong, the father was a well-known professor here. He was just an odd duck. He'd walk around the neighborhood muttering to himself. He got involved in local politics and created a ruckus about the strangest things. It was the son that got the attention of most of the neighbors."

"Why?" Cooper asked, taking another bite of meatloaf.

My mother sipped her tea and set down the glass. She seemed to choose her words carefully. "He had voyeuristic tendencies. Early on when he was in his teens, neighbors caught him peeping in windows. He'd lurk around the community pool staring at women. That wasn't the most upsetting thing he did though."

Cooper and I watched my mother in anticipation.

"He was suspected of killing animals, people's pets," she said. "That was the rumor anyway. A number of local neighbors' pets disappeared from their yards. One of the men found his dog, shot dead, in the back hills of the property behind their house. It's not theirs, it's owned by the Troy Masonic Lodge. That's who the father tried to blame it on. An animal sacrifice he claimed. No one believed that. When the police came and searched back there, they found a number of animals, some were shot, others stabbed, all up in the back near the root cellar. The animals had all been killed by a human hand. Everyone always suspected the son, but no one was able to prove anything. His father, not getting any support for the Mason theory, finally sent his son away to a boarding school in Vermont. Next, we heard he was off to university. By the time Michael returned here, he was a professor so the few of us that remained and remembered him in his youth assumed he grew out of whatever the issue might have been back then. All too strange for my taste though."

"What do you mean root cellar?" As soon as my mother had said that, I clung to it, waiting for her to finish.

"Far behind the house in all those woods is a root cellar. It's been on the Masons' property for as long as both houses have been there, from the 1800s. The door pulls up from the ground. They used it back then to store vegetables and such. The entrance is probably long buried among the leaves and brush. It wasn't even in use back in the seventies when the police found all those dead animals."

CHAPTER 75

Luke's flight had been delayed so he had arrived at Riley's mother's house at close to midnight. The house had been dark except for a downstairs hall light and a small light in what Luke assumed was Riley's second-floor front bedroom. He had texted on his way.

Riley had launched herself on him in a huge hug as soon as he walked in the door. Luke wasn't complaining in the least. Riley had offered him dinner, but he wasn't hungry. They had made their way back up to Riley's bedroom, talked for nearly an hour about everything that had happened and then fell asleep. Luke woke to the smell of fresh coffee and chocolate. The sweet aroma called to him like a temptress.

He shuffled down the stairs wearing a tee-shirt and shorts, rubbing his eyes. A few steps into the hallway a chorus of voices boomed. Luke popped his head into the kitchen. Cooper, Riley, Karen, and Liv sat around the table, chatting and eating.

"I feel like I overslept," Luke said, taking in the scene.

Karen laughed and poured him some coffee. "Nothing of the sort. We haven't been up long. It's only seven-thirty. Liv wanted to share with us her new chocolate croissants. She made a batch yesterday and devoured them all herself. Today she's in a sharing mood."

"These are so good. You have to try one." Liv handed Luke a croissant on a small white plate.

He took it happily. Luke took a bite and savored the sweet taste. "This is delicious. Teach your sister how to make them before we leave."

Liv beamed. Luke took a seat next to Riley and ate the rest of his croissant and washed it down with his coffee. "What's the plan for today?"

"Riley and I were just talking about that. I think while you are interviewing Michael Bauer, Riley and I are going to talk to the Troy Masonic Lodge. We want to see if they will allow us on their back property to look for a root cellar that's there."

Luke wasn't sure of the connection. "What do the Masons have to do with any of this?"

Riley explained what Karen had told them the night before about Michael's history. She added, "I know there were women's clothing and other items in that basement the other day. Yesterday they were gone. He's moved them someplace."

"You really think it's this root cellar?" Luke asked skeptically.

"It's a possibility," Riley responded emphatically. "There's probably only a handful of people who even know it's back there. It's not on Michael's property so even if something was found, he probably feels like they might not tie it to him. I got a good tour of that house, and there wasn't even so much as a cup out of place. It was weird."

Cooper chimed in. "It's worth a look. I know you're lacking evidence. We don't need a warrant if the Masons agree to let us search. Who knows what's back there? Michael obviously felt comfortable enough as a kid to kill animals back there, why not leave evidence?"

Luke got up and poured himself more coffee. He held the pot up offering some to the others. Cooper held up his mug and Luke poured. He set it back down in its holder and snagged another croissant. Liv gave him a huge smile, which he returned. There was an innocence about her that reminded Luke of his own sister.

"Go for it then," Luke said as he sat back down. "Jack told Michael he was bringing photos of suspects for him to look at and see if anyone might be familiar. Jack said he was more than eager to help. He did ask why Jack didn't want to come back to the house. I guess Jack told him that he was already going to be down at the pub, and it was just easier to do it there."

"Why aren't you meeting at his house?" Karen asked.

"He could slam the door in my face and refuse to speak to me. I really don't think, if he is the killer, he will let me in. We doubted he'd be willing to come to the police station, so Jack suggested a neutral location. Riley hooked us up with the pub."

"Which pub?" Karen asked.

"The Troy Brew Pub," Riley responded

"The only one that matters," Liv added laughing. She put her hand on Luke's arm. "Please don't ruin my good vibe there with a shootout or anything crazy."

"Nothing of the sort," Luke assured. "Riley, you said there is a closed-off upstairs room, right?"

"There is. Jack should have everything ready to go. I'll give you directions before you leave. We will leave after you. Just text me when he gets there so we know it's clear to head over there. You'll have to text us when you're done."

Luke spent the rest of the day preparing for the interview. He hadn't heard anything more from the killer via Katie's cellphone. Riley and Cooper compared investigative notes and did some more online research, cross-referencing their lists with universities. All the universities where there was a murder had either a Michael Bauer, Hayes Bauer or Michael Hayes give a lecture series August through the end of October. It looked like the lectures wrapped before Halloween weekend and he'd depart right after. Brie had texted Luke too, letting him know a Hayes Bauer had been at the university the same time as Lily.

It was no wonder why no one was suspicious of him. He had a couple of months to gain everyone's trust. Scoping out the lay of the land, choosing a victim, picking his helpers and committing the crime. Then he'd vanish. It seemed he never went to the same school twice. If he hadn't sent the letter and connected the crimes, he might have never been caught.

Luke pulled together his notes as Riley walked into the bedroom. "How are you feeling about this?" She sat down on the bed.

Luke turned to look at her. "I'm good actually. I thought I'd be freaking out, but I think we all have been able to connect the dots. He's been hiding in plain sight for so long, I'm concerned about what he will do once he sees my face. My guess is he'll play it off. He wants a cat and mouse game and this feeds into it. He could get up and walk away. He could lawyer up immediately. I don't know what he'll do. We will have to see how it plays out."

Riley moved to him, standing in between his legs. She kissed the top of his head. "Be safe."

"Always. I hope your search through the woods is worth it. You need to text me immediately if you find anything." Luke stood and wrapped his arms around Riley. She turned her face up to him and kissed him deeply. He let himself fall into her embrace but his mind was elsewhere.

Riley pulled back. "It's time to go," she said, pointing to the clock on the wall. "It's nearly three and you have to meet Michael at four. Jack will be there waiting for you. Frank is waiting at the hotel. He said he'd come to meet you and Jack when you're done."

A few minutes later, Luke drove off as Riley waved to him from the porch. It was a short drive into downtown Troy. The brewpub sat on the bank of the Hudson River. Parking was ample even on the narrow street. He walked past old brick warehouses until he reached the pub door. Inside, Luke was surprised how crowded it was for the middle of the afternoon. The seating area off to the left was packed with people and the bar was far into the building, also on the left, with more round tables in front of it.

Before reaching the bar there was a hostess stand and steep stairs taking him to the second level. Luke scanned the patrons' faces, trying to see if anyone looked familiar from the photos he'd seen. No one did.

The second floor opened up to another dining area. The exposed brick framed the room nicely. Towards the front of the room, near the windows facing the street, Jack stood with a strained look on his face. He waved Luke over and the two men clasped hands. Jack whispered something to Luke he didn't catch. But as Luke stepped through the open pocket doors into a room that held a fireplace and a large dining table, he understood.

A man seated at the table looked up at Luke. "Det. Morgan, I'm Michael Bauer. It's a pleasure to meet you. It took you long enough to get here."

CHAPTER 76

"Excuse me," Luke said, taken aback. Why was Michael there already and what did he just say? Luke stood, his hands on his hips, staring down at the man seated on the far side of the table.

Michael ran his finger across the top rim of his glass, making it sing. He stopped and looked Luke up and down. "I just meant you came a long way from Little Rock. It must have taken you a long time."

"I see. How do you know I'm from Little Rock?"

"I just left there last week. You were on the news several times about that poor missing university student. I heard they found her body. Gruesome." He shivered and made a face of disdain.

It caught Luke off guard that Michael so easily admitted he had just been in Little Rock. Luke took a beat and sat down at the table across from Michael. Jack stood behind him. "Why were you in Little Rock?"

Michael smiled, showing off a row of slightly crooked white teeth. "I'm a professor, but you knew that. I gave a lecture series at the University of Arkansas in Little Rock. Isn't that why I'm here, why there's been this little charade about a long-ago case? You came here to interview me. You could have just come to my home."

Luke laid the file folder he had been carrying on the table in front of him. He watched Michael carefully. The man didn't blink, didn't show he was uncomfortable in any way. He sipped his water and then ran his fingers along the rim. The noise was insufferable, but Luke couldn't show it annoyed him.

"I'm glad you admit to being in Little Rock. It saves us time. Did you know the victim?"

"No. Next question."

"Where were you that Friday night of her disappearance?"

Michael held up a finger. He scrolled through his phone. "I had some late dinner at a place called Loca Luna. I grabbed a drink at a bar in the same vicinity and went back to my residence by ten."

Luke eyed him suspiciously. "That's a rather detailed account. Do you always keep such records?"

"Yes," Michael said directly, looking up at Luke. He waved his hand. "In my line of work, I'm able to write all of this off on taxes, a detailed record is required. It's easy so I can just refer back as I'm looking over receipts."

"Where were you after you left the bar?"

"I went home and went to sleep."

"Can anyone account for you during that time? Anyone see you come home for instance?"

"There was no one else in my place if that's what you're asking. I wouldn't know if anyone saw me come home, but that's where I was," Michael said with indignation in his voice.

"Explain something to me, Michael. If you didn't know the victim and had a solid alibi for the evening, why then would you think I'd be coming to talk to you about the victim's disappearance and murder?"

"Well I," Michael stumbled. He watched Luke's face and broke into a wide grin. "Well, you got me."

"Come again?" Luke said calmly.

"I was at the bar the victim was last seen at on the night she went missing. Cristina was with her friends. I had been going there for some time while I was in Little Rock. I was there the night she went missing. Now we both know I was there, but I swear I didn't see her after that."

Luke looked up at Jack. He winked at Luke, having also picked up Michael's mistake. Michael dug himself in deeper but didn't seem to know it.

With that, Jack stepped out of the room and left Luke alone.

"If you didn't know Cristina before that night, how did you know the victim was at the bar with you, Michael? How did you know she was last seen at the bar? That's not been on the news coverage at all."

Michael looked around the room. He looked past Luke to the closed doors Jack had shut behind him.

"He can't help you. Look at me, Michael." Luke held up his hand and ticked off fingers with every piece of evidence they had. "You admitted to being in Little Rock at the time of Cristina's disappearance. We have witnesses who saw you at the bar the night the victim disappeared. You are familiar enough with the victim to know her and her friends. You can't account for yourself after leaving the bar."

"None of that is evidence," Michael interrupted.

"No, you're right," Luke admitted. "You know what is though?"

Michael shrugged.

"We have a witness who saw you leaving Cristina's body across from my parents' house."

Michael watched Luke but didn't say anything for a while. Finally, he said, "That must have been difficult for your parents, knowing that a dead girl was right across from their house. I would have liked to have seen your father's face when he found her on his morning walk. It must have been dreadful."

It took everything Luke had not to leap across the table and strangle him. Sweat pooled at his lower back. He stared the man down. "How did you know my father found the body?"

Michael waved his hand like he was swatting a fly. "Little Rock is a small town. You hear things. Kind of like hearing the victim was last seen at the bar. Your witness must be mistaken."

Luke reached in his pocket and pulled out Katie's cellphone. He held it up. "What about this? The texts you made to Katie. Why did you need Cristina alone on the very night she was murdered?"

"I don't know what you're talking about." Michael's words expressed a conviction that the look on his face betrayed.

"That's funny because it was me you were texting with yesterday. In fact, you were texting while Riley was in your house."

"Riley?" Michael asked, eyebrows raised. He never even addressed what Luke had said about Katie. It didn't seem to faze him in the least.

"Yes, she's a consultant with the police. She's from here, Michael. Her family knows all about yours."

"There's not much to know about me," Michael said, looking around the room like he was bored with the conversation.

"You laid out a pretty good case yesterday why you killed all those young women. I know it's not just the case in Little Rock. We have investigators all over, looking into your murders. All twenty-three of them. Yeah, Michael, we found them fairly quickly, too. Cooper was in Atlanta. Riley was up here. Frank in Virginia. We've got you. You wanted to play a game and now you've lost."

The man said nothing so Luke pressed harder. "Do you like being called Michael Bauer? Or should I call you Michael Hayes or Hayes Bauer? Maybe instead of all of that, you'd simply like to be called The Professor. That is what you called yourself in the letters you sent me, isn't it?" Luke sat back and appraised the man.

Michael stopped looking around and looked Luke in the eyes. In fact, the man's sudden and intense eye contact unnerved Luke, but he didn't look away.

"You can't prove anything," Michael said smugly, sitting back in his chair.

CHAPTER 77

I rested on my bed after Luke left, thumbing through a magazine my sister had tossed on my nightstand the previous day. It was a bridal magazine, which at first, I had thought was silly, but I wondered if she was trying to tell me I should get married or if she was marrying my ex-husband. Either way, it was entertaining reading material while I waited for Luke's text.

I had called the Masonic Lodge right after Luke left and asked if we could search the property behind them for an old root cellar. The man who answered the phone had no idea what I was talking about but gave us permission. He told me his name was Steve, and if anyone gave us trouble, just to tell them he had okayed it. He assured me they weren't expecting anyone at the building until late that evening.

Satisfied we'd have full access when the time came, I flipped through the pages of the magazine, taking in the gowns and flowers and thankful that even if I married Luke, I'd never have to plan another big wedding. At least I had no intention of doing so.

I was surprised when my phone chimed nearly thirty minutes earlier than I had been expecting. It was a text from Jack, letting us know the interview was already in progress.

I grabbed my things, yelled for Cooper and hit the sidewalk in minutes flat.

"How far away is this?" Cooper asked as he climbed in the passenger seat.

"We could walk there but driving is faster." I turned out of the driveway and made a left at the end of my road to Pawling Avenue. Three minutes later, I sat at the light on Pawling and Route 2. No cars were coming so I went right on red, and not even a minute later, we pulled into the driveway of the Masonic Lodge. I debated if we should check in with Steve before we hit the woods, but I assumed we were probably safe to just start searching.

"Where is this guy's house?" Cooper asked, looking around him.

I pointed down the road to the right. "It's that white one. You can only see the side of it through the trees, but these woods run from the side of Masons all the way back behind them and Michael's house. It looks like more ground to cover than it really is. It doesn't go back that far. It runs up to a hill and then stops. There is a neighborhood behind us high up on the hill."

"Do you have any idea where the root cellar could be?" Cooper stared off into the woods. His face gave away just how daunting of a mission this would be. The woods, although not deep, were dense. The leaf-covered ground was going to make searching all the more challenging.

"No idea. You heard about it the same time I did. There is only one way to find it. We need to start walking. I'll go east-west and you take north-south, and we will grid search."

The ground crunched under my feet. In some places, the leaves and sticks were ankle-deep. I didn't feel like I was walking over anything like doors. It was hard solid earth. Every once in a while, my path would cross with Cooper's. "Nothing," he'd confirm, and we'd keep walking.

I worried we'd run out of time. I had no idea what was happening with the interview, but I was hard-pressed to believe Michael would simply confess and they'd make an arrest. A serial killer playing cat and mouse games doesn't simply give up when they feel cornered. That's usually when the game playing really begins. I hoped that would buy us more time.

Nearly forty minutes of searching later, from directly behind Michael's house, Cooper's voice echoed through the barren trees. "Found it!"

I wanted to run to him but was afraid of tripping over branches. I resisted the urge but was out of breath anyway from anticipation by the time I reached him. Cooper had brushed off the leaves that covered the doors.

"Someone has been here recently. The leaves and branches were placed on top of here to hide it," Cooper said and pointed to some fresh footprints that had been left in the dirt probably the last time it had rained and the ground was soft and muddy.

The doors were locked, closed with heavy chains and a lock that would not be easily broken. "We need bolt cutters or something to break those."

Cooper looked back towards the Masonic lodge. "Since you talked to Steve, why don't you tell him you found it and see if they have anything we can use. I'd rather stand here and wait, especially if Michael comes back. He could potentially see us from his backyard. I'd rather deal with the confrontation than you. I'll also snap some photos of the scene with my phone, just in case we need them later."

I made my way back to the lodge. A few minutes later, I handed Cooper heavy bolt cutters. Steve had been more than happy to help and frankly a little annoyed there was something on the Mason property that was unknown to him. We had full permission to do what was needed.

Even with the tool, the chains were tough to break. Cooper worked at it and worked at it. He cussed and sweat dripped down his forehead. Finally, as he was just about to give up, the lock broke. Cooper pulled the heavy chains off, dragging them over the wooden doors and dropping them in a heap. He yanked on the metal handle and pulled open one side. When he pulled open the other side, I saw the old wooden plank staircase that led into the root cellar.

Cooper looked at me, wiping the sweat off his brow. "Flashlight?"

I pulled one out of the pocket of my hoodie and handed it to him. Cooper went first. I followed right behind, holding on to the back of his shirt. As we hit the bottom dirt floor, I took in what was illuminated by the flashlight. There were shelves on all sides of us.

The walls behind them looked like packed dirt. It felt like being in a tomb.

Cooper flashed the light on the shelves. It bounced from one area to the other. The shelves were filled with women's clothing and other items. There was a bright purple wool scarf, a gold chain with a locket attached, and right in the middle of it all, a pink mask with a flower on one side. I was sure of it — these were the items I had seen in the basement through the back windows.

Cooper flashed the light to the other side. We both took a step back horrified at what we saw. The flashlight beam bounced off mason jars filled with bones. Small finger bones to be exact. Each jar labeled with a date.

I grabbed Cooper's hand. He squeezed mine in response. Neither of us said a word. There was nothing we could say. We were looking at years of trophies from a serial killer. As Cooper turned to face me, the light brightened the back of the root cellar for mere seconds, but it was enough.

"Cooper, what's back there?" I stammered, thinking that there was no way I saw what I had.

"Where?" Cooper asked, turning, moving the flashlight all around.

I took the flashlight from his hands and pointed it at the spot. In an old rocking chair, painted a vibrant green, sat a skeleton dressed in women's clothing. A long dark-haired wig sat on the skull. The hair flowed over the shoulder bones and down its spine. A woman's scooped neck shirt and flower-patterned skirt covered the skeleton's torso and thigh bones.

I took a step towards it, thinking at first it had to be fake. The closer I came, the more I knew it was real. The remains of a woman who had once been as alive as I was at that moment. I shined the light on the hand, the left hand, which rested on the arm of the chair. There affixed on the ring finger was an antique engagement ring.

I shined the light back on Cooper. His eyes were transfixed on the scene. "We have to get out of here and call Luke and the police now." Even though I said the words, neither of us moved our feet. We were planted in a spot of absolute horror.

CHAPTER 78

Michael was right. Luke knew that the evidence they had gave them nothing more than a circumstantial case. During a silent stalemate between the men, Riley's name flashed on his phone screen. Luke hesitated taking it because he didn't want Michael to get up and leave so the call went to voicemail.

Luke pressed Michael again and again, trying every investigative trick and angle he knew to spark the man, make him angry, push and pull him emotionally. Michael didn't bite. The verbal sparring continued for several more minutes until Jack forcefully shoved open the pocket doors and demanded Luke's attention. He held a phone out to Luke. "You need to take this now."

Luke took the phone and stepped out of the room. "What is it?"

Riley detailed everything that she and Cooper had found. Detectives with the Troy Police Department were already on their way. The management of the Masonic Lodge gave full permission for anything the police needed to do on their land.

"You are absolutely certain this land and the root cellar belongs to the Masons?" Luke asked, cautiously.

"I had Steve dig up his latest land deed documents, and the land survey clearly puts it on his property. There isn't even wiggle room for debate," Riley assured.

"Is there anything down there that ties directly to Michael Bauer?"

"Nothing with his name stamped on it, no. The mason jars correspond to each date of the murders. We have no idea who the skeleton belongs to or all the women's items. Would you know your sister's mask?"

Luke wasn't sure. It'd been a long time. "We'd be better off if we took a photo and sent it to my mother."

"You can do that when you come here. Are you getting anything with Michael?"

"Other than some slip-ups, no. Although he did readily admit to being in Little Rock and seeing the victim the night she disappeared. My guess is he assumed we had witnesses who saw him there. It was better to admit than deny."

"Is there enough to make an arrest?"

"No," Luke said, running through every scenario in his head of how they might even hold Michael until they processed the scene. Given the root cellar was on the Mason's property it was a double-edged sword – good for accessibility, bad because of Michael's deniability. They would have to wait for a complete review of what they found and fingerprint analysis.

They'd have to let him go. Luke ended the call with Riley and called Jack into the main dining room. "Can you and Frank do some surveillance on him until we process the scene and get a warrant to search his house or make an arrest?"

Jack readily agreed and left. Luke wasn't sure what to do – push Michael harder or wait until they processed the evidence. Luke knew for sure now his sister's killer sat mere feet away. He was alone with him now. Luke could take out any revenge he wanted. There was no one in the upstairs of the pub with them. Several scenarios ran through Luke's mind. None of them ended with Michael walking out of the building alive.

Luke thought of Riley and then his parents. He couldn't leave them. His parents would never understand. They'd have lost both their children. Once he got his emotions under control, Luke walked back to the room. Once inside he looked at Michael, sitting comfortably across the table. "Let's talk for a few more minutes."

"We are going to have to hurry, I have things to do," Michael said, looking at his phone.

"Why'd you do it?" Luke asked. "I just want to know why you killed all those girls. What did they ever do to you?"

Michael set the phone down. "I didn't kill anyone. You can try all your little cop tricks, but I'm never going to tell you I did something I didn't do."

"We have you at each university when a girl was abducted and murdered. We've tied you to each location. We have witnesses in Little Rock, in Atlanta and here. They will testify against you. We may not convict you on all the cases, but we will get you on enough."

"That's it?" Michael laughed. "You have me teaching at some universities when girls disappear. What about all the ones I've been teaching at and no one is harmed? How do you account for that? You may have witnesses, but what did they really see? Because if they saw me killing someone, I'd already be arrested. You have no DNA connecting me to any cases. You have no murder weapon."

"We are building our case."

Michael studied Luke's face. "Are we done here?" He stood to leave.

Luke stood and looked him in the eyes. "With your little trophy room we just found, we will get you, Michael, rest assured. Troy PD is playing with all your trophies right now. They have the bones. They have the clothing and keepsakes. They've got it all."

Michael kicked his chair back into the wall. Luke put his hand on his gun.

"You don't even have all the bodies!" Michael yelled.

Michael's face flushed. He looked to the floor. Both men knew his mistake.

Calmly, Luke asked, "If you have nothing to do with these murders, how do you know what remains were found? How do you know so much?"

Michael left, shoving past Luke on the way out. Luke texted Jack to tell him the man was leaving. Luke waited a few minutes and practically ran down the steps and out to his car. The drive back up the hill and out of downtown Troy took forever. Luke hit every light. When he pulled up to the Masonic Lodge, Luke was overcome with emotion. The police presence blanketed the entire area. Everyone had come out to help, and Luke couldn't be happier.

CHAPTER 79

Luke stood with one foot in the Masonic Lodge driveway and the other in the grass. One of the big spotlights that law enforcement had brought in to illuminate the area shined right on him. He was awash in light. I waded through the sea of cops to reach him.

Luke wrapped me in his arms and nuzzled my ear. His hand rubbed a sensitive spot on the back of my neck under my hair. "I can't believe you got everyone out here."

"The tech pulled prints off the handle and from the mason jars. They took our prints just to rule them out. Troy PD is working with the university right now to see if the prints match. Michael is not in the system otherwise. One of the cops said that Russell Sage would have put Michael through an extensive background check including taking his prints so they will have them."

We released each other. Luke looked down at me, his smile fading. "I wasn't able to get him to confess. I don't have any doubt it's him. There were things he said that indicated he knew more, things he couldn't have known otherwise. I'm worried about getting a conviction." Luke looked around seeming to search for something.

"What?" I asked, looking in the same direction.

"The FBI comes out now once we gather all the evidence? Let me guess, they are going to do a press conference on their find." Luke laughed and scratched at his chin. "I need a shave."

I stood on tiptoes and kissed his stubble. "Isn't that typical of the FBI? The locals do the grunt work and they swoop in for the credit. They are good for some things though."

"What is that?" a man's voice said from behind me.

I turned away from Luke. A man with blond hair and piercing blue eyes flanked my side. He stood about Luke's height and wore a dark windbreaker with yellow writing on it indicating he was with the FBI.

He extended his hand to Luke. "I don't know what field office you talked to, but I just spent an hour with Cooper who detailed the entire case for me from start to finish. I'm sorry about your sister. We should have paid attention."

"What's going to happen now?" Luke asked, his voice strained. "I have a murder case in Little Rock to wrap up. Are you taking over?"

"We have this scene to process. It's going to be a long road. Our guys will be working around the clock to process all that evidence and then go through the arduous challenge of identifying all those victims. We'll need your help if you're willing to work with the families you already identified to check on DNA matching. I don't know what's currently available, but we need to start there."

"Michael Bauer?" Luke asked. "What happens to him?"

"I've already sent guys to Michael Bauer's door to see if they could search his house, and he refused. I've got a criminologist who specializes in these kinds of cases flying in from D.C. Once we get prints back and other forensics, we will get the warrant to search his house and bring him in for questioning."

"In the meantime, he's just free?" I asked. I knew the reality of how the criminal justice system worked, but it didn't mean I had to like it.

The man turned to look down the hill at the house. The house had several lights on. The kitchen light cast a shadow of a man. Michael Bauer stood in the back window watching the scene, watching us specifically.

The agent said, "Michael Bauer isn't going anywhere. There are agents around the perimeter and down the road watching him. He will be under our surveillance until we bring him in."

Luke nodded. "I wasn't able to get a confession on the murder in Little Rock or the other cases. Maybe y'all have some better tricks up your sleeves, but Little Rock will want the first stab at him."

The FBI agent frowned. "You know I can't promise you that. If it's what we think, this will be a multi-state case. I don't know who will get him first."

Luke balled his hands into fists at his sides, a sure sign he attempted to control his temper. "There would be no case without us. There'd be no case without Little Rock. I'll fight you on it. As sure as I'm standing here, my Captain and the prosecutor's office will fight you on it."

The agent held his hands up in defeat. "You have my word Little Rock will be my recommendation. Go home, get some rest. I've got your number and will be in touch as soon as we have confirmation it's him. If he confesses anything, you'll be my first call. I promise you that."

The man turned and walked away. Luke slid his arm around me. Quietly, he said, "As much as I want to stand here and watch, let's go back to your place. I'd like to talk to all of you. I need to call Jack and Frank off surveillance. No point having them out there with the feds on watch, too."

Luke walked off towards his car. I waved to Cooper and together we walked back to where we had parked hours earlier.

"Luke okay?" Cooper asked.

"I think he will be. The case doesn't feel wrapped up. I know that's what he's feeling. He's worried about after an arrest. What happens with the prosecution. You know he won't rest until the very end."

Back at my mother's house, my mother was in the living room snuggled in a chair under a blanket reading a book. She had a fire going. As I walked down the hall heading into the kitchen, she called, "I didn't know when you'd all be back so I ordered pizza and salad. It should be here soon. Liv's coming over, too."

I found Luke in the kitchen. He leaned against the counter, drinking a tall glass of water. I didn't think he was crying, but his eyes were red and watery.

"You okay?"

Luke exhaled. "I just want this to be done. It feels close, but still, such a long way to go."

"I understand. Hopefully, the FBI can make progress. I trust their crime scene techs. Cooper just went upstairs. My mom ordered dinner."

"Frank and Jack are on their way, too. Should I call my parents or wait?"

"I'd wait until we get some confirmation. No point getting their hopes up. Anything can happen. What if we're wrong and his prints don't match? I think they will, but could your parents take the disappointment?"

Luke nodded. "I'll wait. I did call Captain Meadows and Tyler. I checked in on Gabe, too. Aaron Roberts lawyered up so we aren't getting anything out of him. If I had to guess he was one of The Professor's pawns, probably like Katie. If it goes to trial, he will have to testify about his actions that night, but knowing what we do now, I don't think it was him who hurt my sister. He isolated her, but he didn't kill her."

As the evening wore on the food was delivered, which my mother insisted on paying for even though we all tried to give her cash. I texted my sister, but Liv responded that she got caught up with a few things and wouldn't make it over. After we ate, my mother went up to her room to read. It was just the five of us left.

Luke turned to Jack and Frank. "I can't thank you enough for helping us. You're the only ones that took us seriously. I hope this is the end. Maybe Michael will spare us all and confess. I appreciate all you've done so far. We couldn't have asked for better help."

Jack slapped Luke on his back. "It was you, Luke. It was for your sister. We are here for her and all the young girls he took."

Frank and Cooper shared the same sentiment. It neared midnight. Jack and Frank left. Cooper and Luke went upstairs. I finished cleaning the kitchen alone. The kitchen never seemed quieter and colder. As I shut off the kitchen lights and made sure the doors were locked, a chill ran down my spine. I pulled my hoodie closed and zipped it. I also nudged up the heat.

CHAPTER 80

At two-thirty in the morning, Luke's phone chimed incessantly. With half-closed eyes and Riley's arm slung across his chest, he slapped his hand around on the nightstand to silence it before it woke the whole house. Luke got the phone in his hand and moved Riley's arm so he could sit up.

He tapped the screen. He had missed two calls from Jack. There were also text messages, but they would have to wait. Luke moved off the bed and sat in a chair Riley had in the far corner of her room. He called Jack. The man picked up immediately.

"What's wrong?" Luke asked.

"I heard through a detective at the Troy PD that the FBI confirmed Michael Bauer's prints. His prints were found on the root cellar handles and the mason jars. They also have photos of him with the skeleton posed grotesquely. There's no question. He's our guy, but Luke, he's gone."

"What do you mean gone?" Luke said, louder than he meant. Riley stirred in her sleep.

"The FBI said they were watching him. The Troy detective, who left about eleven, said the lights were still on in the house, but when they went to serve the search warrant and make an arrest at two, Michael was nowhere to be found. He vanished."

Luke cursed loudly and slammed his fist down on the arm of the chair. Riley woke with a start. She pulled the blanket up around her waist and watched Luke in the dark.

"Are they out looking? What do you need?"

"Nothing right now, Luke, just be on guard. Who knows where this guy is going? The FBI has everyone out searching. I wanted you to know, keep you in the loop, because obviously, the FBI isn't."

"I appreciate that but there's got to be something..." Luke paused. Another text came in. It was from a number Luke didn't recognize.

It read: *He's got me in a sea of headless angels. Come alone, he won't kill me. He wants to tell you his story.*

It was a 518 area code. Luke read the number off to Riley. He didn't even get to the last numbers before her hand flew to her mouth.

"That's Liv, my sister. He has her." Riley scrambled out of bed. She went to the closet and pulled on clothes. She yelled to wake Cooper.

He read the text off to Jack. "Don't get the cops involved. No FBI either. You and Frank come over here. We can do this ourselves."

Luke hung up and reached for his gun. He checked it and grabbed his extra clip. He pulled on jeans and a shirt and the rest of his clothes. Cooper stood in the doorway. "I'm not armed," he said. "With the laws, I didn't carry over state lines. Neither did Riley."

"I've got that covered," Karen's voice boomed from the hallway. Luke stepped around Cooper. Karen punched numbers into a wall safe that had been hidden from view by a small hallway shelf. She pulled out several handguns and ammunition.

Luke was utterly speechless. The last thing he thought Riley's mother would have was a secret weapons stash.

Karen looked back at him. "Don't look so dumbfounded. Riley told you about her father. I never know when there will be blowback from that."

Riley rolled her eyes. "Like you're taking on the Irish mob."

Karen pulled her aside. "Bring your sister home safely." She kissed Riley on the cheek.

The four of them went downstairs and met Jack and Frank who had arrived moments earlier.

"I assume one of you would know where there is a sea of headless angels?" Luke asked.

Jack and Riley shared a look. "It's the cemetery, Luke. Where the Troy victim was found."

Frank swore. "That place isn't fit for daylight. Spooky as hell going back at night."

They drove to the Forest Park Cemetery in two cars. Jack and Frank were in the lead with Luke, Riley, and Cooper following. Riley drove since she knew the way.

"We're here," Riley said, as she pulled up a road marked with a sign for the Troy Country Club.

The farther up the road they got, the darker it became. It was pitch black with only the moonlight overhead.

From the backseat, Cooper remarked, "This doesn't look like any cemetery I've ever seen."

"It's abandoned. You have to be careful walking. There are overturned headstones, large boulders, branches."

Luke texted the killer that he was there and asked where they could be found. He got an immediate response.

Near the headless angel

Riley gave Luke detailed directions on how to reach them. Jack and Frank headed deep into the woods to come up from the right. Riley and Cooper moved in the other direction so they'd come up on Luke's left. They worried the killer would hear them, every step echoed with the crunch of dried leaves or the snap of a branch.

Luke moved down the middle, following exactly what Riley had said. His flashlight only showed glimpses as he moved. "Michael," Luke called out. "I don't know where anything is in here. You're going to have to direct me."

Luke continued his slow progression with his flashlight and gun at the ready. His heartbeat pounded in his ears. He flashed the light all around him, hoping to catch sight of them. Finally, he came to a clearing just like Riley said he would.

Liv sat on the ground with her hands behind her back at the base of the monument. Michael paced in front of her. The flashlight beam hit them just right and Luke saw the ice pick in his hands. Its silver blade reflected the light.

"Michael, I can see you," Luke called. "I'm here now. Let Liv go. If you want to talk to me, you need to let her go."

Michael yanked Liv up by her hair and positioned her in front of his body. "I'm not letting her go. I let her go, you'll shoot me. I know how this works. Put the gun down now. She lives or dies, it's up to you."

CHAPTER 81

Luke knew he wasn't alone. Riley and Cooper and Jack and Frank had their guns drawn just out of sight. But the sight of the headless, armless angel unnerved him. He felt a hundred eyes on him. The dead watched. The victims and their desire for justice stood at the ready.

Luke approached Michael, debating the best course of action. He eyed Liv, searching her face for an answer to an unspoken question.

"I'm okay," Liv responded quietly.

Michael jerked her back, but Liv stood firm. Her eyes were red. Makeup streaked her face. She had on yoga pants and a thin tee-shirt. She shivered in the chilly air.

Luke holstered his gun and held up his hands. "It's just you and me now. The gun is away. What did you want?"

Michael held the pointed blade of the ice pick to Liv's throat. One move and he could stab her easily. Michael looked around the woods on all sides of him, but Luke was sure he couldn't see anything.

"Come on, Michael. You told me to come alone, and I did. Now, what did you want to say?"

Michael bought his attention back to Luke. "How did you find me? How did you figure it out?"

"I didn't. My team did. You told us everything. You said twenty-three victims and you told us the university where it started. That's all we needed."

"That can't be. It couldn't have been that easy. I didn't leave any evidence. No one saw me."

"You did. You had an easy pattern to figure out. People saw you, Michael. Someone saw you talking to the victim. Jordan was her name. They saw you leave with her that night."

"That's impossible," Michael said, clearly agitated.

"It's not. I bet that's why you stopped taking them from inside buildings, isn't it? You worried you'd be seen."

"I worried, yes," Michael confirmed. "But it was too easy. I was at the universities. They trusted me. Young girls are so trusting with anyone in authority. There was no one to stop me. It was easy hunting. I wanted a game. The chase."

Liv struggled against him. Luke wasn't sure if she was trying to break free or just get more comfortable within his grasp. He had an awkward hold on her neck. "Why don't you let Liv go? We can talk. She hasn't done anything to you. She doesn't fit your pattern."

Michael laughed, a sinister deep guffaw. "She saw me that night. She saw me pick up the victim in Troy. I saw her, walking home all alone. She only saw me for a second. I never worried about it. When I followed Riley home the other day, I saw her outside. I knew it was the same girl. She still looks the same. I waited and followed her home, too. I knew then you had found me. Riley came to my house. I should have just killed her and that cop then, but there was no fun in that. I slipped away from the FBI tonight and lured her away like the others. I got you here, Luke. I got you here."

"Why did you want me here?" Riley had been right about Liv. All these years later, she had unknowingly seen the killer.

"I wanted to tell you why I did it. That's all you want to know, right?"

"Okay, you've got my attention. Tell me."

Michael whimpered. He wanted to tell his story. Luke believed that. He wanted someone to listen. Luke was going to listen, and then he would bring him down by force if necessary.

"I was a weird kid. I had no friends, but in college, I met the most beautiful girl. I was happy for a few years. I was normal. We got engaged. But then she tried to leave me. In the fall, right at

Halloween, she broke off our engagement. She said I was too controlling. She said it would never work. I had been with her since we were freshmen. We were about to graduate that spring and start a new life together. She killed my dreams so I killed her."

"Is that the skeleton in your root cellar dressed in women's clothing?"

"Yes, she's mine, and you're taking her from me. I promised her we'd never part."

"You're sick!" Liv shouted and struggled against him.

"If you move again," Michael yelled, he punctuated each word, "I will kill you."

"Liv, honey, look at me," Luke said, making eye contact with her. "Settle down. Let Michael tell his story. You'll be okay, I promise."

Looking at Michael, Luke said, "I get it, man. We've all been there. We've all had our hearts broken. Mine was broken for a long time, too. It's hard to move on. But you killed innocent girls. Girls who didn't do anything to you. They didn't hurt you, Michael."

Michael started to cry. He choked out each word. "Don't you see I didn't hurt them? They were all so perfect. I kept them from hurting anyone else. They are mine now, too. I chose each one very carefully. I watched them, saw how they interacted with others. People liked them. Eventually, they'd hurt someone just like me. They can't now. They're mine. My brides in death."

"Is that why you took their ring fingers?" Luke asked, disgusted. He tried to stay steady.

"Yes. Look at how I preserved them. I kept their clothing and things they liked. I didn't separate them from that. I've honored them."

Liv's eyes grew wider. Luke feared she'd say something to set him off. Luke made eye contact with her, hoping his look would let her know she was okay. Liv finally exhaled without saying a word.

"Michael, was there just the twenty-four, with Cristina in Little Rock?"

"Yes, my mission is complete. We planned to get married when we turned twenty-four. The circle is finished."

Michael kept babbling, but Luke couldn't make out what he was saying. Luke needed to keep him talking. "Why me, Michael? Why did it have to be me? I don't understand why you sent me those letters. Why did you let us figure it out? You had to know you gave us enough clues."

"You were better than I thought you'd be. I thought you'd chase me for a few more years. I was done killing, but I thought the chase would be fun. Like how I got other people involved. The chase was addictive. Manipulating all those people to help me kill. It was a game! I had to kill, but it was the chase that was fun."

Luke had his right hand on his gun at his hip. He steadied the flashlight. "Okay, so you knew I'd chase. What now?"

"You don't know, do you?" Michael laughed again.

"Know what? I'm asking you. Tell me, dammit."

"Your sweet sister Lily. Right before I killed her, she told your parents she loved them. She said it like they could hear her. Then she looked me in the eyes, defiant. She was helpless, tied up and the ice pick right at her heart. She wasn't afraid in her last moments. She was defiant. She was angry. She was the only one who dared to look me in the eyes. She said, 'My brother Luke will catch you and make you pay.' It was her last words."

Luke had kept it together until he heard his sister's last words. His hand shook for the first time. The doubt and fear and grief rushed back like a tidal wave taking him down. He felt his sister there with him. The wave of emotion dragged him under. He had no idea how long he stayed like that.

It was Riley's voice that brought him back.

"Timmy Jacobs!" Riley yelled. Liv's head snapped up and she looked to the woods, following the sound of Riley's voice. Riley yelled it again, louder this time. "Liv, now, Timmy Jacobs!"

Luke had no idea what Riley yelled, but Liv did. Liv slammed her head back into Michael with all of her might and got loose enough to punch her tied fists into his groin. He dropped the ice pick as one hand went to his bloodied nose and the other to his crotch. Once free, Liv sprinted off in the direction of Riley's voice.

Luke reached for his holstered weapon and advanced on Michael, kicking the ice pick out of the way. Luke grabbed the man by the hair. Liv had already brought him to his knees. Luke pointed the gun right at his forehead and steadied his finger on the trigger.

Luke wanted to pull the trigger. He wanted nothing more than to end this scumbag's life right there and then. Save the cost of a trial. Save the families. Put an end to the sick twisted thing right then and there. When Luke looked up, he saw his sister's face. He blinked once and then twice. She shook her head and smiled at him sweetly. Luke knew he had to be imagining it, but it was so real.

Luke pressed the cold muzzle harder into Michael's head, fighting his demons inside. Michael begged for Luke to kill him.

Jack and Frank approached from the right. "Luke?" Jack said, cautiously.

Riley approached from the left. "Luke, this isn't the way. I know you. You wouldn't be able to live with yourself."

"You have no idea what I could live with," Luke snapped. His fight wasn't with Riley. It was with himself.

Luke pressed the muzzle harder and looked into Michael's eyes.

"Kill me, kill me, please," he pleaded and closed his eyes.

Epilogue
Six months later

In the end, Luke had done the right thing in the cemetery that night. He had jerked Michael up off the ground and slapped the cuffs on him. Cooper had my sister safely back at the car, assuring she didn't need medical attention. The four of us had walked Michael Bauer out of the cemetery together, two flanking him on each side. Before I left, I had taken one long last look at the headless angel and hoped I'd never have to see her again.

By the time we had breached the perimeter of the Troy Country Club grounds, the police had already been there. Luke had handed the cuffed man to the FBI agent. "Try not to lose him this time," was all he had said.

In the end, it was Luke who had secured the confession. I brought my sister back safely to my mother. She hadn't said one word about putting my sister in danger. Liv had explained that Michael had shown up at her house in the middle of the night wearing a cap and reading glasses. He had flashed a fake badge and told her that we were all in danger. She had gone with him willingly to help me. It was when she had settled into his car and he took off the cap and glasses that she had realized her mistake.

Over the next two months, Luke, Cooper and I had helped Jack and the Troy PD, Frank and the police in Virginia, and other jurisdictions contact the victims' families so the FBI could secure sample DNA to make positive comparisons to the bones found in the root cellar. It had been a long process, but rewarding. Families could finally grieve, knowing the truth.

Michael had confessed again and again, basically to anyone who would listen to his story of how he had been wronged by the love of his life. It was clear his psychosis ran deeper prior to that. Michael had explained that he had used an ice pick and had another sawing blade to cut off the fingers. The murder weapons he'd discard in each city and buy new ones the next year. He often stole rental cars on the nights of the murders to conceal any DNA evidence. He scouted the car rental places that had no surveillance. He'd return the car and no one would be the wiser.

He'd kill the girls near where he left their bodies but never in the same exact location. Separating the two ensured that less evidence would be found. He was right about that.

Michael had driven to and from the universities from Troy so he'd never have to fly. It made sense. He wasn't going to get sawed-off fingers through airport security. Michael had at least explained to local police departments where bodies had been left so one day possibly the remains of other victims could be found.

Little Rock was tapped to hold the first sentencing hearing, and then from what we understood, Michael would face justice and sentencing in all of the cities where he had taken a young girl's life.

Six months after the night in the cemetery, once all the cases had been closed, we threw a party. Luke had invited all of the family members that we could reach as well as the detectives, many of whom were retired now.

My mother and Jack came down. Liv was on vacation with my ex so she missed out but sent her congratulations to us all. Frank brought his wife, who looked pleased as punch that her husband had finally gotten off the couch and was active again. Jack and Frank had been talking about maybe digging into some other cold cases together. I think they really just wanted more excuses to play golf. Even Emma and Joe were there. They had found a sitter for Sophie. Emma's round swollen belly grew a little more each day. It was going to be nice to have another little one in our circle.

Cooper stood at my side as we both surveyed the scene in front of us. "This is a pretty great party. Think your wedding reception will be this good?"

I swatted at him. "Luke hasn't even proposed yet. Don't be silly. Where is Adele?"

"She's in the middle of a big case, but she will be here next week. You can meet her then."

"How's it going with you two?" I gave him a sideways glance.

"Great," Cooper said, sounding surprised at himself. "She is forever grateful we solved her sister's murder. More than anything, she's relieved she can move on with her life. If nothing else comes out of it, at least we gave her that."

A glass clinked and Luke's father cleared his throat in the front of the room. Spencer commanded our attention. He said loudly, "I'd like to take a moment and say a few words to my son. Luke, we never dreamed that we'd be standing here. We never had any doubt about your ability, but we were so afraid of losing you in the process. You are more than any father could hope for in a son. I could stand here all night listing your amazing qualities, but anyone who has met you knows. We cannot thank you and Riley, Cooper, Jack and Frank for all you have done not only for our family but all the families. There is no closure. The victims will be a part of all of us for the rest of our lives, but in time, we will make our peace with it. Thank you."

We all raised our glasses to Luke and then took a sip. We thought Spencer was finished, but he got the crowd's attention again. "Now, if you could just marry that beautiful woman and give us grandkids, we won't ask for anything else." A chorus of laughter followed.

"Here, here," my mother yelled from the sidelines.

My face reddened, but I quite liked the idea of being Luke's wife. Luke gave a quick but heartfelt speech and thanked everyone for being there.

When he was done, he crossed the room and stood by my side. "What do you think?"

I looked up at him. "I think 'What do you think' is not a marriage proposal."

"Oh, I see, you're getting all romantic on me," he teased. "I have to do it right then."

"You'll have to do it right." I grinned. Was he really going to do it in front of all these people?

Thankfully, no.

Luke grinned down at me like he had a secret plan. I'm sure he did. Luke always had a plan.

Stacy M. Jones

RILEY SULLIVAN MYSTERY #3

MISSING TIME MURDERS

Private investigator Cooper Deagnan blinked himself awake after what should have been the night of his life. He had helped solve Det. Luke Morgan's sister's murder, and in the process met an incredible woman. His life finally felt on track.

Slowly opening one eye and then the next, Cooper's head pounded. He searched the recesses of his mind but came up blank. He was missing time. Cooper had no idea how the party ended or even how he had arrived home.

Rolling to his side, Cooper came face to face with a dead woman. Her eyes open, coldly staring back at him, blood trailing down her forehead from a bullet wound. The cold grip of the gun pressed into Cooper's belly, the muzzle pointed right at her. She wasn't a stranger. She was a one-night stand from Cooper's past that went horribly wrong. How did she get into his bed? More importantly, who killed her?

It's the question men across Little Rock are made to answer when the slayings, known as the Missing Time Murders, paralyze the city.

Access the Free Mystery Readers' Club Starter Library

Riley Sullivan Mystery Series novella "The 1922 Club Murder"
FBI Agent Kate Walsh Thriller Series novella "The Curators"
Harper & Hattie Mystery Series novella "Harper's Folly"

Sign up for the starter library along with exclusive launch-day pricing, special behind the scenes access, and extra content not available anywhere else.

Hit subscribe at

http://www.stacymjones.com/

Follow Stacy M. Jones for exclusive information on book signings, events, fan giveaways, and her next novel.

Facebook: StacyMJonesWriter
Twitter: @SMJonesWriter
Goodreads: StacyMJonesWriter